"Cease this battle!" Urza cried imperiously. His figure blazed with light aback Gherridarigaaz. Dragon and rider descended in a column of mana energy before the storm of angels and falcons. "Cease this battle or be destroyed! I am Urza Planeswalker!"

"Tremble before him!" came a voice in mocking answer from among the angel horde.

Radiant emerged. Her figure was lit with an incandescent heat equal to Urza's. A group of archangels accompanied her, four before, four behind, and four more around the ruler of the realm. Her appearance brought a sudden hush to the battle lines. She was strange-eyed, beautiful, and terrifying.

"Tremble before this petulant god-child, this despoiler of worlds, destroyer of planes. Urza has come, my children, and when Urza comes, death always follows."

A World of Magic

THE BROTHERS' WAR
Jeff Grubb

RATH AND STORM
A MAGIC: THE GATHERING Anthology
Edited By Peter Archer

PLANESWALKER
Lynn Abbey

TIME STREAMS
J. Robert King

BLOODLINES
Loren Coleman

THE COLORS OF MAGIC
A MAGIC: THE GATHERING Anthology
Edited By Jess Lebow

MAGIC
The Gathering®

TIME STREAMS
ARTIFACTS CYCLE · BOOK III

J. Robert King

Wizards
OF THE COAST

TIME STREAMS

Distributed to the hobby, toy, and comic trade in the United States and Canada by regional distributors.

Distributed worldwide by Wizards of the Coast, Inc. and regional distributors.

Cover art by Dave Dorman
First Printing: April 1999
Library of Congress Catalog Card Number: 97-062377

9 8 7 6 5 4 3 2 1

ISBN: 0-7869-1344-4
21344XXX1501

U.S., CANADA, ASIA,   EUROPEAN HEADQUARTERS
PACIFIC, & LATIN AMERICA   Wizards of the Coast, Belgium
Wizards of the Coast, Inc.   P.B. 2031
P.O. Box 707   2600 Berchem
Renton, WA 98057-0707   Belgium
+1-800-324-6496   +32-70-23-32-77

Visit our web site at **www.wizards.com**

To Jeff Grubb:
A great writer, a fellow Alliterate, and a good friend.

ACKNOWLEDGMENTS:

Shared worlds are just that—the shared imaginative property of many people—game designers, artists, editors, authors, directors, marketers, accountants . . . and consumers, too. I will not pretend that the group I thank here includes everybody, but to those listed below, I give my deepest appreciation.

First of all, let me thank the two people I worked most closely with on this book, my two editors, Peter Archer and Jess Lebow. They are gentlemen and scholars, endowed with creativity as well as analytical prowess. Thanks, guys.

Secondly, I am in great debt to the authors who paved the way for this new batch of **Magic** books—Jeff Grubb and Lynn Abbey. I cannot imagine two professionals I admire more. Thanks for taking the lead and inviting me along.

Next, let me thank the summit team I worked with—Peter Adkison, Mary Kirchoff, Emily Arons, Joel Mick, Pete Venters, Chaz Elliott, Scott McGough, Paul Thompson, Loren Coleman, and Lizz Baldwin. It was a great week of synergy.

And, finally, I want to thank Richard Garfield, the man who started it all, and you, the readers and game players, who make the whole world live.

Proogue

Urza says he's sane. Perhaps he is. Measures of sanity among planeswalkers are hard to come by. He has lived for over three thousand years. He heals by merely willing it. With a thought, he steps from world to world to world. His very appearance is a matter of convenience, clothes and even features projected by his mind. How can conventional notions of sanity apply to a planeswalker?

Perhaps they cannot, but his madness began before he was a planeswalker. Three thousand years ago, a mortal Urza battled his mortal brother. Their sibling rivalry turned fratricidal. So began the Brothers' War. In his rage to kill Mishra, Urza enlisted the armies of the world, sank the isle of Argoth, gutted the continent of Terisiare, and wiped whole nations from the globe. He ushered in an ice age. In repayment for all this madness, he became a planeswalker.

Urza says he regrets the destruction. True regret would be a good sign.

It wasn't regret that later sent Urza on his own private invasion of Phyrexia. It was revenge for his brother. Somehow, Urza convinced himself he hadn't killed Mishra, that the Phyrexian Gix had done it. True, Gix seduced Mishra with promises of awesome power and in the end transformed him into a monstrous amalgam of flesh and artifice. But Urza was Mishra's slayer. Not in his mind, though.

1

In the mind of madness, Urza blamed Gix and plotted to get even. His motive was mad, and his invasion madder still. Urza attacked Phyrexia—one planeswalker against armies of demonic monstrosities. He lost, of course. He couldn't defeat a whole world and was nearly torn to pieces trying.

Tail between his legs, Urza retreated to Serra's Realm, a place of angels and floating clouds. There he convalesced, but he never truly recovered. Madness still haunted him, and so did Phyrexia. Gix followed on his tail. No sooner had Urza left Serra's Realm, thinking himself whole and hale, than Gix and his demons arrived. A war began in heaven. That place, like any other where Urza had chosen to dwell, was decimated. Centuries later, it is still shrinking in its long collapse.

When I point out these mad indiscretions, Urza shrugs. He claims he regained his sanity after all that. He credits his newfound perspective to Xantcha and Ratepe—"two dear friends who sacrificed themselves to slay the demon Gix, close the portal to Phyrexia, and save my life. To them, I am forever grateful."

True gratitude would be a good sign, too.

Urza has never, in his three millennia of life, shown true gratitude nor had a "dear friend." I have known him for three decades. For two of those, I have worked side by side with him at the academy we established here on Tolaria. I am not his dear friend. No one is. Most of the tutors and students at the academy don't even know his real name, calling him Master Malzra. The last person who was close enough to Urza to be a dear friend was his brother, and everyone knows what happened to him.

No, Urza is incapable of regret and gratitude, of having dear friends, not that there haven't been folk like Xantcha, Ratepe, Serra, and I, who genuinely love the man and would give our lives for him. But he seems incapable of returning our affection.

That's not enough to declare him insane, of course. As I said, measures of sanity among planeswalkers are hard to come by, but there is something mad about Urza's blithe belief that Xantcha and Ratepe sacrificed themselves, that Serra's Realm and Argoth sacrificed themselves, that Mishra sacrificed himself. . . . It seems everyone and everything Urza claims to care about gets destroyed. And what does that mean for me, his newest dear friend?

—**Barrin, Mage Master of Tolaria**

PART I

School of Time

Chapter 1

Jhoira stood at the edge of her world. Behind her lay the isle of Tolaria, its palm forests and lecture halls overrun with magical prodigies and clockwork creatures. It was a realm of ceaseless tests and pointless trials and worries and work, lots of work.

Before her lay the blue ocean, the blue sky, and the illimitable world. Clouds piled into empyrean mountain ranges above the shimmering sea. White waves broke on the ragged rocks below. Beyond the thin, brilliant line of the horizon, the whole world waited. Her soul mate was out there somewhere, she dreamed. Everything was out there—her homeland, her parents, her Shivan tribe, her future.

Jhoira sighed and slouched down to sit on a sun-warmed shoulder of sandstone. Sea winds sent her long black hair dancing about her thin shoulders. Breezes coursed, warm and familiar, through her white student robes. She'd spent many hours in this sunny niche, her refuge from the academy, but lately the hideaway brought her as much sadness as joy.

She'd been at the academy for eight years now, learning all she could of machines. A prodigy when she arrived, Jhoira was now a formidable artificer. She was also a woman, or at eighteen nearly so, and was weary of the school and the kids, of brimstone and machine oil. She was sick to death of artifice and illusion and wanted something real—some*one* real.

Jhoira closed her eyes, drawing a deep breath of salty air into her lungs. Her soul mate would be tall and bronze-skinned, like the young Ghitu tribesmen back home—keen-eyed and strong. He would be smart, yes, but not like Teferi and the other boys who tried to get Jhoira's attention through juvenile antics and unsubtle innuendoes. He would be a man, and he would be mysterious. That was most important of all. She could not be in love with a man unless, at the core of his being, there was mystery.

She opened her eyes and shifted her weight, one sandal sending up a puff of dust. "I'm a fool. There's not a man like that in the world." Even if there were, she'd never get to meet him, not while she was stuck on this blasted island.

* * * * *

Standing, the silver man awoke. He had moved before, had walked and spoken before. He had occupied this enormous body of metal, peered out of its silvery eyes, and lifted things in its massive hands. Before it had been always as if in a dream. Now he was awake. Now he was alive.

The laboratory around him was bright and clean. Master Malzra liked it clean—clean but cluttered. One wall held hundreds of sketches and refinements of sketches, some in ink, some in lead, some in chalk. Another bristled with specialized implements—metal lathes, beam saws, injection molds, presses, rollers, bellows, drills. A third wall bore racks of cogs and struts and other mechanical castings. A fourth held ranks of assembled mechanisms. A fifth—very few of the school's rooms were square—allowed egress into the room. In the center of the space, a great black forge rose. Its smokestack climbed up and away through the dome above. A second-floor gallery ringed the fringes of the room. Up in those balconies even now, young eyes peered down on the result of Master Malzra's latest experiment. They peered down on the silver man.

The silver man peered back. He felt frightened, awkward, shy. He wondered what they thought about him—wondered and cared in a way he never had before. Everything was like that. He had seen this laboratory many times before, but he never would have used terms like clean and cluttered and bright to describe it or the man who had created it. Now the silver man perceived more than just things. He perceived the organization of things, their disposition, and what they implied about their creator. The laboratory was a study in the mind of Master Malzra—ancient, obsessed, brilliant, tireless, preoccupied, short-sighted, grandiose. . . .

Master Malzra, meanwhile, studied him. The man's gaze was penetrating. Folds of aged skin drew up skeptically beneath one eye. His nostrils flared, but he didn't seem to breathe at all. One soot-blackened hand trembled slightly as he raised it to scratch his ash-blond beard. He swallowed, blinking—but with eyes like that, as hard and sharp as diamonds, it seemed he didn't need to blink at all.

"Any noticeable change in the probe's energy profile, Barrin?" Malzra asked over his shoulder.

It was a strange greeting. The silver man felt somewhat offended.

"A reasonable enough question," came the response—from Malzra's second, a master mage. Barrin stepped from beside an injection mold. He wiped grit from his hands with a white cloth. "Why don't you ask him?"

Malzra blinked again. "Ask whom?"

"Ask *him*," the mage repeated, quirking one corner of his mouth. "The probe."

Malzra pursed his lips. He nodded. "Probe, I am Master Malzra, your creator. I wish to know if you notice any change in your energy profile."

"I remember who you are," responded the silver man. His voice was deep and resonant in his metal form. "And I notice a very definite change in my energy profile. I am awake."

A sibilance of voices came from the balcony.

Malzra seemed almost to smile. "Ah, you are *awake*. Good. As you are doubtless aware, we've made some modifications to you, hoping to enhance your performance, your intellect, and your capacity for social integration." He ground his teeth and could not seem to come out with anything else. Malzra glanced back to Barrin for help.

The mage—lean, middle-aged in a white work smock—approached. He patted the silver man's shoulder. "Hello. We're glad you've woken up. How do you feel?"

"Confused," the silver man heard himself say, then in a voice of wonder, he went on. "Everything seems to have a new dimension. I am filled with conflicting information."

Barrin asked, "Conflicting information?"

"Yes," replied the silver man. "I sense, for example, that though Master Malzra is your superior in rank and age, he often defers to you due to his social disinclinations."

"Social disinclinations?" Barrin prompted.

"He prefers the company of machines to that of people," clarified the silver man.

Titters of humor came from the gallery. Malzra's expression darkened as he glanced up.

The probe continued, "Even now, I perceive that my observation, though accurate, displeases Master Malzra, amuses the students, and embarrasses you."

Barrin flushed slightly. "True enough." He turned to Malzra. "I could run some magical tests, but even without them, it's clear the intellectual and emotional components of the implant are functioning."

"Only too well," responded Malzra ruefully, to the delight of the watchers in the gallery. "Still, I would be just as glad for further tests of these components to occur outside of my company."

"In other words—?"

"Send out the probe. Let it interact with the students. We can monitor its progress," Malzra instructed.

Barrin looked levelly at the probe. Wisdom and magic danced in the man's brown eyes. "You heard what he said. Go out. Explore. Meet some people. Make some friends. We will recall you when we are ready for more experimentation."

The silver man acknowledged these instructions by moving

toward the door. As he shuffled past lathes and drill presses, the probe marveled at the resentment he felt toward his creator. Malzra had referred to him as an "it." Barrin had referred to him as "you."

As if reading his mind, Barrin approached the silver man and patted his shoulder once again. "You were right about Master Malzra's 'social disinclinations,' that he likes machines better than people. What you didn't seem to recognize is that he got flustered in dealing with you."

The silver man's response was sullen. "I recognized that all too clearly."

"Yes," Barrin said, "but that means he doesn't think of you as a machine, not any longer. To him, you are becoming a person."

* * * * *

As the probe and the students filed out of the laboratory, Barrin drew Urza to a wall of sketches. There, in diagrams of lead and ink, the silver man was detailed, inside and out.

"Well, you were right," Barrin said quietly. "Xantcha's heart was the key. Her affective and intellectual cortexes must be intact, as you had thought. We can be thankful that none of her memories remain, or her personality—apparently. Still, I have to wonder about the wisdom of placing what amounts to a Phyrexian matrix into the head of your most powerful and advanced creation. I could have achieved the same effect with an animation spell—"

The master waved off the comment. "I wanted to achieve sentience through purely mechanical means. Besides, there is nothing Phyrexian about the heart crystal anymore. There is not even anything of Xantcha left in it—just enough of a matrix to allow logical, emotional, and social learning."

Barrin winced slightly at the man's choice of words. "Yes, well, that's the other matter. What we've got here is no longer just a machine. You know it, and I know it. So does the probe. You gave him emotions. You need to acknowledge those emotions. You need to *respect* those emotions." Only a blank stare answered him. "Don't you see? This is not just a probe anymore. He is a man—no, more than that—he is a child. He'll need to be guided, nurtured—"

The master looked stern. "I wish you had brought this up before. We could have devised a rubric for handling this aspect of the probe's development."

"That's just it," replied Barrin. "You can't devise rubrics for this kind of thing. You can't chart it out in blueprints. You have to stop thinking like an artificer and start thinking like a—well, like a father."

"I was an orphan at twelve. Mishra and I both. We turned out all right."

The mage snorted just slightly at that. "If you wish, I will act as the probe's mentor in your place, but in time you are going to need to create that bond yourself. And that will mean telling him who you really are—telling him he was created by Urza Planeswalker."

* * * * *

Master Malzra's laboratory had been daunting enough for the silver man and his new intellectual cortex. The corridors and spaces beyond the lab—tutorial rooms, lecture halls, surgical theaters, wind tunnels, test chambers, and countless more laboratories—were overwhelming. In gazing at these elaborate structures, the probe understood at last what a school was: a building designed to aid in gaining new knowledge, communicating it to others, and applying it in invention. This was a revelation. His creators needed to learn. They were not all-knowing angels, driven by logical necessity and an apprehension of the ascendant good. They were ignorant animals, ennobled only by their insatiable curiosity, and some were less ennobled than others.

"I'm Teferi," offered a boy who capered into the silver man's path and stopped stock still, as if daring the half-ton creature to walk over him. "I'm the magical prodigy." He followed the introduction with a snap of his fingers, sending blue sparks bursting through the air.

The probe stopped in his tracks and crouched slightly to get a better look at the young scholar. Teferi's face was small, dark, and impish. Tousled black hair jutted wildly about his gleaming eyes. He wore the manifold white robes of a Tolarian student. At his waist, a leather sash held his personal array of crystals, wands, and fetishes. His feet were bare, in defiance of school policy, though his toenails bore strange legends in bright, glossy paint. He held one of his hands out formally toward the probe.

The silver man extended his own massive hand and lightly shook the boy's whole arm. "I am Master Malzra's Probe." No sooner had he taken the boy's hand than the probe noticed a strange, stinging jolt in his silver hide. "Your handshake is shocking."

The lad pulled his hand away and shrugged, seeming somehow disappointed. "Just a spell I've been working on. Knocks people on their butts. Not golems, I guess. Say, what kind of a name is Master Malzra's Probe, anyway?"

"It is the only name I have," replied the probe truthfully.

Teferi's face rumpled, and he shook his head. "Not good enough. You've got a personality now. You need a real name."

Other young students were gathering in the corridor behind Teferi, and they leaned inward, anticipating something.

"I am unfamiliar with naming procedures."

Teferi gave a confident smile. "Oh, I'm quite familiar. Let's see. You're big and shiny. What else is big and shiny? The Null Moon. Why don't we call you the Null Man?"

The students laughed at this suggestion.

The probe felt a sense of irritation. "That sounds unsatisfactory. null means nothing. Your suggestion would imply I am a nothing man."

Teferi nodded seriously, though a smirk played about his mouth. "We can't have that. Anyway, you aren't really a man. You're an artifact. Arty would be a nice name for you. Arty the Artifact."

The probe could not determine any reason to reject this suggestion—aside from the chuckles of the students. "Arty is a name used among humans?"

"Oh, yes," replied Teferi enthusiastically, "as a first name, but most humans also have a last name. Let's see, you are silver. What else is made of silver? Spoons are, and since you are large, we ought to name you after the largest spoon—a ladle, or perhaps a shovel. Thus, your full name should be Arty Ladlepate or Arty Shovelhead."

These young folk seemed to giggle at any and every suggestion made to them. The silver man became less concerned about their amusement. "Whichever name sounds more pleasant to human ears—"

"Oh, either name will bring a smile to anyone who hears it. Still, Ladlepate sounds a little too uppity, as if you were putting on airs. Shovelhead is much more accessible. I vote for Arty Shovelhead. What say the rest of you?"

The gathered students cheered excitedly, and the silver man could not help being swept up in the mood. At the moment, any name seemed better than no name.

"I shall then be Arty Shovelhead," the probe said solemnly.

"Come along, then, Shovelhead," said Teferi grandly, gesturing down the corridor with his boyish arm. Streamers of conjured illumination fanned out from his fingers. "I have much to show you."

The crowd of students surged up around the probe and dragged at his cold metal hands with their warm fingers. He plodded along among them, careful not to step on their feet.

The entourage of children led the probe along as though he were a visiting dignitary. They arrived first at a large dining hall with ivory rafters and soaring walls of alabaster. Beneath this white vault were long, dark tables crowded with more students who bent above bowls of gruel and platters of hard crackers and cheese.

"This is the great hall," narrated Teferi. "This is where we students eat. The food is specially prepared so that nothing about it could distract us from our studies. Notice the bland colors and mean consistency of it all? The flavors are even more indistinguishable. No one could gnaw on one of those crackers and spend even a moment to contemplate its nonexistent virtues."

The probe could tell that this boy had an acute grasp of the truth behind appearances. "Master Malzra must care greatly about your studies."

Teferi laughed, though the sound was rueful. "Oh, yes. He nurtures our minds like a farmer nurtures grain. He heaps manure on our heads, knowing we will rise up through it, despite it, to bear richly, and then he comes along with a scythe and cuts our heads off to nourish his own appetites. It is a fine arrangement, depending on who you are." He had said this last bit while leading the probe and his companions down the passageway to another chamber, similar to the first, except that the vault overhead was dark, and the students at the long tables were crouched over sheets of paper, quill pens scraping fitfully across them. "Here is part of that diet of manure I spoke of. These students are copying plans and treatises of Master Malzra, Mage Barrin, and other scholars. It is in sedulously copying the scribbles of our betters that we become consummate scribblers ourselves."

The probe was appreciative. "What do these plans and treatises describe?"

"Machines, such as yourself. Gadgets, mainly. He's got a whole mausoleum—um, that is, museum—filled with artifact creatures. You'll be there too, soon enough. Master Malzra has a very active imagination and puts it to great use devising elaborate means to save himself a little bit of labor. He has created numerous devices to more quickly and efficiently cook the gruel and crackers, to more effectively limit the freedom of those under his command, to more completely defend all of us against external foes so that he alone can torment us."

The silver man felt uncomfortable with this new line of thought. "External foes? What foes does Malzra have?"

"Oh, everyone is against him, or didn't you know?" said Teferi lightly as they moved farther down the hallway. He idly conjured a small knife, whirled it deftly between his fingers, and then dispelled it. "At least that's what Malzra thinks. He's got clockwork creatures and actual warriors roaming the walls around the academy at all hours, and clay men tramping through the woods by the sea, and gear-work birds that spy on the island. I myself have never heard of a single real enemy, but Malzra spends so much time creating these machines and recreating them and perfecting them, there must be something more than psychotic paranoia at the root of it, wouldn't you think?"

"I suppose so," the silver man answered.

They came to another room, this one filled with dissected hulks of metal, leaning clockwork warriors, dismantled machines, piles of rusted scrap iron, and at the far wall, a great open furnace. Workers on one side of the blazing forge shoveled coal into the flames and pumped massive bellows. Workers on the other side dumped bins of spare parts into great vats of molten metal. Throughout the rest of the grimy chamber, students moved among the ruined machines like vultures picking at a battlefield of dead. A shiver of dread move through the probe.

Teferi noticed the impulse and smiled grimly. "See, Arty, even if Malzra has no other enemies, his old creations could easily turn on him. They should. They certainly have reason to hate him. Malzra quickly tires of his playthings. I can imagine a legion of metal men such as yourself learning that Malzra planned to melt them down. They could escape across the sea. I can imagine whole nations of clockwork creatures who have fled their creator only to muster themselves in hopes of returning and killing him."

The silver man was aghast. "How could an artifact creature ever seek to destroy the artifact creator?"

"Give it a year, Arty," Teferi said lightly, though none of the students laughed this time. The boy patted the golem's arm. "Give it a year—two at the outside, and you'll be facing that fiery furnace. It's the way of artifice. When you're in pieces in that room, then ask yourself what you think about Master Malzra."

* * * * *

Jhoira was again in her rocky haven from the world. She spent less and less time in the academy and more and more time here, dreaming of far-off places and futures—

A white flapping motion caught her eye. There along the shore, between two fingers of stone, something was moving. It looked like a seagull's wing, only too large. A pelican? A white sea lion? Jhoira blinked, rubbing her eyes. The sea and sky were dazzling here. Maybe it was only a glaring bit of foam.

No, it was more than that. It looked like fabric—perhaps another student? Jhoira slid from the sandstone ledge and eased herself down the tumbled hillside. One edge of the white fabric was tied to something rigid—a spar. It was a sail. Jhoira descended more quickly. Her sandal soles slid on pea-gravel and sand. She thrashed past a brake of grass and clambered down the cleft between two wind-carved stones.

The space gave out onto a wide beach of beige sand, broken by rills of craggy black stone. Above one such rill, a lateen-rigged sail jutted flaglike from a shattered wooden hull. The impact had staved the boat's prow and splintered the timbers amidships. Since then, the rocks had chewed away at the frame, each new wave grinding the hull again on the ragged stones.

Jhoira approached cautiously. So few ships arrived at Tolaria. Most were the academy's own supply vessels, captained by seamen hand-picked by Master Malzra. The island was too remote, too removed from trade routes to attract other ships. This boat must have drifted for some distance off course before crashing. Perhaps it was abandoned. Perhaps its crew had been washed overboard. Jhoira craned her neck as she neared, looking for signs of life in the ruined hulk. Her sandal prints filled with salty water behind her. She reached the stony outcrop and climbed up above the pitching wreck.

It was a small craft, the sort that might have been manned by a crew of five or a crew of one. The deck was in disarray—lines lashing loosely, small barrels rolling with each sea surge. The hatch was open, and in the dark hold Jhoira glimpsed gulls fighting over bits of hard-tack that had spilled from broken crates. The mainmast was cracked, though it still held aloft the raked sail, and the mainsail's sheet was cleated off, as if the boat had been at full sail when it

17

struck the stone. It must have run aground last night, when the Glimmer Moon had been obscured by a midnight storm. The bow was gone entirely, but the stern remained. A narrow set of stairs led downward to a small doorway. The captain's quarters would lie beyond.

"What are you doing?" Jhoira asked herself worriedly as she clambered down the boulder where the ship was impaled, lifted one leg over the starboard rail, and hauled herself onto the pitching deck. "This thing could come loose any moment and roll over and drag me out to sea."

Even so, she crawled forward, reached the set of stairs that led down to the captain's quarters, and descended. She pulled open the red door and cringed back from the hot, stale air within. The space was dark and cramped. With each wave surge, the floor clattered with junk—a map tube, a lodestone, a stylus, a wrecked lantern, spanners, a slide rule, and other indistinguishable items. To one side of the cabin, a small table hugged the wall. To the other were a pair of bunks. The bottom bed held a still figure.

Dead, Jhoira thought. The man lay motionless, despite the tossing sea. His face was tanned beneath curls of golden hair. His jaw was shaggy with a week's growth of beard. His hands, large and strong, were laid across his chest in the attitude of death.

Jhoira backed away. Perhaps this was a plague ship, this man the last to succumb, with no one to throw him overboard. She'd been a fool to climb aboard.

Then he moved. He breathed, and she knew, even if he was plagued, she could not abandon him. Without another moment's hesitation, Jhoira crossed the crowded cabin, stooped beside the bunk, and lifted the man. She had always been strong. The Ghitu of Shiv had to be strong. Shifting the man to her shoulder, she struggled out of the cabin and up the stairs. Navigating the rubble-strewn deck with a man on her shoulder was difficult, and Jhoira stumbled twice. Gritting her teeth in determination, she made the rail. With a heart-rending leap, she reached the rock and clung there.

As if shifted by her jump, the broken craft heeled away from the crag. A wave crashed into it, lifting it up, and with a briny surge, the boat scraped up toward Jhoira and her charge. She clambered to a higher spot on the rock. The wave tumbled back from shore, taking the hulk with it. The mast rolled under and snapped like a twig. Shroudlike, the sail wrapped the splintered boat as it heaved outward on the retreating wave. Broken barrels and other debris boiled in the wake of the boat.

Panting, Jhoira watched the broken mass of wreckage bob out into deeper water. The next wave rolled it once more, and then the ship disappeared. For some time she could see it, moving in the undertow like some white leviathan.

Jhoira waited for a break in the waves and climbed down from the stone. She crossed the sandy berm, tempted to set the man down there. A darting glance up at the hilltop told her that no other students or scholars had seen the shipwreck or knew of the man, but others might come soon. The man would be as good as dead. Malzra did not suffer the arrival of strangers on his island paradise, and the students were sworn to report any such castaways they discovered. Jhoira planned to report this one, of course, but she didn't want anyone else to know about him—not yet.

Strong though she was, the climb from the shore to her hideaway was a hot labor. When she arrived, she laid the man down on the sunny stretch of sandstone where she had spent so many afternoons. She checked for breath and pulse, found both, and set a hand on his brow to check for fever. He felt warm, though that might have been only from the sunlight. There was a better test for fever. Her heart pounding, she leaned over and kissed his forehead.

"Hot. Yes. Very hot," Jhoira said breathlessly.

She removed her outer cloak, snagged a bit of scrub, and propped the fabric up over his face, shielding him from the sun. She retrieved a small canteen from her belt, parted the man's lips, and poured a cool trickle of water into his mouth.

He was beautiful—tan, strong, tall, and mysterious. That was the most important thing of all. The last drops fell from the canteen.

"You stay here," she whispered, patting his shoulder. "Don't let anybody see you. I'll go get more water and blankets—supplies. I'll take care of you. Stay here."

Heart fluttering in her breast like a caged bird, Jhoira hurried away from her secret spot and her secret stranger.

Her footsteps had hardly faded beyond the rocky rise when the stranger's blue eyes opened. There was a gleam in them, something vaguely metallic. It might have been only the silver shimmer of clouds reflecting there, but there might have been something else to that gleam, something mechanical, something menacing.

Monologue

At last, Urza has done it, making a machine that really lives. He's been working for three thousand years to devise such a thing. Now that he has one, he doesn't know what to do with him.

The silver man is engineered to let Urza return in time, even farther back than those three thousand years, to the time of the ancient Thran. Urza hopes the probe can reach the time of that ancient race, some six millennia in the past. If Urza himself could reach such a time, he could prevent the Thran from transforming into the race of half-flesh, half-machine abominations that seek to destroy life on Dominaria, thereby rectifying the error he and his brother Mishra made in opening the doors to Phyrexia.

I've pointed out that unmaking the Phyrexians is tantamount to slaying all of us who have lived in this world since their creation. Still, Urza would rather wipe the slate clean than deal with his past—just as he did at Argoth.

The disturbing thing is, he is making all the same mistakes over again. If he could only have embraced his brother instead of attacking him—if he could only have apologized for his arrogance and obsession and been reconciled—the Brothers' War would never have been fought, the brotherhood of Gix would never have gotten a foothold in the world, and Argoth and most of Terisiare would not have been destroyed. If he had worked with his brother instead of against him, combining their genius and the power of both halves of the stone they had discovered, the pathway from Phyrexia might have been cut off the very day it was accidentally opened.

Reconciliation is not in the man any more than regret or remorse or friendship. Every sin of omission Urza committed against his brother, he repeats now against his own students . . . and his new-born silver man.

—**Barrin, Mage Master of Tolaria**

Chapter 2

The students were gone from the laboratory. Only Master Malzra, his trusted associate Barrin, and the silver man remained among the dark implements and ubiquitous sketches.

"You've learned much in your first day," said Barrin gently. "We have been observing, remotely. You have interacted well."

"I have a friend," the silver man volunteered.

A creased smile played across Barrin's face. "Yes. Teferi, my prodigal prodigy—we know about that."

"He told me many things," the probe continued. His voice was edged with suspicion. "He explained the academy to me. He has named me Arty Shovelhead."

The mage sighed in irritation. "Teferi is a brilliant young mage—my most promising student—but he likes to stir up trouble. He makes things twice as hard for himself, and three times as hard for everyone else—"

"Teferi is a good first friend," interrupted Malzra with uncharacteristic alacrity. He glanced between the silver man and the man of flesh, then seemed to withdraw behind his glimmering eyes. "After all, Barrin, you said the probe has emotions—needs friends."

"Yes," the mage said, diverting the conversation at its awkward turn. "Master Malzra is eager for you to begin the experiments you were created to carry out. That's why we called you back this evening."

22

Barrin moved to one wall, opened a small hatch, and drew forth a long pole three times his height. At the tip of the pole was a small hook. Barrin hoisted the hook to the ceiling, engaged it in a hidden slot, and pulled downward once. A large panel in the dome shifted and then slowly separated from the smooth curve. On hydraulic rods, the panel eased downward from the dome. A large, complex machine of glass cylinders, metal casings, and snaking tubes emerged. Lamplight glowed from the descending apparatus, ten times more massive than the silver man himself.

"This is a time field distortion device," Master Malzra explained. "It is powered by four separate sources of energy—thermal, mechanical, geomagnetic, and of course, Thran. The thermal component provides a molecular time clock, an exact measure of the temporal vector, calibrated in atomic vibration per second. The mechanical component rotates the unit about its axis, thus creating beneath the device a cone of radiation within which the temporal distortion will manifest. The geomagnetic component provides precise coordinates of longitude, latitude, and altitude for the origin and destination points. Thran powerstones, of course, provide the main drive of the machine."

The silver man wondered aloud, "What is this . . . machine?"

"A time machine," Barrin explained. "Actually, it provides travel through time and space both. Tonight we plan to test only the temporal components."

"You wish me to operate this machine?" the probe guessed.

"We wish you to travel in it," Master Malzra replied. "The current design plays havoc with biological creatures. Any organism with a heartbeat, respiration, a sequential digestive tract, and a network of neural pathways that rely on chemical reactions is ill-adapted to time-field distortions."

"They die," Barrin explained. "Metals are much less susceptible to temporal stresses. Silver, of all metals, showed the least resistance. That is why you are made of silver. That is why you were made—to travel through the portal and report back what you have discovered."

The silver man approached the dangling device. His eyes traced out a circle on the floor beneath the massive machine. "Teferi told me about this. Every machine is made for a specific purpose. Every machine is made to defend you and the academy against . . . external foes."

Master Malzra's eyebrows rose. "Teferi knows that much?"

"Everyone seems to," the silver man said.

"Well, then—yes," the artificer said. "This is part of that defense. You must not divulge the information we are relating to you—"

"Of course not—"

"We intend, in time, to send you or another probe or perhaps eventually a person back to the time of the Thran, to divert them from the path that led to these—external foes."

"Send me or another probe. . . ." echoed the silver man, thinking of the fiery furnace, heaps of scrap metal, and workers with shovels.

"This is all utterly secret, of course," Malzra said.

"Yes," replied the silver man.

"Tonight's regression will be nothing so grand," assured Barrin, apparently sensing the probe's hesitancy. "If things go well, you will return in time perhaps as far back as this morning."

"What must I do?" the probe asked.

"You must stand here, within the circle," said Master Malzra. "That is all. You will stand and wait while the machine does its work. When the time regression slows, you must step from the circle to arrive in the former time. You will remain somewhat out of phase in the former time—you will be able to see your surroundings, but no one will be able to see you. This is to protect the time continuity. As the particles of your being gradually align themselves with your surroundings, this out-of-phase effect will lessen, and you will become visible. Whether in phase or out, you will be able to affect your environment, but we ask that you make no significant alterations, again for sake of temporal integrity. We will control your return trip from this end. When you are drawn back to the present, you will make a report of what you have discovered. Do you understand?"

"I understand," the silver man said flatly. "It is my purpose. It is why I was made."

Barrin eyed the silver golem narrowly and shook his head. He turned to Malzra and spoke quietly in his ear. "I don't like it. He's been traumatized by Teferi."

Malzra laughed quietly. "*You* are traumatized by Teferi."

"His emotional cortex is too new."

"He exhibits the correct emotional response to Teferi."

"I tell you, I don't like it."

"He understands. He knows this is the reason he was made."

"What if he meddles in the time stream?"

"Then we'll draw him back through, and we'll know he isn't sufficient to the task."

The silver man stood silent while the men spoke, his acute senses picking up every word.

"I understand you are eager, Malzra, but we have time. If our experiments work, we'll have all the time in the world. Testing a living creature is not like testing a machine. You can't just dismantle a creature, insert new parts, and start him up again—"

"On the contrary, that's what we did just this morning," Malzra finished, turning away from his associate. With a curt gesture, he said to the silver man, "Into the circle then. The power-up phase will take us a few moments."

Wordless, the probe stepped into the circle and stood. He could feel the silent, magnificent weight of the time machine hanging above his head. From the precise center of the floor, he watched Malzra and Barrin.

Barrin used the same hooked pole to trigger a hidden panel in the floor. A trefoil section of stone shifted aside, and an array of consoles rose into the room. Copper coils and pulsing tubes spilled from beneath the control panels. Barrin checked the various conduits where they connected with the floor. Malzra meanwhile worked adjustments to levers and switches.

Fluids began to move through the tubes. A low hum started among the great glass cylinders. Brass fittings buzzed. Even the dome itself rumbled with the mounting sound.

A high-pitched whine rose to echo through the lab, and a thin red beam stabbed from the base of the machine. It lanced through the charged air, just past the silver man's shoulder, and neatly struck the circle scribed on the floor. The ray fluttered a moment before sweeping in an arc. It looped the golem once and sped in its course. In moments, the single spinning beam had widened into a crimson cone that enveloped him.

The silver man stood there, bathed in lurid light, watching his creators. The men were busy at their consoles, drawing up one energy source and leveling off another, directing the beam in its spiraling crescendo, configuring the coordinates of space and time. . . . Light intensified. The artificers' endeavors slowed. The whining hum reached a peak. Master Malzra and Barrin soon moved not at all, frozen in space . . . or time.

The probe understood. The roaring machine and its whirring cone of light had teased the cord of time down to a frayed nub, and then to nothing. With rising fury, the device plucked at the packed skein of past moments. They too began to unravel. No longer motionless, Master Malzra and Barrin moved backward, undoing all they had done. Their arms darted with strange jabs like scorpion tails. More than that, the silver man also moved, or his past self moved. It trudged backward out of the circle just as he had trudged forward into it, only minutes before.

Within the cone of regression, the present-time silver man watched in amazement. His doppelganger conferred with Malzra and Barrin. Their words were lost to the hum of the machine, but the sense of them was clear—reversed syllables that did not inform or enlighten but rather disinformed and obscured. All the while they spoke, the ghost golem knew less and less, and the ghost time machine retracted into the dome above. When the brief conference was done, the past-time golem staggered backward toward the door, ignorant of the hidden machine and all that had been said.

The regression accelerated. Barrin and Malzra scuttled backward about the room, dismantling things, forgetting conversations, reducing conclusions to hypotheses, surrendering step by step the whole march of time. Soon they moved too quickly to seem anything but man-shaped blurs, then were gone entirely. The lab was dark and empty for some time, except the occasional jag of a mouse backing fitfully across the floor.

Eventually the two scholars returned, drawing after them a backwash of assistants and tutors. The galleries above flooded with eager, watchful eyes. The past-time golem trudged backward into the midst of it all. His return was heralded by nodding heads and hands coming sharply away from each other, drawing a brittle ovation from the air. The artificers themselves formed a retreating pocket of space into which the golem walked. He reached a designated spot and settled into immense inertia. There was another time of questions.

Malzra, with a suddenness that seemed almost savage, reached toward the probe's neck, performed some quick manipulation, and shoved the creature's head back on its shoulders. In a moment more, he lifted the metal skull-piece cleanly away.

Within the time machine, the silver man stared, stunned to see his own being so quickly and easily dismantled. The body yet stood, though the casing of the head lay now, as if discarded, on a side table. The inner workings of the golem's head were laid bare. Cogs and cables gleamed beneath a low set of struts. Light leaked through the whole mass. Malzra was busy tugging at a central silver case, the movements of his fingers awakening twitches in the creature's vivisected frame. Another two jiggles and Malzra drew forth the case. He opened it. Inside lay a dark stone the size of a child's fist. He removed the crystal. All final signs of life fled the creature.

The silver man watched in amazed dread as Malzra held high the stone. Gulping backward laughter came from the gallery. Malzra shouted something that ended the jollity and retreated to a table where he positioned the stone in a metal case.

The students in the gallery began to move. Malzra and Barrin busied themselves setting tools into cases and rubbing smears of oil from rags onto their hands. As the room slowly emptied, the dissected golem merely stood, lifeless and headless in the midst of it all.

The regression slowed. The time-traveling silver man's hulk smoldered—heat from temporal stress. He stepped from the coruscating beam. Around him time resumed its forward march. The students headed back into the gallery. The scholars unpacked their tools and wiped their hands clean.

Out of phase and unnoticed by them all, the silver man approached his headless predecessor. He stared into the vacant silver case jutting from the golem's neck. He reached up to his own neck, wondering where the catch was that would allow his skull-piece to be lifted away. His mind, his emotion, his very essence could be hauled up like a hunk of coal and displayed. He was a mere amusement for children. They had called him friend, but in truth he was only Shovelhead. Without that dark stone, he was not even that. The silver man stared into the undeniable image of his own death.

The regression was done. He was suddenly yanked from the time stream and back again, bathed in that rapacious red glow. Master Malzra summoned him to the present.

The silver man arrived. The beam skittered and danced away, withdrawing into the machine overhead. It too withdrew, trailing gray tendrils of smoke from the temporal stress it had endured.

Barrin and Malzra stood, blinking, at their consoles. Tentative, the two scholars released the controls beneath their fingers and approached the probe.

Barrin spoke first. "Are you well—?"

"Are you capable of rendering a report?" Malzra interrupted.

"My frame is quite hot," the silver man responded, "but I am capable, yes."

"How far back did you go?" Malzra asked.

"Back to this morning, to the time of my awakening."

"Excellent," Malzra said as Barrin noted the response on a sheet of paper. "And did you touch or move anything in that time?"

"I touched only the floor, with my feet, and moved only myself."

"Were you approached by anyone, or was there any other indication that your presence was noted?"

"No."

"What did you observe?"

This answer would not come as readily as the others.

"I observed myself dismantled. I observed the core of my being removed. I observed the small, dark, fragile thing that is my mind and self and soul."

Monologue

The first day of life is always the hardest, to be dragged from whatever warm, safe womb in which one is conceived and then thrust into the cold glare of the world. There is much to adjust to—breathing air instead of liquid, for one; being naked and prodded and scrubbed, for another. Worst of all, there is that moment when the cord is cut, and one is suddenly and irrevocably alone.

It is in recognition of such traumas that mothers' arms are made.

You have no mother. You have no father, either. You have a pair of creators, but that is not the same. Neither of us knows how to comfort and protect you. If you need too much nurturing, we may even consider you defective. Perhaps it is because you were designed to be a tool, a weapon—not a person. Perhaps it is because we have not expected to have to save you. We were hoping you would save us.

—Barrin, Mage Master of Tolaria

Chapter 3

It had been nearly a month since Jhoira had observed the lab session in which the silver man awoke. She could remember each detail of Master Malzra's technique. She'd spent the intervening time studying powerstones, like the one placed in the golem's head, and poring over the artifact's design sketches. All of it was preparation for the design debrief she would be required to give. It was the price paid by all the elite students invited to observe the procedure. There remained only one more task before she was ready to write her report—actually interviewing the machine.

She sighed with dread and tapped her fingers idly on the plans. She had hoped to derive a satisfactory description of the golem's intellectual and emotional performance from these plans, her research on Thran powerstones, and first hand observation of the refit. None of these things explained its—his—apparent logical and affective capacities though. She would have to interview him.

Jhoira glanced in surrender at the ceiling of her dormitory cell. Interviewing the machine meant winning past his self-appointed wrangler, Teferi. The boy—and at fourteen, he was *only* a boy—was one part prodigy, one part prankster, and one part pervert. Unfortunately all three parts were madly infatuated with Jhoira. She had done her best to discourage his advances, but he didn't notice subtle rebukes, and he considered unsubtle ones only affectionate horseplay.

If she told him she wasn't interested, he would pledge to make her interested. If she said she hated him, he would respond that hate and love were only a hair's breadth apart—and speaking of hair's breadths, could he have a breadth of hers? She had the inkling that he had made several attempts to devise a magical love potion to win her over.

Just thinking about the young man—the *boy*, he was only a *boy*—exasperated Jhoira. She stood from her desk and paced the small, spare room she occupied in the academy. If only Teferi could glimpse a real man, could glimpse the man she had found at the seaside and had provisioned and kept secret in her stony hideaway . . . No. Nobody could know about Kerrick except for her. That's the way it was and the way it should be. Jhoira sat down on her cot and stared out the window of her cell. Beyond the pitching treetops and the tumbled boulders lay the shore and her secret love.

She shook her head to clear it. The sooner she interviewed the silver man, the sooner she could finish her report, and the sooner she could rejoin Kerrick. Snatching up a sheaf of paper and a lead nib, Jhoira made her way through the door and out into the academy to hunt down the silver man.

She found him in the great hall, crouching to sit on a stump that had been hauled in specifically for him after he had broken three of the academy's benches. He looked dejected, hunkered down at the end of a table. Teferi held court beside him, and a passel of the prodigy's devotees clustered in a laughing bunch around. Carrots were on the menu today, and Teferi had discovered that by levitating them into various holes in the golem's skull, he could create comical ears and a long twisted nose. To these alterations came others—oily lettuce in an improvised head of hair, and large, bulging eyes made of hard biscuits rammed into the machine's eye sockets.

Jhoira shook her head as she approached. If reports were right, this machine was fully aware. He knew what was being done to him, and he cared.

"Does Master Malzra know what you are doing, Teferi?"

The boy looked up, his impish features lighting up when he caught sight of her. "Hello, Jhoira! Have you met Arty Shovelhead?"

"Does Master Malzra know what you are doing?" she repeated angrily.

The fourteen-year-old affected a smug superiority. He nodded toward the mirrored loft where Malzra and Barrin often took their lunch. "Master Malzra is keenly interested in all of my adventures. I'm Barrin's magical prodigy. Of course they know what I am doing."

"This artifact creature is self-aware, Teferi. He thinks. He has feelings. You can't just toy with him like this."

"I can, and I do," replied Teferi. He levitated a pair of radishes to make them hover like earrings on either side of the golem's head. "What fun is it to toy with someone who doesn't have thoughts and feelings?"

Exasperated, Jhoira flung out her hands. "Anyway, I need to interview him."

Teferi smiled. "Go right ahead. I'm his interpreter—right, Shovelhead?"

Behind his mask of biscuits and carrots, the silver man remained silent.

Reaching out distastefully, Jhoira drew a dripping leaf of lettuce from the creature's head, slug-trails of salad oil glistening across his shiny brow. "Did you ever think you might be damaging him, might be destroying him? This is sensitive machinery."

"Master Malzra wants it tested," Teferi replied glibly. He laced his fingers behind his head and leaned back on the bench. "I'm just giving it a rigorous exam. If you're jealous, I could arrange a rigorous exam for you, back in my cell." His friends chorused a thrilled *oooh* at the suggestion.

Jhoira flushed. "I'm not interested in little boys—" she countered, savagely knocking the biscuits from the silver man's face. The golem sent her a look of lost misery "—not interested in tiny, mean, little boys who cut the eyes out of sparrows and stomp roses into the ground and empty their bladders on anything beautiful and good.

That's what you are, Teferi—you're not even a nasty little boy, but an infant who can't control his own body, can't recognize anybody else as real, can't do anything but whine and cry and soil yourself and everybody around you. You're going to have to do lots of growing up before you'll be anything more than a squalling baby." Jhoira punctuated this tirade by yanking forth the variously placed carrots.

Teferi was silent. His face grew pale, as though the flush of Jhoira's features sucked the color out of his. By the time she was finished, his lip was quivering. His eyes were as wide and staring as the biscuits on the floor.

Jhoira reached down, gently, regally, and took the silver man's hand. "Let's go. I have a lot of questions to ask you."

The probe rose, as though his half-ton bulk could have been lifted by her one slender hand. Looking back over his shoulder, the silver man followed Jhoira, dejection and confusion in his bowed shoulders.

* * * * *

Barrin was nettled. He let go of the rail that overlooked the great room and paced in front of it. Through a one-way glass enchanted by the mage himself, they had both witnessed the incident with the carrots and biscuits—and hundreds of other pranks Teferi had played on the hapless golem. These occasions seemed only to mildly amuse Urza. They made Barrin furious.

"I can't understand why you allow it!" he stormed. "Here is the first truly living artifact creature you have created, and yet you surrender him to the depredations of that . . . that vulture!"

"Living things have to live, Barrin," Urza said calmly. "If Teferi breaks down the probe, we'll know it needs to be redesigned."

"Breaks down? Redesigned?" Barrin raged. "That's not what you do with living things. They have to live—as you said. This golem of yours is only a month old. Give him time—"

"Time is all I give him. We'll attempt another regression at the end of this month," Urza said, heading toward the chamber door.

"Meanwhile," said Barrin grimly, "I'm going to ask Jhoira to look after him, to keep him away from Teferi. I really don't understand why you refuse to let me expel that troublemaker."

Urza turned back in the open doorway. "I keep him here because he is a magical genius—driven and destined to greatness. He may be a social nuisance, yes, but I was one, too."

"You still are," Barrin observed tartly, "but Teferi's more than a nuisance. Jhoira said it best. He's selfish. He's dangerous. He hurts people without thought or apology. He takes no responsibility for his actions. I don't care about his potential. Until he grows up, he will leave a path of destruction in his wake."

"You have said the same of me before." Urza blinked, considering. "Yes, I keep Teferi here because he reminds me of me."

* * * * *

Jhoira ushered the silver man into her room. He had to turn sideways to fit through the arched doorway, and once within, merely stood there, as stiff and fearful as an adolescent boy.

"It's all right. I'm not going to bite," Jhoira assured. She gestured the golem in so that she could swing the door closed behind him.

The click of the latch made the room feel even smaller. Despite his stooped shoulders and silent demeanor, the probe seemed especially massive in that moment.

Jhoira skirted around him and busied herself tidying the room. "It's not much, I know, but it's all I need and private." She snatched up a conspicuous undergarment and secreted it within a basket in one corner. "Here's my bed," she continued, nervously straightening the slate-gray blanket on it and fluffing the pillow, as though she expected the silver man to lie down on it. "Here's where I keep my clothes—the student robes hanging in that bone-inlaid wardrobe there, and my knockabout clothes here in this drawer. That's one drawback to being made of skin. You've got to cover it all the time."

That felt forced. Jhoira reminded herself this was a man of metal, no more interested in her undergarments than a doorknob would be.

"Here. He.e's something you'll like." She reached up to a low shelf above her drafting desk and drew down a small metal pendant. It was fashioned to resemble a lizard-man dressed in heavy robes. "This is from my homeland, Shiv. It's metal—not just metal, but Viashino metal. That's some of the hardest stuff in the world." Unthinking, she tossed the trinket to the golem.

One massive hand snatched the item from the air—the first movement the golem had made since settling into stillness. He stared down at it. "It is hard," he agreed in a voice like the distant rumble of a waterfall. "It scratched me."

Jhoira's brow furrowed. She crossed the floor to look. Two small scratches marked the silver man's palm. "Oh, no. I'm sorry. Let me get something for—" She broke into laughter, backed up, and slumped onto the bed.

The silver man leaned forward. "What is it? Did I say something stupid?"

"No, no," Jhoira assured. "I did. It's me. If one of my other friends had gotten scratched, I'd have pressed a rag on it to stop the bleeding, but you can't bleed. Still, I was going to get a rag."

"One of your *other* friends—?" the golem echoed.

"Oh, I'm just nervous. I don't know why." She sat up soberly on the bed. "I don't really have a lot of friends. I don't usually let anybody else in here, and I know you're just a machine, but you seem so real, so much like a person."

"So much like a person—"

She shook her head and fetched a rag from among her drafting supplies. "Still, you could use one of these. I've been going on and on, and there you stand, vinegar dripping from your head." Flipping the rag in one hand, she walked to the golem and began wiping away the liquid. "You know, in my tribe back home in Shiv, they put oil on somebody's head to honor him. It's called anointing. Ghitu do it when you are born, and when you set out on a vision quest, and when you need healing, and when you've just been saved from death." She patiently daubed away the streams of liquid and polished the creature's shiny pate.

"Maybe that's what happened to me," said the silver man. "Maybe I've just been anointed."

"You're lucky it was just oil and vinegar. Knowing Teferi, it could have been something much worse."

"It wasn't Teferi who anointed me," the silver man rumbled. "It wasn't Teferi who saw that I needed healing."

Jhoira smiled sadly, wiping the last of the oil away. She gestured at the pendant. "You can keep it. They're supposed to be lucky. They're good to have with you on a vision quest." She wiped her hands on another cloth and tossed both into the basket in the corner. "Anyway, I'm doing a treatise on you, and I have some questions—if you don't mind?"

The silver man said solemnly, "You are the first person to ask whether I minded anything."

Jhoira nodded distractedly. She drew a large folio of sketches from beneath her drafting table and selected a number of rattling sheets from it. She spread them out on the workspace.

"These are drawings of me," observed the golem.

"Yes. This is the final set of plans for you before the powerstone was implanted—front, back, left, right, top, and bottom views. There's a detail of your torso. You've got lots of room in there. And here's your head," she said as she pointed to each matrix of gray lines and gear-work.

"This legend names me only 'PROBE 1,' " the golem indicated.

"Yes," responded Jhoira. "Master Malzra is not very imaginative when it comes to names. Still, it's a better name than Arty Shovelhead."

One of the golem's massive fingers traced out a bracket that indicated the whole frame of the construct. Beside it was a call out that said simply, "KARN."

"I like this name better. What does it mean?"

Jhoira looked up from the sketch. Her eyes narrowed intently as she studied the golem's gleaming features. "That's Old Thran. I don't know much of the language—even Master Malzra doesn't know much of it—but I know that word. It means 'mighty.' "

"Karn," the golem repeated thoughtfully.

Jhoira smiled again. "Yes. That's a good name. That's your name. Karn." She turned back to the table. "Now these sketches on this side show the powerstone and its integration into the superstructure. The point of my treatise is to explain how an automaton becomes a thinking, feeling creature, simply through the addition of a crystal. I haven't been able to figure it out by looking at these diagrams, even by watching the operation. I can't imagine how a powerstone—especially one that looked dead, like the one inside you—could give a creature thought and life and soul."

"Perhaps it isn't a powerstone," offered Karn quietly.

"Not a powerstone?" Jhoira wondered. "Then what would it be?"

"I don't know, but without it, I am nothing," Karn observed. "I've seen myself without it. I'm just a pile of metal."

"Seen yourself?" Jhoira asked. She turned toward the silver man and took his hand conspiratorially. "Karn, just what is it they have you do in there? I know Master Malzra has been running secret experiments with you at the center of them. He's been building some kind of big machine—I've worked on parts of it—but none of us can guess what it does. And there's been something strange about the school since you arrived, something about the air. It feels like waves moving through a tidal pool or something. Do these experiments have anything to do with that?"

An insistent knock came at the door.

Jhoira's face hardened. "It's Teferi, the little rat." Then, to the door, "Just a moment."

The knock came again. "It's Mage Barrin. I've come for the probe. And I have a request to make of you, Jhoira."

Jhoira hurried to the door, opened it, and bowed slightly. "We were just in the middle of an interview, but we can talk later. Would you mind, Karn?"

"Not at all," replied the silver man, "I would like that." He turned sideways to slide out the arched doorway.

Barrin backed up to make room. "Karn?"

"Yes," responded Jhoira. "That's his name. What was your request?"

Night drew down around Tolaria. The dying sun burnished rooftops of blue tile, giving them a bronze patina. The Glimmer Moon peered palely over the treetops. Hot, dense breaks of jungle chittered with the final choruses of day birds, and night birds raised their first ululating songs. White waves along the shore glowed golden over burgundy seas. Throughout the afternoon, a hot, still column of air had stood upon the isle, but now, before evening breezes, it shifted and uncoiled until trees and students and all shivered in relief.

Jhoira was among them. She crouched in the shadowy lee of the academy's eastern wall, breathing slowly. The culvert where she lurked had been designed as runoff for garderobes, but the building it served became a lab instead of a dorm. A series of grates fastened into the passage and a main sluice gate were meant to secure the passage against invaders. Jhoira first noticed the unused duct in plans of the buildings; she had quite an eye for details on a page. The prospect of having her own entrance and exit to the academy had been enticing. It would allow her to skirt strict curfews. She didn't actually remove the bolts until she had devised replacements that would hold the passage secure to all but her. She was not selfish enough to jeopardize the security of the whole school for the sake of her own private amusements.

Private amusements. She smiled. Kerrick would have been flattered by the title. Their liaison had lasted for two months—surely more than a passing amusement.

Before she reached him, Jhoira had to slip past the guards, both human and clockwork. They would be more vigilant now in the shifting air than they had been in the hot, still afternoon. She dared not open the grate until she heard her friend above. . . .

"There it is again!" one of the men shouted overhead. "Look out!"

"Damned bird!" cursed another.

"Bird, my eye," a third yelled. "They make them in there. They're wind up toys."

She heard her shrieking toy bird dive and harry the men on the wall. It was a simple construction, weighing the equal of two pieces of paper, but it was fast and shrill. She'd discovered the plans in some ancient designs by none other than Tawnos, legendary assistant to legendary Urza. It didn't matter who actually designed the feathery flying machines. It mattered only that she could make them easily and—

"Arghh! It's in my hair!"

"Bash it with a glaive!"

"No! It's in my *hair*, damn it!"

"Hold still!"

"They banned the things. They circulated a memo! That's what they said! Let them guard up here and get these damned things stuck in their—"

The little mechanical birds were as adept at mischief as Teferi himself. During the next exclamation, Jhoira swung the grate outward, rolled from the sluice, closed the metal, set her special pins, and crawled away into the underbrush. There, breathless, she paused. There was a hammering noise above and the sickly flapping of ruined wings. Someone stomped a final time, and there was silence. Then—

"See, it's not a real bird at all. See where the quills are folded into this paper loop? And here, this hard part? That's what smells your sweat. They make these things to dive on us! The twerps are too young, too pasty-faced and frail, to sweat."

"If I ever catch the little prodigy that's making these—"

"He's watching us right now, I'll wager."

"There! There! That's what I do to your invention, you little twerp!"

Jhoira tried not to giggle as she made her way through the dense forest. She knew the path perfectly. It was narrow and shaded, exposed only after the hillsides below the western bank. She moved without breaking twigs or tearing leaves. They were her allies in this deception. As long as no one found the forest path, no one would find the rocky niche she kept above the shifting sea. As long as no one discovered the rocky niche, no one would know about Kerrick.

In an hour's time, she topped the final shoulder of parched earth above the niche. Already the sun had quit the sky. A russet blanket of clouds covered the world. The hooded lantern she had brought to the spot glinted faintly through a crevice. Peering through the crack, she saw the bookshelf Kerrick had improvised from stones and flat slabs of driftwood. The shelf burgeoned with volumes on loan from the academy: Kerrick was an avid reader. He had little else to do during his days and said he hoped to gain enough knowledge of artifice that he could apply for admittance. He was a good reader, a better trapper, and a superior cook. Even now, Jhoira could smell the savory aroma of salt-marsh hare sizzling on a skillet. Kerrick had dressed the creature with wild spearmint and scallions. Jhoira's knees melted.

What the academy served could not even be considered food next to fare like that.

Drawn by those aromas, Jhoira tiptoed around the corner. Beside the sizzling skillet were a pair of slim, bronzed feet crossed over each other. As she approached, she saw the long, muscular legs attached to those feet, the man's ragged trousers, his tattered shirt, his strong hands, clutching yet another book. Then there was his handsome face, his beautiful golden curls. Jhoira's knees melted again.

What the academy had to offer could not even be considered manhood next to fare like this.

He looked up, saw her, and smiled.

Jhoira leapt into his lap and wrapped him in eager arms and kisses. "I've been waiting all day to see you."

Laughter danced in his eyes. "Rotten day?"

"You have no idea," she said between kisses. "There's a little tyrant prig who thinks his job is making everyone miserable—"

"Yes, Teferi," Kerrick replied.

"I've mentioned him before?"

"Often," Kerrick said. "You've said he has a crush on you, but you're the one always talking about him."

"He's a child!" she replied indignantly. "I talk about him like I would talk about a goblin infestation."

Kerrick shrugged. He shifted toward the fire to turn the hare meat, and Jhoira caught a whiff of his musky scent. It was not the reek of worry but the strong animal smell of a man who works beneath the sun.

Over his shoulder, the man said idly, "Teferi seems one of your only friends."

"Oh?" Jhoira replied archly. "I spend too much time out here to have any other friends. And I don't hear you complaining."

"No, you don't."

"Besides, I have made a new friend. He's stronger than you, taller than you, younger than you, more polite . . . definitely more polite."

A delicious flash of jealousy showed in Kerrick's eyes. "Then why are you here?"

"He's a machine!" Jhoira said, rolling the man into another embrace. "He's a thinking, feeling machine, and I think he also has a crush on me."

"Really?" Kerrick replied. "Is the feeling mutual?"

"It is," Jhoira teased brightly, "and a little jealousy will do you some good. You've gotten quite comfortable living here in my secret place."

"Stronger than me, taller than me, younger than me? If you want me to be really jealous, bring out the plans so I can obsess over them."

"You'll have them tomorrow—if you return your overdue books," said Jhoira. "Now, come back over here. Those steaks need another few moments, and so do I." She dragged him with her onto the pallet and drew the scent of him and sizzling steaks into her chest.

Ah, she could put up with a hundred Teferis as long as she had her escape route, her paper birds, and her wild, secret love.

Monologue

What does Urza see in Teferi? The little monster is nothing like Urza at any age. For one thing, Teferi has a sense of humor. That is perhaps his only redeeming trait—aside from his undeniable brilliance. Still, Teferi uses his brilliance only to tear things apart, not to build them up. Urza has always been a builder and a serious one.

On the other hand, Urza's creations—his clockwork men, his war towers, his powder bombs and power armor—have always been used to destroy. The sum of Urza's constant creation is always destruction. Ironic, isn't it?

Do I dare to hope that, in the end, Teferi's constant destruction will bring about a new creation?

—**Barrin, Mage Master of Tolaria**

Chapter 4

Karn stood in the whirling red beam. Overhead, Malzra's machine turned back the tide of time. It was Karn's third trial in as many months. Each test reached only hours farther back in time. Each produced greater temporal stress across his frame. The current envelope was a regression of eighteen hours, beyond which lay almost certain meltdown.

Karn told himself he should be getting used to the vertiginous moment when the gear-work of the universe ground to a halt and then began slowly to turn backward. There was an instant of spinning wheels and whines of protest before time's conveyor reversed. Then came a sudden acceleration: Barrin and Malzra were freed from their immobility. An alien physics took hold. Effect became cause, memories became prophecies, and silver men were disassembled to gulping laughter.

Now as the spool of time rewound, space shifted as well. Within his red cone of light, Karn slid slowly sideways. He jittered through steel engines and furnace casings, his physical form out of phase with the atomic synchronicity around him. In moments, he slipped past the laboratory wall and out into the corridor. He saw himself strolling backward down the hall beside Jhoira. She had accompanied him to the lab, talking of her volcanic home island and how she missed her tribe.

Jhoira and Karn had become fast friends in the last months. She was a mental giant, and he a metal one. Whenever Karn was not in the lab and Jhoira was not studying or sleeping, the two were together. She had taught him to skip stones, which he could do with rocks the size of bread loaves. He had let her ride on his back as he climbed the eastern pinnacles. From the top of the jutting stones, they had seen ships so distant that only their topsails showed above the horizon. Jhoira had shared with Karn her many impressive clockwork inventions—toy birds and frogs and leafhoppers—and fixed a finger servo that had burned out after one of his secret tests. He had borrowed her drafting tools one evening when she fell asleep mid-conversation and had drawn a crudely elegant portrait of her. Best of all, they had made a home for each other, a refuge from the grueling rigors of their posts at the academy—and from the depredations of a certain fourteen-year-old menace.

Karn and his pool of red light drifted out the other side of the corridor. He moved through a set of tutorial rooms. Some were dark and vacant. Others were crowded with tutors, students, and artifact constructs. Many of these structures were basic forms meant to teach the principles of artifice to young scholars. More advanced devices could make beds, tie boot laces, or scuttle like cockroaches. The most mobile of these creations were used by some of the senior students in elaborate off-hours stakes races. Some elite machines were designed to slither into the cells of opposite-sex students to spy for their makers. For every such offensive device, there were three defensive ones that could detect, disable, or outright destroy the offender. The highest-level creations, though—the sort Jhoira spent her days designing and building— were complex components for Master Malzra's time-travel device. He had dozens of his oldest and most promising students working on the project, though none of them knew the ultimate end of the devices they designed.

Onward went the time traveler in his vessel of light. He saw into lecture halls, slid through a sleeping student lying sick and alone in her cell, tore past a pyrotechnic display on the properties of coal dust, and drifted through Malzra's private study. Books and models lined the walls, diagrams and studies hung on stands. In their midst, across a table piled with ancient manuscripts, Barrin and Malzra argued heatedly.

Karn drifted beyond those walls as well. He emerged into early morning in the academy's gardens and passed the twelve-foot-thick outer wall, then he moved through forests. Leaves twirled in odd backward spirals to sucking winds. The sun retreated to disappear below the horizon. Through a vast and settling darkness, Karn glided out toward the distant western shore. It was a place he and Jhoira never explored on their rambles, keeping themselves to the pinnacles and the east. Karn slid through tree trunks and boulders, even long low shoulders of earth at the edge of the island. Afterward, the ground fell away. A series of rough steppes rambled down to the sea.

In what seemed mere moments, the foamy verge of ocean passed some fifty feet beneath Karn's dangling feet. The water seemed to boil, ever receding from the toothy shore. He floated outward. Morning deepened into night. The Glimmer Moon quit the sky. Black midnight shimmered with twilight.

He was hot. He was nearing the edge of the envelope, eighteen hours back and five miles in space. The plan had been for Malzra and Barrin to monitor the temporal stresses on the portal device and recall Karn before he reached meltdown. That wasn't happening. Already his silver chest plates ground against each other in feverish expansion.

Still he drifted outward—

The red pool of light suddenly shimmered out of existence around him. Flailing to stay upright, Karn plunged, as massive and hot as a meteor. Overhead, the sky was starry but moonless. The ocean below was black with night and deep. It roared up to meet him. Flecked waves seized his legs, sent jets of steam from the golem's sizzling hide, and dragged him under. For several long moments Karn was enveloped in a fine cloud of steam bubbles, and then he slipped down out of the foamy stuff and sank through cold, viscous dark. Sandy silt sifted up around him, and then his feet struck the benthos at the bottom.

For a few moments he simply stood there feeling salt water wriggling past all his plates and into the interior spaces of his being. Surely they would recall him now. He needed only wait. Still, with each creeping moment, he felt his temporal displacement draining away. He would soon be in phase with the particles of this time continuum, solid and seeable to anyone who might look. Best not to give anyone a chance. He would remain where he was until recalled.

An hour passed. The last pockets of air in him had seeped out and escaped to the surface some fifty feet above. He'd been bumped three times by an inquisitive serpent and had given up hope of being automatically recalled. Perhaps he was out of range. He would have to find his own way out.

Luckily, among his capacities were an internal clock, compass, and sextant—not that he could see any stars. Even so, with the various improvements Malzra had made to all these systems, Karn had an almost foolproof direction sense. He set out, slogging toward the island.

It took longer than he had anticipated. There were numerous submerged sandbars to climb and other pits to descend into. There was also a coral reef that was too fragile to climb over and too extensive to circumnavigate. He ended up having to smash through, the sharp animal accretions scarring his silvery knuckles.

It was midnight when his head finally cleared the water. Constellations spangled the sky over the black island. In the extreme distance, the academy glowed, a collection of ivory jewel boxes. Within those walls, his other self, his historic self, would be spending the night in voluntary deactivation. Within those walls, Jhoira and Teferi slept, and Malzra and Barrin no doubt pondered the upcoming spacial-temporal trial. The wrapping walls of that school held everything in the world to Karn, and the rest of the island was dark—

Save for that one dim glint near the brow of the sea cliff. The light was so small he had first taken it to be a distant star. Marking its position, Karn emerged from the water and strode up the sloping shore. Water disgorged itself by the gallon from his sloshing innards. He stood and let the purge continue.

What about that light? No one was allowed beyond the walls after dark. Who could be in that niche?

Karn climbed. The rocky cliff side before him was all too easy to ascend after the dragging depths of the sea. In sliding, scraping moments, he had reached the peak. Ahead, in a deep, narrow cleft of stone, the light shone tepidly forth. Karn strode toward it.

It suddenly went out.

He paused, allowing his eyes to adjust to the starry darkness. Something moved in that space—something warm. Karn made out a peering, squinting face and the glint of stars from a small, steel blade. The figure withdrew again into the cave. Karn started forward, his massive feet grinding quietly over the gravel-covered ground.

The person in the cave reappeared, hoisting a curved stick. There came a thrumming sound. Something—a crude arrow— darted swiftly out to strike Karn's hide. Metal rang with the sound of stone cracking. A shattered shaft tumbled away to one side.

A hostile act. A caveman living on the edge of Tolaria. An intruder.

Karn set his jaw and marched toward the cave. Two more arrows struck the golem and cracked off into the rocks. He came on, furious. The man abandoned his bow for a large, stone-tipped club. He bounced it in his hand, growled out a wordless warning, and squinted into the night.

Karn strode to the figure and swiped out to capture him, but the man was too fast, spinning from his grasp. The club descended. Its stone tip shattered and sprayed outward. The hardwood handle jangled in the man's grasp. Karn whirled. He caught the man with the back of one hand and flung him to the ground. The body sprawled against an outcrop of rock and lay still.

Light flared to Karn's side. He spun. Flames roared over him. Fire sizzled away the water in his joints. He lunged past the flame at the second attacker. Arms limned in flame, Karn surged into the cave.

"Karn!" came a shout of surprise and relief. "What are you doing here?"

"Jhoira?" Karn asked. His eyes quickly adjusted to the darkness.

Jhoira trembled in her nightclothes, a smoldering torch butt held in her hand. She must have used the brand to ignite airborne coal-dust, as the students were taught at the academy.

Karn blurted, "What are you doing here?"

Jhoira's face grew resentful and desperate. "You followed me. I can't believe you followed me."

"I didn't follow you," Karn protested.

"Why did you leave the school grounds at night then? What about the curfew?" Jhoira challenged.

"I could ask the same of you," countered Karn.

"Where is Kerrick? What have you done?" she demanded suddenly, and stumbled past Karn to the mouth of the cave. She felt around blindly in the dark until her hand settled on the leg of the man. She shook him. "Are you all right? Can you hear me?" The man did not move.

Karn approached. "I'll carry him inside—"

"No," insisted Jhoira, shoving past him and clambering into the cave. "His neck might be broken. Moving him might kill him." She lit the lantern, gathered gauze and supplies from a shelf, and hurried back out. Kneeling beside the fallen man, she let out a moan of worry. One hand reached to stroke his curly golden hair. "No blood, and he's breathing." She gritted her teeth as her fingers encountered a large lump on his forehead. "You banged him up pretty good."

"Who is he?" Karn asked suspiciously. "What's he doing here?"

"He is Kerrick," said Jhoira with a sigh. She probed his neck to check for injury or swelling. "He was trying to protect me."

"He's not a student," Karn observed.

"No. He's a castaway, and he's my friend." She slipped her arms under the man, lifted him, and carried him inside. "Get the lantern, will you, Karn?"

The golem complied, following like a dejected dog. "You never told me about him."

Jhoira settled the man onto the pallet in one corner of the niche. "I never told anyone. Master Malzra would have him killed."

"But we are friends. We have no secrets from each other," Karn said. He set the lantern on the makeshift table.

"We have secrets. You won't tell me what experiments you are involved with."

"Master Malzra forbade me."

Jhoira smiled grimly, dipping a cloth in a pitcher of water and applying it to the lump on Kerrick's head. "Master Malzra forbade me—or anyone—from harboring castaways, too, so it all comes down to Master Malzra. I keep secrets from you because of him, and you keep secrets from me because of him. That's just the way he wants it. He doesn't want any of us to have friends, to have lives."

Karn felt a wave of sick dread move through him. He remembered what his existence had been like before meeting Jhoira, caught between the quiet apathy of Malzra and the loud antipathy of Teferi. This moment could ruin things between him and Jhoira. This moment could cost Karn the only friend he had and turn him back into Arty Shovelhead.

"Time travel," Karn blurted, his voice anguished. "That's what Master Malzra is testing. That is why I am here. He is testing a device that will send me back centuries or millennia, that will transport me anywhere across the planet."

Jhoira stopped her ministrations and stared in amazed wonder at the golem. "That's why he called you a probe. . . ."

"It is the whole reason I have been created," Karn said soberly. "He instructed me to tell no one about this on pain of being dismantled."

"If he can do this, he can change history—"

"He doesn't want me to change history." Karn suddenly realized he might be changing history even at that moment.

"There's much more to Master Malzra than meets the eye," Jhoira noted, amazed.

"Well," said Karn, kneeling before Jhoira in the wan light of the lantern. "That is the only secret I have kept from you. You know everything else about me. You have studied all my plans. You have watched Malzra assemble me. You even gave me my name, my life. Can you forgive me? Can we still be friends?"

A smile that was one part joy and one part pity broke across her face. "Of course, Karn. You know my greatest secret now, too. I've always trusted you, and I still trust you. Karn, you're my only real friend in the world."

"What is he?" Karn asked, indicating the unconscious man.

"He is my love."

She had no sooner spoken these words than the shimmering tug of temporal displacement laid hold of Karn. He shuddered, shifted out of phase, turned incorporeal, and felt the sudden swift sliding of the red light.

Just before he spun away through the stone wall of the niche, he glimpsed, behind the wondering face of Jhoira, one of Kerrick's fingers draw inward and his eye slit open.

* * * * *

"It's worth the effort," Urza insisted where he sat in his high study. "The Thran became the Phyrexians. If we can divert them from that course, keep them on the path of artifice rather than mutation, we can save the whole world."

Barrin held his hand out and paused, seeming to sniff the air. "What was that? Did you feel that?"

"A temporal anomaly," Urza said. "They have been occurring since we first sent the probe through the time-travel portal. That one was stronger than most."

"A temporal anomaly," Barrin repeated, stunned. "This is what I am talking about. We get anomalies like this when sending someone back eighteen hours. What will happen beyond that?"

"We must stop the Thran from becoming the Phyrexians."

"But millennia? If we could reach that far back in time, you could take a few side trips and rectify all your own past mistakes—leading the Phyrexians to Serra's plane, attacking Phyrexia, blowing up

Argoth, killing your brother . . . why, you could even decide to undiscover the powerstone at Koilos and keep the Phyrexians from reentering Dominaria at all."

Urza's look was sober. "That is what my life's accomplishment amounts to in your eyes? One grand failure after another?"

"Of course not," assured Barrin. "You have done much good, and I do not begrudge you your mistakes. Mages also learn through trial and error. What I begrudge you is the fact that you never take responsibility for your errors. You don't learn from your mistakes. You never clean up after yourself."

"That's what I am trying to do now. I brought the Phyrexians back into the world. Now I am doing all I can to find out how to drive them from it forever," Urza said. "I have learned, but I have much more to learn before I can right this greatest wrong."

"Yes," agreed Barrin, "you have much more to learn."

Missing the intent of this comment, Urza said, "I have seen one piece of the puzzle, but I don't know where it fits yet. Have you noticed the pendant Karn wears?"

Barrin gave a wave of his hand. "A little lizard on a chain."

"Have you noticed how hard the metal is? I tested its hardness. It scratched steel and adamantine and diamond. What's more, it doesn't heat up at all from temporal stress."

Barrin blinked, considering. "What are you saying? That we should build another probe made of this metal?"

"Perhaps. Perhaps," Urza's eyes glinted with possibilities. "I'll have to ask Karn where he got it. If we could forge a probe of it—"

"Should we work out a treaty with the makers of the metal," Barrin asked sarcastically, "or just take over their homeland and drive them out?"

"Start with a treaty, of course. There's always time for conquest later."

Barrin was grim. Under his breath, he said, "Yes, you have much to learn."

* * * * *

In a few months, the spatial displacement capacities of the time machine had been perfected. On one journey, Karn arrived in the Adarkar Wastes, thousands of miles from Tolaria. The place was little more than a brittle blue sky above a brittle white land. Snow and ice covered most of the ground. Bare spots revealed sand that had fused together into great, thin slabs of glass, left from a long-ago battle of fire. Where Karn arrived—this time without the disconcerting fall from the sky—the land was a cracked sheet of glass, sand fused in furnacelike heat. At Malzra's request, Karn gathered shards and brought them back with him.

Malzra tested the samples. He declared them indeed to be from the Adarkar Wastes. He was very pleased with this result and planned to go even farther with the next trial.

Meanwhile, the rills of temporal distortion grew worse. At first these disturbances were subtle and few, slight time-lags passing through the air like mild tremors. The frequency of the episodes gradually increased, from once a week to once a day. The severity went from mere hiccoughs to lapses that spanned four or five heartbeats. Words lagged behind lips. Music lurched up and out of tune. Carillon crews became hopelessly jangled. Goblets were overfilled or dropped. Unbound folios turned traitor in the fingers of tutors and fanned out on the floor. Flames devoured hunks of meat on the grill while neighboring steaks remained raw.

These were minor annoyances only, especially to a creature like Karn without heartbeat or breath to get tangled up. Some of the more infirm tutors, though, had to ride out these time storms by folding to their knees and gasping for breath. As the bands of distortion deepened and grew more common, the school infirmary filled up.

It disturbed Karn. The next time he was called for a time trial, two months later, he brought up his concerns.

"I am not like you," Karn noted. "That's why you made me, because creatures like you cannot safely move through time distortions. Each time I regress through the machine, more time leaks occur, and bigger ones."

Master Malzra studied the golem keenly. The founder of the academy always had a strange intensity in his face and a scintillating focus in his eyes, as though he could see centuries of time crystallized into mere moments.

"Are these . . . time leaks harming you?"

Barrin glanced up from the console he prepared. He nodded approvingly at Karn, nudging him to continue.

"Not me," Karn replied, "but everyone else. They're not safe. You have a lot of aging scholars here and a lot of young children. You are responsible—"

"Have there been any serious injuries?" interrupted the master, his eyes flashing like twin gemstones.

"Not yet, but if we continue these experiments, there will be injuries, and perhaps deaths, across the whole island."

Another nod came from the mage.

Malzra blinked, astonished. "If we don't continue these experiments, there will be injuries and deaths across the whole world. You don't understand, Karn. You have lived mere moments. You have seen only a hundred square miles of land. I have lived millennia. I have seen worlds and worlds of worlds. There are evils at the door, Karn, evils beyond anything you can imagine. I alone know they are there and are knocking. I alone am devising a way to keep them forever out or destroy them when they get in. I alone stand between this world and utter destruction, and you come to me like a nursemaid for these children and old dotards and demand they get goat's milk and nap times?"

Mage Barrin dropped his gaze, head wagging softly.

Karn stood for some moments without responding. He believed, at long last, what Teferi had said about Malzra's paranoia. An impulse urged Karn to confront the man with his own tortured insanity, but the past months had taught him much about dealing with these strange, irrational creatures of flesh.

"Yes. It is a lonely, dangerous struggle."

Barrin looked up, impressed. "One that might, one day, kill us all," he said in quiet reproof.

Malzra took the comments as accord. "Good. I'm glad you both agree. Now, Karn, before you get into the machine, I want you to leave that pendant with me. It may be interfering with the regression."

Suspicious, Karn slowly lifted the pendant from his neck and surrendered it.

Malzra looked it over keenly. "Where did you get it?" There was a greedy gleam in his eye.

Karn opened his mouth to speak, but the words caught short. Malzra's mad ravings still rang in his head. If the master started poking around in Jhoira's room, he might find out her secret. She might be expelled—or worse.

"I found it. It was snagged on a piece of driftwood that washed ashore."

"Driftwood," Malzra said dubiously.

"Driftwood," Karn repeated.

Shaking his head in irritation, Malzra said, "Into the machine then, Karn."

This time the regression took him to a scene of great carnage. The place was evil beyond Karn's imagining. Men, or what had once been men, lay in broken death across the grassy ground. Some were nearly complete, marked only by telltale roses of blood on their hearts or bellies. Others were missing limbs, likely dragged away by the wild dogs that loped shamelessly among the dead. Even less remained of some warriors. They had been torn in half by unimaginably sharp blades or blasted into fragments by fireballs. Smoldering war machines hulked on the horizon. The smell of waste, smoke, offal, maggots, and disease filled the air.

Surely this devastation has been caused by the horrors and evils Malzra spoke of, the silver man thought.

Karn had never felt sick before, but now his silver bulk quivered as with a tarnish that reached to the very core of him. He had been asked to gather some sign of his journey, but he could not bring himself to pry a sword from the hand of a fallen man or pull loose the helm that had failed to save a life. Instead Karn found a single shield, lying alone and bloodless on a windblown tuft of grass. This he lifted and held against him, waiting miserably for the master to recall him.

When Karn returned, he sorrowfully presented the shield to Malzra. The master identified it—a bracer from New Argive. To the silver man's description of the battle, Malzra merely nodded grimly—a battle had occurred in that spot only two days before. Karn had regressed only a day and a half. The master was frustrated and angry. He brusquely handed the pendant back.

"If these are the atrocities you spoke of, Master Malzra," Karn said solemnly as he donned the amulet, "I understand now why you fight so hard."

Malzra's smile—an unusual sight—was sardonic. "These atrocities are nothing, the result of human hatreds. What I fight is the hatred of demons."

Monologue

Sometimes I forget all Urza has seen, all he has done.

The silver man returned from New Argive. We debriefed him and shut down the laboratory. That night, during the reading session in Urza's study, he let the volume he was reading slide down to lie open on his lap. He stared straight ahead for some time. I lowered my book as well and waited. Urza's eyes had that faraway look, and I glimpsed the halves of the Mightstone and Weakstone showing through. Beyond the high windows, sea winds argued among the palms.

"I was fighting a whole world, not just Gix, but a whole world," he murmured.

Cautiously, I ventured, "Fighting a whole world?"

"In Phyrexia. I had gone to fight Gix, but there was a whole world of Gixes. Demons, witch engines, dragon engines, the living dead and the dead living. And at the heart of it all, a god. A dark, mad god."

I wryly imagined the same description coming from an invader of Tolaria.

"I fought to destroy a whole world, but Xantcha—she fought only to regain her heart."

I drew a deep breath of sea wind. "Yes. That one stone was a whole world to her. It is a whole world to Karn."

A gleam of sudden realization shone in Urza's dark, ancient eyes. "That's why they act the way they do."

"Who?"

"The students, the tutors—even you and Karn. Every one of you is defending your own heart, your own world."

He is not mad, not wholly. He is ancient and inhuman, transformed by the millennia, but he is not wholly mad.

"Yes," I agreed. "Don't you remember how it feels? It is a lonely, dangerous struggle, one that will, one day, kill us all."

—Barrin, Mage Master of Tolaria

Chapter 5

Teferi sat on a wind-blasted crest of rock above the restless night-time sea.

It had been quite a feat, reaching this point. Jhoira was lithe and athletic. She had moved quickly and soundlessly from her room after lantern-call that evening. Despite Teferi's invisibility enchantment, she sensed she was being followed. Twice, as she made her way through the empty corridors of the school, she looked back. The first time, Teferi fetched up against a recessed doorway to the forge room. The handle of the door rattled. She peered a long time back in the feverish night, and Teferi dared not breathe. When at last he looked again, she was already gone. He caught up to her in the Hall of Artifact Creatures—a museum where Malzra placed important but obsolete inventions. The place was unnerving enough by day. It was filled with statuesque creatures of metal plate and guy wire, each posed with limbs extended as if beseeching the viewer to reactivate them. At night the museum was downright frightening. Wiry, dog-headed Yotian warriors menaced in their crouches. Backward-kneed *su-chi* lifters seemed behemoths from some far-off world. At the far side of the mechanical menagerie, Jhoira was no more than a fleeting triangle of cloth. The door she exited led to the western laboratory—a half-used structure that was beastly hot in the height of summer and dank in the drear of winter.

Once again, he almost lost her. There was no sign of her in the lab. He cast a spell, seeing the fading heat of her footprints on the floor. They disappeared as he followed. She'd gotten away. Teferi stepped on a slightly skewed grating. It rang with possibilities. He knelt and stared down into the darkness below the grate. Jhoira's tampering had been evident even in the dark—at least to a mage's eye—and the trick of her specially engineered bolts took only minutes to divine. After that, it was easy enough to reach the wall. He saw her slip from the channel as the guards overhead cursed some nocturnal bird. Teferi conjured a real bird to do the task for him, a skycaptain that nearly spooked the men into jumping. With the bird and his invisibility, the young prodigy followed with ease.

Jhoira was not so cautious thereafter. Perhaps, once away from the school, she thought no one would be around to detect her. Perhaps, once near her hideaway, she was too eager to be careful. Even in the patchy light of the Glimmer Moon, Teferi made good time through the steaming woods and to this spot, just above the sea, just beside the mouth of the dimly flickering cave. He dispelled his invisibility, drew a deep breath, and with a smug smile, started into the niche. He stopped just in time.

Teferi saw what lay within, *who* lay within.

In a fit of disgust, he withdrew, unable to bear any more. He'd expected to find something to use against Jhoira, something with which he could extort a kiss from her, perhaps—but not this, another man. Even if Teferi mentioned that he knew her secret, he could not win her heart with it. She would only hate him all the more. He sat there while the sea toiled ceaselessly below and the wind dug its claws into the clouds overhead. He rose and headed back toward the academy, his mind abuzz with questions.

As he pushed past the pawing undergrowth of the western isle, a new thought occurred to him: it was possible there were certain things in life that could not be attained through manipulation and trickery. Nothing he had done had won Jhoira to him. No amount of misdirection, cajoling, humiliation, artifice, boasting, or innuendo had convinced her he was great. Teferi was honestly confused.

He had never met a person so resistant to the obvious truth of his supremacy. She couldn't see any of his overwhelming virtues, determined to focus on the difference in their ages. "Grow up," was all she could ever think to say to him. He *was* growing up. How could he grow up faster? He didn't have a time machine. . . .

That's when he felt the hand seize his shoulder and thrust his face to the ground.

* * * * *

"Teferi knows about Kerrick," Karn said to Jhoira. The silver man hunched just outside the doorway in the nervous light of morning.

Drowsy, Jhoira blinked at her friend. She had gotten back only an hour before, during the sunrise change of the guard.

"What are you talking about?"

"They caught him outside the academy this morning. He was coming back from the western shore."

Her stomach sinking, Jhoira motioned Karn into the room and closed the door behind him. She ran her hand through her tousled hair.

"Now, what's all this about?"

"Teferi's been watching you," Karn said with quiet intensity. "He probably followed you. They caught him on his way back from the shore. He must have seen—"

"Who caught him?" Jhoira interrupted.

"The guards from the western wall. One had seen something rustling in the jungle when he left. The guard followed until she lost the trail but waited on the path for him to return. They interrogated him for hours—they're angry about your mechanical birds and think Teferi conjured them. They got nothing out of him, though, not even the route you used out of the school, and half an hour ago they turned him over to Master Malzra himself."

Shaking her head in irritation, Jhoira swung wide the bone-inlaid doors of her wardrobe and rifled among her clothes. She chose her most formal white cloak, trimmed in gold piping, and slipped it on. Shedding her nightclothes beneath the robe, she selected a belt of gold rope and cinched it angrily around her waist.

"What are you going to do?" Karn asked, stunned.

"I'm going to go defend myself."

"Teferi hasn't said anything yet," Karn pointed out.

"Teferi?" Jhoira asked, angry. "He's holding out for the right price. He'll sell me out as soon as he has Master Malzra twisted around his finger." She shook her head again. "I want to beat him to the punch. I want to confess what I've done, so at least I have honesty on my side." With a final snort of surrender, she turned and bent over her cot, her hands drawing up the covers over a lump Karn had not noticed before. "Let's go."

As the two turned to leave, Karn glanced back at the cot, where he saw the curly golden hair of Kerrick.

* * * * *

Master Malzra was in a state. His face, always alight with a golden inner glow, was bright as a candle. His eyes seemed to cast twin red beams of hellfire. He paced, his blue robes crinkling all about him. In the dim light of the small study he was enormous and powerful, as though he wore one of the suits of power armor he had on display in the Hall of Artifact Creatures.

Before him, fourteen-year-old Teferi looked as small as a sparrow.

"Who are you, then? What are you? A spy? You're too young to be a Phyrexian sleeper. You don't smell like glistening oil. But you are smart and ambitious and incorrigible, just the sort of person the Phyrexians choose. What were you doing beyond the wall? Who were you meeting? Phyrexian negators?"

Teferi kept his eyes averted on the blackwood tabletop where he sat. "I don't even know what you mean by a Fire Ex—Fry Egg—Friar Ecclesian—"

"Don't mock me!" demanded Malzra, pounding the tabletop with his fist.

Tapping an inner reserve of strength, Teferi raised his eyes to meet the glowing orbs of the master, which looked like the multi-faceted eyes of an insect. Teferi drew a deep breath and roared right back at the man, "You're mad, Master. Everyone knows it. You're also a genius, of course. None of us would come here to study if we didn't know that. You know more about artifice and magic than any man for millennia, but you are mad. Fire-Eaters and Fanatics, Demons and Dog-Faced Men, Invaders and Conspirators and Spies—the only invaders that ever come to this island are fish stupid enough to get stranded by the tide or seagulls who have lost their sense of direction and flown away from everything and into nothing. No one wants to get in here, Master Malzra, but I can think of about two hundred students and forty scholars who want out, and that's what I was doing beyond the wall, believe it or not."

In the sudden, stunned silence, a knock came at the door. Mage Barrin shifted from the shadows and went to the door.

While the latch sounded and hushed voices spoke, Teferi and Malzra stared into each other's eyes. There was recognition between them. Despite the vast difference in their ages, the two knew in that moment that they were more alike than different—brilliant, driven, selfish, unstoppable, obsessive, irrepressible, and as deeply flawed as they were gifted. But there was something more to it, an undeniable spark of greatness—unmistakable among those blessed, or cursed, by it.

Malzra's eyes intensified. Teferi felt a *presence* in his mind. Sinuous as a snake, Malzra slithered through his thoughts. The master sniffed among skittering memories, snapped and swallowed them. Fear like a mouse went first into that maw, then jealousy and timid insecurity. The master's mind snapped down images of the forest and the Glimmer Moon. The truth lay beyond. It smelled sour and strong. Malzra wound forward. In moments, he would know. He would know.

Teferi's eyes intensified, too. A cat came prowling among his thoughts—righteous indignation and pride—and it leapt on the snaking mind of Malzra. Fangs and claws, spitting and hissing, fur and scale, they fought in the young man's mind. The battle was ferocious, though only their beaming eyes gave outward sign of it.

Barrin discreetly cleared his throat to break the tension. "Jhoira and Karn are here."

"Another time," Malzra growled.

"She says she's come to confess," Barrin said, gesturing the young woman and the silver man into the small study.

Malzra ended the staring match. His eyes flashed as he marked the Ghitu woman. She was dressed in her formal academy robe, the one she wore when inducted into the ranks of his senior students.

"Confess to what?"

"I am to blame for all this," Jhoira said evenly. "I am the reason Teferi was outside the walls last night."

The young man goggled for a moment at her and then jumped in. "She dared me." All eyes in the room turned quizzically on him. "I'm always trying to impress her, but she thinks I'm too young for her. Finally, she said she didn't want to talk to me again until I did something brave and grown-up."

"That's not what—" Jhoira began.

"You thought sneaking out of the academy would be grown-up?" Malzra demanded.

"I thought if I could get out into the woods at night, I could maybe catch a night loon. They have a beautiful song. They sing to the Glimmer Moon. I made those mechanical birds to impress her—she's not interested in my magic, and I wanted to show her I was an artificer too—but she said only, 'they're fake, just like you.' So I thought, if I caught a real bird, a rare nighttime songbird, and did it without magic, did it by going myself—"

"To catch a loon?" Barrin asked, astonished.

"I had a little chain with a metal collar. I was going to clip it around the bird's leg and put a hood on his head, but they got knocked out of my pocket when the guard tackled me."

"A night loon?" Barrin repeated, incredulous. He turned to Malzra. "I don't believe him. Malzra, I think in this case we could suspend the school's moratorium against mind probes. I could cast a truth spell on him—"

"No—" Something had changed in Malzra's eyes, not a softening, but a hardening, a keen calculation. "No, this was no crime great enough to warrant such drastic measures." A guilty look passed between him and Teferi. "He found a night loon all right, himself, but I daresay this stunt wasn't enough to impress Jhoira. It was not brave or grown-up. It was foolhardy and stupid."

Teferi swallowed and bowed his head. "Yes, sir."

Stunned, Jhoira realized her mouth was moving, but nothing was coming out.

"What do you have to say, Jhoira?" Malzra asked. "Are you impressed by such exploits?"

She took a deep breath and said, "Well, in a way, yes."

* * * * *

After the students and the silver man had left, Barrin lurked among the book shadows of Urza's library. For his part, the planeswalker sat, silent and brooding, at the blackwood desk.

How to say this, wondered Barrin, how to say any of this? "There's more to this, Urza. You know that."

"I know," came the calm response.

"You shouldn't allow the truth of Teferi's words—all that business about genius and madness and paranoia—to distract you from the fact that he was outside the school for more than night loons."

"Yes," agreed Urza wearily. He drew a long, conscious breath, not something he needed to do to live, being a creature of pure energy. Simple acts such as breathing brought him an invaluable connection to the world around him. "There is a Phyrexian in the school. I smell it. It is warded, shielded, wary. Its smell is faint and diffuse, but it is here. A Phyrexian in Tolaria."

* * * * *

The ruby light of the time-travel portal pulsed around Karn. He saw none of it. His mind's eye was turned inward, to the confrontation among Malzra, Teferi, Barrin, and Jhoira. The outcome of that episode a week ago still boggled him. Kerrick should have been exposed, Jhoira and Teferi reprimanded and expelled, and the animosity between them become an unbreachable wall. Instead, the castaway had gained access to the academy by way of the secret passage, Jhoira and Teferi had only risen in Malzra's estimation, and the young prodigy had won respect in the eyes of the woman he always sought to impress. How any of this had transpired, Karn still didn't understand. He had the distinct sense that much of what had taken place in that strange meeting lay in words unspoken and deeds undone.

Time slowed and stopped. Malzra and Barrin stood statue-still at their consoles. The whine of the machine reached a peak. Beyond was dead calm. Then the turbines of time reversed and began rolling backward. It was a dreadful instant, and in it Karn always felt utterly alone. With slow deliberation, Malzra and Barrin moved again, their hands withdrawing along the consoles, undoing all they had done and powering down the machine. The light deepened around Karn. This time, the pool did not shift. Malzra had achieved proficiency in spatial displacement—he seemed to have an especial grasp of that arcane endeavor—and so had set it aside to try to push the temporal envelope. With this trial, all the power of the machine was shunted to the temporal vector.

It began, the dizzy spooling of time. Karn had gotten used to seeing himself withdraw from the pool of light and slump along backward, listen attentively to the two men, and retreat through the door. In the time prior to that, Malzra and Barrin were often busy, breaking down portions of the time machine, removing shiny new components and replacing them with burnt-out hunks of metal and glass. One day, their alterations would reshape this machine so that it could carry Karn back centuries or millennia. . . .

He let his mind drift. On that journey, he would see his own creation and the dead pile of plates and cogs he had been before. He would pass through the time when Barrin was young, was a baby, was in the body of his mother, was nothing at all. It would be a longer journey back to Malzra's beginnings, of course. How much longer, Karn could not have guessed. En route, he would see the man being disassembled piece by piece, just like the time machine before him. He would see each component removed from Malzra—his mania, his paranoia, his obsession, his brilliance, his constant abiding regret and misery. Some of it was part of his original design, perhaps. Much of it, though, the worst of it, must have come from suffering, centuries of it.

The laboratory grew dark. Barrin retreated around it. He drew from each light orb the enchantment that made it shine. He backed out the door, closed it, and locked it. Then came a period of deepening darkness. Karn could almost feel the sun diving silently below the world, a leviathan swimming backward beneath the sea.

It was twenty-two hours now, the extent of their previous success.

In the dead of that recoiling night, someone entered the laboratory. It was not Barrin or Malzra. Whoever it was neither cast light spells nor lit the mundane oil tapers around the walls. There were workers assigned to cleaning the labs, but who would clean in the dark? The intruder moved along the wall of plans, studying them as though he could see without light. He sorted briefly among the piles of parts and drew from his pockets glimmering stones to lay among the others.

A thief.

Karn almost stepped from the circle of light but remembered Malzra's instructions—to travel back in time until his frame neared the melting point. He was nowhere near that now, and in moments, the figure was gone. He thought he glimpsed, in the gray wedge of hallway light, golden curls.

Evening came, in the form of an unnatural dawn. The regression accelerated. Karn waited through the spooling hours as students and tutors jittered through the space, bees in a hive. Morning came. Shadows lengthened and puddled into vast pools of darkness. It was night again.

Karn's hide heated until it steamed.

The thief returned.

It was forty-six hours into the past. Long enough. Karn stepped from the ruby light. His frame fairly sizzled as the silver plates met the air of the former time. The man who had been opening the door closed it. The silver golem made a rapid and quiet passage to the door and eased it open. He peered out, seeing Kerrick withdraw beyond a corner of the corridor.

Kerrick. Jhoira had allowed him into the school, and he was stealing from Master Malzra. There would be more powerstones or plans or parts in his pockets. What use did a castaway have for artifact technology? He must have been delivering these items to someone else. To whom?

There are evils at the door, Karn, evils beyond anything you can imagine.

Karn pursued. He would be out of phase and invisible only so long, and his metallic footsteps would soon give him away. If he didn't catch the thief soon, he never would.

Kerrick fled down a series of curving corridors. At the end of the snaking route lay the Hall of Artifact Creatures. Perhaps he planned on stealing one of the devices in it or copying its design. He slipped the latch and entered the chamber.

Karn hurried to catch the door before it swung closed. He eased inward. His quarry darted away among a cluster of dog-headed Yotian warriors. The silver man followed. His frame was already slipping into phase—he was fading into being. He made his way forward under cover of the mechanical menagerie.

He crouched beside a delver. Its sloping backbone was a vast conveyor designed to bear ores up from mines. Beyond it stood a weathercock topped with a collection of whirring instrumentation—anemometer, thermometer, barometer, cyclonometer. The next beast was wiry and configured like a hunting dog, with long thin legs, a sleek head, and a whiplike tail. Adjacent to it, *su-chi* lifters crouched in their backward-kneed massiveness. It was unsettling to stalk among these metallic brothers, deactivated and nearly discarded, made to stand like statues in this mausoleum. Karn wondered if he would one day be among them, when Malzra's mania had turned to some pursuit other than time travel, or when he had made a better probe to do it.

He was only halfway across the chamber when Kerrick slipped away through the far door, toward Jhoira's secret passage. Karn could not have followed through the tight duct work, but perhaps he could intercept the thief beyond the wall.

Turning, Karn headed for a different door, one that led to the courtyard. He slid the bolt, eased it open, and scanned the yard. Beyond lay a hot and windy night. The Glimmer Moon was a cataracted eye burning behind sultry clouds. Karn was hotter still, his frame smoldering with heat stress. He emerged and stole across the courtyard. Malzra might recall him at any moment. Karn reached the western wall and climbed the inner buttresses. He rose to the battlements.

Beside the turrets, guards stood in lazy clumps. A pair of clockwork watchers perched on adjacent towers, their optics turning in slow fans along the outer wall.

Deep darkness swathed the wall's footing. The grate at the end of Jhoira's passage lay halfway between the mechanical guards, obscured by tall grasses. Metal shifted slightly in the murk. A glint of hair like gold coins showed beneath.

Above, the guards still lounged, conversing, in their quiet knot.

Kerrick slipped from the grate. He scrambled up the weedy embankment and entered the thick wall of jungle beyond. He had not been seen.

Silver skin sizzling with heat, Karn rose to crouch on the battlements and hurled himself into the wheeling night air. He dropped and landed with a thud that brought the heads of the guards around. Karn crouched, half-visible in the silvery moonlight. In time, the guards' attention turned elsewhere. Masked by a rising wind, Karn ambled quietly up into the woods, after Kerrick.

More noises came, necessarily, ahead—the thrash of leaves, the crackle of sticks, the hiss of dew on red-hot silver. Karn feared to alert Kerrick, but speed was the thing. The thief had moved quickly and soundlessly over Jhoira's path, taking with him whatever plans or powerstones or artifacts he had stolen.

Karn followed. His energy stores were taxed by the rapid movements. Heat stress made his joints grind, but anger lent him strength. He topped a rise just as light from the Glimmer Moon lanced through a patch of cloud. Kerrick and two strangers stood beyond. Karn paused, attuning his ears to the whispered conversation.

The golden-haired young man held out a large roll of paper and pointed, saying, "The passage is here. Bring the full company of negators. I will be sure the way is open. I will be sure the guards on the wall are dead—"

That was all Karn heard or saw.

Malzra's machine reached back through time and laid hold of him—every smoldering mote of his being—and dragged him forward. In angry whips of red energy, the jagging light whirred into a solid cone of radiation. The hillside vanished and with it Kerrick and his conspirators. Only the lurid light remained. Roaring in frustration, Karn waited to reemerge in the time stream. Eventually the fabric of the future formed itself around Karn. The cone whirred once more, winked, and was gone.

Smoldering and red-hot, Karn stood in the midst of Malzra's time laboratory. The master looked up from his console. He and Barrin both wore expressions of awe, their eyes tracing the tendrils of smoke that snaked up from the massive metal man and tangled themselves hotly around the time machine. Its own fuselage streamed gray soot and crackled fragilely as it cooled.

Karn stepped out of the transport circle. It was a breach of protocol: he was supposed to wait until Master Malzra summoned him. He further offended by speaking before being spoken to.

"There is an invasion coming."

Barrin approached and gestured the silver man back. "There is a danger of contamination if you step out of the ring—"

"What sort of invasion?" Malzra asked from the console.

"I do not know. I did not see who he spoke to, but he talked of negators—"

"Phyrexians," Malzra replied in grim confirmation.

The mage asked, "*Who* spoke of negators?"

"Kerrick," Karn said. In that moment, he realized he must betray Jhoira's secret, for the safety of the whole academy and her safety as well. Still, the necessity of the crime made it no easier to commit. "He is a castaway, washed up on shore nearly a year ago. Jhoira found him and saved his life. He has discovered a way into the academy and now has taken floor plans of the academy to whoever is in charge of these negators."

Malzra began pacing again, the old fury resurfacing. "They must have a portal to a nearby island or perhaps merely a Sargasso or boat. They knew I would have defenses against portals directly into Tolaria. They are massing somewhere for this attack."

"How do you know all this?" Barrin asked Karn.

"I followed him out of the academy, out of this very room. He took the plans from here," Karn reported. "Beyond the wall, he met with two figures. They talked of the negators."

Malzra was reeling, his face livid. "Damn. Then they know of my time tampering. They could not have chosen a more crucial time to attack."

"When did this Kerrick hand off the plans? How far back did you go?"

"Forty-six hours."

"They could be arriving any moment," Barrin said. "I will alert the guard." He rushed for the door and down the hall.

"It's too late," Malzra said quietly, breathing for the first time in perhaps hours. He caught a whiff of the air that wafted from the open door. "They are already here."

Still sizzling, Karn charged for the door and bolted into the corridor. It was empty and silent, but a smell of oil and metal and death tinged the air. He thought but one thought—Jhoira—and hurled himself down the clattering hall. Malzra called out, but Karn paid no heed. Down a set of stairs, around a long slow bend, and up a rise, he reached the small, round-topped door to Jhoira's room.

He tried the handle, but it was locked. He pounded. The wood jumped in its frame. He bellowed a call, but no answer came from within. Lifting a massive foot, Karn kicked the splintering mass inward and, turning sideways, won through.

There was blood everywhere.

Jhoira had struggled, that much was clear. Now the struggle was done forever. She lay facedown in the center of the floor, and a red pool extended from her matted hair out to the edges of the room. Her sodden robe rested over a body that was half the size it should have been.

There were footprints in the blood, iron shod and spike toed. One led into the wardrobe where Jhoira's robes hung. The door was slightly ajar, and from the darkness within peered a feverishly glowing eye.

Monologue

He is not mad. I should never have doubted him. The madness is what he knows is coming, is what is already here. It surrounds me. Its fangs sink into me. Its claws rend my guts. I can somehow feel the warmth of them splatter my feet in the moment before I die.

—Barrin, Mage Master of Tolaria

Chapter 6

The creature in the wardrobe flung back the bone-inlaid doors, ripping them from their hinges, and emerged.

It was a huge thing, in general configuration human, though with its armor implants, protruding bone spikes, and barb-edged legs, it seemed almost an insect. A pair of steel struts extended its lower jaw, which was tipped with glimmering metal tusks that dripped Jhoira's blood. Its nose had been replaced with another spike, the task of breathing being accomplished through a series of holes bored through the creature's sternum and directly into its bronchia. Its eyes seemed to glow, bedded deep in mirrored sockets, and its horn-studded brow ridge rose into a sagittal crest that also ran with blood. Sharpened tips of bone protruded from shoulders, elbows, fingertips, knees, and toes.

The creature rasped, "Disarm and deactivate yourself, and you will be taken intact. Otherwise, you will be destroyed."

Karn answered by hurling himself at the thing. It was fast, sliding from beneath his descending bulk with all the speed of a snake. Karn clutched one shoulder, but the creature melted away.

It was suddenly on his back. Its scissor-fingers jabbed beneath Karn's headpiece. He remembered how easily Malzra had flung back his skull and removed the powerstone within—

Karn pivoted and toppled, hoping to smash the bug between the hammer of his frame and the anvil of the floor. The monster shifted again, elusive as water, and landed atop him. A red spray went up from the puddle of blood where Karn landed. Gore sizzled on his hot skin. He brought his fists together, pounding the invader's sides.

With a growl and a heave, the beast worked the mechanism at Karn's throat and flung back his skull. Karn could see nothing more, could move little, his limbs jangling around him, but he could feel the spike-tipped fingers slide in around the silver case where his powerstone lay. One yank and the whole assembly would spill forth, and Karn's life would be gone—a fragile crystal clutched in the claw of a Phyrexian killer.

It paused, its fingers catching first upon a small trinket hanging about the golem's neck, the Viashino medallion.

The beast lifted it, looked it over, and softly purred a single word: "Thran."

Karn spoke a different word: "Jhoira."

Gathering together his shattered will, Karn caught up the Thran-metal trinket, broke the silver chain that bound it, and impelled the bauble into the Phyrexian's skull. A gush of hot oil-blood streamed over him.

Screaming, the creature fell back. Karn managed to knock closed his skull-piece and felt his power, his will, reassembling from fragments on the floor. In the next instant, he rose above the crouching killer, the Viashino trinket half-sunk in its frontal lobe. He flung the beast to the ground, and with one stomp of his massive foot, reduced the thing's head into an oily mass of slumped skin, brain ooze, and bone meal. The body trembled for a few moments afterward, but Karn kicked the sloppy corpse aside and knelt beside his fallen friend.

Dead. Jhoira was dead. The rage Karn had felt at his discovery melted now into anguish and sorrow. The silver man crumpled before her. This ached worse than a red-hot frame or a skull-plate peeled back like the rind of a melon.

"They are everywhere," came a stern voice from the doorway. "They are killing everyone. Barrin is dead already. Teferi too."

Karn looked up to see Master Malzra arrayed in battle armor that made him look not unlike the machine-implanted Phyrexian.

"It is too late to stop them. We mustn't thrash at the branches of evil, but chop the root. I will send you back. This whole attack can be averted. Return in time. Return forty-eight hours. Intercept Kerrick and kill him before he can relay the plans. I will guard the machine and fight all comers. I must have Mage Master Barrin back. Let the portal destroy itself, if it must. Let your own frame melt into nothing, but stop Kerrick and his negators."

* * * * *

If I kill him, thought Karn as the smoky beam of the portal danced around him, if I even delay him, detain him, Jhoira will live again.

Beyond the fitful circling of that red ray, Master Malzra worked feverishly at both consoles, his associate lying dead somewhere in the ravaged school.

If I kill Kerrick, thought Karn, it all will be as it was.

Even then, a brace of negators burst through the door. Huge and trussed with steel armor, much like the Phyrexian Karn had already slain, each of these creatures was unique. One had a lupine head and limbs, though its shoulders and torso were human—or once were before they had been pierced in a thousand places by seeking tubes and conduits. Another was a lurching ogre with massive, infolded features, deep, malevolent eyes, and arms as huge as other men's legs. A third was lithe and quick and spidery. These three emerged among spinning shards of the shattered door and plunged toward Malzra.

Karn staggered, almost lurching from the light to drive back the creatures.

Without even looking up from the machinery around him, Malzra lifted a hand and sent out a shocking blast. Three bolts separated from the main surge and caught the monsters mid-chest. Lightning blasted holes where the hearts would have been in humans and raced in crackling fury across the steel frames. Eyes lit from within. Fangs danced with sparks. Muscles glowed eerily where neurons ran, but still the Phyrexians converged.

For the next sorcery, Malzra did not even raise his hand. The spell blossomed full-formed from his mind even as his fingers danced across the consoles. Each of the three creatures abruptly froze, midstride, and fell to the floor, shattering like black ice.

Karn saw no more. In the next moment, all the rest of the world froze. It stood for a shuddering instant, as if on the verge of cracking, and then time began scrolling backward. Broken bits of Phyrexian slid together on the floor and rose up, assembling themselves in midair and retreating toward the door. A gathering spell formed flesh from ribbons of smoke and thrust it into the holes in the creatures' breasts. They obligingly fled outward, rebuilding the door from wood fragments before they departed.

And then time scrolled faster still. The dancing beam shrieked in its frenetic spinning. The world jittered and shook. Master Malzra had harnessed the full power of the device, of its four vectors and its sea-cave turbines, to power this regression. Karn would likely not survive this journey, and even if he did, the machine might not remain to bring him back. But Jhoira would survive, and that would be enough. Jhoira and Teferi, Barrin and the school. If saving them meant losing himself, Karn did not mind. Better to end that way than as a statue in the Hall of Artifact Creatures.

Morning brought darkness to the world; Kerrick entered the laboratory on his last visit and was gone; and evening brought light. Karn waited anxiously through another day and into the morning-twilight beyond. He was already quite hot, his bulk steaming and his plates grinding against each other in expansion. Night deepened. The regression slowed. The light faltered. Karn clenched his hands at his sides and felt the strange, very human impulse to pray—to what god he did not know, perhaps to the time machine itself.

With a light more beautiful than any true dawn, the laboratory door cracked slowly open, and the gray corridor glimmered beyond.

Karn heaved himself from the dissipating pool of light, his own silver bulk glowing a dull red to match that color of the beam. Without pause, he raced toward the now-closing door, grappled the handle, and flung it wide. He barged into the hall just behind the golden headed Phyrexian sleeper.

Kerrick whirled when he heard the door bang raggedly against the corridor wall. Though Karn was still out of phase, his super-heated shell sent wisps of smoke into the air in an aura around his body, and Kerrick saw the shape of the void within.

He turned and bolted. Karn followed. He had not been built for speed, and running taxed his frame. Kerrick darted ahead down the corridor, quickly pulling away.

Perhaps another regression, Karn thought desperately. Perhaps I should be withdrawn for another regression—except the machine may destroy itself to accomplish this one.

Karn was not as fast as the Phyrexian, but he knew the academy and knew where Kerrick headed. Launching himself down a side passage, Karn reached the Hall of Artifact Creatures. He entered quickly, closing and bolting the door behind him.

Karn stalked past deactivated creatures two and three times his size—mechanical mammoths, rovers with the form of steel crickets, spidery devices with hands at the end of each leg. The killer was there, too. Kerrick had entered the chamber from the far end, and he stalked cautiously forward. He was on his way to the west laboratories and would need to pass through the door behind Karn. The silver man eased himself onto a nearby platform and crouched beside the metal skeleton of a clay warrior. There, camouflaged among dead metal creatures, he waited.

Kerrick came. Cautious and quick, he came. A sneer jagged across his lip as he set his hand on the doorknob and pulled, certain he had evaded his pursuer.

Karn fell upon him.

There is an unmistakable sound when bones—whether human or Phyrexian—snap. Kerrick's lower right leg folded below the knee. Shrieking in agony, the man crumpled to the floor.

It was a piteous noise, and Karn, fists balled and ready to finish the man, hesitated. Perhaps breaking Kerrick's leg was enough to stop him, to keep him from escaping the wall and meeting with the Phyrexians. He would be found here by the guard and recognized as a spy. He would be dealt with harshly by Malzra and Barrin, and perhaps they would learn from him who he was, and how many Phyrexians massed, and where. To kill this man insured the Phyrexians would come again, another day, but leaving him alive to interrogate—

Still only half-visible in his phase shift, Karn hoisted the angry man to his shoulders and marched past rank upon rank of artifact creatures. Kerrick arched away from the silver man's burning skin and gave little cries of agony. Prisoner and captor reached the far doorway, passed through it, and started down the corridor beyond.

"I have a spy, a Phyrexian spy!" Karn called out. "Guards! Mage Barrin! Master Malzra!"

Before an answer came, every particle of Karn's being was seized by Malzra's future hand. The machine was drawing him back. There was something different about this summons—its tearing insistence. The silver man jolted under the assault and almost fell. He clutched his captive all the tighter. His frame became griddle-hot. Kerrick thrashed and wriggled. The long dark hallway whirled.

With a shriek of fury, the Phyrexian rammed his fingers beneath Karn's jaw, fumbling for the release mechanism. In reflex, Karn seized the man's hand and flung it violently away. The wrenching movement hurled Kerrick free. He landed, a leg-broken mass, on the stony floor of the hall. Karn staggered back.

The red beam came, a chaotic, stabbing light. The hallway began to dissolve. Karn swung a massive hand toward the Phyrexian, but his fingers closed on wheeling chaos and nothing. Shards of reality slid past in mirror moments. Karn plunged through raveling time.

Something was wrong with the machine, terribly wrong.

The lashing pulses of temporal energy formed a vortex around him, drawing him downward, forward, toward the dark future and its disintegrating mechanism.

The laboratory took fitful shape outside the cone. It winked into and out of existence. A tumbling chaos of red forms blossomed around Karn. For a second time that day, he felt the impulse to pray. The laboratory returned. Malzra's consoles flickered through a shroud of rolling smoke. The master and Barrin labored mightily at the sparking controls. Over Karn's head the time machine swayed ominously, its side panels bleeding soot into the air.

It was disintegrating.

The light orb at the base of the device cracked, sending jabbing rays out in all directions. Where red beams struck, walls turned to dust, machines to slag. Each ray carved a jagged rent in whatever it hit, tearing through the laboratory and the corridors beyond, through the dormitories and the wall itself, reaching out to rend all of Tolaria.

Karn stood in the center of it, shielded beneath the coruscating cone of light.

Then came the explosion.

Red was suddenly gone, red and all other color and all darkness. There was only light in that moment, light like the center of the sun. It came with a fragile shattering sound, as though a crystal had been sundered. A bell-tone keen followed and what might have been thunder if a lightning bolt could be large enough to encompass a whole world.

The air was solid for a moment, an amalgam of gas and energy, then rushed outward. Walls were gone, just as color was before. The rushing inferno rolled out in an incandescent ring from where Karn stood, pulverizing stone and steel and glass. Farther out, the ring devolved into lines of blast as raw energy gathered in radiating avenues. The holocaust obliterated whole sections of the academy and scoured the earth down to bedrock. Other areas remained untouched. Buildings were torn in cross section.

The shock wave pelted outward. It bore a storm of shattered stone and rent metal that consumed with a million gnashing teeth anything it struck. Millennial trees toppled. Stony pinnacles were eaten right through. Green leaves burst into flame. Clouds of dust and ash boiled up from the shuddering forests.

The blaze reached even the sea, and in mile-long arms it boiled water to a depth of five fathoms. It reached to the clouds overhead, flinging some aside and bringing fiery hail from others. It shook the oceans, awakening tidal waves that destroyed coastal villages two hundred miles distant. It was a blast like none felt on Tolaria since the dark days of Argoth.

It was a blast awoken by the same follies of the same man.

* * * * *

Urza stood beyond it all. He had been beside the time portal in the white-hot instant that it exploded. It had taken every ounce of his metaphysical might to gather the particles of his being against the massive waves of power. As mote by mote of matter was blown away from him, he slowly became a being of pure energy. He resolved himself again and again in the first heartbeat of that hailing storm.

In the second heartbeat, he risked it all by reaching out beyond the rolling envelope of destruction and snatching them up, one by one—perhaps not his best and brightest, but those nearest, those who could be saved. Mage Master Barrin was first (yes, the silver man, Karn, had done what he was sent to do, had averted the Phyrexian invasion, though even the facts of that other time loop were as difficult to hold to and reassemble as Urza's own body was), then five other scholars, and eight students. He whisked them up with him in a sudden, spontaneous planeswalk. They would not survive the journey in human form, he knew, and took a moment to transform them all into stone. It could be undone later, when there was time, when there was strength. . . .

Ravening beams streamed past Urza and his company of statues. The death throes of his latest dynamo flung out shrapnel of every conceivable thing. Metal and stone and bone and brain and even mind tore repeatedly through them. Urza held fast against the storm. He rose. He took the others with him.

Now they were . . . where?

The hillside was sunny and green. A gentle, heather-smelling wind strolled easily past the fourteen statues. Urza had saved himself and fourteen others—which meant that more than two hundred were left to die. He had saved himself and Barrin and thirteen others. The negators might have done less damage, but they would have killed Barrin and captured all of Urza devices and the time machine itself. It had been a reasonable trade. Urza had saved fifteen, and kept his work from Phyrexian claws. Yes, it had been a very good trade.

The Tolarian survivors stood frozen and silent in that caressing wind. There was a single, broad-crowned tree at the top of the grassy hill, and it alone moved, breathing the balmy air.

Urza cast the last enchantment he held. It was his final saving act on that afternoon, for he was spent. He would not be able to maintain his physical coherence much longer. It was a feat of will to cast that last spell, to transform Barrin back into flesh.

Stone became bone and muscle and blood. Barrin awoke.

Brows knotted darkly above his intense brown eyes, the man staggered through tall grass to reach Urza.

"Where are we?"

Urza achingly shook his head. "I do not know."

Nodding, Barrin took a calming breath and looked out over the rolling hills, chartreuse beneath the cloud-cluttered sky. "Why are we here?"

A shadow passed over Urza's features. "Tolaria is gone. The time machine exploded. We are the survivors."

The younger man's mouth dropped open, and he gazed with angry appraisal at the other thirteen, arrayed like tombstones in a forgotten graveyard. "Just us? Just fourteen?"

"Fifteen," Urza corrected solemnly. "You and I, five scholars, and eight students."

Barrin crouched suddenly, clutching his knees. "And the rest?"

Urza blinked. He did not need to blink, but it was an old habit that came with disturbing thoughts. "Most are dead. Some may live, sheltered by rubble, but most likely not."

His assistant remained on his haunches. He panted like a dog afraid of thunder. "We have to go back. We have to get them."

"Teleport, if you have such a spell ready. I can do nothing more for a time," Urza replied grimly. "I am spent. As it is, I cannot anchor myself here much longer."

"I have no teleport spells. I had no thought I would need one," Barrin spat. "Then a boat or something. We have to go save whoever may remain."

Already Urza's form faded, his features shifting. The gemstones that had become his eyes flickered. The fire in them guttered near death. "We will find them in time, any who escape the island tonight. Any who do not will be dead by morning."

* * * * *

Karn heaved on the slanting slab of limestone. It creaked. Its far end ground massively against the edges of the rubble field. The voices beneath cried out in hope and terror as light appeared above—not sunlight, but firelight from the raging flames of the explosion. Karn levered the edge of the stone a foot off the ground, and two young students scrambled out. The silver man hauled the block higher. An aged scholar with a bloody head clawed his way free.

"That's all of us," gasped the man raggedly.

"Head for the jungle," Karn ordered as he let the stone grind back downward. "Go through the ruins, not the clear paths. Move through the deep jungle. Get to the sea. Stay away from the clear paths. They are time gashes, and if you enter them, they will kill you."

The aged scholar was still on his knees, cradling a broken arm. His two young students huddled shivering beside him. The man looked about at the devastation. Here and there ragged remains of buildings towered precariously. Between crumbling stacks of stone, the ground had been scoured to bedrock. Bodies littered the smashed edifices, but in the clear paths nothing at all remained but fire-scarred rock. The old man scratched his silver hair just beneath a bubbling gash. He blinked, and blood droplets leapt from his eyelashes to spatter his cheeks.

"Once we reach the sea, what then?" the man rasped.

"Find others," Karn advised as he moved toward the next sounds of screaming. "Find something that floats. Malzra kept boats on the east shore."

It was all he had time to say. He'd rescued seventeen so far, though most of those would die of their wounds or wander into wild time storms that would tear their bodies apart. Karn had already encountered a few such destructive regions, and even his silver bulk, engineered to survive temporal fluxes, had been nearly destroyed. Any creature of flesh needed only to catch his head in a different time stream from his heart, and his veins would burst. Karn had seen it happen many times already today, too many times.

The screaming came from ahead. Karn found a guard pinned under a boulder. The man's upper body had been burned to resemble the purple-black flesh of a date. His lower body was smashed beneath the giant stone.

"Get it off me! I can't feel my legs. Lift it off me."

Grim-eyed, Karn knelt by the boulder, set his shoulder against its bulk, and heaved. The moment the stone eased up from the man's crushed pelvis and legs, a great tide of blood fled out of his belly, and he sank immediately into death.

Karn let the boulder back down. He stood. He could not imagine a worse fate for these folk—half of them only children and the other half fragile old men and women. He could not imagine how an invasion of Phyrexians could have been worse than this. It was a second Argoth, this destruction, and Malzra was a second Urza, more willing to destroy the whole world than let another creature rule it.

If only Jhoira still lived . . . that might make all this carnage less bitter. If only, but her shattered cell was buried beneath tons of rubble, and no pleading had come from it. Perhaps she had escaped. Perhaps she was still out there, somewhere, in the ruined, burning place.

Another shout came from just ahead, where a tower had fallen atop a corner of the north dormitory. Karn marked the swirling temporal storm that roiled in the space between him and the spot, and he strode out to circumnavigate it.

Perhaps she is still out there.

* * * * *

It was near to midnight when the ship slid slowly from its dock and out into the black, rolling sea. Its masts had burned away along with its sails. About three feet above waterline, its bow bore a gaping, man-sized hole where a red-hot chunk of iron had struck it. The boat was slowly taking on water, but Karn and a few of the other survivors were healthy enough to man the bilge pumps.

The rest—only thirty-three in total—huddled together on the singed deck and watched fearfully as the burning island slid silently away behind them. Fires blazed across the island, and weird lights danced in veils that reached through the clouds overhead. Waves surged in fits against the rocky shores, and a hellish moan of tortured winds made the place seem haunted by the ghosts of the fallen. The Glimmer Moon, near to sinking into the hungry waves, watched the whole display with bald accusation.

Thirty-three survivors, mused Karn grimly as he pumped. The light of the burning isle faded behind them, and only turgid cold blackness lay ahead, the sky and sea indistinguishable and menacing. Thirty-three survivors, and Jhoira nowhere among them. How could a Phyrexian invasion have been worse than this?

"It was a terrible trade," Karn said to himself, "terrible and unforgivable."

Monologue

Urza says he did it to save me. He says he let the time machine explode in order to save me and a handful of others . . . and keep his precious designs from Phyrexian claws. In another time continuum, he claims, I was slain by Phyrexian negators, and the school was overrun. Urza diverted that time stream so we could end up here, or so he says.

He is not truly mad. I know that now. He may be lying—a terrifying possibility, for what dark motive would make Urza lie to me? He may be telling the truth—all the more terrifying. But he is not truly mad.

Tolaria is gone, just like Argoth. And why? To save me? Of course not. I was saved from Tolaria just as Tawnos was saved from Argoth, as a side thought.

Tolaria is gone because if Urza could not have it, no one would. Urza is still Urza. I doubt he will ever return to the island he has destroyed, return to rebuild, to declare himself father to the scholars he has orphaned. I doubt it.

Mad or sane, he does not learn from his mistakes.

—**Barrin, Mage Master of Tolaria**

PART II

Times Returning

Chapter 7

Karn stood at the prow of a very different ship—large and golden and fully regaled—when he next saw Tolaria. The isle was only a dark shoulder above the heaving sea. Sky and water scintillated with life and daylight, but that jag of land on the horizon was as dead and dull as a dried bloodstain. Karn shuddered. He remembered that horrible night among the raging fires and toppled walls and time fissures.

The scratches he had suffered that night had all been polished away. Other improvements had been made in the ten years since the destruction of Tolaria. Master Malzra had completely replaced the finger mechanism that Jhoira had repaired. He had also redesigned the latch and coupling device that held Karn's skull-piece in place, lest other foes learn the trick of it as easily as had Kerrick or the negator in Jhoira's room. In his tinkering way, Malzra had worked a piecemeal overhaul of the power conduits throughout the golem's frame, making his reflexes somewhat quicker. Outwardly Karn seemed a new creature.

Inwardly he felt very old. His intellectual and affective cortex—the dark power matrix—remained, and with it sad memories of his first friends. He thought often of Teferi, the young and brilliant mage. He thought even more often of Jhoira, Malzra's best and brightest artificer and Karn's only true friend. Every day that dawned after that hopeless night, Karn remembered his friend and mourned for her.

"What are you thinking?" came a kindly voice at the silver man's shoulder. It was Barrin. He squinted against the bright sea and sky, and strands of silver glimmered in his hair. His eyes reflected the dark wedge of distant Tolaria. "You have been standing here all morning."

Karn turned back to face the approaching isle. "I am thinking of lost friends."

Barrin's voice softened. "It is a difficult return for all of us. But one long overdue."

"It is a place of ghosts," Karn observed. He could feel Barrin's intense eyes focused on the side of his face but did not look at him.

"You never cease to amaze me, Karn," the mage master said incredulously, "a machine that sees ghosts all around."

"Don't you remember the lost students, the lost friends?" Karn asked.

Barrin took a long breath. "Oh, yes, I remember them, and I will be sad to be back where they perished. But I have mourned. It has been ten years. There are new flowers rising among your ghosts."

"I still ache over my friends," Karn replied. "It is as raw as on that first day."

"Perhaps it is something to do with flesh. Mourning is healing. You cannot heal. You cannot truly mourn. You can only ache forever," Barrin thought aloud. He sounded pensive. "We'll have to devise some means to keep you from aching forever."

At last Karn turned toward the man. Beyond Barrin he saw the golden ship, manned by a whole new contingent of students and scholars. Gold-painted rails glimmered in the sea-shine, and white sails reached eagerly toward the isle. At the helm stood Malzra himself, at once ancient and young. The ship's name even told the tale—*New Tolaria*—and for the last eight years, it had been laboratory and tutorial hall and dormitory to all of them, vessel for all of Malzra's pursuits.

It was the genius of humans to discard the old and embrace the new, but flesh was malleable. Silver was not.

"How can I forget this ache and still be me?"

Jhoira stood at the edge of her world. Behind her lay Tolaria, desolated by the blast of Master Malzra's time machine. Before her lay the illimitable sea. She was caught between. Her secret trysting spot had become her home. It was a small place, but dry and clean, appointed with furniture, books, and implements scavenged from the academy.

Most of the old school lay in ruins. The walls that remained were leaning hazards. The walls that had fallen were cairns for the dead. Many of the living had been buried in them too.

Jhoira herself had had to dig for three days to escape the secret passage where she had been when the inferno began. She spent the next three days digging up the final few others who were trapped alive. She and eight others—all young students, resilient, canny, and agile—withdrew from the death-smelling place to Jhoira's secret niche. They, of course, made forays back into the ruins, to bury the dead and salvage equipment and food stores. These trips were far from safe. On the first such excursion, the group lost four of its members who wandered into extreme time rifts and were torn apart. Jhoira and the remaining four learned to avoid such rankling crevasses of time.

Some zones were dark and dry, their flora withered away. These were fast-time areas, where a week might pass in a day. Such places received perhaps a day's worth of sunlight and rainwater in a week and so became chill deserts. The darker and drier the zone, the faster the time in it and the more extreme the rent between it and the temporal flow of the rest of the island. Other zones were bright and wet—steamy swamps. These were slow-time areas, where a day took perhaps a week to pass. In such areas, the sun was intensely bright, moving visibly across the sky, and rain came in constant, short, drenching downpours. Most slow-time areas had not had time to adjust to their new climactic conditions, flooded to their edges and filled with drowned trees. In others, time moved so slowly, the fires of the original blast still stood in orange curtains.

Extraordinary time shifts proved impassable to Jhoira and her companions. Crossing such verges boiled blood and shredded skin, caused some limbs to die of deprivation and turn gangrenous and others to burst as interstitial tissues swelled. Such were the fates of the first four who died. The survivors were careful to map and avoid the violent time rifts. They ventured with trepidation into more moderate time fissures and found them difficult to enter and leave. Changes in inertia caused walking into a slow-time area to feel like wading forward into hardening cement. Emerging from slow time to fast time often resulted in extreme dizziness and sometimes loss of consciousness.

Even so, the final survivor of the school came from an extreme fast-time peak, which fused inexplicably with a slow-time slough beside it. From the normalized zone stepped an old man named Darrob. He had been only a child of twelve at the time of the blast but, five years later, he emerged a gray-haired madman.

There was only one true benefit Jhoira and her companions discovered from these time shifts—slow-water. Water resisted temporal change, retaining the speed of its former milieu awhile before gradually absorbing a new pace. Water that flowed from a certain extremely slow-time zone had preserving qualities, slowing and even stopping the aging of anyone who drank the thick stuff. Jhoira had no real idea how it worked, but she knew it did, at least for the short term. It was by drinking slow-time water that she had stayed young—seeming only twenty-two.

Despite this rejuvenating drink, death stalked the survivors of Tolaria. In the sixth year, their numbers were dwindled from six to five. Out hunting snakes, a fifteen-year-old boy fell down the sea cliff, broke his neck, and was dragged out to sea, even as the others swam helplessly after him. Two years later, a pair of eighteen-year-old lovers carried out a suicide pact, leaving only Jhoira, old Darrob, and another young woman. This last withered soon after, wasted by some interior disease. Her ashes nourished the rose bushes she had so patiently planted and pruned and nurtured. In the two years since her death, the roses had gone wild, spreading across the nearby boulders in a savage, fragrant blanket.

Old Darrob was dead now, too. Three months back, he had succumbed to the rattle in his chest. Jhoira had buried him beside the slab of sandstone where Darrob had loved to lie, a great silver lizard soaking up sunlight. His years in the dim depths of fast-time had taught him to love the sun. He had been Jhoira's last companion and, though mad himself, her final hold on reality. Since the day of his death, Jhoira had felt her own soul going wild, like the thorny rose.

She was alone now, yes, but she always had been. The nine who had lived with her had been companions, not friends, not confidantes. The only true friend she had ever had was Karn, and he was not even human. Jhoira often wondered what was wrong with her. Perhaps she had been taken from her people too young. Among Ghitu, a girl was not a woman until she had gone on a vision quest. Jhoira had never gone. She was twenty-eight chronologically and twenty-two by all appearance, but her soul was still the foolish and frightened soul of a child. That child had made one desperate lunge toward adulthood, had opened her secret heart to one man, believing love could not be fooled. It could be. It always would be. The man had proven a monster. Now, forevermore, Jhoira would be alone. It was a miserable way to live, but it was at least that—a way.

The island had become hers. At some point in the forty mad seasons since the blast, her fierce desire to escape the forsaken land had become a fierce desire to protect it from invaders. At first she referred to this new mania as Malzra's Malaise—a fear of invaders, destroyers. Now she was beyond such light and self-conscious wordplay. She was the island's protector, its guardian spirit. She was the ghost woman on the western shore, forever watching for nearby ships, forever fashioning arrows as Kerrick had taught her, forever designing and building whatever mechanisms she could for the defense of the land.

And now, with unmistakable intent, a white-bellied sailing ship sliced through the spitting billows, making straight for the eastern ports of the island. Jhoira had not forgotten her dream of glimpsing her soul mate on a ship such as that one, but such were the fantasies of a child. Love could and would and forever must be fooled.

Jhoira watched the ship a moment more before withdrawing into the niche, fetching up her bow and quiver of arrows and heading out to intercept the landing party. With the whole of the island between her and the docks, and over a hundred time rifts slicing through the center, Jhoira would not beat them to the shore. It didn't matter. The island's natural defenses were formidable enough.

* * * * *

Barrin inhaled the salty scent of the eastern bay, remembering the smell of saw grass and palm. He sensed nothing of death or decay in the air and was glad. Perhaps time did heal all wounds. Perhaps Tolaria had forgiven—or at least forgotten—its despoiler.

Barrin glanced back toward Urza, who helmed the golden galley *New Tolaria*. It had become his floating workshop, mobile and elusive, beyond the reach of any petty government. From the moment the refitted and renamed ship had slid out of dry dock, Urza had been its unquestioned master. Captain Malzra, the students called him, and he proved a deft helmsman. Somewhere in his three and a half millennia, the man had learned to sail. Better still, Urza's knack for teaching seamanship equaled his talent for teaching artifice. He did not so much instruct but demonstrate and inspire. The young scholars needed only watch the master hoist the main or scale the ratlines before they all wanted to do it as well and as quickly as he.

Of course, being a functional immortal with a body of pure energy can make even the oldest planeswalker a marvel in feats of strength, agility, and speed.

As *New Tolaria* rounded the stone jetty at the mouth of the bay, Urza manned the helm, and his young crew worked their posts with a quiet ease that allowed them long looks at the land ahead. Barrin, too, studied his erstwhile home.

The eastern docks remained largely intact, though the pilings were desiccated from neglect, and thorny weeds had volunteered in the rotting planks. Two ships of the former Tolarian complement lay half submerged dockside, their upper portions scored with burn marks, and their lower portions so covered in barnacles they seemed made of stone instead of waterlogged wood. As each wave rolled, long and even, across them, they rocked indolently in the basins they had hollowed for themselves.

On the opposite edge of the bay, a sinister slough of dark water lay, its surface churning as though it boiled. A time rift, Barrin realized. Urza had described such phenomena after returning from one of his planeswalking scouting excursions. He had spoken in depth about the physics of the rents but could answer none of the important questions, such as—what happens to mortal flesh that ventures into or out of one? Urza's only response to such queries was, "We'll have to find out when mortal flesh encounters one." Barrin had made sure the students were taught how to recognize temporal anomalies and warned what dangers might surround them. He had even devised illusory models and magical simulations to prepare the explorers, but all he could offer was supposition. The experiments with mortal flesh were yet to come.

Urza steered clear of the time rift and the other hazards in the bay and brought *New Tolaria* smoothly into the deep-water inlet. He shouted orders, and one by one the last few sails were taken in. Released by the wind, the ship lounged aft and piled up glassy mounds of water before it. It slowed to a near stop, Urza leaned on the rudder, and students eagerly crowded the starboard rail, each wanting to be the first to leap to the dock and tie off the ship. Two young women were the first with the strength and daring to jump, and three young men followed shortly after. Their laughing comrades hurled to them thick coils of line, which they swiftly hitched onto the pilings. The great vessel lulled once to the fore with the last of its lazy motion and then settled in on its moorings.

More students leapt to the dock and received the gangplank hoisted down to them. It no sooner boomed into place than the five ensigns and their five exploratory parties were trooping in orderly fashion onto the dock. The ensigns were the oldest students—in their mid-twenties—left from the school at Tolaria, and their parties were picked from late-teens who had volunteered knowing the dangers they would face. These groups debarked with the easy strides of conquerors. The white robes of the former academy had been replaced by rugged canvas cloaks and capes, with leather leggings, knee-high putties, and iron-edged shoes. In moments, the explorers filed off the dock and gathered in clusters, receiving orders. Then, to north, south, west, and the angles in between, they set out.

Barrin watch it all, apprehension knotting the muscles in his neck. If it was Urza's island and he felt so safe on it, why were mere children being sent out to explore it? The touch of Urza's hand on his back made the knots redouble.

"We are home again, Barrin," Urza said, deep satisfaction in his voice.

"We are at the door, knocking," Barrin replied. "We aren't inside yet."

Urza studied his longtime associate and friend. "After all your lectures about owning up to my mistakes, returning to right the wrongs I have done, how can you criticize me today?"

"They're only children, Urza—" Barrin began.

"They are grownups. They have been thoroughly trained. They know what to expect. They know what they risk," Urza replied evenly.

"They're only children. Not grownups, not probes, not machines," Barrin finished.

"If anything should go awry, I am linked to them and can reach them at a moment's notice." Urza paused, seeming to hear a voice speak to him out of the wheeling blue sky. "In fact, the first party of explorers is summoning us. They have discovered a time rift." He reached out and grabbed Barrin's hand, saying simply, "We go."

Barrin felt the world fold in around him and Urza. They were planeswalking.

After complications had arisen with Urza's trick of turning planeswalking mortals to stone (four of them had been cracked en route and hemorrhaged massively when returned to flesh), he had devised better spells for keeping mortal flesh alive through a planeswalk. The enchantment currently in effect reduced Barrin from a three-dimensional construct to a two-dimensional one. In this compacted form, he was protected against the trials of sudden vacuum, volcanic heat, and absolute cold encountered in a planeswalk. Barrin's lungs could not explode because they were no more than flat sheaves of paper. Urza hung there beside him, attached and pulling him through to where the world opened up again.

When it opened, the two scholars stood suddenly on a bald brow of sand. Before them, the land dipped away into a grassy swale. There three students stood, staring in astonishment toward a sharp-edged ravine. The air in the ravine looked dusky and turgid, tiny flecks of dust catching and scattering the rays of the sun. Beyond the deep furrow stood an old-growth forest, but within it, the ground held only short, scrubby plants with tender purple blossoms. Small white rocks lined the base of the valley. At the lip of the ravine crouched the team ensign, a powerfully built blonde woman. Beside her hovered a young man with long black hair. They spoke to each other in hushed tones and gestured into the yawning rift, which emitted a sound like a breathing giant.

"Let's see what they have found," Urza suggested.

He released Barrin's hand and started down the hillside. With each step, puffs of dust rose from his feet, making him seem to walk inches above the ground.

That's the way he would prefer it, Barrin mused to himself as he followed. The two scholars passed the group of whispering students, who startled back, lost the thread of their conversation, and receded into watchful silence. Urza and Barrin continued until they stood behind the crouching ensign and her comrade.

"You summoned me?" Urza said by way of introduction.

The ensign stood and snapped to attention, "Yes, Captain."

"What have you found, Ensign Dreva?"

"A time rift, Captain, just as Master Barrin had indicated in his reports." Dreva's eyes were a bit wider than normal, and she stared into space. "A fast-time rift, I would suggest, judging from the apparent darkness and the lack of water. We have conducted a few experiments. I can repeat them. Rehad?"

She reached out to the young man next to her, gesturing for something, and received a long, leafy branch he had gathered in a nearby forest. Despite her formal demeanor, the affection between ensign and student was obvious in the lingering way the branch was passed, hand to hand.

Ensign Dreva turned her attention back to the captain. "Watch the foliage on the end of this bough."

She raised the branch and swung it slowly into the air above the ravine. Something invisible seemed to take hold of the dangling end, making it jitter and sway, and the ensign dug her feet in and tightened her grip on the bow to keep it from being yanked out of her hand. The leaves quickly grew brown and curled into dry crescents. Next moment, they rushed downward from the branch to the floor of the ravine, where they lulled before turning to dust. Meanwhile, the leafless twigs twisted, their bark peeled away, their wood cracked and grayed, and the entire branch came to resembled the hoary claw of a forest hag. The ensign withdrew the stick and laid it beside two others, similarly transformed.

Urza's smile, small and unaccustomed, showed his delight at these findings. "Excellent work. Using a living branch to probe the rift was an insightful innovation."

The ensign flushed. "Thank you, Captain Malzra."

"There are some who doubted whether you would be equal to the task—" Urza turned his mysterious smile toward Barrin "—but I was confident."

"Thank you again, Captain," Dreva replied. "I suggest we continue probing the edges of this time rift and set warning markers. Though most likely the blast that created the geographic ravine also created the temporal anomaly, we shouldn't assume the boundary of the one will be the exact boundary of the other."

"Well reasoned, Ensign," Urza said. "Continue. Report in if you discover anything else of note." He turned, shouldering Barrin toward the privacy of a nearby hilltop as the ensign sent Rehad and the other students to the forest eaves to gather more branches. "It seems to me they are doing quite well, these children you speak of."

Barrin stared down at the tangled grass at his feet. "The dangers here are your doing and my doing, not theirs."

"If they will live here with us, build here and study here, they must inherit all the evils of the past," Urza replied. "It is the responsibility of every new generation to understand what has come before, if only to decide what to keep and what to discard."

The philosophical debate was interrupted by a warning shout from the verge of the forest. Barrin and Urza turned. Ensign Dreva stood at the edge of the wood, grasping something in one arm and urgently summoning her comrades with the other. The students flung down the branches they had chopped loose and ran. Urza and Barrin ran too.

Dreva pulled savagely on a tree limb. Other students, two young men and a woman, reached her and added their muscle to the task. Moments of shouted orders and position-jockeying gave way to groans as the students hauled hard on the limb.

Barrin pelted toward them, wondering what could be so urgent about pulling the branch from a tree, and then he saw.

It was no tree they pulled on, but Rehad, standing just within the forest edge. One hand rested on a fat green bole, just beside a branch he had been intending to cut off. He was trapped in a slow-time rift, one arm extending beyond, and his companions were doing all they could to pull him out.

"Wait!" Barrin ordered. He struggled to form a spell but was too late.

Rehad's arm, bloodless from being trapped beyond the time continuity of his heart, was no match for the pulling might of the ensign and the three others. It dislocated. The tissues caught in the lacerating edge of the time stream tore and gave way. The arm came off in their grasp. Gore dribbled slowly from the ruined shoulder. Ensign Dreva and the students landed in a sloppy heap on the grass, the severed arm among them.

Barrin and Urza came to a stop just before the temporal rift.

Rehad's face was slowly twisting in pain as the initial shock of the injury gave way to rending agony. Urza lifted a hand and pressed it into the wall of slow time. His fingers trembled as they sank into the hot, thick air. Had he blood in him, that limb might well have become stuck, like Rehad, but the master inhabited a body of focused energy. Even so, the time difference tugged at him, sending crazings of energy in twisting spirals along the surface of the distortion. With an effort of will, he maintained the forward motion of his hand and slowly gripped the man's bleeding shoulder.

All the while, Rehad was turning, eyes wide and mouth dropping open in a scream. He shied instinctively back from Urza's grasping hand, but the master anticipated the move. He caught the grisly joint and clamped down hard, stanching the killing blood flow, then, with grim deliberation, slowly drawing the young man toward him.

Behind Urza, Ensign Dreva and the students had risen. The severed arm lay on the ground at their feet. Rehad's blood painted their leather leggings and canvas cloaks. Two of the students were crying, and the third gaped in terrified disbelief. Dreva herself was close-mouthed and dry-eyed, though her face was bone-white. She shook her head in raw regret.

Barrin moved to comfort her.

She ducked away, grabbed the fallen arm, and pushed up beside Urza.

"Put it back, Captain. You have to put it back," she implored, jabbing the limb toward him.

Gritting his teeth, Urza gently pushed her aside. He was pivoting Rehad around so the man would emerge with brain and heart aligned, so that he could escape the time trap as gradually as possible.

Dreva staggered back. She blinked at the sanguine thing in her grip and tenderly kissed the back of the hand. Her lips parted in quiet words: "Oh, Rehad, forgive me." She lay the limb at her feet and, in a sudden rush like a panicked deer, darted away.

"Ensign Dreva!" Barrin shouted, seeing where she headed. "Come back!"

She was deaf to it, already hurling herself past the toothy edge of the fast-time ravine. There came a splash of energy as she plunged into the time shift. Rings of temporal flux whirled on the air around her. Waves sank into the ground and rose into the arcing sky. Within their dancing midst, Dreva's airborne form withered. Flesh wrinkled and dried. It cleaved to atrophying muscle and showed bone beneath. Once she had completely entered the envelope, she fell to earth in a sudden rush and was lost to sight beyond the rim of the ravine.

Barrin bolted after her, down the grassy swale and to the verge of the fast-time rift. There he staggered to a halt and gaped.

She was dead already, her dry, deflated skin teaming with vermin.

Barrin turned away, sickened. When he at last mastered his gut, there was nothing left of Ensign Dreva but scraps of canvas and leather and a bleached skeleton.

* * * * *

They sat aboard *New Tolaria* that night. Urza had planned a banquet to celebrate the island's reclamation. Trenchers of salt-pork stew steamed beside vast loaves of marbled bread and mounds of fresh oranges.

The mood was anything but festive. The day had been a chastening failure.

Rehad was below-decks, bandaged extensively and lying in a drugged sleep. Rejoining his arm was beyond the skill of the crew's best healers and beyond the power of even Urza Planeswalker. It lay now in a wooden case within a pocket of extreme slow time, in the vain hope it might be rejoined in the future. Meanwhile, Rehad's leader, his love, lay in a pocket of extreme fast time, her skeleton perhaps even now scattered by the tiny scavengers of the ravine.

These two were not the only casualties. Each exploratory party lost at least one member, and one party was wiped out entirely. Urza performed two other rescues like the one he did for Rehad, and Karn assisted in shepherding a young woman from the recursion loop she found herself in. The only non-organic members of the crew, Urza and Karn had the best resistance to time distortions, though their systems were greatly stressed by these operations.

The crew ate their victory dinner not in Old Tolaria, as Urza had hoped, but on *New Tolaria*. They ate in near-silence. The waters of the bay lapped, black and thirsty, at the gunwales of the great ship, and beyond the beam of the lanterns, the island and sky were black with night.

From the darkness came a woman. She was tan, keen-eyed, and mysterious. A savage skein drew her dark hair back sharply over her head. Garbed in ragged but regal clothes, she seemed an avatar of the isle itself—alien, angry, and forbidding. She strode up the gangplank and onto the deck, pushing past the stunned guards.

Urza stood.

Barrin rose, his mouth dropping open in recognition.

It was Karn, the silver man, who first spoke her name, in a voice like a rain-swollen waterfall. "Jhoira!"

"Master Barrin. Master Malzra," the woman said in a greeting that combined awe and animosity, "I never thought you would return. I wish you hadn't. After today, you probably wish you hadn't, either."

Monologue

I was overjoyed to see Jhoira. Her death had weighed heavily on me and on Karn as well. She was much changed, of course, hard-muscled and hard-eyed. The impulses of wonder and forgiveness had been winnowed out of her. She had ceased to be a student of the academy, becoming a native of the island.

As the island's native advocate, Jhoira spoke strongly in its defense. There, before Urza's new passel of students, she laid out all his past sins, planted like thistles across the island and grown up now into great killing forests. Quite openly, she berated him for his time machine. The tampering that had brought about the blast had riven the tapestry of days on the island and left it a jumbled mess.

She talked of the other survivors who had, one by one, perished, leaving her alone.

Even more powerfully, she spoke of how life here had continued. Fast-time forests had died and fallen away, giving place to new plants and animals, to an arid tundra ecology with its own balance of predator and prey. Slow-time forests had turned into swampy jungles, hot and steamy—refuges for thousands of creatures that could not have survived on the island before. Within all these details, I sensed how the years had changed her too.

"We are, Master Malzra—" she had said at the end of it all "—we are your children of fury, orphans who have grown up in your absence, no longer yours, no longer beholden to you. Many of us hate you, Master Malzra."

He listened through it all. I'll give him that much. And then, into the unhappy silence that settled, Urza spoke, and what he said filled me with even more admiration.

"I understand. But I am committed to return, and I don't want to fight you, my children of fury. I want to be reconciled. It will be a thorny way, I know, charged with the thistles I myself planted. But I am committed to return."

"You'll need an advisor," I said, "a guide. Jhoira, I can think of no one better than you to help Master Malzra understand the mistakes of the past and avert them in the future."

There was one final, anxious moment, and then something in her broke. The mad sheen of defiance cracked, and I saw beneath it a lonely woman fearing but needing to be among others.

"Only because if I refused, every last one of you would die."

I tried to look grimly chastened, but I was elated. Urza was pleased too. The fearful students and scholars were both jangled and relieved. Someone—even this frightening wild woman—had to guide them through the terrors of Old Tolaria.

—Barrin, Mage Master of Tolaria

Chapter 8

When most of the crew awoke the next morning, Jhoira was already on deck. She had drawn aside to trade stories with Karn. Though fierce and formidable around other humans, Jhoira laughed and spoke easily with the golem. They were an impressive pair—the wild woman and the silver man. Her flesh was as smooth and brown as the sandstone shoulders around the bay, and his as mirror-bright as the sea they had crossed.

Karn told her of all the students and scholars he had rescued, and how he had searched late into the night for her, allowing the refugee ship to leave only as the Glimmer Moon sank in the sea. Jhoira told her own stories of rescue and loss. All of this passed without the long, awkward silences of the night before, as though not a moment had gone by between these long-separated friends. They walked along the shore and reminisced, skipping stones in the choppy waves, until the deck was teeming with crew, and the smell of freshly brewed tea drew them back aboard.

Jhoira drank eagerly, burning her lip with the piping stuff. She smiled at Karn and said, "There are certain drawbacks to being a 'wild woman' and among them are forgoing real tea from a porcelain cup."

The crew broke their fast with a second feast, those going ashore knowing the meal would have to last them until they made camp at the center of the isle. Jhoira predicted, with a caravan of fifty, it would take the whole day to thread their way past the worst time rifts and through the mildest ones.

Jhoira's tone of gloom returned as she described to the crew the temporal distortions of the island. They resembled the physical topography after the blast. At the detonation point was a wide temporal basin like a blast crater, where the explosion uniformly ripped away the natural flow of time. Near the edges of this slow-time crater were a series of concentric rills of time, tightly packed fastzones. The center would be unreachable except for avenues of force that radiated spokelike from it and joined the outer island with the inner. Many of these avenues were deep slow-time rents, though others allowed a gradual descent into the crater. Others still had admixed with the fast-time shells nearby to make bridges of normal time. Beyond these concentric fast-time rings were large, irregular regions of extreme time shift, many contiguous square miles of territory unreachable to those outside—sheer time plateaus and deep time canyons. In these areas, whole new ecologies had evolved and cultures with them.

Bearing only the clothes on her back and a long walking staff, Jhoira led a pack-laden parade of scholars and students up the winding forest paths between temporal canyons and plateaus.

Urza followed just behind her. He carried a large wooden case with ornate inlays of brass and ivory. It looked terrifically heavy, but his strides were weightless, and his questions came easily despite the panting of others. Perhaps he had cast an enchantment that let his feet glide among the gorse, or perhaps microscopic machines did the walking for him.

Barrin came next, carrying the stowed tent that would hold him and Urza, as well as clanking pots and an assortment of swaying parcels.

Behind him, Karn carried the burden of ten men. Throughout the line, other, smaller automata ambled beneath heavy packs. The rest of the company consisted of aging scholars and young students, at once eager and fearful about what lay ahead.

"Karn, come up here. I want you to see this," Jhoira said.

She gestured toward a wide, glaring, and desolate swamp filled with the ghost-gray corpses of drowned and burned-out trees. The water in it was black and seemed infinitely deep. Insects hung in static suspension above the mirror waters. Some were poised just before death, the goggle eyes and gaping mouths of fish stretching the surface tension below.

"I call this Slate Waters. Here the fires from the original explosion went out only seven years ago, after drenching rains. Before then, a pillar of smoke rose above the spot. By my calculations, in Slate Waters the equivalent of ten days have passed since the blast. Step in there, and you'd need a time machine to get back out."

Karn stared at the spot. It reflected darkly in his hide. "My time-traveling days are done. Master Malzra is intent on other pursuits. I'm not much needed these days." The words sounded at once relieved and disappointed.

Jhoira studied her old friend. Provisions hulked up from his massive shoulders.

"Don't worry, old friend. *I* need you." She patted his side and pivoted. "Now look over on this side of the path. That's a temporal plateau. I call it the Hives because of the domed mud huts that its residents build across it." She pointed to a region that was forever in twilight, the land sunk in a vast pall.

Scattered forests of short, scrubby trees clung to the hillsides, a gray and torn fabric of woodlands that looked all the more spectral because of the blur of their wind-rattled leaves and rapidly growing boughs. Here and there, in clear patches among these stern woodland copses, rounded hovels took rapid shape, proliferating like chambers in a mud-daubers' nest until whole dim villages could be discerned in spots, and slender footpaths marked the ground between them. The villagers themselves moved with unseeable speed. As quickly as a particular settlement would mound into being, it would dissolve away again, ephemeral as bubbles atop boiling water.

"Five of their generations are born and die during one of our years," Jhoira said levelly to Urza, who had taken the occasion to stop and stare.

Barrin, coming up behind, asked breathlessly, "Five generations of whom? There were no natives on this island."

Jhoira's eyes were keenly fastened on Urza's face. "I can only assume these were students of the academy, caught in extreme fast time, as unable to escape their rift as we are to enter it. They are fifty generations removed from your school. They have lived a thousand years of tribal history since then."

Barrin was stunned silent for a moment. Then he said, "They see us right now, don't they? The hour it will take us to march past their land will be four days of their time. We are statues to them."

"Yes. Unreachable, inexplicable, nearly immobile statues," Jhoira affirmed. "They can hear us, too, but our speech is deep and long and meaningless, like whale-song. Haunting and otherworldly. They've become a different race from us. Soon they'll be a different species." She began walking again, and the line of students and scholars stretched out behind her. "There's an even more fearsome sight in another time plateau ahead. But first, paradise."

All down the lines, scholars and students traded intrigued looks and hunkered down beneath their burgeoning packs. Jhoira led them up a meandering hillside, past stands of cypress and creeping vines on the left and a gray place of tumbled downs on the right. For some time, the hives of mud and stick were still visible, boiling and receding among the trees.

Eventually, the party reached a new place, a highland with rolling green embankments and thick forest growth. The native flora of Tolaria thrived here on the bright hillsides. Fat-boled trees were green from root-clusters to crowns. Vines like vein work coiled along every stem. Broad leaves lay in a series of dense canopies above.

"This is a mild slow-time area, where sunlight and rainwater are gently enhanced, where creatures and plants live in abundance, where the heat of the canopy is matched by the cool of the forest floor. The hills allow enough runoff to keep the land from becoming deluged, and the hollows where water collects are deep and clear and cool. It is paradise. I call it Angelwood, after the fireflies that light it at night. Whenever I have grown exhausted from my cliff-side vigil, I have come here to swim and climb and breathe again. That is perhaps the best part, breathing again."

Eyes all around the group turned hungrily toward the garden of delights. Sweat-dotted brows eased.

Among the vast tree trunks, large bright birds flew dreamily through curtains of light and shadow. Beneath them, water bounded down a sloping face of stone and emptied into a clear brown channel. After coiling among the forest's seeking roots, the waterway slid into a nearby vale, forming a deep, cool pool before spilling into another stream at the far side. Beneath the surface of the water, the silvery gleam of fish shone.

"Why didn't you make this your home?" one student asked, pushing brown hair back from her eyes. "The game is plentiful, the nights are warm, the water is pure, and you would live longer there than anywhere else."

Jhoira was grim. "You can't live in paradise."

She set out again. The company behind her lingered, a few sipping on canteens, but most just standing and staring. One student made a point of scrawling a crude map on a piece of paper, apparently intent on returning to this spot when time allowed.

Jhoira led the group up toward a wide level place where an outcrop of ancient granite had been worn down like a filed tooth. Aside from the eastern pinnacles, this summit was the highest point on the island. Its gray crown was scoured clean by the blast, dead trees lying in parallel lines all about the peak. Young trees sheltered by the fallen logs rose in the midst of the devastation, a future forest. From the top of the rock, the views were clear from the pinnacles in the east to Jhoira's niche in the west.

There, atop that worn-down stone, the company of fifty paused to catch breath and shake out weary legs. The intimate vistas of Angelwood were replaced by the panorama of what Jhoira called the Giant's Pate. In the east, the sea was a quicksilver curtain streaming down from the white-rising sun. *New Tolaria* was a dark and tiny silhouette against it, crew resting about the deck in the quiet of morning. The shore was a beige ribbon, silky and coiling.

Inland, forest and briar, marsh and meadow made shifting patterns of green and gray, shade and daylight. It was a verdant land.

Not so the westward isle. Its distant shore was a bright orange pile of rankled rocks, among which Jhoira's niche nestled. Closer to the Giant's Pate, the ruins of Old Tolaria lay. They were gray and blighted. The onetime logic of walls and paths was still obvious in the maze-work of foundations, but most of the buildings had been razed by the blast. Here and there part of a structure remained, sometimes in gutted, unnatural towers with open sides and decrepit backbones of stone. Though not an actual crater, the slow-time field of Old Tolaria was noticeable in the bright shimmer of the air over those ruins and the water that lagged in cellars and leaning doorways.

Nearby the glaring section that was Old Tolaria was another district, a place of deep darkness in a literal canyon. It lay in the morning shadow of the Giant's Pate, but its gloom was intensified by the high, leaning walls of the canyon and the vast time shift within it. The floor of the space was indistinguishable, and some of the students whispered it was a crack right through to the underworld.

"It looks like a good place for ghosts," one said.

"If I were dead, I'd choose a home like that," another answered lightly.

"It looks like a scar in the world," ventured a third with awe, "a bad scar, one that tried to close and heal but only festered and grew deeper."

"You are more right than you imagine," Jhoira said. "That is a very deep chasm and a sheer fast-time precipice. But there is a bottom to it, and there are creatures trapped in it."

"Like the tribes in the Hives?"

"No," Jhoira said flatly. "Look there. You may not be able to see it while the Giant's Pate casts its shadows—sometimes it can't be seen even at the height of midday, but there is a fortress down there."

Urza's brow furrowed in concern. "A fortress?"

"Perhaps it is only a kind of commune, but what I have seen of it looks savage and braced against attack."

"What have you seen?" Barrin asked.

"Spiked battlements, for one, a causeway of suspension bridges between high guard towers, flying buttresses that look like they are fashioned of dragon bone, windows as black and smooth as onyx, fiendish adornments, and thick-cast tiles of clay. I have the notion they would prefer to make everything of steel, if they could make it, but iron is the best they have and not much of it. It has taken many hours of distant observation to piece that much together. I would not suggest close scrutiny: I've seen harpoons fly from that space, spear deer, and drag them in."

Barrin blinked in confusion. "This barbarous culture arose from refugees from the academy? Students of ours?"

"Again, no," Jhoira said. "You remember that man, Kerrick, whom you found with the broken leg, whom you interrogated as a Phyrexian sleeper? The man I had let into the academy? Remember that he escaped an hour before the blast? He must have been trapped in that fast-time gash—he and whatever Phyrexian negators he had summoned to Tolaria."

* * * * *

Through a two-story-tall window of polished obsidian, K'rrik watched the new arrivals. They stood atop the gleaming peak at the height of the island, a summit always visible to K'rrik and his retainers here in the depths of the abyss.

Jhoira was among them. She seemed, in fact, to be leading them. She had been a canny foe during the century of his imprisonment in this time-gash. She never entered range of the harpoon crews— and more's the pity. He had much to repay her for. Betrayal to Urza Planeswalker was chief among the offenses. Putting a harpoon through her gut and hauling her across the jagged lip of the chasm to burst like a fist-clutched skull—that would have been glad repayment of her debts.

She probably still called him Kerrick. She probably still thought of him as a golden-haired boy, but a hundred years had turned

Kerrick to K'rrik, had made the smooth-skinned Phyrexian sleeper into a hoary warrior.

If there were some way to bring Jhoira over alive, not masticated like the goat and deer carcasses they feasted on, K'rrik would at last consummate their "love." That was her other great offense, her persistent virtue in the face of his advances. It was galling that flimsy chastity should stand against the might of Phyrexia.

Of course, if he could drag her across whole, he himself could have escaped this abyss. It had taken the death of half his negator minions—twelve of the twenty-four—to finally convince K'rrik to suspend his escape attempts. Even so, with each new generation decanted, he sent one in ten out to seek escape—a tithe to his eventual return to Tolaria, to Dominaria.

This ten percent attrition was no great loss. He still commanded a mighty nation of two hundred Phyrexians. They filled every corner of the chasm. Generations of them worked in the deep dank of the waters at the base of the canyon. They hatched, netted, and gutted the various species of blind scavenger fish that were their major diet. Other Phyrexians, for generations, drilled deep into the chasm walls in search of buried veins of obsidian and the basalt stones the palace was built of. Scant resources had been the only real limit to K'rrik's inventive genius. If he could make steel or powerstones, his artifact creatures would have overrun the isle eighty years ago. As it was, what little iron the miners found was more precious than gold. It was constantly oiled with Phyrexian blood to prevent rust. An iron sword like K'rrik's was a kingmaker. It made him unopposable in the arena and maintained his power. Thus the miners who found scant veins of iron were essential to his power base, the figurative foot soldiers of his regime. By carefully distributing these slivers of iron among real foot soldiers, K'rrik controlled a private army engineered to be loyal only to him. These killers used draconian measures to ensure the compliance of all the others. K'rrik presided over the army and the nation because he had created both and was the smartest, strongest, and most vicious of them all.

To these native talents, the Phyrexian sleeper had added enhancements to himself of bone and steel and, eventually, even spawned tissue implants. He was indomitable in the arena. His once-smooth shoulders were now adorned with tusks hollowed out to inject scorpion-fish poison in anyone he fought. Similar spikes jutted from his elbows and knees. The spikes were back-barbed like arrows so that once they sunk into flesh, they ripped it out in great chunks. His torso was braced by a black-steel frame that prevented his spine from being broken and allowed him to break the spines of others. He himself had wielded the cleaver that removed his outer two fingers of each hand, making room for more venom spikes. The century of imprisonment in the abyss had done much to perfect his form.

Now, gazing through the thick, dark glass of his upper throne room, K'rrik saw the means by which he would at last escape his prison—the power of his old foe, Urza Planeswalker.

* * * * *

It was a bitter pill for Master Malzra, Jhoira could tell. The man stood there, gazing into that black jag in the ground. His eyes saw more than most eyes did—they gleamed with an acute, penetrating judgment. Surely they saw past the shrouding murk to the Phyrexian colony that lay within it. Surely Malzra peered into that black pile of basalt and obsidian to the wretched creature at the heart of it—malicious and brooding, growing a year in strength for every month outside.

Kerrick was the man. Even without preternatural sight, Jhoira knew that. Of course, he was no man, but a monster wearing the skin of a man. She knew he was at the nexus of that vast infection and that he would be powerful now, perhaps the equal of Malzra himself, perhaps his superior.

Karn's eyes, too, saw more than most. He drew Malzra, Barrin, and Jhoira aside from the others.

"It is no secret to any of you what I was made for—to travel down the throat of time. Perhaps I have found my new purpose here, to enter that place and destroy them." The suggestion was made with a mild, matter-of-fact tone, but in a voice like the myriad whisper of trees before a summer storm.

A knowing glance passed between Malzra and Barrin.

The mage said through a grim smile, "I seem to remember just such a journey, from my study of arcane lore. There was once upon a time a planeswalker who went into Phyrexia to destroy it. He was armored much as you are, Karn, but was nearly destroyed in the attempt."

Malzra nodded. "It is a good analogy. What we have here is a pocket Phyrexia. And in Tolaria." His all-seeing eyes were suddenly hooded beneath angry brows. "Jhoira, you spoke last night of the children of fury I have left in my wake—the orphaned mistakes that have, in my absence, grown up to defy me, to hate me, to harry me and slay me if they can. I see now just how true your words are." He blinked and drew a deep breath, two actions that signaled a powerful shift in the mind of the man. "Better not to create such foes than to be forever fighting them."

Barrin looked with admiration at him.

The sun glinted from Malzra's lifted eyes as he marked its march across the sky. "Already the sun begins its descent. Come, take us to Old Tolaria, to a place where we can safely make camp. Somewhere outside the slow-time slough in the center of the blast. Preferably on high ground nearby, where time follows its normal courses."

A solemn look crossed Jhoira's face. "I know just the place."

She turned, heading for a path down from the Giant's Pate toward the decimated academy below. Squinting in tired amazement, the students and scholars on the hilltop watched her go. Many of them were worn out from staring into the impenetrable blackness of the Phyrexian rift and exhausted from the nettling worry that the cleft awoke in them. They had unpacked meals of press-bread and jerky. When Jhoira marched on, they glanced a question at Master Malzra and Barrin. The two men took their last survey of the spot and started after her. Flashing on the brow of the hill, Karn also set his feet to the path. With angry sighs, the students jammed their half-eaten lunches back into their packs, hauled the parcels to their shoulders, and stomped onward down the trail.

Jhoira took a path that had been carved out by her own feet during her rambles. It passed a number of other time rifts, these small and severe, some as narrow as an arm's breadth but a mile in length. Jhoira called these the Curtains of Eternity because anyone who ventured into them would be instantly torn to pieces. There was no need to instruct the party to stay strictly to the path.

Beyond loomed the labyrinth of riven buildings that had once been the Tolarian Academy. The march line stilled to silence as they approached the necropolis. The older members of the company had lived in these gutted hulks, had had friends who died in the cross-sectioned towers and lay even now, skeletal, beneath the piles of cut stone. To the natural dread that came upon them all in descending into that dead place, there was added the drag of slow time on their hearts and lungs. To step onto those ravaged and rubble-strewn streets was to sink into a nightmare made real in stone and bone and ash. Eerily, the sun shone bright and merciless in that flagging place. Those who glanced up toward it saw the fiery ball fleeing visibly toward the horizon.

During their tour of the old town, Jhoira led the group to a particularly disturbing sight. It was the statue of a young man running. Both feet hovered impossibly above the ground. His mouth was wide in despair. His eyes were clenched tight. His hands groped out madly. His white robes were lit with a diffuse orange glow that enwrapped him and rose into an onion-shaped dome over his head. The young man was ensconced in a pillar that shone with fiery light. Just ahead of him, floating still in air, was a heavy cloak, caught in the moment before descending to enfold him.

Jhoira watched the faces of Malzra, Barrin, Karn, and the older students and scholars, looking for recognition. They stared bleakly for some time, their minds unraveling the mystery before them.

At last, Karn breathed the name: "Teferi."

"Yes. He was caught in flames when the blast occurred. Only a moment of time has passed for him in these ten years. When I discovered him here seven years ago, I fetched a heavy cloak, soaked it in water, and flung it into the air to engulf him. In another few years—a split second of his time—he will be wrapped in it, his burning robes extinguished. Perhaps a few years later, he will tumble to the ground. Perhaps in ten years, he will see the *New Tolaria* and strive to reach it. Then, of course, he will be torn to pieces." Her face hardened. She gnawed at one lip. "That damned cloak is all I can do for him. I've studied the time fissure, performed experiments, tried everything I could imagine, but he's caught and cannot be saved."

Stunned silence followed this revelation. Fifty sets of eyes traced out the doomed figure, frozen in fire, unreachable, but only an arm's length away.

At last, Malzra spoke words that comforted them all. "The first area of study for our new academy will be techniques to rescue this young man."

Jhoira wore a grim expression as she turned away. She led onward at a stern pace. The young students, some only children of twelve or thirteen, followed close behind. Older marchers paused at Teferi's Shrine, as some were already calling it. Master Malzra, Barrin, and Karn themselves brought up the rear of the procession.

The marchers felt their sunken spirits and slowed hearts rise again as they climbed the headlands on the southern verge of the ruins. Beyond lay a wide, level place covered with tall, dry grass. The parched blades made a familiar and soothing noise in the warm afternoon winds.

Despite Jhoira's steady pace, evening deepened across the hilltop by the time Malzra, Barrin, and Karn reached the summit. There the master looked about with his piercing eyes. He marked the closeness of Old Tolaria, of the Curtains of Eternity, and beyond it the Phyrexian canyon where his foes, even then, multiplied.

"You were right, Jhoira," he said simply. "This is just the place." He walked to the pack of one of his young, tired hikers, drew a tent spike from the gear stowed there, and, with the sheer force of his hand, drove it deep in the dry ground. "Just here, we will build our new academy."

Monologue

I was bone-weary and soul-weary that first night when, by lantern light, we erected our tent city. We cleared fire circles, set stones to hem them in, gathered firewood and water for the evening, and sat down to dried meat, press-bread, and a little hot broth. I had been the one all along telling Urza he must return to Tolaria, must rectify his past mistakes and embrace the children of fury. But in glimpsing those children for the first time—whether the tribal folk of the Hive, the unseeable Phyrexian hordes in the gorge, or the ghosts of the dead that almost palpably haunt the ruins of the academy—I fear I was perhaps wrong.

Forgetting the past, fleeing the death it holds, shrugging off the wounds—this is the way mortals live. Yesterdays are supposed to remain dead. It is the gift of time. Each new generation is supposed to be born ignorant of the horrors that came before. How else can any of us live?

And, yet, perhaps I was right after all. Urza is not mortal. He cannot afford to forget, any more than time can afford to forget. The world is not large enough to let him go from mistake to mistake, leaving destruction in his path. He has to clean up after himself. In a way, his mania to return in time was a desire to remember, to own up to the past. He likely would have come to this conclusion with or without me. Of course, now that Urza has decided, we might as well assist his every endeavor, for he won't change his mind for another millennium or so.

I only hope, after all this temporal fiddling, I have the blessing of dying after a normal human span—not before and certainly not after.

—Barrin, Mage Master of Tolaria

Chapter 9

The heavy wooden case Malzra had borne on his back turned out to be an elaborate desk. He unfolded it next morning to the surprise and delight of the breakfasting students. The surface of the thing was smooth ebony composed of various panels. Each black wood panel slid out of the main compartments on hidden joints and fused seamlessly with its counterparts. The end result was an extensive, smooth tabletop, as wide as Malzra's arm span and twice as long. The work surface rested on cabinets with many small drawers and compartments. By some ingenious trick, the whole thing—cabinets and drawers and all—had collapsed easily into a compact box. More marvelous than even these capacities: no sooner than the desk was fully set up, Malzra drew open drawer after drawer, producing styluses, spanners, rule rods, compasses, protractors, a set of angle edges, and roll after roll of plans. He smoothed the last down atop the workspace, struggling to get them to lie flat until Barrin set a stone on each corner of the sheets.

Barrin and Malzra stepped back, allowing the gathering crowd of students to look on grand vistas in lead and ink. There was a soaring central hall, with room to seat four hundred students and scholars, a series of balconies overlooking the grand space, and an empyrean vault open on one side to show the dense forest canopy. There were fanciful towers, rounded and lean like exotic gourds, some topped with guard stations, others with fire towers, and others still with observatories that bristled with optical paraphernalia. The outer wall was an enormous bulwark of earth and stone, with a notable absence of sewage grates and duct work. Long, curved corridors, great banks of jeweled-glass windows, an aviary, aerial docks, a gymnasium, a large, rock-lined pond, gardens and groves. The dormitories provided private rooms that were bright and open—no longer the cells of the previous prison. Every aspect of the design was marked with imaginative ornamentation—octopodal figures, fantastical sea prawns, Tolarian drake-head appointments, four-winds motifs, devices drawn from the naval architecture of *New Tolaria*, gulls and kingfishers, anvil-headed storm clouds, tridents and coral and nautilus shells.

This was not the stern infirmary of the previous Tolaria. This was not a prison. Asceticism had given way to aestheticism, strict artifice to fanciful art.

"Of course," Malzra said to no one and everyone at once, "we will have to move the eastern gate from there—" he pointed to a place on the plans, and the corresponding location on the topography before them, "—to there, allowing easier access to the safe path and Angelwood beyond."

Barrin assessed his friend. "I'm glad to see you've not turned the school into a fortification after seeing the Phyrexian rift."

Malzra smiled tightly, drawing a new plan to the fore. "They are the ones to be imprisoned, not us. Look, here. This is the first building. It will be everything to us to start with—great hall and sleeping quarters and tutorial space. In time it will be my private lab." He indicated a large lodge with walls of stone rubble and a peaked roof held up by tree boles felled and lashed together. According to the schematics, the initial roof would be thatch, but in time it could be converted to shake and eventually to slate. "It will stand there, on that rocky ridge at the edge of the tent city. We start building it today."

Breakfasts were forgotten in the ink-and-parchment visions of a bold, bright future. The whole encampment gathered around to hear their assignments.

One ensign and his contingent were given guard of the camp, charged with setting up posts, building palisades, organizing a day-and-night patrol schedule, and assembling an arsenal. The guard group's duties would include the investigation and marking of temporal danger zones, as well as exploration into techniques for rescuing Teferi from his pillar of frozen time.

Another ensign and her team were sent out to thoroughly survey the ruins of the old academy, cataloguing whatever could be salvaged—block and brick, wood and steel, furnishings and artifacts. She was also charged with making recommendations for a site and structure that would be a memorial to the students and scholars who had died in the blast. Barrin volunteered to join this group, as he was keenly interested in the proper disposition of any remains the group might encounter.

A third group—called the food commission—was sent out with Jhoira. They sought glades where they could set rabbit snares, pools in which to string lines for fish, and verdant fields for planting. Malzra urged Jhoira to make the best use of mild fast-time areas, where hares and fish and crops could mature in weeks instead of months.

Another team took up picks, shovels, levels, stakes, and twine. They began clearing the location of the new lodge and excavating a foundation per Malzra's plans and elevations. Karn accompanied this group, intent on lending his strength to the earth-moving tasks.

The last group accompanied Malzra himself on a return trip to the Giant's Pate. There they initiated further study of the Phyrexian gorge and suggested strategies and devices for the extermination of their century-old foes. Malzra spoke of an ancient and minute device, a tiny crystal attuned to the Glimmer Moon and suspended like a lodestone in a drop of water. When the moon rose, the crystals were drawn upright and emitted a high-pitched tone that dismantled Phyrexian blood, breaking glistening oil to its component parts. By mass-producing these "spiders," as he called them, and introducing them into the gorge though one of the rivers that flowed into it, they could hope to slay the whole army of Phyrexians before any of them knew what had happened.

With the quiet and determined efficiency of refugee ants digging a new hill, Malzra's company marched out across the strange and hostile hillsides of Old Tolaria. The tents that had sheltered them the night before fluttered, empty and clean, in the hot, shifting air of summer. The columns of fire that had held up the black vault of night now smoldered in gray slumber. There was a sense of expectant hope in the air. Around axe-wielding arms and bent shoulders and shovel-prodding feet, there arose the airy vision of a new academy taking shape all around them.

* * * * *

As the last sharpened logs were set in place about the tent camp and the foundations of the new lodge, a cool breeze moved through the surrounding forest. The summer's labors were done. Autumn had arrived. Workers paused. They breathed deeply, straightened their tired backs, and lifted grimy, streaming faces toward the sun. Life at sea had been no idle existence for the crew of *New Tolaria*, but at least it had not held the daily back breaking task of wrestling the earth—piercing it, digging it, lifting it, hauling it, dumping it, compacting it. The grit at sea had been largely salt, which washed easily enough away and provided the skin certain natural protections against insects. This grit was good, black earth. It coated everything evenly, never completely washed away, and smudged the books and scrolls that the scholars and students studied in their off-hours. They were a brawny, tanned, industrious lot after their long months of labor, starting to look like Jhoira, like natives of the island.

The cool breeze riffled tents where students rested or studied. It fanned flames where a midday meal of fresh-water fish sizzled. It kicked up dust from wheeled litters that dragged dressed tree boles into place for the lodge's nearly complete vault. It rattled the roll of animal skins that would, when complete, become a great dirigible to lift Malzra's Phyrexian war machine. The breezes seemed all too eager to bear the dismantled machine into the air. Most of all, the refreshing wind buoyed heat-weary workers, promising of cooler days and more rain.

Barrin drank in the air as he marched up the hill that led into the palisades. Autumn would mean tall, dry grasses, ready to be scythed and sheaved and draped into a roof for the lodge. The place would be warmer and drier than the tents and more resistant to mosquitoes and snakes. The prospects of real beds and real pallets was enticing, too.

Even so, Barrin's uplifted mood came not from hopes of future comfort but from the completion of long labors. The ruins were fully scavenged. Every bit of useable stone had been hauled to the site of the new academy, many of the rougher pieces already incorporated in the mortared lower walls of the lodge. Barrin's team had also discovered the wreck of the Hall of Artifact Creatures and rescued from that shattered place many operable pieces of machinery. These Urza had used to construct five *su-chi* lifters, units designed to perform the heavy tasks of the construction projects.

The most important result of these scavenging efforts culminated today, though, and Barrin had climbed into the encampment to gather Urza, Karn, Jhoira, and any others not immediately employed to come see the result.

"It's finished," Barrin said simply, brushing dust from his hands as he stood before Urza.

The planeswalker glanced up distractedly from the plans for his war machine, nodded, and gestured to a pair of students to remove the face plate they had just attached to the metal framework. One of the young men gave him a look of consternation, to which Urza replied sternly, "We have to deepen the belly of that piece or the incendiary devices won't slide smoothly from the payload chamber. They might get jammed, they might explode within the superstructure. Now do it!"

As the students set to work, Barrin repeated, "It's finished. I'd like you to come see it."

Urza turned back toward his plans, which showed a fuselage of thinly tapped metal. The device, shaped like a horseshoe crab, hung beneath a great sack of heated gasses.

"I'm in the middle of something. Can't it wait? Schedule a formal ceremony. I'll attend."

Barrin's eyes hardened slightly. "Two hundred students and scholars died in that blast, Urza. Another twenty have worked long and hard among the ghosts of those two hundred, trying to find a way to honor them and remember them. If you won't come for my sake, come for theirs."

"While you are mucking about in the past," Urza snapped, flinging a hand out toward the half-built war machine, "I have been devising a means to save the future. Just this morning we learned why the spiders didn't work—not enough moonlight in the cleft to activate them. This is our only hope. I have to complete this machine, or your monument might stand for all of us. I'm thinking about our future."

In a gesture he rarely made, Barrin took hold of the master's arm. He felt the hot surge of power beneath the man's skin. "Come see the memorial. It is why we are working for the future."

Urza took one more exasperated look at the fuselage, where the students swore quietly over their turning wrenches. He waved them off.

"Come along, you two. Set those tools aside, and come along. We are going to look into the past."

They stared at him for one uncertain instant before his stormy brows convinced them to drop their wrenches in the dirt and rise to follow.

Urza issued a similar command to all the students and scholars he and Barrin passed on their way out of the encampment. Scores of tasks were abandoned half finished, and the folk of Tolaria flocked up behind their two masters. They had specialized in those long, hot months of summer, the guards different in dress and demeanor from the gardeners and hunters, who were different in turn from the artificers working on Urza's war machine, and so forth. In that spontaneous parade down into the time-slough of Old

Tolaria, all the scholars and students were one again, as on the day they had marched into the island. Jokes and laughter flowed out in the stern-faced master's wake, the sound of it not deadened or dragged down by the steady decrescendo of time.

Barrin wondered about this happy spirit. He and his scavengers had always adopted a solemn demeanor among the ruins, not that much ruin remained. Despite the short days in that slow-time spot—Barrin and his crew had only ten hours of sunlight during the sixteen-hour summer days—they had been diligent. The foundations of most of the buildings were still there, rectilinear crazings of stone moving through the hard-packed earth. Rainwater had gathered in the exposed basements of a number of buildings. Grasses had volunteered in many of the cleared areas. A few short walls remained intact, but most of the structures that had survived had been reverently pulled down. The cut stones were carefully sorted and stacked for use in the new buildings. Even the field-stone rubble lay in piles in the new camp. As a result, the old school now seemed almost a park land, with quiet meadows, wandering paths of stone, and placid pools. The ruins were ruins no longer. Barrin's mood, too, lifted as he felt the final leveling of the temporal descent, and the parade wound its way into the heart of the place.

A plaza had been laid, dressed stones set into an even mosaic between the two stunning sights there. On one side was Teferi, mouth still gaping and eyes still screwed tight, the eternal flames of his robes enveloping him, and the wet cloak descended only a finger's-breadth. The leaning corner of a building remained behind Teferi, helping to shield him from the intense sunlight.

As Urza and Barrin paused beside this living shrine, Jhoira emerged from the throng. She stepped up beside them and stared bleakly at her imprisoned friend.

"He is trapped, like me. Alone. Abandoned. Neither dead nor alive."

"We'll save him, Jhoira," Barrin assured. "We'll find a way.

"He can't reach us. We can't reach him." Her voice held desperate anger. "If he tries to emerge, he will die."

"Yes. We must save him before then," Barrin replied.

"Every night, I wrack my brain. I can't sleep, thinking about him. There must be a way," she insisted. A trembling hand traced across her jaw.

Barrin took her hand and led her away from the spot. "Come. I have something else to show you."

On the opposite side of the courtyard stood the memorial to the others slain in the blast. The base of the monument was the old foundation stone of the former academy. Urza had wanted the stone brought to the new school, but Barrin was adamant. He said it should mark the beginning and the end of what came before. The side of the giant block of stone bore both its original inscription—Academy Tolaria, Established 3285 AR—and a new inscription—Destroyed 3307 AR. The front of the block bore the names of the dead. On the other side was an inscription in the ancient tongue of Yotia, which meant in translation:

> The souls of a man who dies
> Standing in the teeth of fate
> Are the souls of all men,
> Gone on ahead that we may remain.

The hollow interior of the stone held all the bones unearthed by Barrin and his team, interred as they lived and died—together.

The stone was surmounted by a sculpture from the sketchbook of old Darrob—Jhoira's final companion in the months before Urza's return. Though his mind had been too fragmented to allow him to communicate well in words, Darrob was an accomplished artist. Perhaps the most common image in his drawings was a seeking figure, gaunt and wind-torn, holding out a lantern and peering toward the future with eyes like twin, hopeless pits in his skull. Barrin had taken the metal remnants of ruined artifact creatures and welded them, one to another, into a statue of that bleak, searching soul, leaning ever against a ceaseless and silent gale.

Jhoira stared sadly. Barrin stood beside her still holding her hand. Urza took in the whole sight at once. The long caravan behind spread out in a semicircle to either side. All of them—student and scholar, artificer and guard—grew silent as they studied the memorial. Soon, only the wind spoke.

Barrin stood in that awed hush and felt an emotion swell through him, something that was as much joy as it was despair, something that darkened his eyes and made his lips clamp in a tight line.

"On behalf of all of us left here after the blast, Master Malzra," Jhoira said at last, "I want to thank you for this. It is right that this is the first finished building of the new school."

"Yes," replied Urza with a decisive nod, "yes, it is right."

* * * * *

The new lodge was completed just before the wet drear of winter, and the embers in its two great fireplaces did not go out until spring was warm on the hillsides. Though better than the tents, the accommodations were still tight. The finished fuselage of Urza's flying war engine took up one corner, sitting atop the rolled animal-skin balloon that was to haul it into the sky. The nighttime floor beyond it was filled to its edges with sleeping mats and the daytime floor with tables of food being prepared and eaten. Books and plans were crammed into cobbled nooks in one corner, and artifact experiments crowded another. So cramped were these accommodations that Jhoira and her food-gatherers chose to sleep and eat on *New Tolaria*, where hammocks and bolt-head meals seemed almost luxuriant. Aboard the ship, she also had more room to pace the nights away, designing and discarding means of saving Teferi. It was a long, wet winter, and the only saving grace of it was the drive of Urza and Barrin to push forward all of the projects begun.

By the first breezes of spring, a second building was half completed—a round-walled dormitory with each room opening outward to the forest splendors of Tolaria and inward to a central courtyard. Even without doors on the rooms and shutters on the windows, many of the scholars and students opted to move into the structure and brave the first days of spring. By the middle of that season, most artifact study had migrated to the central courtyard of the dormitory, and there was room for all in the lodge.

Today the winds were right. Mild and even, they flowed from the east, past the harbored *New Tolaria* up the very path they had taken back into Tolaria. Breezes coursed over the Giant's Pate and straight out above the Phyrexian gorge.

"Ten years have passed in that gorge since our enemies first saw us, our return," said Urza, sniffing the sea breeze as it breathed through the new academy. "Surely they have not been idle in that time. They are tenfold stronger than they were on that first day and perhaps twice as numerous. Every day we wait gives them another week to prepare. It is time."

He spoke these words to Barrin, but everyone who took breakfast in the lodge that morning heard him, and they all knew what he meant.

"Today, we attack," Urza said.

Most of those breakfasts went unfinished. Students rushed to their posts, excited and terrified by what the day might bring.

Moments after this announcement, crews hoisted the balloon of animal skin and the metal fuselage from the corner and bore them up toward the crest of the Giant's Pate. Behind them went more workers with massive bellows hooked to specially designed forges meant to heat air. Ropes borrowed from the docked *New Tolaria* followed in their turn, and crates of dark orbs carried gingerly by pairs of workers.

"It is crude, I know," Urza said with chagrin as he sat across from Barrin, who was rapidly filling his mouth with too-hot forkfuls of fried loon eggs, "but until we have full laboratory capacity, I am not willing to cobble together an ornithopter. Besides, this floating behemoth can hold one hundred times the number of powder bombs as an ornithopter."

"Even four thousand bombs may not be enough to destroy them. And if any Phyrexians remain in the gorge, we will be in grave danger," Barrin pointed out, hissing between scalding sips of tea.

"They are working on something, Barrin, a way to escape," Urza replied. "They've been searching for an escape for a hundred ten years of their time. They mustn't have the metals or powerstones for anything but a few crude artifact creatures, or they would be sending them out after us. They must be developing some new mutation, some new strain of Phyrexian that can escape their time rift. If one of the four thousand bombs penetrates to their bio-labs and destroys generations of research, we will have bought ourselves another few years."

"Yes," Barrin agreed. He brushed off his hands and rose. "Yes, today is a good day for this. I'll go brief the flight team."

Urza caught the man's shoulder and shook his head. "No, let me do it. I'll be the one on board with them."

* * * * *

By midmorning, the great war machine of skin and metal was fully inflated atop the Giant's Pate. Its air-bag shone in the sunlight gold and brown, crossed in a thousand places with sewn seams. Beneath, the metal fuselage gleamed, its base spotted with dew from its early morning trek. Strong winds up from the bay tugged and teased the dirigible, and its anchor lines moaned. The ground team worked busily among these ropes as well as the three long tethers that would guide the machine out over the rift. Barrin led the team through checks of the capstans bolted into the stone. Karn was there as well, prepared to lend his titanic strength to haul on the lines.

Meanwhile, the flight team of five was receiving its final instructions from Master Malzra. One team member was assigned to each vector of the balloon's movement—an officer of altitude, another of radius, and a third of tangent. Through a system of signals, these officers would instruct the ground team to accomplish the desired movement through a combination of rope trim and wind utilization. As Malzra's most accomplished artificer, Jhoira was made officer of altitude, in charge of the elaborate onboard forge bellows that provided the machine its lift. The final two fliers, a scholar and her protégé, were the school's best cartographers. They would lie prone in belly-holds on opposite ends of the device and would each make maps of what they saw. Their work would prove invaluable in determining what sites to bomb, what resources the Phyrexians likely had, and what strategy to use in future strikes against the stronghold. Malzra, the final member of the team, was captain. Receiving information from the mappers, he would send instructions to the flight officers to position the machine and, at the precise moment, release salvos of incendiary devices.

"The sixth bay is full, Master Malzra," reported a dark-haired, young woman, breaking in to Master Malzra's briefing. "Five hundred powder bombs. Two more bays, and the full complement of four thousand will be loaded."

"Good," Malzra responded. His eyes seemed especially dark this morning in the gleaming sunlight. With a nod, he dismissed the woman and turned back to his anxious team. "Jhoira, remember, at all times we must remain at least a thousand feet above the top of the gorge—at the same height as the Giant's Pate. Even there some Phyrexian projectiles might be able to reach us. Fifteen hundred feet will be safer. The bomb bays and mapper bays are shielded, but projectile penetration is possible and could cause a chain of explosions that would destroy the machine."

The crew had known all these facts before, but their repetition in the shadow of the leaning, leaping device widened eyes and brought uncomfortable gulps.

"If a projectile pierces the air sac, we will release all bombs and ballast and signal to be brought back. Escape will be impossible until we reach the Giant's Pate. Any who fall atop the time rift will die immediately. The scarp below the Giant's Pate is too sheer and littered with fallen trees to allow any safe landing," Malzra said. He studied the grave young faces arrayed around him. "I hope you have said your good-byes, should we not return. If not, I have brought a messenger." He indicated a fleet-footed girl, who obligingly tapped a shoulder satchel with quills and parchment. "Avail yourselves in the next moments. We must be aboard once the final bomb bays are full."

Four of the five crew members turned quickly to the girl, selecting quills and nibs and beginning to scrawl what might be their last words.

Only Jhoira stood, resolute and ready. "Karn is here, and we have already spoken," she said by way of explanation to Malzra. "The only other person I would send a note to is Teferi. Of course, any note to him would burn up before he could read it."

Malzra's eyes narrowed in assessment of the young woman. "You must concentrate on the task at hand, Jhoira."

"Teferi never leaves my mind," she replied. "If I could trade places with him, I would. We needn't both be forever alone. He saved me once, you know."

"I did not. But if you cannot maintain focus, I shall have to find a different officer of altitude—"

She dropped her gaze. "I'll fight all the harder, thinking of him."

"Good," he replied. "Let's take our positions."

Malzra laid a hand lightly on her shoulder, directing her with him toward the waiting craft. His touch felt almost searing.

Jhoira walked beside him.

Shiny and glowing in the morning, the craft loomed up before them. It bucked slightly under the restless winds.

Reaching the machine, Malzra drew back a rope slung across the doorway. He gestured inward and gave a gentle bow.

Jhoira preceded him into the vessel. She crouched as she scuttled down the tight passage. Her feet made small pings on the plate armor below. The bomb bays crowded either side of the passage. Ahead, the tangent-officer's crawlways cut across the main corridor. The radius-officer would remain in a seat on one side of the craft, monitoring the lengths of rope anchoring them to the Giant's Pate. Jhoira's post was in the exact center of the vessel at the juncture between the fuselage and the balloon. She had sight lines in every direction and had memorized the height of the various landmarks. She also had an open shaft downward for a visual check of the ground position. A harness of hemp held her suspended in this empty column of air. The rig was designed to pivot in a complete circle but otherwise provide a stable base. To one side of it was the forge bellows that Jhoira would stoke and tend to keep the machine aloft. To the other side were a set of instruments—anemometers, barometers, compasses, spyglasses . . . Jhoira climbed into the seat and strapped herself in.

Malzra, in a similar rig in the belly of the craft, ordered through the speaking tube, "Stoke the forge for liftoff."

"Aye." Jhoira complied, feeling small shudders in the fuselage as the other team members clambered into their positions.

She faintly heard instructions spoken into tubes that went elsewhere. Beyond the superstructure, anchor lines were one by one drawn loose, and the ground crew took up the three lines that snaked around the capstans.

"Cast off," came the order in all the speaking tubes.

The craft lurched up from the rock. The nervous chitter of metal against stone was gone and the rattling resistance with it. Jhoira pumped the bellows before her, fueling the fire in the black box. A hiss of red air roared up from the forge. The vessel rose farther, heeling away from the stone. Beyond snapping lines and stretched skins, the bright brow of the hill retreated. The folk clustered thickly atop it, toiling at the capstans, were diminished. Soon their faces were only knots of exertion. Then there were no features at all, only bent backs and sinewy arms like extensions of the stout ropes themselves. A shadow-painted face of stone slid by below, descending suddenly into vast distance. An immense bowl of land opened up. The Giant's Pate became only a ground-down prominence on one edge of the basin. Lines that had once seemed massive now looked all too thin, stretched across the plummeting spaces.

"Take us up three hundred feet to thirteen hundred," Malzra's voice came. "Let's come in from above, give us time to survey the pit and choose our targets.

"Aye," Jhoira responded.

She slid back the door to the coal chute, allowing a few more shards into the firebox. A lever spread the black stones across the embers. She pumped repeatedly on the bellows. Hot air jetted into the vast air sac above, and more tepid air spilled from the lips of the balloon. Impatient, the machine rose higher, its lines tugging it in an arc back toward the Giant's Pate.

Malzra issued course adjustments, signaled to ground crews by the tangent and radius officers. The tethers slackened, and the machine swooped out on new winds over the black wound of the Phyrexian pit.

"We're getting clear visuals," the map scholar said into her speaking tube. "A main fortification at the center of the cleft, perhaps a hundred yards square, with many turrets and towers, elevated battlements, and scores of heavy ballistae, each targeted on the rim of the gorge."

"Thirty-three ballistae, by my count," the student broke in.

Jhoira peered down the shaft. She could make out the black form of the main structure and the bristling array of spear throwers atop the towers and rooftops. Even as she watched, the long shafts foreshortened.

"They are redirecting them at us," she noted urgently.

"Maintain altitude," Malzra ordered. "Remember, they have ten seconds to our every one. They can respond, regroup, and regear quickly."

"The main fortress seems to be perched on a rock prominence in the center of a deep lake. I cannot make out the contours of the bottom," the chief cartographer reported. "I'm surprised by all that water. Fast-time rifts tend to have little water. It looks as though numerous streams empty into the gorge."

"Any sign of structures that might be laboratories?" Urza asked. "I'm looking specifically for spawning facilities."

"There seem to be fish hatcheries in various places in the lake," replied the mapper. "I can make out figures moving among the sluices and nets. As to laboratory structures, I could not begin to guess."

The assistant cartographer said, "There are various caves and what might be mines in the walls of the gorge—"

He broke off as the tip-tilted ballistae flickered in sudden, violent motion. Before any of the crew could blink, a flight of thirty-three massive shafts leapt into being twelve hundred feet below. They raced up with preternatural speed, going from being wickedly barbed jags to being large as lightning. They rose to within a hundred feet of the ship's belly before slowing and curving off. The ballistae bolts lingered a moment on the winds and then tumbled. Their heavy heads drew them quickly back downward, and they sank toward the temporal envelop where the Phyrexians were trapped. Striking the verge of the fast-time gorge, the bolts accelerated to blinding speed.

The crack of those thirty-three shafts smashing through rooftops was like manifold thunder. A cheer went up from the flight and the ground crews.

"Excellent," Malzra said. "Maintain tangent, radius, and altitude. Stay directly above them. They'll think twice before sending another salvo. I am dropping the payload of bomb bay five."

There came a great ratcheting sound as the doors of the bay swung slowly downward. Out tumbled the powder bombs. Just such devices had been employed with devastating effect at Korlis three millennia before, though they had been dropped in tens on marching troops instead of in hundreds on a stationary fortification. Now the black objects, which seemed merely tumbling stones, rolled slowly in their swarm, gathered speed, and pelted down into the fast-time rift. They struck the envelop *en masse*, making a distant, ominous patter. Accelerating to the speed of the rift, they struck.

Light leapt from the cleft. Orange flares in their hundreds illuminated the previously veiled depths. Jagged roof lines and battlements shone in sudden relief. The cartographers scribbled frantically. Then smoke obscured everything in a deeper shroud, and blackness settled again.

The sound of the attack lagged a moment behind this brief, pure flash, but when it came, the roar was amplified by the basalt fort, the glassy water beneath it, and the rocky cliff faces all around. It seemed a great beast had awakened, furious, from sleep. The noise filled the air for some moments, and then all was silent. Smoke— gray and white and black in curdled rills—bled from the gap.

"That got their attention," Jhoira shouted, giving a whoop.

"Cartographers," came Malzra's call, "target acquisition?"

"Too much smoke," replied the scholar. "Give it a few minutes to clear."

"That will give them a few hours to regroup," Malzra responded. "Altitude, radius, tangent—has our position held?"

"We've gained height," Jhoira said, "after the bombs went. We're up to about seventeen hundred feet."

"Bring us down to twelve," Urza commanded, "and anticipate the next payload drop."

"Radius is steady."

"Tangent is steady."

"Down to about twelve hundred feet."

"Payload six away."

* * * * *

The first wave of attacks slew over a hundred and fifty of K'rrik's minions, toppled three towers, blasted away the roof of the upper throne room and, worst of all, sent blazing death into the spawning lab. Vials of brain and placenta burst and oozed, recombination matrices ended in tatters on the floor, vats of glistening oil ignited in enormous jets, mutant stock burned to cinders, and the decanted, half-mature killers that K'rrik had been breeding to survive the time rift were roasted alive. The destruction was almost total. Almost.

Out of chaos came order. The fires from the initial onslaught were already extinguished, the dead and dying thrown to the fishes, and the ballistae recalibrated for greater distance. K'rrik ordered all able-bodied beasts to salvage whatever specimens, equipment, and plans had survived from his breeding laboratories. The remains were taken below the castle, into the caves. Urza's crude bombs might have blasted holes in roofs and walls, but they would not crack the basalt extrusion on which the castle sat and would not completely wipe out a century of research. All hope of escape and victory rested in that ragged refuse, in the half full jars of cracked glass with their skittish placental inhabitants. Some of the creatures would survive, and K'rrik's clawed and tentacular horrors carried them as tenderly as human mothers with their babies.

All of this had happened in the hour after the first attack. As the smoke cleared enough to make out the dim line of the airship above, guards spotted more of the bombs resting in the air below it. They looked like pepper on a white piece of paper. It was an easy thing to predict where they would strike and evacuate the areas.

K'rrik stood, furious and humiliated, among his folk. Sizzling chunks of fire struck the roof of one guard tower and the adjacent section of wall. The resultant chorus of flares and pops shook the rest of the fortress and echoed through the chasm. Hunks of stone pelted outward and hailed across the Phyrexian host, who flinched away. The tower came to pieces, pulverized by the attack. The weakened wall crumbled away, crushing an armory lower down. Fires flared up wherever there was wood or cloth or skin to burn, and the armory ignited. A cloud of flame and soot shot up in a vast column, its top rolling and boiling.

K'rrik watched. The filed teeth in his enhanced jaw ground into their opposite gums, cutting bloody rents in the flesh.

"What are you going to do?" barked a creature next to him. It seemed more a giant flea than a man, its head three times the size of K'rrik's and its pale, naked body humpbacked and twisted. "You can't let this go on!"

"Yes," K'rrik responded grimly. Pus-colored blood was suddenly jetting from the creature's severed back as K'rrik withdrew his sword. The monster tumbled from the wall where they stood, its body bouncing twice along the buttresses before striking the black foundations of the fortress and bursting in a white mass. "Yes, I cannot let you question my authority."

K'rrik turned to another Phyrexian, this one more manlike, though he had the infernal head of a haggard goat. The commander ordered, "Tell two ballistae crews to fire three rounds every half hour, half-cocked rounds that will fall short. Have crews ready in the water to retrieve the shafts. Cover the rest of the ballistae with dead bodies. I want Urza to think he has destroyed most of our ballistae, and nearly disabled those that are left. I want to draw him downward. Once they are in range, fling the dead from the ballistae and fire all simultaneously. Aim for the flying machine's bomb bays."

Nodding his understanding, the goat-faced man headed off on his mission.

K'rrik snarled at the minions around him, "As for the rest of you, put out those fires. And keep watching for more onslaughts. Anyone injured will be killed. Anyone killed will be defiled. It is your duty to fight and to live."

* * * * *

The third, fourth, and fifth drops went as well as the first. Bombs hailed down. Fire and smoke came up. The sound of tumbling towers and shrieking beasts rose to meet them. On the second drop, Jhoira had learned the trick of spilling heat from the air sac at the moment the bombs were released, thereby preventing the machine from lurching upward. This technique allowed for quicker follow-up attacks, greater accuracy, and less time spent reeling.

Until the sixth drop. The gorge below was a gray scar, so full of smoke that no fortification was evident within. Still, the cartographers had picked out landmarks on the edges of the cliff and could, from memory alone, pinpoint important sites to strike. They were above just such a site now—what had looked like a throne room or great hall—and Malzra issued the now familiar warning.

"I am opening bay two."

Jhoira paused a breath and then bled the air from the forge. She knew immediately that something was wrong. There came no grating ratchet. There was no sound of tumbling bombs. There was only the sudden loss of height as hot air spilled from the sac.

"The mechanism is jammed," came a shout over the speaking tube.

Jhoira ground her teeth as she struggled to shut off the bleed and pump the bellows. The dirigible sagged on its lines, dipping below the crest of the Giant's Pate. The deflated sac rattled in a sudden downdraft. Jhoira heaved at the bellows, and jets of red air roared into the sac. It began to reinflate.

Loud shouts of metal came below, ballistae shots hammering into the fuselage. The speaking tubes were flooded with screams. Then came another wave of ballistae shots only a breath after the first. They penetrated. Spearheads struck powder bombs. With a dull roar, they ignited. The explosion spread. Bomb bay two blasted away. The metal fuselage fragmented. The machine mounted up on a wave of fire. What remained of the fuselage rammed up beneath the air sac.

Jhoira was suddenly inside the balloon, the air around her baking her skin and burning in her lungs. She was aware of a great emptiness beneath her. Half of the fuselage was gone. The rest was shoved in a tangle of lines inside the skin sac. The other crew members were dead—the officers of tangent and radius, the cartographers, even Master Malzra. She was about to die too.

"I'm sorry, Teferi," was all she could think to say.

The ragged metal fuselage dropped from the air bag and slued sideways. It tugged the deflated dirigible down behind it. The whole mass plummeted toward the Phyrexian gorge below.

Coals from the tilted forge sprayed out around Jhoira. Cursing, she clawed her way from the harness and climbed into the tangle of ropes. She clambered over them, seeing through their webwork as the vast gray gorge rushed up to swallow her. One of the ropes was fatter than the others and tighter. She grabbed it and felt the insistent tug of life on the other end.

"Karn is up there," she gasped to herself. Karn and the rest of the ground crew.

She fought her way out of the flapping folds of skin and the taut net of ropes and clambered up that one fat line, the one that pulsed with life. Hand over hand, she dragged herself up the rope, toward the Giant's Pate and away from the Phyrexian fortress.

There was too much rope, too little air, too much rock.

The world roared up with crushing weight. She climbed.

The ruined dirigible was about hundred feet behind her now. It struck the fast-time envelope. Waves of time-distortion roiled out around it. The war machine plummeted in a sudden preternatural rush. The rope snapped taut. It flung Jhoira free. The capstan ripped from its mooring and surged through the air. There came a white-hot explosion within the rent. The sky and ground fused into a single sheet.

"I'm sorry, Teferi." Jhoira struck earth, and all went black.

Monologue

We do not make machines, I now realize. We make only fire and death.

The blast surprised all of us, even Urza. He survived through a great concentration of will, holding his corporeal form together, but unlike the explosion that tore apart Tolaria, or that which tore apart Argoth, Urza had not anticipated this one. He was struggling to keep his body solid even as his crew members were no more than red particles on the wind.

And there is no time machine for bringing them back.

The blast surprised all of us. I summoned a wall of air, trying to catch the falling craft, but only slowed its descent. In the midst of the fumbling hopelessness of it all, I saw Jhoira ambling spiderlike up the main line toward safety. That was the greatest surprise of all, though it shouldn't have been. Jhoira's force of will equals that of Urza.

—**Barrin, Mage Master of Tolaria**

Chapter 10

They sat at Jhoira's bedside in the makeshift infirmary. No pallet, no cot—here she had an actual bed—Barrin's, volunteered by him for the purpose. The infirmary was soon to be a kitchen attached to one end of the great hall, but now, amid newly mortared fireplaces and stacks of iron-worked spits and grills and pots, she lay in coma. She was the only one injured in the wreck of the dirigible. All the others were killed.

Except Urza. He and Barrin sat on cook stools just next to the bed, and they spoke in low tones.

"She's become another Teferi," Barrin said sadly. "Three months, and still no response. Lying there, an arm's length away but unreachable."

Urza watched the still woman, his eyes glimmering darkly. "Physically, she is well. You saw me lay hands on her. You saw the wounds close and the breath begin again. She was whole the moment I laid hands on her. I can't understand why she does not awaken."

"Her wounds are deeper than you can reach, my friend," Barrin replied.

He fondly brushed her hair back from her forehead. Her face was losing its olive patina after all this time beneath roofs and blankets. Her hair was darkening from the roots outward. It was as though the years were being one by one revoked from her, and she was becoming again a mere child.

"She survived Old Tolaria, through ten years of abandonment, isolation, and want. Then we came back, and we all thought she would return to us. But she didn't. Karn was her only friend. She was withdrawn and haunted. Every time she saw Teferi—spoke of him, thought of him—the horror of those ten years came welling back. She felt trapped, like him. An arm's length away from us but always alone."

"She could stay in this coma forever," Urza said.

"No. She is fighting. Either she will win or lose. It will not be forever, but it may be a long time. Last time, she fought for a whole decade."

Urza lifted his eyes, seeming to see straight through the wall and even through an oblique curve of the world to some dazzling place that lay beyond it all.

"Serra's Realm had once restored my health. I would take her there at once if Serra remained, if the place weren't shrinking, if I hadn't led Phyrexia to it. . . ." A cloud passed over his features and they grew iron-hard. "We have to keep up the fight. Everywhere I have gone, those monsters have followed. Everyone I have befriended has been wounded or killed by them. I would destroy myself if I knew it would stop them, but they will never quit. I must fight them as long as I live."

"And what if you die before they are defeated?" Barrin asked soberly. "Who will fight them then?"

All light fled Urza's face, and it was as black as a mask. "Yes, who then?"

* * * * *

Karn heaved the massive keystone into position atop the archway. The stone grated against its neighbors. Sand sifted down from its settling bulk. Silver hands lingered in uncertainty on the huge block.

"Does it look straight?"

Behind him, Barrin looked up from Malzra's field table and squinted along a sight line. The keystone gleamed like a jewel in the morning sun, its polished edges reflecting the Tower of Artifice and the Tower of Mana in the background.

"Yes, Karn. It looks straight."

The silver golem nodded and then asked, "Will it stay put?"

This time, Barrin was too busy with his sketches to look up. "Of course it will stay put."

He sighed. The stack of floor plans and elevations before him were the latest creations of Urza for his new academy. Already, after five years of intensive, year-round building, the school was nearly as extensive as it had been in its previous manifestation: dormitories, lecture halls, laboratories, great halls, guard towers, curtain walls, gates, gardens, and now a new infirmary. Not that many of the academy's hundred and ninety students were ill or injured. Most were too young to have any serious health problems aside from homesickness. Whatever injuries or illnesses occurred were treated with placebo pills, gauze, and Urza's healing touch. No, this grand new two-story infirmary was not so much a necessity as it was a monument to the school's perpetual patient.

Jhoira had not awakened. She had indeed become another Teferi. For his part, the young man was now wrapped in the wet cloak and beginning a tumble that would take him another handful of years to complete. Jhoira had meanwhile grown pale, her hair dark brown again. She did not awaken. Barrin had discovered that water from slow-time rifts helped to sustain her health, and Urza provided his healing touch daily. Nothing improved. Urza had devised a machine that liquefied whatever food was offered in the great halls and pumped it into her stomach. Karn, meanwhile, had developed the habit of picking wildflowers for her from the hillsides of Angelwood and bringing them to her bed. He too often stood vigil there, choosing to spend his nights in her company instead of deactivated.

Her plight weighed heavily on Barrin and Karn as they worked on the new building. Both moved sadly and slowly, as though building a mortuary rather than an infirmary. There was anger in them too, frustration at their inability to save her.

Karn trudged up beside the desk and stood, gleaming in the bright, hot sun.

Barrin shielded his eyes from the glare and said irritably, "Can't you let yourself tarnish a little?"

"Master Malzra forbids it," Karn replied truthfully. Then, with a tone of sarcasm he had been slowly developing over the last fifteen years, he said, "It would bother you less if you wore a sack over your head."

Barrin cast a reproachful look at the golem. "I think maybe it's time to design a new helper—one with a thicker skin, if that is possible."

"If you're after compatibility, try a helper with a thicker skull."

"Thicker than Arty Shovelhead's?"

"Teferi was a better companion than you—"

"An old shoe is a better companion than you—"

A sudden buzz tore through the air between the two. They shied instinctively back, gaping at empty space. Something darted, the size and speed of a falcon, above the treetops. It circled and dived down toward them again. It glinted metallic.

Barrin swore, stepped to the desk, and hauled a sword from it. As the thing swooped by again, he swung the blade. It cracked against the silvery shoulder of the device, but the metal bird soared again, ripping leaves from their boughs as it shot through the forest. The rattle of its passage faded briefly and then returned with a swift crescendo. Growling, Barrin hefted his blade again and watched the mechanism shriek inward.

Karn stepped into the path of the attacker. He reared back, balled a fist, and hurled the massive thing at the flying target. It crashed amid a jangle of slivered struts and sprung coils. The artifact creature fell back in the dirt. Its metallic wings glinted, shuddering to either side. Spikes thrust outward all across it. An assortment of round, rending blades emerged, whirling violently.

Astonished, Barrin and Karn gazed at the broken mass as it whined furiously. They were so amazed by the display that neither noticed Master Malzra approach from behind. The artificer watched with amused interest. It was only when the mechanism had nearly spent itself and shimmied into stillness that the master spoke.

"It was only a prototype. The final falcons will stoop at hundreds of miles an hour on the gorge—arriving even before the sound they make. They will smell Phyrexian glistening-oil blood, home in on it, penetrate the beast's hide, and begin a shredding procedure."

Panting heavily, Barrin turned toward the man. "How many of them will you build?"

As many as I can, given our supply of Thran powerstones. If I could only design and build my own stones, I could fill the skies with these creatures, could perhaps protect the whole world. With the stones we have—and the ones I hope to uncover at three Thran sites I have found—I can make perhaps a thousand."

"Three Thran sights?" Barrin asked, eyebrow canted. "You are planning on sending students to dig?"

"Yes," Malzra replied. "They'll be taken aboard *New Tolaria*, and the ship will return with a new load of students, whom I've chosen from the best and brightest the world has to offer. I have the itinerary right here. And since I, myself, need to remain for research—"

"Yes, yes," Barrin replied irritably. "How many years will I be away this time?"

* * * * *

"Teferi is covered in your robe, now," Karn said gently. He sat by Jhoira's bedside in the completed infirmary. "He's not being burned anymore. You've saved him." He didn't add that the boy would likely rise, now, and make his way toward the outer world and be killed in the curtain of time.

Jhoira was too fragile to bear that sort of news. She looked pale and small in the bed. Her arms and legs were weak from years of stillness, her eyes were lost beneath lids forever closed, her mouth was red where the tube of Malzra's feeding machine descended.

"The new students are arriving today," Karn said, changing the subject. "Barrin has been out collecting them the last three years."

Karn glanced up at the rafters of the building. The academy was at last complete. Malzra had ceased his new building designs. He now poured all his energy in the arsenal he was creating to eradicate the Phyrexians in the gorge. He spoke of the battle as a "dress rehearsal for global conflagration." It was his new mania. The minds of all the scholars and students were trained on the task. One team had developed a battery of long-range ballistae, which were stationed in a ring around the site and were employed in a day-and-night peppering of the fortress. Another crew had devised a set of catapults, which delivered powder bombs as quickly as they could be concocted. Rivers had been dammed and diverted away from the gorge to empty the Phyrexian fish hatcheries and starve them. Meanwhile, every student spent hours every day assembling the delicate and complex clockwork falcons Malzra had designed. He would do just about anything to slay Phyrexians.

On the other hand, in these ten years, what had he done to save Teferi or Jhoira?

Reaching in delicately, Karn grasped the tube that ran from Malzra's feeding contraption into Jhoira's stomach. Bracing himself, the silver man hauled slowly on it, withdrawing the hose. It emerged with a jolting, sucking motion.

Karn set the tube aside and said gently, "Come with me." He lifted her limp form in his arms and, with reverent step, carried her out the door.

It was a long walk past the towering buildings of the new academy and through the western gate. No one stopped him, though everyone stared. Karn was well known among the students and scholars, the ever-present builder and guardian. Jhoira was known too, the never-present ghost of the former island. In all accounts, they were dear friends, and half of those who glimpsed the pair believed she had died at last, and he was taking her to be buried.

The other half assumed Karn was acting at the bidding of the inscrutable master.

Karn carried her away for his own purposes, and hers. Bypassing the killing time pits and pinnacles, the silver man bore Jhoira through the thick forests of Tolaria, across tan shoulders of sandstone, and to the secret niche she had kept on the western edge of the island. Her things were still there as she had left them ten years ago, as she had left all of Tolaria ten years ago.

"It is time for you to come back," Karn said heavily.

He brought her to the sunny ledge of sandstone where she had loved to stand and gaze out to sea. He climbed onto the stone and sat down. Jhoira was small and cold, cradled in his lap. Salty air rose warmly around them, lifting and gently tossing Jhoira's hair. The laboring waves below worried stones to pebbles and pebbles to sand. The sky was endless in blue. Mountain ranges of cloud slid in slow panorama through it. On the horizon of the vast ocean, a tiny white sail shone—the returning *New Tolaria*.

"You always said you would be here, on this stone, when you would first see your soul mate arrive." He glanced down at her unmoving form, and desperate sadness welled in his voice. "Wake up, Jhoira. You have slept too long."

Only her hair moved, lifted by the caressing breeze.

"You have to come back, Jhoira. Despite his best intentions, Master Malzra has turned the school into a fortification, the students into a young army. He's bringing more students, to do the same with them." Karn gazed desolately at the pounding waves. "You wouldn't have allowed that. You were the soul of this place. Remember how I was before Master Malzra gave me that dark crystal—what he called an intellectual and affective cortex? Remember what I was like before I had a soul? That's what the island is like without you."

Still, there was only the slow shift of breath in her, the arms and leg in languid repose.

"Look out on that huge dark sea. You see that scrap of white. It is Tolaria's hope, returning. I know you have been faraway. I know your soul feels tiny, lost amid rolling breakers and heaving gales, but it is our best hope. Return."

There came a fluttering at her eyelids. Karn held still, not daring to believe. Jhoira's breath deepened, and she seemed to settle against him. Her eyes again were closed.

"If you don't wake now, you may miss your soul mate."

"I've . . . dreamed—" a voice came, as thready and elusive as the wind, "—I've . . . quested. . . . I know how to break through. . . ."

"What?" Karn blurted stupidly. He peered at her, but she was unconscious again, her figure as limp as the wet cloak she had thrown over Teferi.

Karn stood up, the woman in his arms. He felt as though he had a heart in his chest, for all the thrumming ache of it. Was she awakening, or was it only the wishful thinking of a silver man given to fantasy? Feeling as though his burden had doubled, he staggered back toward the distant academy. Which healer would know how to waken her again? What if she never woke again? How had he lived these ten years without her?

* * * * *

K'rrik stood in the midst of his deep mutant lab, sunk in the lightless bedrock beneath his castle. For twenty years, the spot had been exposed, no longer shielded by water—ever since Urza Planeswalker had diverted rivers from the gorge to kill off the fish they ate. K'rrik had dammed the far end of the gorge, thereby making a shallow, stagnant lake, where at least scavenger fish could be bred from the waste poured into the pool. For forty years, powder bombs and ballistae bolts had rained down on their heads. Urza must have been clearing the island's forests as fast as he had cleared Argoth's. None of it, not brimstone hail, lightning shafts, flood nor famine, had reached this deep cavern and its precious contents.

In great vats of obsidian, melted and cast for this very purpose, K'rrik's latest generation of negators was gestating, maturing. Vast, pulpy heads, hideously distorted bodies, arms as sharp and thin as swords, legs that could lope at the speed of jackals, clawed feet that could crush a man's skull as if it were merely a melon. In two years, this sixth batch of modified negators would be ready to emerge from their vats, full-formed, ready to scale the walls of the gorge and struggle through the vast rending curtain of time that surrounded them. Perhaps they would die, like the five previous harvests. Perhaps they would win through, too weak to hunt down the man at the heart of K'rrik's torment.

The man? The god!

Whatever happened, K'rrik had already harvested their flesh, sampled it, improved on it. The seventh batch would be stronger yet and ready in another decade. In no more than twenty years of Urza's time, his beautiful garden academy would be overrun with Phyrexians, bred to walk uninjured through the worst time storm, and—this was the best part—bred to be utterly faithful to their master, K'rrik. To them, he was more than an ancient sleeper, more than an indomitable and unkillable warlord. To them, he was a god—

He was Yawgmoth incarnate.

* * * * *

It had been six months since Jhoira had first reawakened in the silver arms of her old friend. The healers and Malzra himself had been incapable of reviving her, despite their intense and sometimes rigorous interventions.

Karn's touch had worked the magic their hands could not, bringing her around again a week after the first occasion. The moment of lucidity had been brief and feverish, but Jhoira again said she had been on a vision quest and had seen a way to "break through." To this cryptic revelation, she added that she knew how to save herself—and Teferi—then she lapsed back into unconsciousness.

Since that time, Karn had refused to aid in any more war efforts. He spent his time sitting at her side, gently speaking to her through the long hours of night, telling her anything he could think of, even reading stories of Shiv from the academy's library. It was just as in the old days, the two of them making a home for each other, withdrawing from the ignorant outside world that recognized and welcomed neither of them. Jhoira responded. Soon she had awakened every hour or so and remained awake for minutes at a time. Karn forced broth and bread into her on these occasions, refusing to allow Malzra's tube to be in her throat anymore. In another month, she had been able to sit up, and her arms and legs had grown stronger.

At that point, she had called for paper and writing implements and tools. She sketched out a complex machine that even Malzra could not quite visualize—long tubes and pump chambers, with large gears bearing huge sails of gauze windmilling up from wide troughs, a massive turbine driven by teams of workers. . . . When Barrin and other scholars expressed their reservations about the large, costly design, none of them spoke of dream delirium, but the thought lingered in their words.

Karn gathered a passel of young, bright students from the new batch that had arrived on the island. He brought them to the infirmary and equipped them with whatever tools and resources Jhoira directed. They worked tirelessly, these children, forever guided by Jhoira and her vision.

Three months later, their creation was wheeled to the center of the slow-time slough where the Teferi monument stood. The creator was also wheeled to the spot, on a cart Jhoira had had modified for the purpose. The whole of the academy gathered as the woman's young protégés rolled long, flexible tubes out of the slow-time area, over the hills, to a nearby rift of extreme fast time. While they worked, discreet murmurs of dubiety circulated among the crowd.

Jhoira rolled herself up beside the hulking machine she had first glimpsed in her coma. She rapped on the side of a metal reservoir. The thunderous sound drew the attention of the group.

As they quieted, she began to speak, "The principle is simple. Water resists time change. We have witnessed this. We survivors of the first academy used the properties of slow-time water to stop aging. So, too, fast-time water is reluctant to give up its pulse. This machine draws fast-time water from a nearby rift that contains an underground spring. The pumps here fill the reservoirs with water. These sets of cranks then power the wind turbine and the gauze sails. The windmill blades dip into the reservoir, drawing water into the gauze. Wind from the turbine blows through the gauze and produces a thick fog of fast-time water. The saturated fast-time cloud will create a safe corridor of passage into the time pit where Teferi is, and safe passage back out again."

Silent doubt gave way to silent admiration.

"Have any organic creatures successfully passed into and out of this fast-time cloud?" Barrin asked sensibly.

Jhoira's countenance sagged. "This machine is the result not of artifice alone but of vision—Ghitu vision. We have not tested the device on living creatures, no."

"I will enter it," Karn said, his voice like the quiet rumble of gravel in a breaking wave. "I was made to withstand temporal distortions that would kill any living thing, and I believe in Ghitu vision."

Barrin, looking chagrined, continued his objections. "Yes, Karn, but just because you might be able to walk safely into the pocket that holds Teferi does not mean he could walk safely out again."

It was Karn's turn to stare downward in defeat.

"I will go with him," came another basso voice, and all attention turned to the bright-eyed and bearded speaker.

"Master Malzra?" Barrin protested. "It's out of the question. We need further tests, animal tests, before any of us steps into the cloud—"

"I believe in this machine," Malzra responded simply. "It is a fine design. It is the first glimmering that any of us have had about crossing severe rifts. I believe in this machine, and—" he paused to send a mocking wink in Barrin's direction "—since I am the reason Teferi is caught there anyway, I owe it to the lad to help get him out." He gestured toward Jhoira's protégés, clustered in an anxious knot beside the pump mechanism. "Fill the reservoir."

Brightening, Jhoira nodded toward the students, who began

plying the pumps with all their might. The tubes hissed and gurgled for a time before the first brown splashes of water entered the reservoir. The liquid spattered the base of the trough and immediately evaporated, leaving a residue of dry dust.

Jhoira was distressed to see this, but Malzra crossed to her and patted her shoulder. "It just shows that the water retains its fast-time properties. Be patient. The pumps will do their work. It is a very good design."

Water flooded up from the pump tubes and rushed out along the base of the trough. It shimmered and splashed with preternatural speed, rectangular waves coursing over its rising surface. The students continued their work at the cranks. The water level rose. It seemed to be teaming with fish, so energetic was its surface. It reached the halfway point along the wall of the reservoir and crept upward. The crowd around the tank watched in anticipation.

Malzra stood beside Karn as the gauze-covered blades began to windmill through the trough. After a complete revolution of the blades, workers manning the turbine began cranking. A hot, unnatural wind jetted from one end of the device, striking wet gauze and sending a thin spray outward. Wind bore the vapor along, spotting flagstones between the machine and the alcove where Teferi huddled beneath his soaked robe. The spray entered the slow-time pit and crept slowly over him. Those gathered near the shrine strained forward to make out any movement across the crouched figure—the shift of wet fabric, the quickening of drip lines. As the crank teams set up a powerful rhythm, the mist thickened into a white wall of fog, opaque and dazzling in the sunlight.

Jhoira nodded to Malzra.

He studied the roiling wall of fog before him. It churned in a dizzy dance, the suspended particles of water as vital as they had been in the trough.

"Well, Karn, it seems creature and creator will step together into this time machine."

The silver man stared at the turgid mist. "I can precede you and provide report."

Malzra flung away the suggestion with a simple shake of his head. "We go, side by side." With that, the two strode to the rolling edge of the fog and stepped inside.

The mist enveloped Karn with sudden force. It felt like the rush of sea water when he had fallen into it from his time-travel cone. He could sense the wet flagstones beneath his feet, but the fog tore over him like a gale. Bracing himself against the rolling blast, Karn reached a hand outward to make certain Malzra was beside him. Through the impenetrable white air, as thick as paint, it was impossible to see the man. The buffeting wind coursed around something solid. Karn's hand swayed outward and struck another hand, reaching. Malzra took hold of the silver man's fingers and clung tightly.

The winds slackened. The violent forces tearing along Karn's armor plating diminished to a washing flood, and then a gentle caress.

Malzra's voice sounded pinched, as though he were caught in a great vise. "The time differential . . . is leveling . . . off."

Karn responded easily, "You are having trouble breathing."

"I don't need . . . to breathe," came the reply. Again the winds softened. "We should walk. We are nearly . . . time adjusted now. Hours will pass on the outside for every few minutes we spend . . . in here."

Shoulder to shoulder, they pressed forward, in line with the sifting fog. Though time in the fog was compacted, space remained constant. In only five steps, white mist turned to gray, and they could sense the looming corner behind the Teferi shrine. The boy himself lay in a barely distinguishable huddle on the ground. Karn was thankful he hadn't stepped on him. It might not have mattered. Teferi didn't appear to move beneath that wet cloak.

Except that he was panting. . . .

"Teferi," Malzra said, the old roundness returned to his voice, "rise. We have come to take you out of here."

A small shiver moved through the cloak, and a young, breathless voice emerged, "Who are you? Angels?"

Malzra laughed, but it was Karn who replied, "It's me, Teferi. It's Arty Shovelhead. I'm here with Master Malzra."

The boy tugged the cloak back from his head and stared into the thick darkness. He could not have seen more than a pair of towering figures wrapped in dense fog.

"What is happening? There was a big lightning bolt out of the clear air, and thunder so loud I couldn't hear it, and then everything was flying and burning, even me. Once I could get my feet under me, I ran. Everything was blinding and boiling hot, and then all of a sudden comes this darkness and you two."

"We've come to take you out of here," Malzra repeated.

The gray cloud around them suddenly dimmed and grew black. Night had fallen in the world outside. Only the Glimmer Moon, streaking bright beyond the fog, lit the niche.

Feeling a new urgency, Karn reached down, drew off the cloak, and lifted Teferi by his hand. "Come along. Hurry now. Jhoira is waiting."

"Jhoira?" the boy said as he staggered to his feet. "I'll be glad to see her."

"Come along."

Monologue

After the first hour of cranking, I moved among the crowd, organizing the students into teams that took shifts powering the pumps, windmills, and turbines. If the flow of fast-time fog had ceased for only a moment, Urza, Karn, and Teferi could have been torn to shreds on the verge of their time pit. The teams worked all through the night. I fortified them with a number of white-mana spells I know. All the while, Jhoira and I remained beside the machine to monitor it for stresses and possible breakdown. No crises came—as Urza had said, it was a good design.

The real crisis was one of hope. It had occurred to me after the first hour that Urza and Karn might have been torn to pieces by the time cloud only moments after entering it. They might be lying dead just within the wall of steam, unseeable to us. How long would we keep up our labors? Days? Weeks? Months? I could tell that these same dark musings were plaguing Jhoira, though neither of us voiced our concerns. It was the middle of the next morning before I overheard these questions muttered among the crank teams. It had been a weary and sleepless night for all of us—the fatigue of labor overlaid with the fatigue of welling doubt.

"How long do we keep this up?" I asked Jhoira quietly during the blazing afternoon.

"We keep it up until the machine breaks or the master and Karn emerge."

I felt heartened by her words. Here was a woman who had struggled out of a ten-year coma to design a machine worthy of Urza himself.

A quick march up over the hill told me our labors would soon end. The water in the fast-time rift would not last into the night.

I was coming down the slope to report this grave news to Jhoira when I saw a terrifying sight. The windmills ground to a halt, the turbines ceased their whining, and the thick, life-giving wall of fog roiled and dissipated on the wind. I started to run until I saw Urza, Karn, and Teferi standing there, having just emerged, alive, from the time pit. The crowd of students let out a spontaneous whoop and surged up around the three refugees. I hurried down toward them until I saw another knot of young folk, clustered quietly around Jhoira's wheeled cart. In the next moments I reached her side. Her eyes were shut, her hands limp at her sides, but blessed breath coursed smoothly in her chest.

"She stayed awake until they emerged," one of the students said with quiet reverence, "and then, a moment later—"

"Rest, dear girl," I said fondly, stroking the sweaty hair from her forehead. "Sleep awhile more. We'll wake you again. We'll always wake you again."

—Barrin, Mage Master of Tolaria

Chapter 11

Teferi had not adapted well in the months after his rescue. The explosion had been horrible, of course, and the fire afterward, but he had been utterly devastated by the fact that the world and all his former friends were nearly twenty-five years older. Teams of healers had gingerly counseled the victim about his ordeal, focusing on his slow-time isolation.

"What isolation?" he asked. "I was alone for three seconds! When you're on fire, you don't care if you're alone. The fourteen years before the explosion were more traumatic. Talk about isolation! I had no peers. Every equal of mine was five years older than me. Now they're almost three times my age! Jhoira's forty. Malzra's probably five hundred and forty. What about Teferi? Oh, he's still fourteen!"

It was another wound Urza couldn't heal.

Neither, apparently, could Teferi. After weeks of counseling, Teferi told the healers to leave. When they wouldn't, he cast an itching enchantment on them. They struggled to maintain their decorum but soon were scratching like a pack of mongrels. They fled.

Teferi stalked out of the infirmary. He marched across the finished academy.

"That wall wasn't here before," he growled, and flung a spell at it. Green coils of energy leapt from his fingers and lashed into the grass at the base of the wall. Ivy grew rampantly up from the ground, overwhelming the limestone wall. In moments, the redoubt was buried deep beneath a riling green mound. "Look at these lovely towers." His hand flung out again. Moss sprouted all along the rooftops of blue slate and hung down in gray beards.

Teferi's tantrum began to attract a crowd of students. Heads popped from behind shutters. Faces appeared in doorways. Students emerged to follow the tempestuous lad. They all knew him from the Teferi monument and excitedly crowded up to see the teenage hermit in action.

Teferi whirled. "Get out of here. I'm tired of being stared at! You've had nearly fifteen years! Look at something else!"

The students shied back from him, but the moment Teferi stalked onward, they followed.

Drawing a deep breath, Teferi bellowed. "Then look at this!"

The student robes of Old Tolaria opened obligingly down their back panel, allowing for various necessary functions—and this unnecessary one.

A new generation of students glimpsed Teferi's infamous "Breech of Etiquette." Many of them turned in disgust. Others laughed, some even checking to see if their work suits would allow a similar display.

Teferi was apparently dissatisfied with this response and added to his visual display an olfactory one. He cast a spell that sent a stink cloud through the whole academy. The crowd shut their mouths and squinted their eyes and ran. Doors and shutters slammed closed. The community that had stared at Teferi continuously for over a decade at last closed their eyes to him.

And he disappeared.

Eventually, the squelching cloud dissipated enough that students and scholars ventured back into the streets.

Barrin and Malzra were livid, a week-long experiment ruined. Their anger only deepened when the prankster was nowhere to be found.

"Look everywhere," Barrin commanded the students in the streets. He hissed to Malzra. "We've not saved him from fire and time only to lose him to stupidity."

The whole school was mobilized. It seemed they were being invaded. It was too bad Teferi was gone, for he would have loved the sight.

Jhoira emerged into the din. Students and scholars trooped like army ants through the academy, opening every door, looking beneath every bed, poking at every curtain and tapestry. Her brow was creased in consternation.

"Teferi, where are you hiding?"

A smile came to her face. It was as though she could read his mind.

* * * * *

"I knew I would find you here," Jhoira said quietly as she approached her niche on the western edge of the isle.

Teferi didn't look up. He sat on a sunny slope of sandstone and stared out at the glimmering sea. He had come to this spot once before, ages ago, and discovered Kerrick and Jhoira trysting within. Teferi's heart must have broken, but he hadn't betrayed her secret, even in the face of Malzra's questions.

Jhoira remembered the time. To her it was ages ago, but for Teferi, it had been only a matter of months. Ages. Months. What did they mean on Tolaria? Jhoira herself seemed little older than in those days. Slow-time water had kept her outward age around twenty-two, and the coma had left her seeming younger still. Her inward vision quest had restored her. It had saved Teferi and her as well. She had discovered a way to break through the temporal wall that isolated him and the social wall that had isolated her. They were perhaps not soul mates, she and Teferi, but they were metaphysical twins.

Jhoira eased up to the rock and slid into position beside him. It was as though she were reenacting that low moment ages ago, though now Kerrick was gone. It felt right to sit beside Teferi instead.

"I'm glad you're here. It's a good place to be, when you're feeling trapped between Tolaria and the world."

The muscles along Teferi's jaw clenched. He stared out to sea.

"If you have to be alone, it's the best place in the world."

"You don't understand," Teferi broke in.

"Yes, I do," she said. "Yes, I do." She reached a hand out to him.

He didn't take it. "We're farther apart than ever. When you were eighteen, you always told me to grow up. Well, look, now you're forty, and I still haven't taken your advice."

"This is Tolaria," Jhoira said philosophically. "Time doesn't matter. You'll see. In a few years, we'll be the same age."

He heaved an angry breath. "A few years—an eternity, a horrible eternity."

"Not so horrible," Jhoira said, "when you've got friends."

At long last, he took her hand. "Thanks, Jhoira. Thanks."

* * * * *

Seven years had passed since Teferi was released from his temporal prison. In that time, he had at last become a man—a young man, to be sure, but at twenty-one, he and Jhoira seemed the same age. She had been partaking of slow-time water for two decades. Most of the scholars and students over the age of thirty were also allowed to drink slow-time water once a year—the frequency required to halt aging. More frequent drinks caused strange illnesses. Since no one understood the long-term effects of the stuff, its use was strictly regulated. Those younger than thirty were forbidden the drink at all. Teferi, at one point, had to be reprimanded by Barrin for drinking fast-time water in hopes of growing up sooner.

In the seven years that he had been free, young Teferi had distinguished himself among the pupils and shown a new maturity. His pranksome nature eventually played itself out, though he still had a sharp wit and, occasionally, a sharp tongue.

Among Teferi's most ingenious innovations was organizing a squad of "temporal spelunkers"—students interested in studying the effects of movement into and out of steeper time gradients. They modified Jhoira's machine to create longer-lasting artificial bridges into drastic time shifts. Teferi even pioneered using existing rivers to cross temporal curtains. By submerging oneself completely in water and holding a large glass jar of air inverted over one's head, a spelunker could be carried along by the current and, cushioned by the water, slowly readjust to a different time. Through such discoveries, the academy was able to establish laboratories in moderate fast-time areas, where a month of experimentation could occur in a week.

The most visible effect of these accelerated laboratories was the rapid proliferation of Malzra's falcon attackers. Their intricate mechanisms were manufactured more quickly than powerstones could be found. The crystals came in only sporadic numbers aboard *New Tolaria* as it made its rounds from Thran site to Thran site.

Meanwhile, Malzra had been busy designing another set of guardians. He took the sensor systems from the guards he had built for the walls of Old Tolaria and merged them with various locomotor apparatuses—bipedal structures modeled after long-legged and fleet-footed emus, preferentially quadrupedal frames based upon the feline physiology of panther-warriors, and even octopedal devices made for ambling over any terrain type and up even the sheerest surfaces. Each of these devices was armed with specially designed pincers and blades for piercing Phyrexian flesh, an array of sight-targeted quarrel launchers, and a core packed with explosive powder, to be activated when all other systems are spent and an engaged foe has incapacitated the sensory or locomotor systems.

The resulting machines were collectively known as the Guardian class—a fearful assortment of artifacts. The two-legged variety were Tolarian runners, capable of great bounding speeds, their mirrorlike torsos bearing eight quarrel ports up each side. Where wings would be on emus, scythe blades emerged to snap together before them. These artifact creatures were meant to fight on open fields. The four-legged machines were known as pumas, sleek stalkers that would patrol the forests from the treetops and drop soundlessly onto any intruders. Their daggerlike claws could bear them swiftly up even sheer tree trunks and could take off a man's head with one swipe, slicing his neck into three equal disks. These claws sharpened themselves each time they were withdrawn into the machine's pads. The final type—eight-legged beasts—were called scorpions, with pincers fore and aft and the dexterity of any spider. As yet only half a dozen of each of these beasts existed, but their gleaming hides and dark, gemstone eyes were enough to frighten even the older students. Given the need—and given Teferi's fast-time laboratories— armies of these creatures could be created in a single year.

With patrols of runners, pumas, and scorpions on the ground and flights of falcons in the sky, Malzra felt he could ensure the safety of his isle. In addition to these forces, Malzra instructed students on the creation of ornithopters. Five were currently being built.

The academy had become an armed fortification, despite the efforts of Barrin and Jhoira. They had ensured, however, that it was still a human place. They emphasized learning and experimentation over arms production and scheduled celebrations and festivals to help break the tedium of work. Even so, the black blight of the Phyrexian gorge never went away, and every tender thing that came into being in the walls of the new academy did so in the shadow of that horrid threat.

Then they found it—the dead Phyrexian lying at the top of the gorge, having clawed its way up the cliff. It had used the properties of normal-time river water to help cushion its passage, climbing a thin waterfall. Even so, the beast was macerated from the crown of its bony head to the last spike in its scourgelike tail. The fiend's pink skin was ripped, revealing mounds of gray muscle over a hulking skeleton. Its once-long claws had been worn to bloody nubs in its tortured climb to the top of the chasm. It had passed through the shredding blades of time and somehow survived to reach the top. After two hundred years of experimentation and mutation, the Phyrexians had bred a beast resistant enough to time change to climb five hundred feet through the curtain of fast time. In two more generations, they would be strong enough to escape the gorge and fight. In four more generations, there would be hundreds of them. With their fast-time advantages, the Phyrexians could produce four generations of hybrids in eight years of time outside.

This was why Malzra planned the Day of Falcons. Even as he geared up for all-out war, he devised a swift, preemptive air strike. The attack had two objectives. Minimally, it would slay Phyrexians, perhaps even the new generations, and buy time for Malzra to complete his arsenal. Maximally it could exterminate every last beast in the gorge and thereby end its threat forever. Barrin approved the plan, which required no risk to students or scholars and employed the seven hundred fifty falcon mechanisms already created.

At long last, the Day of Falcons arrived.

* * * * *

Atop the Giant's Pate, Barrin and Karn watched Malzra climb into the framework of his newly completed ornithopter. This command-class mechanism carried remote sensors that were linked to the prototype runners, pumas, and scorpions deployed in a circle around the gorge. It also bore a payload of fifty powder bombs, a complement of sixteen quarrel ports, and wings capable of being swept back alongside the main struts to allow for swift diving. From this aerial command seat, Malzra would monitor and direct the coming attack.

Barrin squinted into the bald morning sun. He held his hand visorlike over his eyes and peered from the Giant's Pate out toward the edges of the island. Thin tendrils of red smoke appeared on the western rim of the isle and frayed out on the sea winds.

"Jhoira and her three squads have reached the shore and set up their posts. They are the last of the thirty-eight launch squads. The falcon fleet is ready to be deployed."

Urza strapped himself into the command seat. His usual blue robes were replaced by a charcoal-gray suit replete with pockets, tool belt, and armor at the shoulders. He wore boots laced to the knee, and his gemstone eyes were shielded by a dark crescent of polished obsidian.

"If this works today, perhaps we can send millions of these beasts into Phyrexia itself, and not a single Dominarian will have to fight."

"What about you?" Barrin asked levelly. "You are a Dominarian."

"Don't you ever stop worrying?" Malzra asked. "I will fly over the gorge, drop my payload of bombs, and rise out of reach of anything they could hurl my way. It'll be just like flying over the deserts of the Fallaji. Besides, I'm only a diversion, a smoke screen to hide the assault."

"The falcons themselves will hide their own assault. That's why we're taking the trouble of launching them at the edge of the island. They'll outrun sound itself in their dive. The Phyrexians will neither hear or see them until they are torn apart by them. Your bomb salvo only risks you and your new ornithopter."

"We both know I might possibly survive a fall through the temporal bubble around the Phyrexians—"

"Could you survive the moments afterward, surrounded by hundreds, perhaps thousands, of the beasts? Planeswalking cannot save you when the distances are temporal."

With a snort, Malzra activated the great Thran device. It shivered to life. Its wings accordioned out and began to beat. The machine rose, slow and animated, into the skies.

"This is a battle I must fight and win." Malzra soared away from the Giant's Pate.

Just before the wings' whirring drowned out all sound, Barrin shouted, "There is another battle, a much bigger battle, you must fight and win."

Karn watched the machine climb into the sky, beyond the reach of words. The silver man said, "The crews have prepared your ornithopter, Mage Master, as you requested. They included a payload of fifty bombs."

After a long, drawn breath, Barrin said, "I hope I will not need it. Master Malzra might survive a fall into the time bubble, but I am quite—" he broke off, as though he thought better of what he was about to say.

"You are quite human, yes," Karn agreed, his eyes still focused on the shrinking ship, "and I have been near him long enough to know Master Malzra is not."

The not-human in his not-bird spiraled upward above their heads in a maneuver designed to catch the attention of every beast in the gorge—and to signal the falcon crews at the edge of the isle.

* * * * *

"There's the signal," Jhoira said to herself. She peered into the rising sun, where Malzra rode in bold spirals. "He'll start his bombing run any moment." Turning, she called to her three squad captains, "Falcons ready?"

"Squad Fifteen ready," replied Teferi, who stood beside an array of twenty falcon creatures.

Each bird occupied a small metal launch platform, anchored by a foot-long spike driven into the wet sand. The small creatures shimmered in the early light, their metal pinions folded against their legs, and their eyes glinting with predatory hunger.

"Squad Sixteen ready," came the report of its captain.

"Squad Seventeen ready."

Jhoira paused a moment, surveying the gleaming rows of bird creatures, fifteen rows of four each. They and their six hundred and ninety comrades could well save the isle. "Loose falcons!"

Sixty pairs of wings flashed out. Sixty artifact creatures crouched a moment, gathering themselves to leap into the air. Then the wind was filled with the sharp slap of metal wings. The falcons rose in a great glittering cloud, camouflaged against the silvery work of the sea. The great rush of them upward, of wings and cogs and seeking probes, was something horrific.

Jhoira glimpsed another mass of glimmering wings along the shore in either direction. In moments, though, even her own three squads had ceased to be individual birds and become only a writhing swarm, an amorphous swirling monster, and then it too was gone, through the ceiling of clouds. All across the island, there was no more sign of the flocks of killer raptors.

"Gods speed you," Jhoira said to the cluttered sky. "Gods speed you."

* * * * *

Urza reached the peak of his spiral into the sky. He folded the wings of his ornithopter back beside the struts. The nose of the craft lost lift and dropped toward the black rift below. Urza blinked placidly behind the obsidian crescent that shaded his gemstone eyes. Wind shrieked over the triangular wings. The isle rushed up to meet him. Easing the airfoils outward, he caught lift and corkscrewed low above the black cleft. The craft leveled into a furious strafing pass.

Black ballistae bolts soared out in a spiky forest all around him.

Urza triggered the hold, pouring powder bombs down onto the much-scarred fortification below. Each tumbling incendiary device plunged into the fast-time envelop and rushed fiercely to impact. Shrapnel and smoke belched out in a line below Urza. He banked, soaring away from another barrage, and stared with delight at the boiling cloud of destruction. They would not see the doom that rose at the edges of the island, rose to descend and pierce the walls of their time prison and slay them.

Nor did he see the bolt that rose with fiendish speed and smashed through his port wing and dragged him down into the Phyrexian pit.

* * * * *

Amid rolling clouds of smoke, shrieks of glee arose. Every throat and air sac and proboscis in the Phyrexian rent hooted as the ballistae bolt transfixed Urza Planeswalker's flying machine. It dragged on the wing. The ornithopter listed with agonizing slowness. Would the man have time and sense to planeswalk from the falling wreck? The smoke thickened, obscuring the view of all beasts below.

K'rrik surged to the rail of his observation tower and grasped it. Even as he gripped the metal, he saw one wing of the machine dip into the fast-time envelop and send rings of distortion ripping out from it. The sudden inertial change hurled the rest of the ornithopter, rider and all, into the gorge. That was all he saw, smoke boiling up to obscure anything else.

K'rrik spun to shout down into the riot of dying Phyrexians and burning buildings, "To the south wall! Capture the planeswalker!"

* * * * *

Stunned, Barrin and Karn saw the ballistae bolt lunge up from the black gorge like a darting fish, lance the wing of Urza's ornithopter, and drag the listing thing down into the lashing currents of fast time. The flying machine whirled once, hung up on the surface of the envelop, and then, before Barrin could send out a saving spell, slid down into the vast murk of the gorge. Smoke and darkness obscured all else.

Barrin turned, darting down the slope of the Giant's Pate.

Karn called after him, "Where are you going?"

"You said my ornithopter was prepped," came the shouted response, flung over Barrin's shoulder as he ran.

"What should I do?" Karn asked.

"Do anything you can, but be quick. Minutes are hours."

The silver man suddenly wished he had the controls that would summon the runners, pumas, and scorpions.

That useless thought was swept away by a sudden shrieking roar, descending from everywhere and nowhere at once. Karn had hardly lifted his brow when, from every corner of the heavens, shooting stars fell in a great converging ring. The whistle of their flight rattled the silver plates across Karn's body. With a series of booms that came so close to each other as to sound like a ceaseless peal of thunder, the lightning-swift creatures lanced down the sky.

They punched through the time ceiling and accelerated to blinding speed. They seemed to ricochet between the rock walls of the gorge.

Do anything you can. The words rang in the resounding air.

Karn shifted his silver bulk. He lifted the Viashino luck charm to his mouth for an awkward kiss, and bolted down the steep slope of fallen trees between the Giant's Pate and the gorge. In clumsy moments, he reached the black lip of the space. Without pause or thought, he hurled himself within.

* * * * *

It happened too quickly, the impossible ballistae bolt through the wing, the sudden unresponsive stick, the listing turn, the tug of fast time, yanking Urza and his machine down into the envelope. Before he could think to planeswalk, he was immersed in the vast, churning field of the gorge. Then all of thought and will and power were channeled into holding himself together against rending, dispersing distortion.

His hands turned to protoplasmic mush. His feet evaporated. The wave of destruction clambered up his limbs, to knees and elbows, hips and shoulders, until heart and head both were melting into air. The temporal field tore not merely particle from particle, but wave from wave. The core of his being dissolved. Urza had to think his body and mind and soul, had to plan them and stare at the immutable design of them to force chaos back into order. Again and again, he resolved himself, red clouds of pulverized meat accreting into the figure lashed in the ornithopter's seat. All the while, the ruined bird-machine and the ruined man wrangled in a tangle between worlds of light and darkness.

Suddenly he was free and falling. The last angry torrents of flesh recombined, and he plummeted. The air was dark and dank and foul. The scent of glistening oil was overwhelming. Sulfur smoke roiled from the bombs he himself had just dropped, and beneath those ropy columns, armies of monsters converged. They slithered in gray-skinned masses, slime and bone and horn, clambering over each other like swarming roaches.

Urza fell.

There was not enough strength left to planeswalk. Even if there were, his powers would not allow him to step through the gates of time. There were spells, though.

With a weary thought, Urza cast a flying enchantment on himself and stopped his descent. Ragged, panting if only as a reminder of the physical form he cast, Urza hung for a moment in midair. With another effort of will, he began to rise toward the surface of the gorge. It was like ascending through great pressurized depths toward the air and light above.

The first ballista bolt was a surprise, ripping through his liver and tearing out his right lung before pulverizing his sternum and snagging in his rib cage. Pain was a sensation like any other, useful for orienting him in his physical form, but this screaming, hopeless pain shattered his concentration for a moment. He shut off the claxon of agony, reshaped his body with a thought, letting flesh shrink away from the shaft until the bolt tumbled free. He grew a new liver and lung from the pulverized muck of the old ones.

But this was work, and it distracted him a few moments. He fell again. The air rushing up around him was a flashing mass of smoke, oil-reek, and black shafts. Two more bolts pinioned him in his plummet. By the time they, too, were out and the organs they had skewered were regrown, Urza Planeswalker came splashing down in five feet of foul water.

From a nearby causeway of carved basalt, hordes of gibbering monsters—star-shaped eyes and great shags of barbed hair and curved claws and teeth indistinguishable from each other in their scythelike savagery—hurled themselves into the water. The horrid splashing of their deformed figures seemed the slap of shark tails in frenzy. In moments, Phyrexians surrounded Urza and rushed in, biting great chunks from him.

He thrashed against them. Lightning roared out from his hands beneath the water. Phyrexians died in scores, but more came.

Whenever he fought free of them and began to rise through the air, arrows and ballista bolts ran him through, and he sank again into the churning flood.

They would not kill him, though they could. They would only harry him until every sorcery was spent, every last trick gone to the graveyard, then they would net him like one of their scavenger fish and haul him up to be flayed alive by the man standing there on that smoke-wreathed bridge.

K'rrik.

* * * * *

K'rrik's vast host gathered in the arena at the center of the city. It was an elevated circle of black basalt, carved out like a giant funnel, rings of balconies and seats converging on the small, central platform. Though used most often for gladiatorial contests—many of which featured K'rrik himself—the central space was not bounded by any rails, walls, or gates that might contain the warriors. Battles began on this stage but ranged the whole arena. Competitors were not only expected but encouraged to use the topography, weaponry, and even citizenry of the arena in their fight. The outer rim of the stadium was lined with a variety of barbed and spiked weapons provided by the state—bone, stone, and horn, but of course no iron. To get a metal weapon, a gladiator would have to wrest it from the claws of a spectator. Often obnoxious crowd members lost arms or tails, taken up as makeshift cudgels and whips, and sometimes smaller beasts were used whole.

It was not a gladiatorial battle scheduled today, though. This crowd had assembled for a state execution. They still brought their weapons in hopes that they might get a chance to join in the fun.

In the center of the arena, Urza Planeswalker hung, lashed to a much-scarred column of obsidian. The pillar was traditionally used to execute traitors, who were mauled to death by gibbering horrors. With Urza, the mauling hordes were needed to keep him weak and defenseless while K'rrik flaunted his new prize. The largest of his three executioners was little more than a massive fist of flesh, with two tiny eyes positioned under a pair of jagged pincers. At intervals, the beast lunged in and eviscerated Urza, dragging his steaming entrails onto the polished basalt. The other two beasts were jackal-headed spiders, waiting to leap in should Urza overpower the other killer.

K'rrik paced before the knot of them, hissing with laughter. Though given to excited ovations whenever the planeswalker was assaulted, the gathered throng of beasts was otherwise silent, straining to hear every word of their ruler, their god. He spoke to them not in the dulcet tones he had used to ply Jhoira all those years ago. He spoke to them in no human language at all, but rather in the growling, crackling tongue of Phyrexia.

Urza, who could drink down languages like water, knew what he said.

"Children of Phyrexia, scions of the greater god Yawgmoth and his son K'rrik, newts and negators and spawn of time, behold the man who brought us here. Behold the man who opened for us the gateway to this new paradise, to Dominaria—"

This statement was punctuated by a brutal lunge from the pincered beast. Rent viscera spilled in a fetid flow on the floor. A throaty howl erupted from the gathered throng. Even as the monster withdrew and K'rrik began again to speak, Urza's innards writhed on the floor. They drew themselves by force of will back into the murdered man.

"He has a long, honorable history of aiding our coming domination. In the caves of Koilos, he and his brother Mishra sundered the powerstone that had locked us away from Dominaria, thus opening the way for us. During Urza's subsequent war against his brother Mishra, followers of our patriarch Gix were welcomed into both armies, and Gix even made a Phyrexian out of Mishra. When Urza learned of his brother's conversion, he was so delighted, he loosed a catastrophe across Dominaria to slay its greatest armies, sink its mightiest nations, and soften the way for us to invade. He forsook his world, his trusted associate Tawnos, and even his own son, Harbin, all of which we have inherited."

"Harbin!" Urza cried out in despair, just before his gut was ripped open again and there was no breath left to scream.

"Allying himself with our comrade—the newt Xantcha—Urza traveled to Phyrexia under the pretense of war. In truth, he was drawn to us like a gnat to a great lantern. He desired to join us, to become one of us. To show his good faith, he led an army of us to the Realm of Serra, where we initiated a war of conquest that brings the angel realm to its knees even now. He betrayed the woman who healed him and gave us her plane as a trophy."

The hisses and groans of delight almost drowned out the sound of spilling blood.

"Now, our eternal champion, our spy in Dominaria and throughout all the planes has come to us. He has come to pay homage to Yawgmoth and the Son of Yawgmoth—K'rrik. He has come to grant us the world! He has given us his brother, his associate, his son, his best friend, and now, he gives us himself. Once he is dead, no one on Dominaria can stand against us."

Into the roaring ovation came a high-pitched whistle. The keen was omnidirectional and ear-splitting. Those Phyrexians with ears clutched them in sudden reflex. Those with knees crumpled to them. Even the massive pincer beast fell back, its fistlike head clenching and flexing beneath the onslaught. Only two creatures remained upright—K'rrik and his captive. Together they saw a vast silver corona slice through the time envelope and shriek toward the rim of the arena.

For one flashing moment, the machines were etched vividly in the sky—a circle of razor beaks and raptor talons and wings that glared like lightning. They crossed paths in a vast spiral and, in precise succession, punched one after another into the beasts at the base of the arena.

One monster's inch-thick skull shattered like glass as a falcon smashed into it. Another was split open from neck to navel and spilled gray-blue organs out over its shag-furred lap. Beside that creature, a crane-necked monster was undone when a falcon bit through its neck in a shrieking pass. The creature's eyes darkened, and its head tilted and dropped away like the crown of a felled tree.

Whenever a falcon tore cleanly through a beast, it would continue on to attack the next one, killing two or three in progression. Whenever a falcon was caught in a particularly resistant ball of muscle or cage of ribs, its wings stabbed outward. Spinning saw blades emerged from its frame to mince whatever meat lay about. Phyrexians penetrated by falcons jittered in death spasms, their punctured bowels or chests or brainpans boiling with vicious motion.

In an instant, the three hundred beasts in the lower seats were slain. They crumpled and jittered and spilled downward in a wave of death that crept visibly up the arena. Falcons darted like electrical jags from beast to beast, dropping them wherever they stood. More metallic birds roared in and impacted.

In the second instant, the remaining seven hundred Phyrexians took up their own defense. They swung blades and clubs to bash the birds from the skies. The tide of slaughter slowed but did not stop. The shriek of silvery wings was joined by a manifold roar of fighting and dying Phyrexians.

In the midst of it, tied to the obsidian post, Urza at last recovered fully from the pincer beast's attacks. His abdomen reassembled. His flesh knitted in glowing health. He lifted his head. The jackal-headed spiders cowered back from the quicksilver cyclone that ravaged the stands all around. With a summoning of will, Urza reached out to the mountains of Tolaria and drew from them the power for four spells. A red flare arced out from Urza, burning away his ropes and impacting the pincer beast. He amplified the kindled blast with his own mounting fury. The massive monster went to shreds of meat before him, blood extinguishing the fires there.

The jackal-spiders pivoted in sudden amazement.

Urza flung out two other spells, fireballs splashing across them and sizzling them away. His own figure steaming with the rage of the moment, Urza stalked past the smoldering heaps of his attackers, seeking the Phyrexian at the heart of all this.

But K'rrik was already gone.

Karn plummeted.

He passed the ravening time envelope. It tore futilely at his wires and conduits. Heat sparked across his frame. His orientation meters went haywire, and he could not distinguish up from down, past from future. Then, in a sick rush, he was through and plunging into the fast-time gorge.

That was the worst feeling of all. Something in Karn responded to that place, something at the core of his being. Though he sensed the reek of oil-blood and decay in the air, though he saw the wicked outline of the monstrous city below and knew Urza was there somewhere, trapped or dead—still there was a harsh rightness to it all. It was a vast, desolate beauty that he could not help being drawn to. At first, he could not imagine from where rogue feeling arose, but then he knew. It was the core of his being. The powerstone that provided him mind and heart and soul, it had come from these monstrous creatures. Karn had come from here.

Karn landed in a brackish lake. Filthy water coursed into every seam and hollow of his body. He struck the muck bottom—bones and decay over bedrock. Heaving himself upward, Karn stood and discovered his head cleared the surface. The rock wall of the gorge towered before him. He turned, for the first time clearly seeing the demon city Kerrick had built.

From a volcanic outcrop at the base of the canyon rose a bristling collection of towers, walls, spikes, and battlements. The gorge walls all around the city stared out at it with deep, black mines, like mourning faces, twisted and dribbling. The waters where Karn waded teemed with ravenous creatures, many of which even now converged and nipped at his silver frame. Above the city, clouds of mechanical falcons circled in a great storm.

Urza would be at the center of that storm.

Ignoring the snapping jaws and battering tails, Karn trudged toward the city.

The tide had turned. Most of the falcons were spent. Many Phyrexian negators remained. Urza's enchantments were used up. The artifact creatures he had summoned were being dismantled in the claws and fangs of his foes. Over grisly steppes of dead, K'rrik's nation converged on the center of the arena to slay Urza.

He could perhaps muster the strength to planeswalk, though the trip would merely take him to some other dark corner of the time rift. There he would die when K'rrik returned. Better to fight now and decimate his forces.

Suddenly, into the bleeding, black arena came a silver figure—Karn. He advanced in his slow and ceaseless way, casually tearing arms and stingers and tails from his assailants and continuing on. They swarmed him, but he carved a path through them. They piled on him, but he dug his way out.

An infernal court came with him. Smoke bombs struck among the advancing circle of Phyrexians. Shrapnel sprayed out in a killing ring. More glistening oil mixed with what already painted the seats, and here and there it caught fire.

Urza gazed up through the rising ring of sulfur smoke. There frozen in time above the gorge was the figure of an ornithopter. It hovered low over the temporal envelop. Urza thought he could make out the shadowy figure of its pilot. Better still, uncoiling in silvery promise from the craft came a slender metal cord. It looped down into the time rent, unwrapped, and swayed within paces of Urza.

Suddenly, the silver man was there, too. He clasped the strand in one powerful arm and caught up his master in the other.

How slowly they rose above the shrieking hordes. Thrown scythes and arrows pinged from Karn's skin or buried themselves in Urza until he could will them outward again. Soon, though, they were beyond reach of any thrown weapons, and then beyond even the few ballistae that were still operational. They took one final glance at the shrinking city of devils, littered with the remains of his falcon engines.

"I've only given them more metal . . . more powerstones . . . to fight us," Urza gasped out grimly.

Then the coruscating edge of the rift enveloped them.

Monologue

Even as I flew them from that vile gorge, I knew this meant full-scale war. We would have ten or twenty years to ready our arsenal. K'rrik would have one or two centuries. But all-out war would certainly come.

And this time, the battlefield would be all Tolaria.

—Barrin, Mage Master of Tolaria

PART III

Journeys

Chapter 12

It was a decade later when Malzra called them together in the new Hall of Artifact Creatures.

This hall was no mausoleum and no mere museum. It was a working laboratory, a robotics infirmary, an assembly line, a military staging ground, and a tutorial hall that offered instruction to humans and artifacts alike. Karn's touches were apparent throughout the place. No machines were interred here. The exhibits contained only living, active mechanisms, which spent periods of voluntary deactivation on view. The plans of the various inventions were stored in an archive along one end of the huge chamber, available to scholars, students, and artifacts themselves.

The command center for Malzra's island defense lay here as well. As a result, the place bustled even in the depths of night. Some of Malzra's runners and scorpions were stationed here permanently, and a puma reported in each afternoon, but the main body of machine defenders were stationed remotely around the island. A hundred of the troops were posted in fast-time curtains around the academy. They could leap from cover even before an assault could commence. These machines were rotated into and out of service every day, due to the ravages of fast time. Another hundred served in slow-time curtains—the long-term defenses. They were rotated into and out of service twice a year.

"Between them and our corps of sorcerers, led by Mage Master Barrin, the island's defenses are complete," Malzra said as he paced before the wall of schematics. Mechanical and biological troops were laid out in ink and paper in this private corner of the Hall of Artifacts. "Five hundred large-scale artifact creatures, seven hundred and fifty new falcon engines, a fleet of thirty ornithopters, and even a new dirigible."

Barrin, Jhoira, Teferi, a handful of senior scholars, and Karn sat in the tutorial space and studied the layouts, though the island's defensive systems were well known to all of them. Malzra's presentation was quickly becoming a tedious review.

"In the past five years, we have repelled five Phyrexian incursions and slain over a thousand negators."

"We know," Jhoira reminded him impatiently. "We were the ones who fought those battles.

Malzra turned from his pacing and glanced up, blinking. "There will be more. The creatures will be deadlier and more numerous. With ingenuity, foresight, and grit, the systems we have developed should be enough to repel these attacks. For the time being, the island is safe—"

"Master Malzra," Jhoira interrupted, "we know all this."

"I hope so, since I am going away," the man said quietly.

That brought back the attention of everyone but Barrin. The mage master leaned back in his seat in appraisal, watching the response of the others.

Jhoira stood, alarm in her voice and on her face. "You're leaving? Again? What about the Phyrexian gorge? What about concluding all the business of the academy?"

Barrin rose as well. "He is going on academy business. As to the Phyrexian gorge, Malzra has spent the last half hour reviewing the defenses and our tasks in maintaining and upgrading them."

"That's not what I am talking about," Jhoira said, crossing arms over her chest. "He has unfinished business—"

"Our senior student is reminding me of the 'children of fury,' " Malzra said, cutting through Jhoira's objections and Barrin's apologies. "She is reminding me of my pledge to clean up the messes of my past—chief of which would seem to be this time-torn isle and the monsters I brought here—"

"And the children you brought here—"

"And," added Karn quietly, "the machines you brought here—"

"Thank you," Malzra said not unkindly to the added comments, "but in the way of young folk, you have underestimated my capacity for pernicious destruction. No, the ills I have done here are nothing next to the ills I have done elsewhere, in the world at large."

He walked back to the drawings, reached up with hands that seemed almost to glow in that dark corner of the Hall of Artifacts, and drew down a large pallet. Behind it lay a map of the Phyrexian gorge. Lines of lead detailed the woundlike fissure—dark and narrow, overrun with evil.

"This is our most up-to-date rendering of the gorge." With a sword-sized pointer, Malzra gestured at the drawing. "Here is the gladiatorial arena, and here, the palace of K'rrik, and here, the breeding laboratories. In these hovels beside and beneath the water, K'rrik's minions dwell, nearly a thousand strong, the number growing by ten each day. Unless extinguished, they are fomenting a threat that will one day overrun the whole island."

With a swift and fierce gesture, Malzra tore down the map, revealing beneath it a much larger schematic—what looked like a series of nesting dolls in cross section.

"This is Phyrexia—nine stacked planes, one within another. This top layer is the only one where a human might survive, for a few hours. It is inhabited by dragon engines, some five hundred feet in length, and creatures discarded as useless, creatures that would make our runners and pumas and scorpions seem like mechanical fleas. The dense forests in this region are made of semimetallic plants—poisonous, with razor-edged leaves—that grow in the light of the ceaseless lightning storms that fill the soot-black sky. Each layer downward grows worse—with mutilated priests, demon hordes, witch engines, titanic worms, poison and acid and fire. At the base of it all, there is a figure deeper, darker, more hideous than any Dominaria has ever known."

To himself, Barrin whispered a name. None heard that name, but the look of solemn dread on his face made the others wince.

"I have awakened this creature. I have drawn him here. That is how deep and ancient my mistakes are. I am responsible for the plague of Tolaria, yes, but also for the gradual collapse of a realm of angels, the long ice age of this world, the destruction of Argoth, and the very introduction of evil into the world. That is the scale of my failures. All of that is what I strive to undo. K'rrik is a nightmare, yes, but one man's nightmare. K'rrik's lord is the nightmare of a whole world—a corporate, unconscious, and universal terror. As certainly as K'rrik is arming himself to take over this isle, the creature I will not name is arming himself to take over our whole world."

There were no interruptions now, only sober eyes.

"To fight such a creature and his millions of minions, I need . . . we need a much different arsenal. I go to begin work on it," Malzra said.

At last, Jhoira had regained her voice. "How can you be responsible for all that? How could anyone be responsible for all that? Even if you were responsible, how could you—or any mortal man—hope to undo all those evils? You would have to be Urza Planeswalker to have any hope of—" She broke off mid-sentence, her horrified glare of comprehension bringing paralysis to her whole being.

"Nevertheless, I must go," Malzra said, "and I go alone, for now. It is a very dangerous place I am going. In time, if I am successful, I will bring all of you with me to help."

Trembling, Jhoira had regained her seat. "You're not going . . . you're not going to Phyrexia."

"No," said Malzra fondly.

He crossed to Karn and reached out toward his neck. For a moment, the silver man withdrew as if fearing the master would unlatch his skull piece and deactivate him. Instead Malzra lifted a pendant from the golem's neck and held it out before them all. A lizard-shaped trinket of very hard metal dangled, glinting, in the dark air.

"Not Phyrexia. I'm going to your homeland, Jhoira. I'm going to Shiv."

* * * * *

Urza descended. It felt nice not to have to walk. It felt nice to indulge himself in the luxuries of being a planeswalker, to forget about the worrisome business of feigning breath and blinking, of being asked to join in dinners. For him, eating was only a nuisance. Despite his many almost limitless powers—stepping plane to plane with little more than a thought, casting all colors of magic at high levels, living beyond the terrors of ravaging time, seeing to the essence of things, smelling Phyrexian blood at a hundred paces— portraying a convincing human was a task that was at once vexing in its minutia and exhausting in its limitations. It was a small and tedious job, but a necessary one.

Except in times like these.

Urza descended past great rafts of sulfuric cloud and banks of rusty steam. His ceremonial robes shrank inward about him, becoming a suit marked with drake-feather pads to deflect the volcanic heat of the landscape. His sandals transformed into thick leather boots that laced to the knee. Hair braided itself tightly to his head, proof against stray fingers of flame. He needn't enter a landscape this way, dropping from such a height, but he wanted to survey this land before alighting upon it. And, frankly, he enjoyed the ride.

Urza had descended once before this way, returning to the ancient, ruined wasteland where he and Mishra had first discovered the Thran site of Koilos. That landscape, blasted by a force that sank continents and brought a millennium of winter to the world, could not have been more tortured than this one.

Backlit mountains jutted in a devilish ring against the sooty horizon. At their tilted tops, steamy lakes glowed evilly in haloes of brimstone. Twisted piles of rock slumped down the sides of these silent sentinels, and rivers of stone pulsed and glowed like arteries. Among them, black courses formed networks of cool veins. Black and red alike, the rivers plunged into a great steaming ocean of bubbling lava, beside which sat twisted columns of stone like dejected statues. The magma vented gasses in mile high jets, rock-spitting coronas, and foamy, belching chunks that sizzled nastily along the shore.

Urza descended. He landed atop a knob of stone that overhung this seething sea of fire. Beneath his feet, the rock was maroon and warm and rumpled, like a glob of blood pudding. All around him, the air was hot and thick with noxious fumes. Urza breathed and reminded himself what a good thing it was to be immortal.

He lifted his gaze. There, above him, magnificent in the dead glare of the place and the roiling gloom of the sky, was what he had come to see: the mana rig.

It crouched on a massif of basalt, vulturelike on broad talons of stone and cast clay. These talons ended in myriad claws that reached in a webwork down the rock face to the boiling caldera below. The extrusion looked like a gigantic heart, and once it functioned that way. In ancient time, the tubes that crisscrossed it drew lava up from the boiling pit and pumped it into the immense facility above.

The rig was a thing to behold. At either end of it, a pair of bowl-shaped heat shields each held aloft a great city. One, tucked back from the ocean of fire, was an ancient monastery, its conic temples and towers stacked in a decorous hive into the sky. The other, hanging out over the brimstone sea, was a colossal forge of Thran design. It was here that the incredibly hard Thran metal had come from. Urza had arrived in Shiv to explore this site. Between the two cities extended a long storage and production facility with high, cathedral-like walls and tapered archways. In that spot, Urza would begin to assemble the weapon that would turn back the Phyrexians forever.

Jagged script crawled along the base of the bowl-shaped heat shields. Within the structure would be more script, perhaps undisturbed libraries of it. The rooms and halls, the mechanisms and walls themselves would be chronicles in metal and stone of the minds of the builders. He would learn to forge Thran metal, yes, but more, he would plumb secrets of the greatest artificers the world had ever known—secrets that had made them into the very enemies he now faced.

Urza strode from the warm shoulder of stone, making his way past ropy lines of cooled magma. His gemstone eyes scanned the eroded edges of the volcano. He would have to circle north and east, past a giant steaming fissure and a pair of twin cliffs washed by tides of superheated rock. It would be a five-mile walk to reach a structure one mile away—an uncomfortable walk. He was immune to the destruction of fire and poison but not inured to the pain they would cause.

To his clothing, Urza imagined a silver-gilt wrap that flung back the red heat assailing him on all sides. The wrap took form, and he felt his other clothes cool and sigh, venting heat. A veil of fine-ringed metal mesh assembled itself before his face. Thus garbed, Urza climbed the difficult mountain passes.

Of course, he could simply have wished himself into the structure, but to walk a land was to know it. Geography would force him to trace the same paths as generations of others, perhaps as the Thran themselves. He would approach the rig as they had, would see it the way they had. It was much like holding a book upright when learning to read, though it is perfectly possible to read upside down and backward.

Already the alien script of this place was beginning to resolve into meaningful words. There were trails here—broad, smooth, patient trails. The stone over which they ran was etched with claw marks. Paths led to various prominent points—lookout posts. If they were currently manned, Urza could see no sign of it. Whoever used these trails moved in the open and at a measured pace. They were man-sized creatures. They ruled this place and routinely defended it. Urza lifted the pendant about his neck and stared at the robed lizard dangling there.

Other creatures frequented the hillsides too. They had made various rank nests beneath tilted stones and within lava tubes. Though hidden from sight, these spots reeked of furtive movements, worry, and quick death. Spies. Some of the sites were burned out from within. The bones of their inhabitants lay in ruin at their entrances in warning to others. Other spots, invisible to mortal eyes but plain to Urza's all-seeing gaze, were yet occupied. Tiny eyes gleamed, rat-like and blinking, beneath dark brows of stone.

Goblins. Urza smiled gently. Poor, wretched monsters, vermin more accursed than rats. Once he had taken hold of the facility, he could bring a few dozen scorpion engines to clear out the infestation.

Until then, he had a long walk. Unless a goblin emerged to bar his way—and descending from the clouds had probably done much to convince all watchers to merely watch—Urza would not engage any of the beasts.

He entered a vast defile and wandered the length of it. In black-eyed cave mouths, goblins crouched. They whispered to each other and blinked in resentful appraisal but did not emerge. Urza's instinctual mind marked their positions while his higher mind analyzed the structure that hung overhead.

A third part of his psyche roamed a different defile, one glimpsed long years before. In it, two vast armies engaged in a death match. Urza had believed the vision to show the Thran driving the Phyrexians from the world. It took him millennia to realize the Thran had willingly become the Phyrexians, that Mishra had willingly transformed himself too. Only in that bitter realization had Urza begun to regain his sanity, to recognize the enemy in himself.

Something emerged from the lip of stone at the mouth of the defile. Many somethings. Their rust-red robes melded so naturally with the cliff sides that Urza had not seen them until they were rising from every crevice and steam vent across the stone. They moved with a silent, sinewy grace. Some slid out on all fours, clutching the ground with four-clawed hands and feet. Others strode out on hind legs and brandished thin, wickedly barbed polearms. They posted themselves in Urza's path and planted muscular tails behind them. The nearest ones drew back mottled hoods from their heads. They were reptiles, lizard men, with short, toothy snouts, small, bright eyes, and craggy skulls. Their scaly skin gleamed gray-green and red in the fiery light of the caldera.

Jhoira had called them Viashino.

The largest Viashino in the party of thirty-some approached Urza. It held its hook-edged polearm out before it. The creature glared into the planeswalker's eyes. Slivered pupils stared, unblinking. There was intelligence in that alien gaze, but also fear and resentment. It hissed angrily.

Urza's mind scrolled through all the languages he had learned in three millennia, many of them only written, never spoken. This tongue was not among the ones he had heard before, but for Urza to know a language was only for him to breathe it in.

"Ghitu are forbidden this high," the lead creature hissed.

To understand an alien language was one thing; to frame a response in it was something else. Urza wondered if he should have brought Jhoira with him as a native liaison. He could planeswalk and snatch her up even now, but the rattle of polearm butts on volcanic scree convinced him not to endanger her. He kept his constructions simple.

"Do I look Ghitu?"

"Who are you, then?"

"I am Malzra of Tolaria. I have come to see the rig."

"It is forbidden."

"I must see the rig. You cannot stop me."

"Perhaps I cannot," the warrior said, his eyes glinting like metal, "but our champion can."

From the rear ranks of the Viashino, eight lizard men emerged— not eight, but one the size of eight. It was not a Viashino, though, but a young Shivan drake. The massive creature slithered forward on hands and feet, tail lashing viciously behind it. A predatory grin drew black jowls back from rows of daggerlike teeth. The thing's eyes were small and keen beneath horned brows. Scaly spikes rose across its shoulders. In place of the robes of the others, this brute wore a leather harness, as though it were often used to haul heavy machinery.

No dumb beast, though, the drake reared up and snorted, "I am Rhammidarigaaz, champion of the Viashino. Feeling so arrogant now?"

Urza tilted his head in admission. Were he a mere man, he would be terrified at the prospects of battle, but Urza could sidestep the fastest blows of this creature, could shock him mercilessly until he fell dead, could enervate him so he could not attack, could summon armies of artifact creatures to swarm the hillside and dismantle these creatures. Subtlety in dealing with such creatures was a lesson hard learned over the last few thousand years. It was not fear that informed his next actions, but a concern that he not reveal too much about his powers—just yet.

"Arrogant? No. Confident? Yes." Urza waved the monster forward.

Rhammidarigaaz came on. The shouldering might of the drake was like a mountain moving. Urza did not flinch away. Without changing appearance, his robes hardened into armor that would bend only when he willed it to. The creature clutched him in one massive claw, nails clamping down. Urza did not struggle. Rhammidarigaaz hoisted him into the air and snorted hot breath over him.

It regarded the unmoving man. "Shall I bear you to the dungeons or kill you now?"

"You will let me go," Urza replied placidly, "and take me to your king."

"Our bey does not entertain vagrants," Rhammidarigaaz sneered, "and I cannot let you go. You have seen our homeland. You will remain our captive or die."

"I foresee a different future."

The beast clenched its claw. Urza's robes crumpled in slowly around him, but he gave no gasp of pain. The Viashino watched in awe, half-expecting blood to rim the man's eyes and lips.

Instead, Urza repeated his request. "Release me, and take me to your bey."

Enraged, Rhammidarigaaz opened his jaws in a roar and lifted Urza into the gap. Teeth dripped hot saliva across his head. The monster shoved him inward.

As placid as ever, Urza reached up into the drooling jowls of the thing. One hand clutched a great, slimy tooth above him, and the other a tooth below. He flexed his shoulders.

The drake's jaw distended. Like a dog with a stick rammed in its mouth, Rhammidarigaaz gagged and rolled his head. He hissed a cloud of acidic breath. Lizard-men scattered, but the man in the maw did not relent. Rhammidarigaaz tried to clamp his jaws together. A great clacking sound answered. He howled with pain. Yanking Urza from his mouth, he hurled the man to the ground. The beast clutched one jowl with a twitching claw.

Urza rolled across the volcanic dirt and rose to his feet. He clutched in his hand a dripping drake tooth.

"Now you will take me to your bey." Urza's gaze brooked no discussion.

Rhammidarigaaz dropped the claw from his mouth. Scaly hackles bristled across arched shoulders. Hot plumes of death jetted from his nostrils. Twin flames swept over Urza.

He stood in their midst. Poison and pulverized rock sluiced past him. In moments, he was lost in the dense blaze.

The Viashino who had fled once did so again, backing farther from the battle. Rhammidarigaaz vented his fury until lungs were flat and throat was raw. In the aftermath of rolling smoke, there was no sign of the invader.

Lizard men ventured timidly from the rills where they had sheltered. A purring growl that must have been laughter circulated among the creatures.

As if stepping around a corner in space, Urza suddenly appeared. The gory dragon tooth still hung in his grasp.

"Enough bravado. Now take me to the bey."

Rage blossomed blood-red in the drake's eyes. His claws sank deep into the volcanic earth. Its haunches gathered to spring. Jaw dropping wide, Rhammidarigaaz lunged through air to swallow Urza whole.

The planeswalker grimaced. With an offhand gesture, he flung an arc of magic across the beast.

He transformed into stone. Rhammidarigaaz, the champion of the Viashino, became a statue frozen in terrific motion. He seemed even more massive and fearsome in that aspect. His jaws gaped wide. His eyes glared blindly. His whole figure was caught in the act of a leap he would never finish.

Urza shrugged. The pulpy tooth waggled in his hand. "Well, now instead of a champion, you have a gargoyle." His voice grew steely. "Take me to the bey."

Though none of the Viashino warriors approached, the largest called out from the lee of a nearby boulder. "No. If this is what you do to our champion, what will you do to our bey?"

It seemed a reasonable observation, and thus, by extension, these could be reasonable lizard men.

Urza approached the drake statue. He took a few visual measurements. Positioning himself carefully out of the line of charge, Urza set the drake's tooth back into the spot it had occupied. It no sooner touched the creature than it fused to his mouth. Urza took a step back. Next moment, the dragon's stony semblance fell away.

Rhammidarigaaz vaulted in his attack. He soared past Urza and crashed to the ground before a pile of cooled magma. His toppling bulk shattered the stone bulwark. Chunks of rock bounded out. Viashino scattered farther. The drake's tail lashed the ground. He rolled twice and fetched up against a rocky knob. There he lay, miserable, a twisted mess of wing and claw and scale.

Urza gazed bemusedly at the creature. He addressed all the lizard men. "I could go to the bey without you to guide me, but there may be more mayhem."

The drake rose. He probed his jawline and gasped out wonderingly. "My tooth. It's back!"

"I can kill, or I can heal," Urza said plainly. "You decide."

Viashino and drake exchanged sullen glances. The leader of the lizard men nodded meaningfully to their champion.

"I r-regret my actions," Rhammidarigaaz stammered resentfully. "Violence is not the way."

"All is forgiven. This is a lesson I took years to learn as well," Urza said. He gestured up the trail toward the mana rig. "Shall we proceed?"

With a wounded bow—not quite courtly but not quite mocking, the drake led Urza up the path. Viashino warriors fell in line behind them.

* * * * *

Jhoira stood in the east forest guard post along the path from the academy to the harbor. It was a small, remote tower, provisioned for three guards with a single cot to allow a sleeping shift. Tonight the battlements and the short length of wall were manned by only two, but Karn did not need to sleep. He stood below, beside the locked iron gate, and watched through an arrow loop in a curved section of wall. Nothing would get past him. Nothing ever did.

One end of the wall verged on a deep fast-time rift where a contingent of eighty runners and scorpions were stationed. Anything living would be slain by the temporal curtain, and anything unliving would be swarmed by the academy's machines. The Glimmer Moon shimmered from their silvery shoulders and watchful optics. On the other end of the wall was a steep cliff at the edge of Angelwood. The puma patrols would slay any monsters moving through the forest and the falcons any moving through the air beyond.

It had been ten years since Jhoira had lounged away the day in one of the warm pools of Angelwood. She looked no older outwardly, but inwardly she felt ancient. The slow-time water that sustained her and all the older scholars and students preserved her body, but her spirit was no longer that of a child. She had been on her vision quest. She had learned how to "break through"—not merely to save Teferi from his isolation, but to save herself as well. She had found not a soul mate but a spiritual twin and had found that she had discovered her destiny. It was not a life of bright seas and distant shores, though. It was a life of Phyrexians, forever bubbling out of K'rrik's dark kingdom.

Tonight would be no exception.

"All clear down there, Karn?" Jhoira asked, pacing the top of the rampart.

"All clear, Jhoira," came the response in a voice like distant thunder.

"We have a full complement of runners tonight?"

"Yes," he replied quietly.

Jhoira sighed. Karn was not much of a conversationalist while he was on watch. Her education complete, the academy built, and her post among the scholars secure, Jhoira had had her fill of lectures and demonstrations, experiments and designs. She could have used a little conversation.

"How many negators do you think we will see tonight?"

"The average number at this location is one for every watch of the day and three for every watch of the night," Karn noted.

"That number might change now that Malzra is gone—gone to Shiv," Jhoira said sadly. "I don't know if I would even recognize the place. I was eleven when I left it. That was over forty years ago."

She shook her head, picking up a chip of stone from the top of the battlements and hurling it off into the forest. The stone ricocheted off a pair of trees, sending a deep and mournful echo through Angelwood.

"I'll probably never see the place again."

"Malzra said that he'd be back to collect you, once he had prepared the way," Karn noted.

"By the time he's done that, I certainly won't recognize the place," muttered Jhoira bitterly. "The Viashino and goblins will be massacred, the drakes will be enslaved, and the mountains will be leveled into fields of glass."

Over the years, Karn had developed a nascent sense of humor

that relied heavily on irony: "You have great faith in Master Malzra."

"Master *Malzra*? Do you know who Master Malzra is? He's Urza Planeswalker! He's caused every great disaster in the last three thousand years."

"Yes, I know," Karn said quietly. "I overheard Barrin and Urza on numerous occasions when they thought I was deactivated."

Jhoira growled, tossing her hands into the air and staring daggers at the silvery figure below. "You might have mentioned it."

"Urza seemed to want it kept secret."

"Didn't it shock you? Didn't it seem impossible for the man to be a three-thousand-year-old legend?"

Karn's silvery head shook slowly. "I am a man made of silver. My best friend is a Ghitu genius who is fifty years old but looks twenty. I dwell on an island where a day might pass in minutes or years. No, Malzra's real identity didn't shock me."

"Aren't you outraged? Here's a man solely responsible for every wicked thing that has happened to our world. He makes messes and leaves—"

"He has given Barrin a beacon," Karn said.

Jhoira's rant was caught for a moment short. "He what?"

"Barrin has a beacon, a jewel-handled dagger that is magically linked to a pendant around Urza's neck. Barrin can summon him at a moment's notice should the war turn suddenly. He can appear as quickly as the island's native defenders."

Jhoira shook her head. "You're defending him. Don't you see? Urza should have stayed here until the Phyrexians were no longer a threat. He's the reason the Phyrexians are here at all—"

"We are the reason the Phyrexians are here," corrected Karn. "You and I are the reason K'rrik is here. Urza might have been the reason they came, but we are the reason K'rrik got in. It's up to all of us to get rid of them."

Even as these words sank in, Jhoira glimpsed, in the deep distance, the movement of something vast and multilegged, scuttling like a giant flea. Karn struck the alarm.

A contingent of five runners darted emulike from the fast-time rent beside the wall. They loped forward along the trail. Their legs ratcheted in the darkness.

The distant monster wheeled about, retreating.

In moments the runners closed in. They flashed silver in the light of the Glimmer Moon. The small snap of quarrel rounds rattled though the forest night.

The Phyrexian shrieked but turned. It was small and fiendish between the solemn trees.

The scything sound of the runners' scimitars ended in five pairs of meaty thuds. One by one, their internal charges went off. Hunks of meat and blood and mechanism leapt up into the air. In moments, there was only smoke and the tangle of legs, monster and machine.

"We brought K'rrik here, Jhoira," Karn repeated in the drifting silence.

"Yes," she agreed, "and we need to get rid of him."

* * * * *

"Yes, Majesty," Urza said graciously as he bowed before the lizard lord, "I am a planeswalker. I, and all Dominaria, need your forge."

Urza made a broad gesture, taking in the high hall, its rings of balconies, and its conic vault. He had seen much of the ancient facility on his way in—the coke chambers and blast furnaces, the mold rooms and rollers, the ancient gear-work and chain drives. He had seen enough to know that the forge was capable of producing far more than trinkets—if it was given over into the right hands.

The bey was an elder Viashino. A gray-grizzled wattle hung at his neck, and a bright red crest topped his head. Robed in purple, Bey Fire Eye stood at an ornate rail, the equivalent of a throne for a species with neither the physiology nor the need to sit. The rail was carved from one wall of a giant piston chamber. The circular space had become a pulpit, protected from attack on three sides. Its symbolism was clear—whoever stood within the ancient piston chamber embodied the power of the arcane machinery all around. Fire Eye exuded that power. His eyes were small and implacable as they moved across the gathered throng in his audience chamber. He glowered especially at the young drake who had been sent out to best Urza.

At last, Fire Eye spoke, "What would you build with this forge?"

Urza blinked, taken aback a moment. "Machines. Living machines, like this one." He reached out into empty space, and in his hand appeared a large sheet of paper—the plan of the silver man, Karn—and spread it on the floor before the bey. "Men like this. I will make them from your metal. I will make them to defend our world."

The bey stared for some time at the plans before hissing out his response. "This machine will work?"

"I will show you, yes," Urza said emphatically. "I will bring a prototype made of metal. An old model—too soft. You will see. He works well."

Again, the silence. Urza was not accustomed to waiting for the decisions of others, but he needed these creatures. They knew more about the rig than any other beings on the planet. They knew the secrets of making Thran metal.

At last, the bey spoke again, "You may make your metal men with our forge—on two conditions."

"Yes?" prompted Urza.

"First, there is a certain ancient enemy of ours—"

"The goblins?" Urza guessed.

"No. The goblins are a menace, yes, but our patrols are more than able to dispatch them. The enemy I speak of is the fire drake Gherridarigaaz, mother of our champion. She has plagued us since her son joined us," the bey said. "You must halt her attacks."

"It will be done," Urza replied, "and the other condition?"

"Second, grant us as our property into perpetuity the prototype creature you speak of."

Urza stared a long while at the lizard lord, sitting there

enthroned on the massive piston. His gemstone eyes lifted, searching the darksome balconies above, as though an answer would lie there. "It is quite a sacrifice you ask."

The bey nodded placidly. "Among our people, sacrifice for the tribe is the highest honor."

There was wisdom in this saying. Urza thought of all the sacrifices in this war so far. As always, the Phyrexian threat came screaming back to the fore of his mind.

"Yes," said Urza Planeswalker, "you may have him."

Monologue

With Urza gone, things are quiet here at the academy. We have had the usual Phyrexian incursions on the borders. They are only tests, of course, and by killing off each of these beasts, we are only helping K'rrik perfect his invasion force for the day when they will all come across. But, for now, we are safe, and we build more machines.

I can only wonder what Urza is doing on the other side of the world. I can only hope that the lessons he has learned here at Tolaria have made him more human again. Human or inhuman, I pray he succeeds. Otherwise, we are all doomed.

—Barrin, Mage Master of Tolaria

Chapter 13

The line of Tolarian runners darted across the grove, their long legs flashing like swords. Sunlight slanted through the forests to either side. The lead machine coursed along a deer path, mounted a gentle slope, and emerged onto the crest of a summit where it paused. The others loped up alongside the it. Hydraulics whined as the machines turned, surveying the plains below.

At the far end of the fields, Angelwood bristled with moving figures—Phyrexians. Fangs and claws and barbed tails flashed among the tree boles and undergrowth. Skin as pale as bone gleamed sickly. Leathery folds of hide, knobby shoulders, jagged scales, barbed manes, and eyes like slivers of midnight . . . they were monsters of mutation. Now some of the scavenged bits of metal from fallen falcons and runners and pumas were making their way into the beasts' bodies. Not merely war armor, not merely body weaponry, these hunks of metal were badges of violent valor. They were kill trophies, recovered from fallen machines.

On the fields ahead, metal troops gathered to oppose these monsters. Runners in their hundreds flooded onto the belly of the land. Pumas bounded down from treetop glades and stalked through the tall grasses that verged on the Angelwood. A large phalanx of scorpions filled out the center of the army.

The runners on the summit creaked and moved aside, making

room for a new arrival. A large runner, fitted out with saddle and control panel, vaulted into the cleared space. Its rider stood up in the saddle and lifted an olive hand to her brow, peering out across the battle.

"Karn, get up here," the rider called over her shoulder.

A gleaming figure labored up the deer path behind her and stomped to a standstill.

"I am not built for speed, Jhoira," the golem said simply.

Ignoring the comment, Jhoira said, "The main body is coming straight through Angelwood, as the falcon watchers reported. They must have mined their way into the cave complex on the southern edge of the forest. It's just as well. Angelwood is a mild time slough. While most of our forces stop the advance, we'll be able to move through the forest eaves and reach the cave mouth where they are emerging. We'll cut off the advance and then hammer them from the rear."

"How will six runners, a young woman, and a silver golem stop an army of Phyrexians?" Karn asked, his metal frame whining in doubt.

Jhoira flashed a smile over her shoulder and sent her runner bounding down the slope ahead. "You'll see."

The other runners followed. They were fleet-footed, striding like ostriches. Their three-pronged feet scrambled across the shifting stones as they half-slid, half-ran from the hillside into the verges of the forest. They wove their way among great black boles and crashed through damp undergrowth. To one side, the dark dome of the Phyrexian gorge hulked. To the other, Angelwood glowed, infested with hundreds of slow-moving, shambling monsters. Ahead lay a mossy mound of stone. It was a volcanic extrusion, a wound in the earth, riddled with caves. It was through those thousand catacombs that the demonic troops had emerged into the forest.

Jhoira directed her mount up the ancient rill and into the slow time of Angelwood. She charged up the mounded pile of stone, knowing even then that fiend hordes moved through the caverns beneath her. The other five runners bounded up behind her. Karn toiled in silvery languor at the forest's edge. Jhoira's runner leapt up a knob of stone and scrambled across it to the other side. Before them loomed a sheer drop into the mouth of the main cave. Jhoira halted. The five other runners bounded into position beside her, their legs whining in complaint.

From the mossy cave mouth emerged a steady stream of Phyrexians, ambling four abreast into the hot undergrowth. The monstrous column fed the army massing on the plains. The tide could be stemmed right here.

Wishing Karn were faster, Jhoira wrangled her mount up beside a leaning boulder and drove the machine against it. Servos realigned, and the main thrusters of the modified runner flexed. The great stone grated heavily in its cradle. It tilted. Sand sifted from beneath it and rained down over the cave mouth. With one more shove, the runner sent the stone over. Jhoira frantically brought her mount back beneath her. It regained its balance on the verge of the cliff.

The boulder rolled out, tumbled for a moment in massive silence in midair, and smashed down atop a trio of hulking Phyrexians. The stone split like a peeled orange. Golden oil-blood, shattered bone, and pulped muscle mixed with stone shards and sand. The column of monsters behind the site drew reflexively back into the cave. They bunched up at the head of the army. It was now or never.

Jhoira rode her runner over the edge of the cliff. It came to ground on the oily ruin of the boulder and the beasts. Beside it, five other runners dropped. They landed on wheezing legs and pivoted. Crossbow bolts, sixteen from each runner, pelted into the Phyrexians massed in the cave. The ninety-six shafts struck and stuck in meat and bone. The vanguard of the Phyrexian line crumpled, and those behind withdrew a few paces more. It was enough.

Jhoira led the charge into the cave with her runner. It clambered over rock shards and the bodies of Phyrexians. The five others followed. She drew the slim sword that rode at her waist and brought it slicing down through the carapaced head of a negator. It gurgled but flung out its massive arms to drag her down. Leaving the blade in the thing's head, Jhoira vaulted from the saddle. Her mount charged on, out from under her, and swung its scythe blades to engage the fiend. To either side of it, the other runners latched onto their quarry. Ten blades swept out and caught five beasts.

Jhoira, meanwhile, ran toward the cave mouth. It would take only moments before the self-destruct mechanisms activated. . . .

The first, biggest blast came from her own mount. It macerated the beast that it held and sent Jhoira's sword flinging up into the ceiling of the cave. Bits of gore spattered the walls. The blast threw Jhoira free. She crashed among dewy leaves as the other five bombs ignited.

Fire and smoke, bone and stone, waves of belching sulfur . . . with a great, roaring rumble, the top of the cave went to pieces. It collapsed, slowly and magnificently, across the army of fiends, mashing them. Rubble sealed the passageway, mortaring it with glistening oil. The shattered hillside slumped downward in a vast landslide, and like a figure out of a dream, the silver man solemnly rode that slide down to ground.

He clambered from among the tumbled stones and charged to Jhoira's side, drawing her up in concern. "Are you all right?"

The woman smiled tightly, bloody scrapes across her face. "Well, we sealed off the advance."

Karn raised his head and stared warily into the forest.

Many of the lumbering monsters that had emerged ahead of the blast had turned at the sound of it. They converged in a fierce semicircle on the silver man and his friend.

"Yes, we sealed off the advance. Now we can attack them from behind like you said."

Jhoira staggered weakly to her feet and saw the approaching hordes. She sighed in resignation. "I don't imagine you could pick me up and outrun them—"

"I'm not built for speed," Karn answered sensibly.

A solemn nod was Jhoira's reply. "We didn't get rid of K'rrik, you know."

Karn seemed to consider. "We fought. That is all anyone could expect."

Jhoira looked up sadly at the golem and saw, reflected in his silvery hide, the hundred fiends tightening their circle. Some had teeth as long as swords. Others clawed their way forward on limbs as gnarled, strong, and numerous as mangrove roots. Lupine heads and barbed hackles, coiled stingers and bone-studded jaws, naked haunches and cloven hooves, pulsing poison sacs and pulsing brain sacs. . . .

"It has been a pleasure being your friend, Jhoira of the Ghitu," Karn said with elaborate solemnity.

She smiled brightly. "If I have to die—and all of us have to—I am glad I die beside you."

With a ululating cry, the monsters rushed in upon the pair. A forest of fangs and claws and stingers converged. Karn shielded Jhoira with his silver bulk.

There was only shrieking and blood and limbs flung outward to thrash the trees. Amid talons and teeth came blue flares of magic. Some coalesced into dagger swarms that buzzed like bees through the melee. Others spattered eyes and woke in them cannibal rage. Still others melted tooth and bone into chalky pools. Growls and gurgling. Blood and burning. Death and dismemberment. In moments, the furious carnage spent itself.

The forest grew still again.

Karn turned, confused. Jhoira emerged from the haven of his arms. There was someone else beside them suddenly, a blue-robed man with gray-brown hair. He brushed his hands together as though he had just closed a rather dusty door and then withdrew his fingers into sleeves designed for spell battle.

"Ah, here you are," Barrin said matter-of-factly. "The main battle is going well. When I heard the explosion here, I thought it must have been the work of you two."

Jhoira breathlessly surveyed the killing grounds. The forest reeked like an abattoir. "The fiends. You killed them. You cast a spell."

"A series of sorceries," Barrin replied. "Some of my best summonations and enchantments. They were well spent, though, and I can get them back. That's what libraries are for. I couldn't have gotten you two back."

"Gotten us b-back . . ." Jhoira repeated absently.

"Urza needs you in Shiv," Barrin said.

The master had been gone for a few months, and in the escalating Phyrexian war, Jhoira and Karn hadn't had much time to wonder about the success of the mission for Thran metal.

"I summoned him to aid with the battle—one of the reasons it is going well. Anyway, he says he's struck a deal with the Viashino. He needs you to be a liaison with them. He needs you and Teferi and a number of other students and scholars to help run things with the lizard men. I will stay behind with most of the academy. We will carry on this war until you return."

"And me?" Karn asked. "Does he need me?"

"Yes," Barrin said, his expression darkening. "Yes, Karn, he needs you perhaps most of all."

* * * * *

"No, the gray lever, not the red one," shouted Jhoira down the line of steaming pipe-work. Remembering herself, she repeated the instruction in Viashino.

Her dialect of the language was, of course, Ghitu and therefore somewhat difficult for the lizard men to understand. Even so, after half a year of working daily with lizard men, Jhoira was the only human who could speak Viashino at all. Urza couldn't exactly be called human. Just now, the creatures she spoke to cast quizzical looks up the foggy line of pipes.

"Gray, you know—the color of your blood. Red is the color of mine." Jhoira was almost frustrated enough to bite her own hand to demonstrate what she meant.

One of the younger lizards, a Diago Deerv, gestured emphatically at the appropriate lever. The scaly imbecile to his left grabbed the red lever anyway. Diago dealt a slap of his webbed hand—a bit of correction used by many members of Viashino society—reached over, himself, and drew the right lever.

A blast of steam came from the pipe stack behind Jhoira, venting into the black heights of the cavernous room. The stench of sulfur and superheated rock permeated the place. It boiled across the unseen vault, jiggling loose the condensation clinging there.

Hot drops pelted across her sweating back. Jhoira drew up a cloak of drake feathers, standard issue for workers in the lava pits. The feathers were proof against even the hottest temperatures, and yet they wicked sweat and heat away from the skin. Beneath the cloak, she wore only a loose, light shift of linen and similarly loose pantaloons. Her feet were shod with drake-feather slippers, and she had matching gloves in case she needed to handle any of the red-hot controls.

The vitreous pipes began to glow as lava came pumping up them. The heat of the chamber redoubled. In a few minutes, it would be a veritable oven.

"Let's get up to the blast furnaces," Jhoira instructed.

The scales of the lizard men prickled from faces, arms, and tails, struggling to bleed heat into the air. Wide-eyed and panting, the Viashino nodded their eagerness. It was one gesture they had picked up from their human colleagues.

"Good. Follow me."

Climbing over a jumble of dark tubes, unused and cracked from centuries of neglect, Jhoira led her contingent to the wooden ladder. Its iron rails would be too hot to touch, and even the wood was bearable only with drake-feather gloves. Jhoira ascended. Diago Deerv followed. His comrades came in his wake. Jhoira reached the hatch above, turned the thick metal wheel that disengaged the locking mechanism, and flung back the hasp. Hot air roared up around her as she clambered from the shaft.

Those in the chamber above—a bright, airy, space filled with giant, fat-walled furnaces and great slag buckets—turned to watch the sooty and sweating creatures emerge from their infernal under-world.

Among the workers in the furnace room was Teferi. The young man had traded impish games for a keen forcefulness of will and a relentless search for knowledge. Tall, lean, and wiry, Teferi was handsome and clear-eyed. His dark skin was yet unmarked by the care wrinkles of age, but his brown eyes held an amazingly intense focus. Though chronologically he was one-third Jhoira's age, they seemed physical as well as metaphysical twins now.

"Jhoira," he said, approaching her. The mage and the artificer were equal partners in this endeavor, overseeing the full deployment of the mana rig. "How many conduits do you have working now?"

"Twenty-five, if this one holds," Jhoira responded.

"That should be enough to fire all five furnaces," Teferi noted with approval. He flashed her an appreciative and dazzling smile.

"It's only a tenth of the major pipe ways," Jhoira replied. "I still can't get it out of my head there should be a lot more to this facil-ity than making metal. The power this place could draw from the volcano would be sufficient to run fifty furnaces, but there aren't fifty here. They must have used the power for something else."

Teferi moved in close to her, and a hint of his old capriciousness glinted in his eyes. He was still arrogant enough to use magic to enhance the twinkle in his eyes.

"I tell you, the answer lies in the taboo halls. I've been begging you for months to explore the place with me—"

"And jeopardize the alliance?" Jhoira hissed.

"As long as the drake Gherridarigaaz lives, the alliance will not be broken," Teferi said. "Come on. Say you'll come with me."

Jhoira sighed in resignation. "Once the metal works are fully operational. Until then, we have no time for messing around."

"That could be years," Teferi pressed.

"Well, make years into months, and you won't have to wait so long."

* * * * *

The approach to Gherridarigaaz's aerie was forbidding in the extreme. The lands in a ten-mile radius were goblin territory, and in it the voracious creatures were as thick as maggots on a carcass. In a two-mile radius, the dragon's nest was surrounded by a boiling sea of lava. The aerie itself perched atop a jagged pinnacle of stone that stood like a crooked finger in the center of the caldera. Other tumbled monoliths lay in the bubbling basin. They were spaced just far enough apart that no terrestrial creature in its right mind would try jumping stone to stone to reach the nest.

Neither Urza nor Karn were known for being in their right minds. Neither were they exactly terrestrial. They stood silently on the rocky verge of the magma pit. They had been in Shiv for over a year and still felt they walked the surface of an alien world. The audible shuffling of goblin feet, furtive and feral, in the wastelands behind them only added to the impression.

Urza stared for some time at the distant drake's nest, a huge encrustation of tree boughs woven together with black pitch and fired clay. He stooped, picked up a large stone, and hurled it with incredible force across the surface of the caldera. The stone skipped twelve times before melting away into nothing.

"We are, each of us, capable of leaping stone to stone to get there," Urza said idly.

"Yes," Karn replied.

Urza nodded, his nostrils flaring. Any living creature would have been poisoned by the gasses venting in twisted columns past them.

"I could cast a sorcery allowing us to lava-walk or to fly."

"Yes," Karn said.

Urza stooped to lift another stone, but thought better of it and squatted for some time, watching ghosts of steam promenade across the lava.

"I could conjure my own fire drakes and send them to slay this one."

"Yes," Karn said laconically. "You are Urza Planeswalker. You can do anything. You can wish us into the nest and wish Gherridarigaaz from existence. You can do anything you want. You are Urza Planes-walker."

It was Urza's turn to be laconic. "Yes."

Karn turned toward the scintillating man. "You can do anything, so why did you trade me away for an army of Thran-metal artifacts?"

The planeswalker's eyes hardened. "You answer your own question. Why wouldn't I trade one silver golem for an army of Thran-metal men? There is a great war coming. We must all make sacrifices."

"But you sacrifice me."

He had hardly spoken the words when, with a sudden, vertiginous whirl of movement, the cliff top melted away. The scarlet sea and sooty sky disappeared as well.

Karn stood still. Urza was planeswalking them into the aerie. A human could survive that trip only by being carried in a protective embolism, or turned to stone, or made a flat creature of immutable geometry. Karn merely rode as he was. Urza had sent him on more troubling journeys.

They arrived. The sooty sky remained above. The rest of the world was replaced by a vast, woven bowl of wood and clay, the lair of the fire drake. One corner was filled with a midden of bones, bleached and bare in the brimstone breezes. Beside it lay the half-eaten hulk of a small whale. It had apparently been plucked from the water like a herring caught by a kingfisher. The reek of the rotting sea creature was borne outward on clouds of flies. It mixed with the stench of sulfur and another smell—savage and salty and keen-edged like wood smoke—

Gherridarigaaz. The great drake herself lay in the opposite corner of the nest. She seemed at the moment only a huge pile of red skin, scales, feathers, and fur. Her great muzzle oozed twin streams of smoke. Soot tangled languidly among her spiky brows and rangy mantle. A pair of massive claws lay beside her face. Wings of skin folded over her flanks. The creature's scaly tail coiled on the rock-hard base of the nest.

Urza stepped toward the creature and said, without preamble, "I am Urza Planeswalker. I can kill you with a thought. I will kill you with a thought if you make any move to harm us, and I will kill you unless you cease your attacks upon the Viashino settlement."

The drake slowly lifted her head. Giant lids drew back from slit-pupiled eyes, filled with gold and black striations. The beast spoke. Her voice was vast and purring. "Not much for parley, are you?"

"Our message is understood," Urza said with finality.

"Understood, yes," the drake responded. "Obeyed, no."

"You have no alternative," Urza said.

"I do have an alternative," Gherridarigaaz corrected. "Death is an alternative."

"What creature would choose death over life?"

"A mother would," came the immediate response. "You have clearly not been a father."

Urza cast a long glance at the silver man at his side. "I have been a father."

"Oh, yes," purred the drake in remembrance. "Urza Planeswalker. I'm well enough aware of human mythology. Yes, you had a son. Harbin was his name. You blinded him when you destroyed Argoth. Some say you even sank his boat and killed him."

"I tried to keep him away from the war," Urza replied as if in reflex. "What I did, I did to save all Dominaria."

"You sacrificed your son to save the world," the drake said. "That is the difference between us, Planeswalker. I would sacrifice the world to save my son. I will not give up the fight to free him."

"Rhammidarigaaz chose to leave you. He chose to join the Viashino," Urza pointed out.

"Your son chose to join the war."

Urza's features drew into an angry knot. "I could kill you now."

"Yes, you could, Planeswalker. History says you would, but why, then, am I still alive?"

Urza cast one last, fierce glance at the creature. "You have been warned." With a thought, he and the silver man departed the fiery aerie.

* * * * *

Barrin ran. Fronds slapped him. He thrashed through underbrush.

The thing behind him was huge and sinuous. It slithered in his wake—a giant python, muscular, fleet, silent and cold-blooded. Its horned head was as large as the mage master himself. If it unhinged its jaw, it could swallow him whole. Two man-sized bulges distended its gut already.

"There have to be sorceries to defeat this thing. I know hundreds of them. It's just a matter of thinking . . . something about swamp-walking—?"

The mage master ran. He had been in the heat of combat when the thing had broken through the line. The beast's sudden appearance had interrupted a complex casting. Mana burn had lashed Barrin. He had fallen back. Jangled, he had wracked his brain for a defense but found none and ran.

This thing wasn't Phyrexian. It was summoned. The python had been invoked by a Phyrexian capable of casting spells. That was new. Apparently K'rrik had been decanting time-resistant mutants long enough to raise a wizard from their ranks, a wizard or two—or perhaps a small army of them. The giant serpent behind him was not only a terrifying man-eater, it was also a harbinger of greater evils to come.

Breath sawed Barrin's throat. Vines clawed his arms. The creature's cold breath billowed out around him. It almost had him. He redoubled his speed. Think! Think! Treacherous ground stole his feet. With a curse, Barrin tumbled. He crashed through a brake of undergrowth and smashed against a tree.

The serpent coiled into view. It reared up on a broad, shimmering belly of scales. Its mouth glimmered with teeth. Its jaw yawned wide and dislocated.

Barrin clawed behind the tree trunk. He hissed instinctually and glared into the thing's eyes.

"What is that summonation spell Teferi is working on? A creature that can cross time streams . . . Not the imps, but the other one—Teferi's Duck? No, that's wrong."

The monster coiled rapidly around the mage. It looped the tree and lunged.

"Teferi's Drake!"

A yellow-skinned dragon phased into being beside Barrin. It spread its wings in the tight confines of the jungle, and its head darted about angrily. Though the python was gigantic, in the shadow of the drake, it seemed only a worm beside a chicken. The drake's head jabbed downward. Its beaklike mouth snatched up the python.

The serpent riled in the monster's mouth. One of the man-sized lumps in it convulsed too, whether in defiance or digestion, Barrin couldn't tell. Arching its neck backward, the yellow drake sucked down the python and swallowed it in one gulp.

Barrin slid back down beside the tree, panting in dread. If he had been killed by that python, there would have been no one left to summon Urza, no one to lead the students. And there would be more giant pythons, more minions of evil. More Phyrexian mages . . .

How many wizards does K'rrik have?

Into his musings came the acute realization that the summoned drake stared down at him. Its eyes were at once empty and accusing, like the eyes of Karn. Then, as suddenly as it had arrived, it phased out of being.

That was the flaw in Teferi's spell. To date, the creatures he summoned could cross time rifts but remained in existence for only minutes. Barrin had known of this side effect, but he had been desperate. The drake had been created only to fight, disposable.

How like Karn. . . .

* * * * *

Karn sat on a stone escarpment on the mountain side of the mana rig. The ceramic arteries beneath the structure glowed with pulsing lava, pumped up from the caldera below. Within the plant, massive articulated arms would be cranking huge shafts. Steam shot in vast columns from the top of the rig. The whole thing rumbled and roared in a foul-tempered fury. The rig seemed a great beast, crouching in the red-black sunset, hissing into the sky, slurping from the lava pool.

They had brought it to life. After a year and a half of labor, Jhoira and Teferi and Urza had brought it to life. Jhoira had proven herself yet again the critical connection between Urza and the folk under his command. Teferi had come into his own as an innovative leader and mage. Together they had achieved an uneasy alliance between the human students and the Viashino workers. Urza, meanwhile, strong-armed the drake Gherridarigaaz out of attacking the facility. Even his presence was enough to reduce the constant goblin border battles to only sporadic incidents. The mountaintop was ruled by an iron fist in a velvet glove. All had progressed according to plan, and the first new castings of Thran metal were only moments from being poured.

They had brought it to life, but Karn felt dead.

Perhaps it was because Teferi had replaced him as Jhoira's closest companion. Their work to vivify the facility had made the close contact necessary. Their species had made the close contact welcomed. Karn felt no jealousy about this growing relationship and even was happy for Jhoira to have a friend made of flesh and bone. But between her work and Teferi, Jhoira no longer had time for long strolls or afternoon conversations with the silver man. He wished again for those bleak days together in the guard towers of Tolaria, but that was not what dragged at Karn.

No, the feeling of dread and death came from the sentence on his life. When all was said and done, he would belong to the lizard men. Urza had offered to move his intellectual-affective cortex to a new shell of Thran-metal, though the man could not promise Karn's mind would move with it.

With a sudden roar, the facility erupted into motion. Though the forbidden sections of the rig remained dark, windows across the rest of it flared with light. The very walls of the great machine rumbled and glowed. The patient roll and plunge of the facility's crankshafts and pistons accelerated to a deep and trembling drone. Jets of steam above the facility coalesced into a great, sooty cloud that blotted out sun and sky both and enwrapped the rig and the silver man in a choking fog.

He sat awhile longer, shrouded in gloom. The forges would be firing, the metals forming, the molds filling. Within the structure, a new army of metal men was being born. Outside of it, an old metal man was being killed.

All around him, small red eyes emerged from nearby crevices and caves. Unseen by the downhearted golem, goblins ventured up to the very verges of the rig, stood atop each others' shoulders to peer into windows, and set hundreds of tattered claws to whatever loose plate or door gap presented itself.

In one place, they found their way inside, hundreds of them.

Monologue

I do miss Urza, Jhoira, Karn, and—yes, I'll admit it—even Teferi. Their labors on the island before they left have given us a solid defense against Phyrexian incursion. I can only hope their labors in Shiv will do the same for the world itself.

K'rrik's machinations advance exponentially. Just because our artifact machines can repulse his current generation of negators does not mean they will repulse the ones that emerge in a few months—let alone any more negator mages who might make it out. We tracked down and slew the one who had summoned the python, but there will be others.

The students, colleagues, and I work hard to improve and adapt our designs, to suggest new machines and to create new spells, but even our fastest fast-time laboratories run at half the speed of K'rrik's.

It will come down to a final conflict—both here on Tolaria and out in Dominaria at large. To win our little war here, we'll need Urza and Jhoira and all the others. To win the coming conflict, we'll need a new machine, one designed by Urza himself, one that can

J. Robert King

adapt to anything, one with firepower greater than that of the whole island.

Urza started a design before he left. Perhaps he has finished it by now.

—Barrin, Mage Master of Tolaria

Chapter 14

"This is our salvation," Urza said.

He paced before the array of plans. They filled the semicircular wall of his high study in the mana rig. The room was an approximation of his library back on Tolaria, though the books that lined the shelves here were largely Thran, unreadable to anyone but Urza. Tonight, the shelves served to hold tacked plans, the latest wild imaginings of the artificer genius. With a slim pointer cast of the new batch of Thran metal, Urza indicated the sleek structure of the device.

"It is a flying machine, made entirely of Thran metal. It is driven by a matrix of powerstones, which take up much of the hull. With these stones, it is capable of faster-than-sound travel. Power can be diverted from the drive systems into various gun batteries—"

"What is it for?" Jhoira asked.

Among the group gathered, including Teferi, Karn, and a handful of other top scholars, the Ghitu woman seemed the only one willing to question the master.

Urza pivoted mid-sentence and looked at her, blinking. "Why, it is for war, war with Phyrexia."

Jhoira's brow furrowed. Teferi's hand clamped over her arm, but she spoke all the same.

"The metal and powerstones needed to construct that ship could

207

be used to make armies of warriors, which would be more effective against armies of fiends."

"Armies are slow," replied Urza. The lamplight of the darksome study glimmered from his queer eyes. "This machine will be able to move like lightning for quick strikes against specific targets—targets such as dragon engines and landing craft."

"How many such engines do you suspect the Phyrexians will have?"

"Perhaps hundreds," Urza said grimly, "perhaps thousands."

"Shouldn't we plan to build hundreds or thousands of machines like this?" Jhoira asked sensibly.

Urza looked nettled. "There aren't enough active powerstones on Dominaria to build two of these devices and any mechanical defenders."

Jhoira sighed, crossing her arms. "As fantastical and appealing as this idea might be, it seems to be impractical in the extreme. Unless we find some underground trove of powerstones, we must make the best use of the few we have."

A fiery light glimmered in Urza's eyes, and he seemed on the verge of snorting. He placed the tip of his Thran-metal pointer on the table and pressed upon it. The rod trembled with the master's anger. Instead of breaking, the metal only made a jagged line across the obsidian top. Wheeling, Urza tore the plans down from the wall, crumpled them, and flung them savagely in the corner.

"No more delays. I want the prototype Thran-metal man completed this month."

* * * * *

Teferi finished undoing the final bolt, pulled away the age-crusted grating, and gestured Jhoira into the dark crawlway beyond.

"The plans say that this space leads into the heart of the forbidden zone." His eyes gleamed with mischief. "The secrets of the mana rig await."

Jhoira glanced around again, trying to make sure no Viashino patrols were coming down the passage. "I think this is a mistake. If the lizards find out—"

"Tribal law forbids Viashino from entering the forbidden zone. It says nothing about humans," Teferi said, and his smile glinted in the dark space. "Besides, you promised. The metal works have been running at full capacity for a year now. I'm well overdue."

A laugh of resignation came from Jhoira. She shook her head, staring in amazement at the handsome young man. "Yes, Teferi, you are well overdue." She paused. The cloud of bygone days passed over her eyes. "You followed me down another passage like this, once."

Teferi only smiled.

"Some things never change."

So saying, she drew a dimly glowing powerstone from her pocket and waved it in the cobwebbed crawlspace before her. Taking a deep breath, she entered it.

Teferi followed closely behind. The space was tight, its height slightly shorter than Jhoira's thigh, its width slightly thinner than Teferi's shoulders. The effect was claustrophobic. Instead of an actual crawl, the two explorers had to move forward with an inchworm motion. Even so, the shaft did not seem an air duct. The floor was too solid, the walls were sided with moldings, and in places along it, constricting the space further, dull-edged hooks jutted from the walls.

Getting caught on one of these for a third time, Jhoira halted. She half-turned, panting, and let the dim glow of her powerstone reach out through the passage ahead. The walls, ceiling, and floor regressed to a gray-black square of emptiness. A cool, dank breeze came from it.

"There's got to be a reason it is forbidden," Jhoira whispered, sending sibilant echoes both ways from them.

"Yes, because whatever is in there is valuable, precious—"

"Perhaps even deadly," Jhoira finished for him. "It occurs to me that since this was your idea, you should have been the one leading."

Teferi didn't respond immediately. The sudden silence made Jhoira nervous. She craned her neck to make out the man. His powerstone flickered, and wedges of light danced wanly about them.

"Jhoira," he said at last, voice awed, "these hooks in the wall. You know what they are?"

"Triggers for deadfalls," she ventured wryly, "or poison darts?"

"Lamps," Teferi said, answering his own question. "These are lamp sconces. Look."

He lifted his powerstone toward the small curl of metal jutting near the top of the wall. The stone pulsed brighter as it rose, showing up a small, shiny parabola, and in front of it, a clip in a sconce. Teferi positioned the glowing rock in the clip, and suddenly it flared.

The explorers fell back, shading their eyes. Bright ribbons of light coursed out around them. Soon their eyes adjusted to what had once seemed a blinding glare, and they saw the hallway clearly.

That was what it was, a hallway made for creatures much shorter than the two humans. The floor was composed of venous marble, the walls of riveted metal, and at even intervals along the passage, lantern sconces hung.

"Who was it made for? Viashino?" Jhoira wondered aloud. "They'd have as much trouble as we are getting down this passage."

"Maybe the ancient Thran were little guys," Teferi speculated.

Jhoira shook her head. "Don't you remember the stories of Urza and Mishra finding the first ornithopter? Its seat and controls were human sized. No, this must have been someone else."

"You mean that someone other than the Thran built this place?"

"No," Jhoira responded, "I mean that the Thran built this place for someone else to run."

"A slave race?"

"Perhaps." Jhoira pivoted. "I see something ahead, off to one side. It looks like a doorway."

"Lead on, but be careful. Some of the Thran slaves might still be around." Teferi withdrew his powerstone from the sconce, and immediately the hall was plunged into darkness. It took awhile for their light-acclimated eyes to adjust to the murk.

Taking a deep breath, Jhoira inched forward until she reached the doorway. It was a short opening and narrow. The space beyond breathed hot, dry air past her. Cautiously, she extended her power-stone into the swimming blackness. It showed up a set of ceramic pipes, conduits crawling over each other like the viscera of some great leviathan. As her eyes grew accustomed to the darkness, she could make out, low in the tangle of tubes, a number of the greater pipes glowing faintly with the heat of the lava they carried.

Teferi crowded up beside her and confirmed her thoughts. "This is where those other channels empty. They are meant to power the machinery in the forbidden zone."

"We've accounted for only thirty percent of the lava tubes. If the other seventy percent were used for these other devices—"

"What would take that kind of power? What if it was mutagenic research, the kind of thing K'rrik's been doing?" Teferi volunteered.

Jhoira was dubious. "I can't imagine using such thermic power to create clone creatures. K'rrik certainly doesn't have that kind of power. Mutagenics comes more from tampering with the power of growing things. Remember the stories of Ashnod? Vats and chemicals and muscular fusion—"

Teferi's reply was wondering. "You really listened to all of Urza's lectures?"

Pushing onward down the corridor, Jhoira said, "The cool, dank air comes from ahead. There must be a big room up here."

Crawling, they came to a tight bend in the passage—a kink, as Teferi called it. Beyond, the passage widened and dipped into a debouchment with a pair of open doors. The chill in the air was undeniable here. The rustle of clothes slipped outward into silence before coming echoing back at them.

Jhoira extended her arm, powerstone held on her open palm. The light was too feeble to show up anything. Even with Teferi's glowing crystal alongside it, the space ate up the light.

"Well," Jhoira speculated, "either we venture blindly forward—"

"To fall into some open pit or other—"

"—or we try to find another light sconce or two."

"Here's one," Teferi said, slipping his powerstone into the bracket. As light leapt blindingly outward, Jhoira fitted her powerstone into a niche on the opposite side of the room.

The resulting glare filled the vast chamber, driving shadows back beyond a vault of riveted ribs. Metal struts and trusses lined the walls and ceiling, shot through by more tangles of pipe-work. The countless tubes—bristling here and there with valves and pressure gauges, pumps and release valves—entered the room through walls and floor, snaked in writhing piles of pipe across the chamber, and converged on a great central mass encased in scaffolding many stories high. To compare the network of tubes to vessels surrounding a giant heart would be to vastly underestimate the number of tangled channels. They formed a veritable thicket, through which the central mechanism was hardly distinguishable.

"What is it?" Teferi wondered, staggering to his feet before the massive machine.

Jhoira rose also. "Maybe you were right about the mutagenic experiments."

"Let's go see."

Teferi brushed dirt from his coveralls and started forward. He clambered over a dust-mantled manifold, noting the small ladders and causeways that gave access to them all.

Jhoira followed. Each footfall sent lint rolling up into the air. "It looks like the forbidden zone has truly been empty for some time."

"Unused, but not empty," Teferi ventured, pointing to a small, three-toed footprint on the far side of a cluster of pipes.

An adjacent channel held a three-fingered hand print. More tracks led away from the spot, into the lurking shadows behind the main mechanism.

"It's as though somebody watched us approach and scrambled away when we lit the place."

A wary look crossed Jhoira's face. "We've seen enough to make a meaningful report to Urza."

Teferi ignored the implication. "There's a porthole on the side of the main machine. It's only ten paces farther."

Without waiting for her approval, the young man strode onward. His footfalls obliterated the skittering tracks he had discovered. Jhoira fell in step behind him. Shadows deepened. The glare was reduced to triangular bright spots cast in kaleidoscope across the metal-plated bulk of the mechanism. Teferi and Jhoira reached the porthole. Teferi wiped centuries of dust from the face of the glass.

A dagger of light stabbed through the porthole glass and glinted across something within. The explorers crowded together at the window and gazed in.

"By the stones of Koilos!" Jhoira gasped.

That huge gem—the powerstone that had sundered at the touch of Urza and Mishra, driven the two into their fratricidal war, and opened the door to Phyrexia—could not have been a larger, more perfectly formed crystal than the stone at the center of the dark chamber. Beside it, glimmering in their hundreds, were many more gems, fist sized and double that, all lying in a dark jumble. If charged, any one of them could have powered a dragon engine.

"That's why this place is forbidden," said Teferi with awe. "It is a trove of powerstones."

"Not a trove," Jhoira said. "This is a machine for making them." In the moment of that staggering realization, Jhoira made a second. She hissed, "Teferi, we aren't alone."

The two whirled to face a toothy wall of short spears, thrust their way. Behind the savage shafts, small red eyes squinted in wicked little faces. Light from the wall sconces outlined the creatures' rumpled brows, their pointed ears, their wiry frames, and the obscene proliferation of bristly hair from ears and moles and shoulders.

"Goblins," Jhoira said.

Teferi raised his hands to cast a spell, but a ragged net fell over them both, interrupting the enchantment.

The net cinched tight. The wall sconces went dark. The spears converged.

* * * * *

They came from everywhere. They came from the caves where they had hidden from the Viashino patrols. They came from crevasses that sliced down into their underground warrens. They came even from the forbidden zones of the mana rig itself.

Goblins.

They came from everywhere, and they came in their thousands. Many of the hip-high invaders were the red-scaled Destrou clan that inhabited the hillsides around. They bore polearms surmounted by sharpened ram's horns, which curved close enough to their heads to leave ragged cuts along the creatures' shallow pates. Their long ears were pinned back—a sign of all-out war—and their prominent noses flared with battle howls.

Others were gray-skinned Grabbit goblins, somewhat smaller than the Destrou but nastier in combat due to their tendency to bite with small, serrated, and invariably filthy teeth. They also employed body slams, wearing studded-leather jerkins, breeches, and putties. Hurling themselves screaming into battle, Grabbits swarmed their victims, biting and spinning, shredding with teeth, claws, and hunks of metal, bone, and stone sewn into their clothes. They were savage, relentless, and formidable foes—but they weren't normally allies of the Destrou.

Nor were the third group of invaders, the silver-scaled Tristou goblins. Tall and thin, Tristou occupied the distant ridges of the caldera. Not normally a warlike race, Tristou were bone-rolling oracles and goblin visionaries given to week-long trances that yielded lengthy and largely unintelligible predictions of doom. Since the arrival of Urza, Tristou prophets had foreseen an upcoming war that would unite the goblin tribes. It would be an all-out battle against the Viashino.

The day of that war was at hand.

The Viashino and their human allies had desecrated the holy necropolis. Destrou sentries had captured two humans peering into the gemstone tomb. No goblin had looked upon that sacred place in a century of centuries for fear he would be struck dead by the ancestral spirits that dwelt in the stones within. These two humans not only gazed into the space but shone a light into it and hadn't even the courtesy to drop dead.

The united tribes determined the violators would drop dead— the violators and their Viashino allies. Word of the atrocity spread like wildfire from Destrou patrols in the necropolis, to the Grabbit warrens that riddled the volcanic hillsides around, through the steam tunnels and the guard posts stationed at the head of the sulfur vents, and to the distant oracle caves of the Tristou. The wave of angry whispers crashed upon these far shores and then returned, bearing on it a unified army of thousands of goblins. They bore torches and scourges, claw-headed warhammers, notched cleavers, dart-tubes, acid bladders, nets, daggers, teeth, claws, and the will to use them in all-out war with their neighbors.

They would fight to the death, and the two human hostages they held would assure their victory.

* * * * *

Urza had been working over his prototype Thran-metal man when the alarm went off. He looked up, gemstone eyes glinting in frustration. Whenever Jhoira and Teferi were off-duty, the alarms were almost continuous. Closing his eyes, Urza rubbed his temples. The sites were only mental projections, of course, but thus were all the more susceptible to psychosomatic ailments such as muscular tension and nervous spasms. He opened his eyes again. The half-assembled metal man stared blankly back at him.

It wasn't working. Thran metal grew. He had not recognized that fact before. He had assumed only that Jhoira's trinket necklaces were fashioned in various sizes. Now he knew that the large lizard pendants had grown from small ones.

The pieces of the Thran-metal man were growing too. His chest plates were already grating against each other and binding up the shoulder joints. Worse, the clockwork gears ground together, breaking off cogs, bending shafts, shattering flywheels. Even as Urza sat there, considering the slowly deforming mechanism, a great clang announced the sudden catastrophic failure of a strut in the creature's pelvis, and a groin plate slumped ignominiously.

Urza slouched back in his seat, wondering how long this alarm would be allowed to blare. The mana rig was like a giant bucket, amplifying the clamor until it was unbearable. Around the ringing corners of his mind, Urza chased an elusive thought . . . something about aligning growing parts according to the geometry of life, so that the pieces could expand in concert rather than in opposition. . . . A sphere shape or a three-dimensional oval, with internal mechanisms organized in nested shells, would allow for the growth of each level and that of the whole. Even in the shrieking air, he recognized the irony of designing a machine after the plan of Phyrexia with its nested planes. His gaze strayed to the abandoned plans for the Thran-metal ship—it was ovoid. Perhaps he could use the concentric organizational plan to structure . . . to allow the Thran metal . . . organization with the . . . make a growing—

"Enough—!" shouted Urza at the reeling ceiling.

The alarm was suddenly louder, jarring into the room with a flung-back door. Urza whirled angrily, seeing the silver man crouching in the too-small space.

"What is it?"

"Goblins. Goblins everywhere. Three tribes. The Viashino are losing," Karn said in a rush

"That's it," Urza growled, standing and growing a war cloak about his shoulders.

The stylus he had been holding grew into a glimmering staff, and he strode ahead of the silver golem, out the door and toward the battle.

* * * * *

The forge room was chaos. Viashino workers in their leather coveralls fought side by side with disheveled, human students. Wrenches and spanners flashed among double-bladed paortings, wrist daggers, and dragon-headed throwing axes. The lizard men fought in ragged clusters, backed up against the vast, glowing furnaces they tended. With desperate jabs and off-balance swings, they held at bay the loud, lapping tide of goblins.

They were everywhere. Gray Grabbits swarmed at the front. They hacked and gnawed at knees. Red-scaled Destrou crowded up behind their short comrades and swung ram-horn polearms above their heads. Here and there hooks caught lizard-man sleeves or wattles and dragged the victims onto the impaling gray horns. Behind that line, a few silver-skinned Tristou held the center of the floor and flung fire and lightning into the defenders' ranks.

Viashino were falling. Already seventeen workers and four warriors lay in pools of gray blood among the advancing goblins. Grabbits fed violently on these dead forms. Two more lizard warriors hung smoldering on the sides of furnaces. They had been backed against the sizzling metal, and their skin adhered. A few flailing minutes followed, and then the cooked reptiles turned to coal. Two human students also had died, one impaled on the end of a stolen paorting, and the other beneath the toothy tide of Grabbits. The remaining defenders, outnumbered, ill-armed, and overheated, languished in the verge between fire and spear.

Diago Deerv brought a gaping wrench down on the head of a Grabbit before him. It staved the beast's skull. He kicked the body among the mass of its comrades, giving them something besides him to eat.

"Where is Jhoira?" he gasped out to the workers around him. "She'd have an idea."

"An idea?" roared a nearby mechanic. A goblin torch rammed against his chest. The lizard man reared back on his tail and kicked the fire-wielding monster back among his fellows. The torch set another pair of Grabbits aflame. "We need an army, not an idea."

Diago blinked at the burning Grabbits. "Sometimes an idea's worth an army." He whirled, pulled a forge pole from its rack beside him, and slipped its hooked end into a large latch on the side of the forge.

"What are you doing? We're fighting goblins, not forges."

"Get back!" Diago shouted forcefully.

His comrades fell back, and in the next moment he flung open a slag gate in the side of the forge. Out poured a river of molten metal, spilling across the goblin hordes. Even the heedless and senseless Grabbits retreated from the blistering flood. Many weren't quick enough, swept under the tide and exploding as every liquid in their bodies turned instantly to gas. These small blasts sent red-hot spatters of metal out to burn other goblins.

Panting behind the flood, Diago gasped out, "Gives us a moment to breathe."

The warrior beside him was prickly, his scales jutting out all across his body. "I'd rather die by spear than by fire."

Diago looked up, toward the wide stairway that led down into the forge room. "Maybe we won't have to die at all."

Another tide rolled down the stairs—Viashino warriors, fully armed and armored, their paortings gleaming in a thicket as they waded into battle. Above the tide of warriors, another figure came, floating above the floor and emblazoned with fiery light. Urza Planeswalker drifted down, a second sun above his army. From his fingertips, bolts of power lanced outward. Where the red crazings struck, goblin bodies flipped up into the air. They tumbled like charred toys before clattering to the ground.

The straggling defenders let out a cheer.

Urza hovered into the center of the forge room. He lifted his hands together overhead. A white light awoke between his fingers. It shone across metal struts and trusses that hadn't been illuminated in millennia and then swept out in stunning waves. Rings of illumination moved over the gathered monsters, stilling them in the midst of battle. Upraised cleavers did not fall, frozen in air. Scourges followed one last course before going limp in the hands of their wielders. The magical staves of the Tristou flared and became rods of fire before fizzling away into sifting ash. In his last labor before the stilling waves of magic lay hold of him, Diago hauled hard on his hooked staff, drawing the slag sluice closed and stopping the flood of metal.

Next moment, even the war cries died away. All eyes turned to the floating figure.

Urza shouted over the throng. His voice was guttural, a collection of growls and harsh barks. The words, nonsensical to humans, made sense to the goblins and their ancient lizard foes.

"Surrender, all goblinkind. Throw down your weapons or face immediate destruction."

He made a sign, and three goblin figures—taller and more elaborately mantled than their fellows—rose into the air. The three chieftains kicked in struggle against the invisible claws that gripped them. They drifted toward the imperious figure.

Below them, among the goblin rank and file, nerveless claws opened, letting cleavers and axes fall to the floor. Grabbits withdrew, bloody mouthed, from corpses. Destrou dropped to one knee in sign of surrender. Tristou stood, spells forgotten on quivering lips. Even as they did, the pacifying waves of white energy gently cycled among them.

"I will speak with your chiefs about terms of surrender," Urza announced to the room.

He made a final gesture, bringing the floating creatures to a stop before him. They hung uncomfortably in the air, their robes of state trailing in bloody tatters.

Urza examined them. His uncanny eyes rested on each in turn. The Tristou chief was a wizened old creature, his eyes large and solemn behind a nose as withered and dark as a date. His robes were once fine—midnight blue with silver piping, though a scorch mark showed where his staff had blazed away. One claw had been burned brutally. Beside him, the chieftain of the Destrou was a warrior female, clad in gray leather armor from which taut red arms and legs protruded. She wore the scowl of bitter undefeat and kept her eyes lifted defiantly in the presence of her foe. The third chieftain was a mad imp, its small body wrapped in bloodied armor studded in teeth and metal shards. It fought angrily against its captivity.

"I am the lord of this rig," Urza said in forceful goblin tongue.

"You and your folk will withdraw. None of you will be left within five miles."

"These are our ancestral homelands," objected the silvery Tristou.

"You were permitted to live here until you attacked," Urza pointed out. "You have brought about your own exile."

"Our attack was provoked," the Destrou warrior chief said. "Two of your lieutenants desecrated our sacred necropolis."

"That does not matter," Urza said dismissively. "You have been utterly defeated. Withdraw from this facility and the lands around, or I will slay every last one of you who remains."

"We hold these lieutenants captive," the Destrou continued. "We hold them in a death cage. It is linked to me. At a moment's notice, I can make the cage collapse with them inside, killing them instantly. If I die, they die."

Urza studied the warrior woman. "You are lying."

"Their names are Jhoira and Teferi," the warrior chief replied.

Urza began a response, but the words jumbled on his tongue, and he quieted. He breathed, perhaps for the first time since entering the forge room.

"Take me to them. I must see they are alive."

"No," the Destrou chief replied. A file-toothed smile spread across her face. The tables had turned, and she savored the shift. "But you may speak with them." She nodded to the Tristou oracle, who used his charred claw to draw a black circle in the air.

Noises came from the circle—the jabber of goblins, the crackle of a fire, the shift of midnight winds.

"Teferi, Jhoira," Urza called, "can you hear me?"

A shifting sound came, and the clang of metal. "Who is it?" came a woman's voice."

"It is Urza. Where are you?"

"We don't know. A dark cavern. They have us in a strange cage."

"Is Teferi with you?"

The young man's voice answered, "Yes."

Urza's features darkened. "What is this they tell me about you desecrating their sacred necropolis?"

Teferi sighed. "We went into the forbidden zones. That must be what they mean."

Urza turned to the silvery oracle. "Your sacred necropolis is within the rig?"

"It is sacred to our ancestors. They dwelt in it, long before the lizard men," responded the Tristou with a twitch of his prune nose. "They dwelt in it with the old masters."

Before Urza could respond, Teferi offered, "It looked like it was designed for them. Everything is goblin sized—corridors and ladders and consoles. Viashino couldn't have operated or maintained any of the machines we saw."

The silvery oracle blinked placidly back at Urza.

"Are you saying your ancestors served the Thran?" Urza asked in hushed tones.

"There's more," Jhoira interrupted. "That sector of the rig—the largest sector—is devoted to making powerstones."

The planeswalker, despite himself, turned white.

The oracle spoke into the following silence: "Now, do we surrender to you, or do you surrender to us?"

Monologue

Urza arrived today with strange and marvelous news. He has just brokered a peace accord between five races.

Yes, Urza Planeswalker—defiler of Argoth, scourge of Terisiare, bane of Serra's Realm, destroyer of Tolaria, he whose name has become synonymous with mad and savage war—Urza has brokered peace. Viashino, Tristou, Destrou, Grabbit, and human now work hand in claw within the mana rig. To make matters more incredible, the two human prisoners of war caught desecrating the sacred necropolis of the goblins have been set in charge of returning the goblins to their ancient homelands in the rig and training them once again to run the machinery there. And, most incredible of all, what Jhoira, Teferi, and their goblin hordes will be producing are powerstones—large and perfectly engineered for whatever task Urza wishes.

He seemed mad again, relating all these things to me. He seemed as delighted as if he had just finished designing some vast, improbable, and powerful machine. In a way, that's what he has just done.

I was sad to report less stellar results for my own efforts. K'rrik's negators are growing more powerful by the week. Our laboratories can hardly keep up with the old designs. New versions of our runners are still months away from their initial trials. The spells we have marshaled have succeeded in blocking whatever summoned creatures and artifacts the Phyrexian mages have conjured, but we cannot keep up with their studies. I sense a final conflict coming. Even if K'rrik's forces do not overrun us soon, we will deplete our resources and workforce. Whether they win in a moment or in a million moments, they will win.

It was with this assessment that I pleaded for Urza to return and bring Jhoira and Teferi with him. He shrugged off the request, saying he had complete trust in me. He reminded me of the beacon, saying I could call on him at a moment's notice, and that was the end of it. He couldn't wait to return to his mana rig and the marvelous machines it would produce.

I cannot help feeling abandoned. Urza has learned much, indeed—he no longer forgets his past obligations, only ignores them.

—Barrin, Mage Master of Tolaria

Chapter 15

"This is our salvation," Urza said.

He addressed the same group of scholars—Jhoira, Teferi, and Karn at the head of the group—in the same study where he had first presented the design. The plans hanging behind the pacing master, however, were completely rethought. Thran metal was used only in key places. The rest of the structure was wooden.

"It will be capable of faster-than-sound travel, will be able to planeshift, will be fitted out with powerful offensive weapons, and is designed to bear its crew into the most hostile Phyrexian environments. It will be the ultimate strike weapon, arrayed to penetrate the enemy's defenses and destroy the heart of their attack."

Urza paused, as if waiting for Jhoira's objections. She coughed discreetly in her hand but offered no comment.

"One of the key changes to this design, you will notice, is its wooden hull. Given the properties of Thran metal—specifically its tendency to grow—I have determined that it is best used in conjunction with living materials, in this case wood—a specific kind of wood." Urza set down the pointer he had been using. "Given the excellent progress you have made in the new alliance, I feel the time is right for me to take a brief absence to secure the wooden components."

The once-silent crowd was suddenly on its feet, protests coming from them all.

"What are you talking about—"

"—bring us to this inferno and then leave—"

"—how are we supposed to keep them from killing each other—"

Jhoira's voice rose above the others. "—only reason the accord has worked as well as it has is because you are here, the everpresent and incalculable foe."

"Let them think I am still here then," Urza said. "If you want, I can even arrange a few illusory appearances during my absence. I'm speaking of only a few days away."

That assurance quieted much of the objection. Jhoira was still dubious, "What if it is longer?"

Urza seemed to consider, his eyes twinkling, and then he gave a small shrug. "You will manage. You always have. In the meantime, I have some new specifications for Thran-metal castings—the fittings for the ship. I want you to get started on them. Also, I have these specifications for the size and shape of the powerstone I need for the ship's engines. Jhoira, I want you and Teferi personally to oversee its creation."

* * * * *

Urza descended into the heart of a dense jungle, into the heart of an ancient dream.

It was called Yavimaya. Its ancient trees reached three thousand feet into the sky and three thousand feet into the ground, and three thousand years into the past. Just beneath Urza's feet—shod in gold-gilt sandals, suitable to his role as ambassador for all Dominaria—spread the tumbled landscape of treetops. Multiheaded crowns nodded sagely in the high winds. Among their shifting forms, giant limbs twisted, as large and brown as whole hillsides elsewhere.

In the hollows of some of the massive boughs, clear waters gleamed in wide and twisting lakes, thirty feet deep above smooth-skinned bark. Daily rains filled these raised lakes. Their verges hung with shaggy curtains of moss, and elven settlements crouched at their edges. Waterfalls cascaded from the lakes, down bows or empty air into the darksome forest below.

Urza did not stop among the elven folk. He sought none of the forest's inhabitants individually but all of them collectively. He sought the spirit of the forest itself—Yavimaya.

In places, a magnificent tree had succumbed at last to the colonies of worms and termites that riddled its city-sized trunk, or to the rot of deep roots in lightless slime, or to the implacable time clock within it, and had fallen. Many dead giants leaned against their neighbors, forming vast decaying ramps down into the murk. On such slopes, whole new ecologies of undergrowth and grazing beast and sharp-eyed hunter grew up. Other trees, the titanic ones that could not be held aloft in their creaking plummet toward ground, opened vast pits in the forest canopy, giving view down thousands of feet, past the mounded and rangy bulk of the world trees to the tangle of roots at their base.

Urza entered one of these empty shafts now. He watched in appreciation as the huge sprawl of tree summits rose to close out the sky. Only a large, ragged hole remained overhead. All around him, single-tree forests shivered bright green against the blue sky and its scrolling clouds. The high brakes of branch and bloom gave way to lower ranks of coiling vine and draping lichen. They in time surrendered to dark, cold, plunging depths, reached only by manifold waterfalls and the ever-dimmer sunlight. The air turned cold, wet, and biting.

Urza formed a thick, woolen cloak atop his silken robes of state. The fabrics fanned out on the cool wind, making him seem some great black spider descending an invisible thread.

In time, his gemstone eyes adjusted to the murk. He saw whole new worlds around him. The curved boughs were inhabited. Giant antlike creatures swarmed blackly over a knot in one of the ancient trees. The rotten center of the knot formed a great archway that gave into an enormous interior chamber. As Urza slid downward, he peered past guard ants poised at the brink of their colony and saw into the teeming blackness inside. There hunks of fruit and severed segments of leaf and dead carcasses of tree goats were borne along in caravans to inner storage places. Translucent white larvae lay in careful nests tended by tireless workers. A queen, who was the size of a parade of elephants, laboriously dragged her moving bulk, leaving a trail of wet globs in her wake. Just below the colony, placid herds of long-horned cattle grazed on terraces of bark. These beasts were tended by the ant creatures as though they were mere aphids in a garden.

A sheer drop lay beneath the cattle fields. A few hundred feet farther down, giant cobwebs clung. They held rolled white pouches—some vaguely cow-shaped, others ant-shaped, and still more with human or elven form. Urza was careful to steer clear of the sticky strands of web in his course toward the bottom.

Wherever life could cling, it did. Villages of elves dwelt on shallow swoops of tree bark. Forest sprites lived in spangled beauty among the deep dew fields. Dryads peered out distrustfully at him from folds of bark, and naiads glared from the silvery cascades that dropped from aerial lakes. Tree goats bounded up the sheer faces of the tree boles. Black-and gold-skinned cats stalked among fields of moss. Beneath it all, on the tangled roots at the base of the trees, druids appeared once in a while. They stared up at Urza in fierce resistance before disappearing beneath the ground.

He gazed down at the root cluster. As vast as the boughs above, the roots of the trees climbed over each other in a muscular jumble. In places, the tightly laced structures held dark pools of water or small banks of new tree growth. Where the roots did not connect, though, were triangular wells of darkness. During millennia of growth, the trees had depleted all the earth beneath them, drawing it up their boles. The result was a vast emptiness under the root cluster, broken only by more waterfalls and fat taproots. At the distant base of this murk, waters toiled in perpetual darkness. This was the realm of the forest druids, crisscrossed by thousands of causeways, stairs, and cave passages.

They would put up a fierce resistance to any program Urza might suggest. They would know of Argoth.

As Urza settled his gold-gilded feet on the root bulb of a massive tree, a sudden dread rose through him. This place was uncannily like Argoth. Its elves descended from those who had fled the forest he and Mishra had destroyed. There were ghosts here, the ghosts of Urza's past, but he had not come to commune with ghosts. He had come to discover the future.

Urza lifted his hands in invocation. "I am Urza Planeswalker. I have come for an audience with Yavimaya. We must discuss the coming war. I wish to ally myself with you. We must confer upon the fate of our world."

* * * * *

Multani had known the invader even before he spoke his name. The forest recognized the monster much as a body recognizes a contagion it had once suffered.

Defiler of Argoth, Destroyer of Elves, Terror's Twin, the End Man, Slayer of the People of the World—Urza Planeswalker.

Even as the man descended through the foliage of the upper forest, Multani surged up the bole of a great magnigoth tree. He gathered himself in myriad surges of sap and pulses of green wood. From the roots of that ancient colossus to its spreading crown thousands of feet above, the magnigoth came to exquisite life. The soul of the forest quickened every twig and leaf and tendril. Multani could have flexed the massive roots like the tentacles of a squid and marched the enormous tree through Yavimaya. He could have reached out with any of the magnigoth's hundred thousand boughs and snatched Urza and crushed him. He could have slain the man ten thousand times, in clouds of mold dust or swarms of arboreal spiders or lashing storms of boughs, but he did not, not yet.

This man was no mere man. He had become a power since Argoth. He had drawn the might of the land into him and was perhaps a match for Multani and Yavimaya. He had become a planeswalker and could wink into and out of existence with a thought. It would take a careful trap to capture this one. It would take all the mesmerizing force of the forest's mind to drive from the planeswalker any thought of escape. Only then could he could be contained. Only then would Argoth have its vengeance.

Until then, though, Multani would seduce the planeswalker into a trap. He watched patiently, following Urza down the trunk of the great tree. He would marshal the might of Yavimaya and lead Urza into doom, just as surely as Urza had led Argoth into doom.

A pang jagged through Multani. The man was calling on the land. He was summoning its power as he had back in Argoth. He was daring to compel the forest he said he had come to consult.

Multani sifted all the faster downward, hurrying to reach the spot where the man stood. No matter how many creatures Urza summoned, this was Multani's forest. He would take them back, free them from the bidding of the Defiler.

To treat with Yavimaya, Multani thought bitterly, you must treat with me.

* * * * *

Urza had finished his invocation, but the forest had not answered. He stood for some time, letting the verdant air sift over and around him. He could wait, of course. The forest knew he was here, sensed his power as assuredly as he sensed its, but Urza was never content to wait. He always felt better if he could tinker.

He reached into his vast reserves of sorcery and summoned forth a swarm of sprites.

A flowing cloud of gold and silver cleaved from the treetops high overhead and danced down on the breezes toward him. Urza watched in silent amazement. Though the cloud was still a thousand feet above, his gemstone eyes made out the tiny darting creatures within it. Winged and delicate, the sprites approached, a high song in their tiny throats. The melody ranged hypnotically through many tonal structures, sinuous and ineffable. Soon Urza could make out words in the song.

Return among us, child of ages.
Sing the reconciling song
And burn the pages where long
The sages condemned thee.
Sing, forgetful, sing
Of mild, regretful things
Before the forest's nodding head.
Let dead bury dead and then
Arise to sing again.

The words plucked strangely at Urza's mind. He remembered those voices, small and chimelike against the waterfall roar of wind in the leaves, remembered sprites fighting among druids and elven archers, their voices raised then in fury and condemnation. These creatures sang, instead, of reconciliation. They sang as though they were miniature Barrins.

Delighted, Urza moved to cast a second summoning spell. The sorcery was never completed. Already the forest responded. New ambassadors arose.

To the convolute roll of the gnat song came also a slow, low, gulping sound. It came from among the roots of the oriatorpic trees—shadowy gnomes within their barrows. Their tones made a basso counterpoint to the whistle-high melody.

O nations, rise into the dawning light
Where, bright, our generations' hope has come.
Speak, O dumb, and dance, O lame, the night
Of blame advances round to sun
And morning comes again.

Urza stood in the midst of the swelling chords, daring to hope that this ancient forest had grown up outside of the pall cast by Argoth's death. Perhaps short-lived sprites and gnomes would simply not remember that time. The folk who would not forget, could never forget, would be the elves. Urza needed to know their mind.

As though summoned, they came—elves of the high forest.

They came from behind every tree, from within every fold of root upon root. Their eyes were bright and wide in the gray twilight of the place and glowed, luminous and green. They came, singing too, their voices at last providing the main body of the chantlike round of the other creatures:

> Hello, Urza, we know of you
> From dark times past that nearly slew
> Us, every mother's son, and tore
> Our bodies limb from limb. That war
> Was hateful, true, but now we live
> In peace and health. We wish to give
> You all you ask, to save
> Our world from such a grave
> As once you dug that terrible day.

The three groups of singers converged around Urza. Sprites danced in glowing daisy chains in the air around him. Shadow gnomes scuttled from their burrows to crouch like toads upon the moss beds. Elves treaded with preternaturally light footfalls among the roots. Urza listened to their singing—his mind could hear each strain separately and all of them together. His foot lightly tapped the root ball where he stood.

He heard another voice, a deep rumble more massive and hollow and mournful than even Karn's. The sound came from all around, as though the air itself spoke. The clammy breath of it, though, came from behind Urza. He pivoted, seeing only a vast wound in the base of the tree. The gouge was three times his height. Bark had struggled hard to close over the gash. Great rolled lips of wood still strained to come together. Next moment, those same bark lips drew apart, and smaller rents in the side of the tree opened above. Knots rolled beneath. The wound spoke:

"Welcome, Urza Planeswalker. We are Multani, spirit of Yavimaya." The face in the wood was utterly mournful, the mask of tragedy with only shadows for eyes. "We remember you."

The planeswalker bowed his head and actually dropped to one knee on the root cluster. "Forgive me. What I did three millennia ago, I did to save Dominaria from hideous invaders."

"To Argoth, you and your brother *were* the hideous invaders," replied the voice, haunting as a chorus of the dead.

"I had to sacrifice Argoth or sacrifice the whole world," said Urza, almost pleading. "I did not doubt Titania of Argoth would have made the same choice were she strong enough to."

"Titania had been strong enough before they were despoiled," the tree spirit replied.

"As I said before, forgive me—"

"We are not Titania. We are not Argoth. We are Multani of Yavimaya. We have welcomed you," the voice said, and the lagging chorus of sprites, gnomes, and elves resumed.

The melody coursed, coy and yet somehow cloying, through Urza, like the dank wind moving through his robes. There was a wild geometry to the tones as they twisted in and out of each other. The notes trickled upon Urza. Waves of sound lay beside waves of energy, nudging them into their pattern. He closed his eyes a moment, struggling to assemble a response to Multani. Whenever a pair of words connected in his mind, though, they were soaked apart by the gentle nudge of the song.

"We would speak to you at length of this coming invasion."

Urza nodded, his eyes opening. He was slightly startled to realize he was standing. When had he risen to his feet? The question melted away on the pulsing song. Such matters were unimportant. There were allies here. There was music. For the first time since his ascension, Urza felt true joy. The sharp-edged box of his intellect softened into a warm, hazy buzz, like a swarm of bees—or a swarm of sprites.

"We would first treat you to a festival dinner to celebrate our newfound association."

Yes, thought Urza, I am hungry.

There was something wrong with that thought, something Urza could not quite identify. He couldn't remember the last time he had eaten. Of course he was hungry. If the forest's fare was as sumptuous as its music, he would eat himself sick. Surely there would be wine, and other delights to the appetites. Urza would indulge them all.

There was something wrong with that thought too. The nagging objections bubbled up, drowned, through the flood of music:

> Return among us, child of ages.
> Sing the reconciling song
> And burn the pages where long
> The sages condemned thee.
> Sing, forgetful, sing
> Of mild, regretful things
> Before the forest's nodding head.
> Let dead bury themselves in dead
> Sing, forgetful, sing.

When had he begun to sing? When had he ever not sung? Urza's voice, deep and resonant in the edifice of sound, moved among the smiling tones of the sprites and gnomes and elves. The mouth of the tree opened wide. The company of fairy folk guided Urza forward. He paced, solemn and happy, into the yawning space and down the throat of the enormous tree. There would be a feast in these deeps. There would be more music and lights and festival.

Except that all of it was behind him now. Darkness and wood and the irresistible power of Yavimaya pulsed in the very heart of the gigantic tree. Then, these things were all around. The mouth spoke one last time.

"We would speak to you at length, also, of the last invasion."

With that, the tree's mouth closed. Its throat as well. Urza, caught in wood and the thick darkness, wondered dimly where he was, and how he was, and who he was. He would be able to think, were it not for all the pervading mind of the forest, curing him like cedar smoke, changing him, preserving him in place.

But not preserving him. Urza felt his body dissolving away into wood. His fingers were the first to go, each burning with incandescent agony. His every nerve sizzled beneath the skin. His bones turned to chalk and rubbed away in the sooty gnawing of the heartwood around him. His fingers and toes, harvested slowly by the massive tree, turned into mere minerals.

"When Harbin, son of Urza Planeswalker, landed upon Argoth,

he sought a green limb to replace a spar on his flying machine. In its mercy, the forest showed him a fallen limb that perfectly suited his needs. In repayment, the man returned to the heart of Argive to bring back armies of ravagers to harvest the forest. Men and machines felled ancient trees, slew druids, hunted creatures into extinction, pillaged, burned, raped, destroyed, all to the glory of Urza and his brother Mishra. Slowly, they ate away at Argoth, killing Titania, her spirit."

The words were needless. Urza had become Titania. His body had become a vast forest. He felt in every tissue of his being the destroying, despoiling work of his own armies. Minute creatures invaded his body and, mote by mote, turned him into mere minerals, mere resources.

Urza would have screamed, but he was no longer Urza. He would have planeswalked from the spot, but that would mean leaving his body, the forest, behind. He could only hang there, encased in wood, and endure.

Monologue

Urza is arriving in Yavimaya even as I write this. I know the forest's position, as unreachable and forbidding as Shiv. He hopes to return in two days' time. Knowing Urza's sense of time—and guessing about the reception Yavimaya will have for him—I'll give him a week before I become unsettled.

This could well be the pivotal point for Urza. He has shown he is capable of building human alliances, and more than that—building coalitions among many races. Perhaps by creating an alliance with Yavimaya, he can make amends for Argoth. Perhaps no amount of penance could ever make amends for such atrocity.

We have our own atrocities under way in Tolaria. Just today I led a charge of scorpions against Phyrexian entrenchments at the border of Slate Waters. Given the physiology of my mechanical forces, a pincer movement naturally suggested itself. We flanked the main body of Phyrexians left and right and trapped them in their trenches. They were caught between us and the temporal curtain. I sent scorpion units flooding into their dens. Meanwhile, I drove a wall of wind down the middle. Flushed from cover, the beasts fell back into the time curtain at the edge of that charred swamp. I ordered a charge. We hurled them into the rift.

That passage would have killed any human. It did little more than further jangle these fiends. Even so, the extreme slow time of Slate Waters halted the Phyrexians in a thick wall. I ordered the scorpions to fire. Quarrels stormed out in a killing gale. The front line of Phyrexians was nearly sawed in half. They were spewing glistening oil in a cloud before them by the time a human contingent arrived to reinforce us.

One young woman tore a hunk of cloth from beneath her armor coat and doused it with oil from a fallen scorpion. She stuck the cloth on a spent quarrel, ignited it, and hurled the thing into the gap. It entered the spray of glistening oil. A dull orange glow spread from the spot. The fiery quarrel hung strangely in the air as slow flame rolled laterally out along the Phyrexian lines.

We stopped firing. We stood, staring in a mixture of exultation and dread. Languid tendrils of flame coiled out around fiendish arms and legs. We watched as our foes ignited. The cheer that came from us when hair and carapace were limned in flame devolved quickly to a groan. Eyeballs ruptured from the heat. Limbs were blasted away. The deep, horrid roar of dying monsters struck us.

"Back!" I yelled.

Even I was cemented in place when the blaze went critical. White hot, the flash was blinding. We fell back then by instinct alone. Clutching our eyes, we clambered over stalled scorpions and mired dead to escape the coming blaze. When the blast at last emerged from Slate Waters, most of us were half a mile into the forest. Even so, it flung us to our faces and, like the warriors on Argoth of old, we could only pray the sun-bright blast would someday end.

It will be another Argoth, this conflict. The Phyrexians press us day and night. Their numbers grow greater with each sally. Their magical might will soon be the equal of mine. The students are weary of fighting, and though I have employed my most awe-inspiring battle spells, I am not a charismatic leader. Jhoira and Teferi were better suited for that. Urza, despite all his inhumanity, perhaps leads best of all.

—Barrin, Mage Master of Tolaria

Chapter 16

Jhoira stood on the lofted control platform at the nexus of the mana rig. To one side of her stood Teferi and to the other, Karn.

Teferi watched over his workers—the goblin hordes that tended the crystal-manufacturing wing of the factory. It had been nearly two years since the Viashino-goblin war had concluded, and the forbidden zones were now fully functional. Each of the three clans of goblin—the silvery Tristou, the red Destrou, and even the irrepressible gray Grabbits—had aided in the cleaning and repair of the facility. In doing so, they had risen to their individual levels of ability. Chieftain Glosstongue Crackcrest of the Tristou had become the nominal leader of the three clans, but a certain manic Grabbit machinist had won over the masses with his antics, his nonsensical but volatile speeches, and his instinctive and incessant gladhanding. Though all decisions were made by Chief Crackcrest, they had to be approved by Machinist Terd.

The gray creature even now climbed to the observation post. He scrambled up a ladder engineered for goblins considerably larger than he. His much-spattered coveralls jangled with small shiny tools that no one had ever seen the goblin use—bits of metal Terd wore like talismans or awards. Despite his inability to perform actual work, the creature was in constant motion. His eyebrows—great knotted tufts of hair that were even more prominent than his prominent nose—were raining sweat down on his knobby chin. As he grabbed the rails of the control platform and pulled himself up beside Teferi, Terd gave a bright, sharp-toothed smile. It was one of his proudest features. A goblin with a full set of teeth was a rarity. One with white teeth was a messenger from the gods.

Terd kowtowed obscenely, tipping a little rag of felt that he considered a hat. "The rock thingies all ready." Terd's reports were no more explicit than his speeches. Interpreting them typically took a tedious game of charades.

Teferi gave a long-suffering sigh. "The ore conveyers?"

Terd shook his head with such abruptness that an umbrella of sweat unfolded from him onto all those around.

"The crystal presses?" Teferi guessed.

Terd pursed his scabby lips in thought and then whipped his head as though he were trying to rend the suggestion with his teeth.

"The Thran-metal molds?"

Ecstatic, Terd touched a withered finger to his nose. "Yes, yes. We make rocks today? Yes?"

Teferi shook his head. "Not until the ore conveyers and crystal presses are ready."

"You make Terd a pretty big rock."

"Yes," Teferi assured.

It had been one of the incentives provided the goblin workers that, once a month, when the rig was in operation, each would receive a small crystal—in fact only a cast-off shard from a cut stone. Even if a goblin had happened to get hold of a larger stone, none of the crystals from the rig would be imbued with power until it was charged with mana. Even the smallest of stones would permanently drain the mana from a large tract of land. To power a stone the size of the one Urza had designed for his flying ship would require the mana destruction of a whole world.

"Terd use his stone to be big magic man. Terd become big king of goblins."

"Yes," Teferi humored, "and that will be a bright day for us all."

"Terd go tell goblin scum—'Work faster! Work faster!' Then he be king sooner."

"Go do that."

Even as the irascible little fellow scuttled away down the ladder and shouted commands to his kinsmen, a very different liaison officer climbed the opposite ladder. Diago Deerv had proven himself a capable and level-headed lizard man in regearing the Thran forges. Now with the ancient enemy of the Viashino occupying half of the rig, it was only creatures such as Diago and Bey Fire Eye himself that kept the creatures from all-out revolt—Diago, the bey, and Jhoira's continual reminders that Urza would return any day.

Jhoira was not the official manager of the Thran forges. That job fell to Karn, the very creature who was promised to the lizard men in payment for their labors.

Diago rose to his full height on the platform—he had grown in the last four years—and looked Karn directly in the eye. "We've finished the castings Master Malzra requested. We ask that you come to approve them."

Karn nodded. "I am waiting for a report from the lava batteries. Then I can come with you."

Diago took a deep breath and spoke with a strained voice. "With the completion of these castings, we have fulfilled the terms of our agreement. We ask for payment of the price owed us."

Before Karn could answer, Jhoira interrupted, "Actually, we have still not successfully created a Thran-metal man." She glanced warily between reptile eyes and silver ones. "Those were the terms of our agreement."

"You've abandoned that project," Diago objected.

"Actually, no," Jhoira said quickly. "We have a new design, one that takes into account the metal's growth patterns."

"May I see these plans?" Diago asked.

"Tomorrow," Jhoira said. "I will provide them to you tomorrow. We can begin our castings then."

Diago wore a suspicious expression. "And once these new machines are cast—"

"Yes," Jhoira said, "then you will have your price. You will have the silver man."

Diago bowed low and backed down the ladder.

Jhoira, Karn, and Teferi traded sober looks.

"You don't have any new plans, do you?" Teferi asked.

Jhoira shrugged. "I have old plans—for Tolarian runners. I'll modify them tonight, taking into account Urza's nesting-doll pattern of construction. It'll hold them off awhile more. It may even prove a useful fighter for the Phyrexian wars."

That mention brought all of their thoughts around to Barrin and besieged Tolaria.

Jhoira spoke for them all. "I hope Urza returns soon."

* * * * *

Every axe-blow that struck the trees of Argoth bit into the man's limbs. Every fire that mantled his magnigoth trees flared through his veins. Every killing blast and grating landslide enervated him.

Urza was on the island. Urza and Mishra. Their names were plague and famine, fire and flood. From opposite ends of the land they tore at each other. They converged, and whatever stood between them was destroyed by their fury.

The man in the wood watched as ancient trees leaned and crackled and fell. Their bulk did not even rest on the root cluster before vast machines yanked and hewed and hacked them into beams and joists and planks—but mostly scrap. Bark and thin branches, leaves, and buds became only mounds of debris over which the killing machines rolled. Black snakes of smoke coiled into the troubled sky. There they joined great mountains of darkness, hovering as though in mourning.

What could drive those killing brothers? What passions?

And yet, the question seemed false. It was forced into the man in the wood from the outside. He knew just what drove them—ambition, curiosity, competition, vitality, and all of it enwrapped in a thin, tragic blanket of distrust. What drove them? The highest intentions and hopes. What directed them? The lowest emotion—fear. They were monsters, yes, but only because of their power. Were it not for their machines and their armies, they would not be monsters, but only little boys.

That thought brought a surge of anger from around the man. He railed. As sharp and tenacious as resin, reproof flowed into him. Urza and Mishra were true monsters. They despoiled all they touched. Their very flesh was corruption. Their only motivations were pure hatred.

The man in the wood resisted the welling flood of recrimination, holding his breath. He pushed back against the thoughts. They overtook him anyway and soaked into every pore and poured into his lungs—for every man must breathe.

There was something wrong in that thought, but the distinction drifted away on a fresh wave of agony. In that screaming space, there was no room for any excuse, any forgiveness, but only the undeniable sentence of guilt.

At the man's throat there came another sound of screaming and more visions. Not trees burning now, but people—white robed students. Not axe machines and levelers, but loping artifact creatures, some like headless emus, some like pouncing pumas, some like giant scorpions. Not armies of Argivians and Fallaji, but armies of fiends and negators, of killing monsters. They swept over another island, far away, not Argoth but . . . but . . . the name would not form in his mind.

In the face of this new, horrific assault, the armies of Urza and Mishra seemed civilized and noble. Felling trees seemed nothing in the face of burning children. An idea lurked there, something about the better war to fight, the war that could prevent the apocalypse.

That thought, too, was squeezed out of being in the furious fist of wood around the man. If only he could think. If only he could hold a thought in his head—a thought of his own . . . but then there was only pain.

* * * * *

Barrin watched from the gorge tower. It was the highest spot in the academy. Poised beyond reach of Phyrexian weapons, it curved out over the wall to peer into the dark swath. This spot was manned day and night, and of late, mainly by Barrin. From here he could gauge the movement of K'rrik's forces to any of the four bridges from the time pit. From here, Barrin stemmed the fiendish tide with long-range sorceries and enchantments. Intelligence gathered here allowed him to deploy his machine and human forces to intercept the attackers. And here, perhaps most importantly of all, lay the triggering mechanism for the beacon pendant Urza wore.

Barrin had just activated the beacon.

It had been nearly three years since Urza had gone to Yavimaya, and no one had heard from him. He could be dead, Barrin knew. Though planeswalkers were extremely long-lived, they could be killed, especially if their life-force became unfocused or dissipated. Still, it was a very difficult thing to kill a planeswalker, but not so to trap one. A planeswalker could be trapped in deception. If Urza did not think he needed to escape, he couldn't. If he forgot he could planeswalk, he could be trapped indefinitely. With Urza's fragile sanity and top-heavy psyche, such tricks could be easily accomplished. If he lived at all, he was trapped.

Perhaps, though, the beacon blaring into Urza's mind would startle him out of whatever malaise had laid hold of him.

Of course, there was a third possibility. Perhaps Urza had moved on. Perhaps he had gotten what he had wanted out of Tolaria and Shiv and Yavimaya and had gone some fourth place to assemble it all.

Whatever the cause of Urza's absence, the beacon summoned him. He must return to Tolaria in the next year, or there would be no Tolaria to return to.

The Phyrexians had just discovered a new bridge out of their pit: a deep spring that fed the academy's wells. One moonless night, they had poured up through every well head and cistern in the academy. The forces of Tolaria rallied and thrust back the monstrous intruders, fighting in their own home as they had fought beyond its walls. The beasts were slain wholesale, grates were affixed over any access to ground water, and new guard posts were created. The Phyrexians had yet to exact their worst death toll. Their dead bodies poisoned the water. Any who drank from the school water supplies in the next days developed a flesh-eating disease that turned their muscles to bloody mush and made bone as brittle as crackers. Twenty-three students and scholars died before the source of the contagion was discovered.

All water for drinking or washing had to be brought from distant wells beyond the school walls. Now, Phyrexians could rise right in the midst of the academy.

The Tolarian fortress had disappeared out from under Barrin. The siege had suddenly turned into a jungle battle—dark, desperate, chaotic, and finally, hopeless.

Barrin's hand squeezed the jeweled dagger that triggered the beacon. The enchanted item would convey to Urza whatever Barrin saw, whatever he thought—scenes of flesh-eaten friends and overrunning foes. Barrin said a silent prayer that Urza lived, and that Urza heard.

* * * * *

Jhoira paced uneasily before the line of Thran-metal defenders. Just behind her, Diago Deerv marched. His scaly hide bristled with nervousness as she looked over the machines. They were flawless. The original plan of the Tolarian runner had undergone numerous changes, including a more ovoid body, a deeper bend to the legs, and more capacity for armaments. Jhoira had overcome the difficulties of growing metal in this design, and these twelve fighters, if they ever reached Tolaria, could well prove indispensable in its defense.

If they ever reached Tolaria . . . she had stalled the lizard men for two more years, waiting for Urza to return and broker Karn's freedom. The man had not returned. Jhoira had decided he was dead. Once the Viashino and goblin tribes decided the same, the tenuous peace of the rig would be at an end.

Worse yet, news of Urza's long absence had at last reached the ears of the Shivan Drake Gherridarigaaz. She had resumed her strafing attacks on Viashino patrol posts, had cut off trade routes to the Ghitu tribes of the sea shores, and had dropped numerous boulders into the vent shafts above the city. Her son, who had willingly defected to the Viashino cause, decided he wanted to return to her. Apparently he was a typical child runaway, more intent on making a point than on gaining true independence. The Viashino had adamantly held him to his alliance agreement. The young creature went from being their champion to a caged and chained traitor.

What would they do about Urza's agreement? With the return of the fire drake, half of the bargain Urza offered had fallen through. This morning the other half was in danger.

What would it matter? Jhoira asked herself. If Urza is dead, Tolaria is destroyed, there will be no flying ship, and there will be no hope for Dominaria's delivery from Phyrexia. If Urza is dead, Shiv might well be the nicest place for Karn and the rest of them to live out what remained of their lives.

The words she spoke were somewhat different. "Excellent work, as always, Diago. You and your workers are extraordinary craftsmen."

"Judging from your tone, you have no more reason to delay the payment of our price," Diago said as the two of them reached the end of the line, where Karn stood.

Jhoira's jaw clenched. Muscles in her temples hardened. "No, Diago. I will delay no longer, but I offer you a different bargain. Instead of taking this one silver golem—nearly half a century old and battered and filled with all kinds of emotional entanglements— I offer you these twelve Thran-metal warriors."

A harsh edge entered Diago's eyes. "The agreement was for the silver man."

"Yes," Jhoira agreed, "and now I am offering you a different agreement."

A metallic hiss came from the lizard man's teeth. "No. We know how to build these creatures. They are not intelligent. We wish to have the silver man, to learn how to build an intelligent creature."

"But, he's not just a silver man, Diago," Jhoira said. "He's Karn. He has worked beside you all these years. Don't you care what he wants? Doesn't it bother you to make him your property, your slave?"

"We all are slaves to the tribe. To serve selflessly is the highest honor," Diago said. "Yes, he is Karn, a comrade. When he is given to us, he will be part of our tribe. He will be our greatest defender. He will teach us how to make armies of intelligent machines."

"Karn can't teach you that," Jhoira said. "I know more about his construction than he does. Master Malzra's the only one who really understands his emotional and intellectual abilities. Would you imprison me? Would you imprison Malzra?"

"We do not imprison creatures."

"What about Rhammidarigaaz?"

"He agreed to join us. And, as for Karn, Malzra agreed to grant him to us," Diago said. "And Karn can teach us how to build an intelligent machine. The secrets are inside of him. We will gain them. . . ."

"Enough," Karn said to Jhoira, cutting off her response. "I will go with them. I will teach them what I can. It is the highest honor to serve."

Open-mouthed, Jhoira watched as the lizard man and the silver man turned and walked away into the depths of the humming mana rig.

Monologue

They are everywhere. We cannot stand. We will not last the day. All will be dead. I still clutch the beacon, yet Urza does not come. We all will be dead.

—**Barrin, Mage Master of Tolaria**

Chapter 17

Barrin stood, white-knuckled and wide eyed, in the gorge tower. He clutched the beacon dagger in his hand and gaped as the world disintegrated around him.

A great roaring tide of Phyrexians swept toward the walls.

As a whole army, they were terror personified. As individual creatures, they were worse still. Many of the beasts were gigantic—white and meaty, seeming to have taken their forms from the blind shrimp larvae that infested the gorge lake. They scuttled on sharp, darting legs, their scaled backs hunched in heinous intent over minuscule eye nubs. Barbed antennae tasted the air. The warm brine of human blood drew them on. Others had wolflike figures, all warped and elephantine, with a mane of mange over leathery skin speckled in black and pink. Only their heads diverged from the lupine plan, small, yellow, puffy, and indrawn, like the heads of jaundiced babies. A vast number of the company were human or semihuman, though their bodies had been torqued and tortured into forms unrecognizable—leering death masks of flayed muscle, spidery arms with sinews realigned so that radius and ulna became opposing pincers, rib cages inset with spikes of stone or metal, bellies implanted with poison bladders that splashed foes in acid, hips that were no more than winnowed bone and tarry ligament, and legs that ended in sharpened spikes of bone. Most of the beasts bore weapons stripped from ruined runners or falcons. In a few places, machines of K'rrik's own design shambled among the monstrous hordes.

"We ourselves have armed them," Barrin whispered.

Against this onslaught of horror came the defenders of Tolaria. Barrin activated an array of powerstones, linked to mechanisms across the island. What falcons remained streaked down in furious flight. The white vapor trails behind them traced a converging fan across the sky. Impacting along the surging front, the falcons seemed to be allied lightning strikes. They brought with them a vast, rolling thunder. Fiends were hurled back into the chopping jaws of their fellows. The falcons' incandescent arrival was followed by the ratchet and whine of their shredding mechanisms. Blood—glistening oil and some substance that was bug-black, slime-green, and a shade of lavender that might have been pretty if it weren't steamy and acidic—fountained amid bounding chunks of meat and bone.

Barrin's delight at this grisly assault was short-lived. The hordes behind only splashed through the remains of their comrades and pressed the charge. Barrin squeezed the dagger handle and simultaneously signaled the second wave of defenders.

Hundreds of Tolarian runners lunged up from their trenches at the base of the wall. The machines loped into combat, their scythe wings poised to strike. They darted out, long-legged and fearless. The twang and whoosh of quarrels sounded from the ports that lined their bellies. Shafts soaked in anti-oil—a biologic poison designed to separate Phyrexian blood—thudded home in the pelting lines of monsters.

Phyrexians released a corporate shriek that rattled stones and sheared leaves from their branches. Another line of dead and dying went down, these not in a slick slough but a quaking mound of muscle and bone. The monstrous charge followed on, clambering over the fallen.

Tolarian runners met them, striking with twin blades. Some of the beasts were cut in half. Others were torn open at the belly and ran on a few paces before light fled their eyes and they rolled wetly in the dirt. A few were unstoppable. Though runners hung from scythes buried in their bellies, the beasts advanced, dauntless. They and a healthy horde of fiends surged into the waiting phalanx of scorpion engines.

Urza's scorpions were not designed for speed. With six legs, massive pincers, and darting tails, they were made to stand and fight. They held their position as the beast army fell on them. The first monsters literally fell, legs cut away. Their bleeding bulks dropped atop the stooped shoulders of the scorpions, who merely shrugged them off to snag the next comers. More Phyrexians lost their legs. A third wave leapt onto the backs of the beasts only to be undone by darting tail stingers.

The dead mounded up. In time, the machines' pincers became pinned beneath tons of oozing flesh. All the while, fiends fought onward into a hail of shafts from human guards on the walls.

Then, the first Phyrexian won through. It was a giant creature with a body as bulbous and pitted as an old gourd. It lulled past furiously stinging tails, rolled over the wall of dead, and crashed mightily against the stone rampart around the school. White arrows stood in a thicket across the beast's figure, but they did not stay it. The thing lunged again, smashing into the wall. A jagging crack opened from the battlements to the footings. More monsters clambered past the buried scorpions and reached the wall. They added their bulk to the giant's assaults or scampered up the cut edges of stone or flung tentacular digits to haul themselves over.

In moments, the walls would be breached, Barrin realized. They were already breached. The wells and cisterns poured monsters into the midst of the school. The battlefront had broken into a thousand pieces, and every scholar and ever student would fight the legions of hell alone.

Not entirely alone—Barrin's fingers danced across the glittering gemstones. He called all remaining pumas from their forest posts into the school. He awakened every mechanism in the Hall of Artifact Creatures—from Yotian warriors to Tawnos's clay men to *su-chi* loaders and conveyers and logging machines. Every last one would fight today—on this last day of Tolaria.

His summonations done, Barrin turned and descended into the dark spiral that led to the yard below. He would fight, too, with spells and staves and this dagger that had proven no other defense—and even his nails and teeth and bones, if it came to it. When it came to it.

Urza was dead, and soon all of Tolaria would be.

* * * * *

In the midst of all the shrieking wail of forest fires and trapped animals and tortured elves, the man in the wood heard a greater conflict: Phyrexian cries, mascerating machines, whistling arrows, men screaming, children dying, and in the throat of them all echoed one name.

Urza! Urza! Urza!

He knew the name of the Defiler. He knew the Bane of Argoth, but this Urza was a different one—a benevolent creature of great power, a mentor, an advocate, a protector. These voices did not cry out in hatred and rage, but in need and hope, in supplication. They cried out to a very different Urza.

They cried out to him.

In the deafening clamor of their voices, Urza remembered who he was.

The mind of the forest pressed in upon him with sudden violence, straining to quell the thought. After five years of torture and penance, Yavimaya's fury was spent. The forest had come to know the man it had so hated. It had subsumed him into its web of life. No, Yavimaya's fury was spent, and its rage was nothing beside the fury of the battle that summoned Urza.

He forced back the mind of the wood. He recomposed his being from the drifting shreds of it within the vast tree. He brought his mind into sudden, keen focus.

Yavimaya made one final grab at him. Multani, the soul of

Yavimaya, impelled himself into the form of the awakening planes-walker. He fused with the forming figure, struggling to root him in place, but it was too late.

Urza vanished from the heart of the tree. He was suspended for only a sliver of time in the fold between worlds, but during that moment he could feel a presence imprisoned within him: Multani. In a single instant, his captor had become his captive.

There was no time to think of Multani. Urza stepped from the wheel of eternities into a precise moment, a precise space. Walls of ancient, gray metal took shape around him. Large windows of dark glass, levers and gears, fire belching from glowing forges. It all came into being. None of these things mattered; only the sharp-eyed and dark-skinned Ghitu woman in their midst mattered. She had been crouched over a set of plans, arguing some point with a gesticulating goblin, when Urza arrived.

Jhoira whirled about, slack-jawed.

"Gather your best fighters. Tolaria is overrun. I will return and take you there."

He was already fading from being before his orders were complete. The shocked stare of Jhoira followed Urza into the spinning spaces. He sensed a similar amazement from Multani. That amazement redoubled the next moment as Urza stepped into the chaos of Tolaria.

The walls were breached. The guards along them were merely boneless heaps or red streaks on white stone. Phyrexians poured like roaches through the gaps. They flooded up from shattered grates hurriedly fastened over well heads. They swarmed through burst doorways and down stone corridors. They fought those who could resist and fastened teeth on those who couldn't. Throughout Urza's field of sight, monsters tossed students and scholars like white rags.

Urza rose from the dirt where his feet had alighted for a moment. He floated straight into the air and unleashed red bolts down the ring of wells in the main courtyard. The blasts of energy sailed down the throats of the channels. They flashed past the shadowy forms that scuttled upward. At the waterline, a sudden inferno erupted.

Red water and black-charred bodies geysered from the wells. The ground around each well head mounded up in swollen distress. In the next moment, rock and mortar and dirt cascaded down into fire-fused plugs. The wells were closed. The Phyrexians below would drown.

Urza spun about and cast another sorcery. Red beams darted out to each jagged breach in the walls. Limestone grew molten. It folded over the creatures struggling through the gap. It solidified. The wall was once again whole.

Urza kept rising. He hurled more fire outward, rings of the stuff. Force hissed from his hands in arcs of steam and coalesced over the walls to sweep away the raging throng. The vanguard of the attack turned to black statues and then sifting ash. Flames broke out in a great ball. Dancing orange fire shimmered across the black surge and headed toward the verges of the forest.

Still the killer, aren't you? said a mind within Urza. *You would slay every bird and beast to kill the creatures that oppose you.*

The wall of fire whirled in one last red roar before dissipating, not singeing so much as a leaf tip. The accuser within fell conspicuously silent. Urza allowed himself a small smile—until the next wave of monsters emerged from the eaves of the woods and stomped forward among twisted bodies and piles of dust.

"This is the horror I sought to stop in Argoth all those years ago," Urza explained to the presence within him. "This is the horror I still fight, but there will not be another Argoth."

Again only silence answered.

Urza's eyes glittered in their gemstone aspect. Extending a hand outward, he made a certain sign. One wing of the Phyrexian host swung in upon the other. Fiends leapt on fiends, bit through brains, sliced off heads. With another sweep of his hand, Urza dragged fallen beasts from the dead pile by the wall, digging free his ranks of scorpions. The machines hauled themselves from the slimy darkness where they had been buried and clambered toward the new line of advance.

"That should hold them for a moment," the planeswalker told himself. He drifted back down within the walls.

Below him, scores of machines, students, and scholars fought against the ubiquitous foe. Among them, one gray-haired man battled with an especial fury. He carried only a dagger but made it work like a sword—slashing, striking, parrying, piercing. Already around him on the dusty ground, monsters lay in piles. The dagger he wielded called to the pendant around Urza's throat. Even more, though, the man drew him. He sank a fatal blow in the dinner-plate eye of the creature he fought, and it spilled sloppily out of his way. Urza alighted where the beast had been and for his efforts got a dagger in the gut.

He smiled tightly, "Barrin, good to see you as well."

Turning white, Barrin drew his blade from the master's belly. It emerged, bloodless, and the man's belly and shirt formed themselves behind the retreating knife.

"Urza, I th-thought you were dead," he yammered stupidly.

"Not quite. I have mended the wall and staved off the main attack," Urza said urgently. "But this must end today. I must go kill K'rrik."

"We cannot last," Barrin gasped, almost pleading, "outnumbered, outmaneuvered . . . out of breath."

"I will bring reinforcements." So saying, Urza winked suddenly from existence. Like a man stepping across a hall from one room to another, Urza strode across the corridor of worlds and stepped into the forge-room of Shiv.

A sizable assembly awaited him. Jhoira was at the front of the group, with a rank of twelve modified Tolarian runners behind her—creatures of Thran metal. The platoon of humans numbered thirty-five, and included Teferi and all the other scholars and students brought to the land nearly a decade before. They were serious now, grown-up, and fire-hardened, like the metal they so expertly made. Beside them was a contingent of forty lizard men, including Diago Deerv and the picked warriors of the bey's personal bodyguard. The young fire drake Rhammidarigaaz accompanied them, along with Karn, the silver man. Next to these clean and orderly troops, a ragtag collection of jumpsuited goblins clustered. Many bore the crude tribal weapons they had brought to the rig five years ago. Others carried only the largest, heaviest, sharpest, or most wicked-looking items from their toolboxes.

Jhoira stepped forward with a military snap, accompanied by Diago Deerv and a scrappy little goblin with eyebrows that reached beyond his nose. This warrior gave what it considered to be a rigid salute. Jhoira addressed Urza.

"Your troops are assembled. Your allies have provided more than token forces."

"I see that," said Urza, his eyes flashing on Rhammidarigaaz and Karn. He indicated them and turned to Diago. "You realize, of course, that these two prizes of yours may be sacrificed in the coming battle."

"Sacrifice for the tribe is our highest honor," Diago responded with stern sincerity.

Urza's eyes passed one more time over the forces. Despite their numbers and their resolve, they would not be enough. He breathed deeply and said simply, "Come with me."

The planeswalking wave that swept out from him encompassed them all in an eye blink. It bore with it Urza's latest enchantment—a mass effect spell that turned the troops two dimensional while in the space between worlds. Thran-metal walls melted away to whirling chaos. Ancient enemies—Viashino, goblin, fire drake, human, and machine, hung flatly together in the emptiness, and then the company resolved out of air into the boiling battle of the Tolarian courtyard.

There was no time for orders. There were no columns marching into battle. There was only space for a breath and pivoting on one heel and striking whatever horrific figure loomed blackly up out of battle. The jangle of Thran-metal paortings joined the clang of goblin axes on carapace. The silver man fought with bare hands and gargantuan strength. The fire drake, the only beast that was a match in size for the gibbering monsters, slew with tail and claws and teeth and breath—all.

Tolaria's defenders gave a ragged cheer as the monsters faltered.

But it would still not be enough.

Urza planeswalked again. He left Tolaria for the lofted aerie of the ancient dragon, Gherridarigaaz. In moments, he appeared in the woven nest as he had before—sudden and stunning, businesslike.

"It is I, Urza Planeswalker," he announced.

The drake was huge and red against the great weave of tree bough and tar. She raised a grizzled head and regarded Urza angrily. "I thought you were dead."

"I can regain you your son, Great Gherridarigaaz."

Her head came erect. "Say on."

"You must fight for me. You must fight for me and the Viashino and the goblins. Your son fights for us, even now. I will take you to the place where Rhammidarigaaz is, and you must fight side by side with him, ally yourself with us, and save us in battle, and your son will be returned to you."

A suspicious glare entered the beast's narrowing eye. "Fight whom?"

Urza's eye was a sharp mirror of the drake's. "You must fight the enemy of us all, the creatures that would kill every last one of us, the monsters at the door."

"Ah, yes," said the drake slyly. "Urza and his Phyrexians."

"I have no time for games," Urza said sternly. "Come with me now and fight to regain your son, or do not come at all."

The drake lifted herself to her full, impressive height. She drew her wings tightly about scaly shoulders and darted her massive head in beside the planeswalker. "I go."

Urza took hold of the beast's shaggy mane and climbed onto her long neck. "Unfurl your wings," he ordered, "and prepare a gout of flame."

The drake complied. Her leathery wings stretched to their full extent.

"We go," Urza said.

With a thought the deed was done. Urza and the dragon folded into immutable geometry. Planar creatures, they careened through the pitching corridor of space. In moments, the veil of that middle place dropped away, replaced with rushing treetops and a bright, cloud-cluttered sky. Urza and his drake regained their third and fourth dimensions. Wings unfolded into rushing air.

Ahead, the Tolarian academy huddled on the hillside. Ropy black pillars of smoke rose from it. Gherridarigaaz gave one magnificent sweep of her wings. Pitching treetops rolled away. The drake broke out over the battleground. Below, monstrous creatures ran in their loping hundreds toward a thinly defended wall.

Drawing a deep breath, she hurled fire down on the Phyrexians. They burned away to greasy black smudges on the littered earth.

A cheer rose up from behind the academy wall. The great dragon soared and banked out over the Phyrexian gorge. Ballistae bolts leapt up from the rent and cracked past her wings. With a single surge, she climbed beyond their reach.

"Yes," Urza shouted to the creature through the wheeling winds. "Fight beside us, and you will have your son."

Then he was gone.

He stepped from the back of the wheeling beast.

The next moment he appeared elsewhere, in a peaceful corner of Tolaria.

His feet came to rest on a dam of rubble and mortar. The mighty barrier diverted water from the Phyrexian gorge. To one side of the broad pile of stone lurked the dark dome of K'rrik's fast-time loop. To the other side lay a vast, blue reservoir, water saved from the dank depths of the gorge. The lake was placid and mirror-still, far from the mad battle. Fishes darted through its depths. Trees around its edges cast their souls in its surface.

"Forgive me," Urza said simply.

Force blasted from his lowered fingertips. It pulverized the dam and hurled Urza into the air. Rocks separated. Water burst forward. The flood turned suddenly white, bearing in its brunt scouring teeth of rock and lime. It roared over the precipice and punched into the gorge. The belly of the lake slumped downward and followed.

Urza plummeted into the blue wall of water. It bore him along. It would disguise him.

It would protect him.

He would not be torn by crosscurrents of time.

He would not be impaled by ballista after ballista.

He would not even be seen in the jetting flood.

And once within the time rent, he would destroy the spawning grounds where these Phyrexian monstrosities were made, would hunt down K'rrik and kill him, and would cleanse Tolaria forever of the Phyrexian menace.

* * * * *

Jhoira brought her Thran-metal sword crashing down onto the head of a gigantic fiend. She split the creature's sagittal crest and sent it sprawling back against the broken wall of the infirmary. The beast's divided head came to rest against the sill of a second-story window. Within that window, more monsters preyed on the bed-bound patients. Giving a roar, Jhoira climbed the sloping corpse of her foe as though it were a staircase. Her sword crashed against the glazing and sent a spray of glass within. Roars and screams burst outward. Another swipe of her blade bashed flat the toothy shards of glass at the base of the window. She clambered over the sill.

Many of the patients were already dead. The rest had put up the best resistance they could with crutches and canes for weapons. One of the more alchemically minded students had made impressive use of the various anesthetic compounds in the chamber. He had also concocted blast powder in small vials and kept three Phyrexians at bay by casting exploding philters at the feet of the attackers.

Coming up behind them, Jhoira swung her sword at the thick, reptilian neck of one of the monsters. The Thran-metal blade sliced through flesh and bone like a knife through water. The head lolled free and toppled toward Jhoira, its eyes rolling and rows of triangular teeth snapping. By instinct alone, she caught the snarling thing by one pointed ear and thrust it away from her.

One of the beast's comrades—a giant with a wattle of bristly flesh—spun about to engage her. Its jaws roared open for a bite that could cut her in half. Again in reflex, Jhoira rammed the snapping head in the path of the teeth. The head clamped its dead bite on the living beast's tongue. Jhoira hardly had withdrawn her hand before the larger Phyrexian chomped down on the severed head. Bone and tooth crunched and burst outward in a tangle of flesh that lodged itself chokingly in the giant's wattle. It gasped and staggered aside, retching. Jhoira ended its agony with a jab up one nostril and into the creature's frontal lobe. It fell with a sick roar, wrenching Jhoira's blade from her hand and pinning it under its body.

A sharp pain exploded in her side. Jhoira flew limply across the room to crash into the wall. Something stalked toward her, a huge something with gray-scaled skin, small insectile eyes, and ears that flared into venomous spikes. It cast aside cots with the same ease it had cast her aside. Jhoira struggled backward but got caught in a tangle of canvas and broken wood. The beast lunged. Its claws spread wide.

Abruptly, against its gray bulk, there was a small figure in white. In one uplifted hand, the figure held a metal case filled with vials of the yellow-gray powder. Next moment, vials and case both were gone, rammed among the teeth. The monster's head blasted away, pelting the room with its pieces. The vacated corpse slumped heavily atop Jhoira.

"Are you all right?" Jhoira shouted into the sudden calm.

Her rescuer had spoken the exact same words. He rolled the dead bulk of the beast off of her, ducking away, and pried her sword from the other body.

"I'm all right," they assured each other, again in unison.

Jhoira gladly received the blade. She thanked the slight young man who handed it to her.

"Do you think you can make a stand here? Do you think you can hold the door and keep more of these things out?"

"Yes," the young man said bravely. "Yes, if nobody climbs in the way you came."

Jhoira struggled up and staggered to the window. The yard between the infirmary and the academy wall was nearly deserted now, occupied only by hundreds of dead Phyrexians, humans, Viashino, and goblins. Even Rhammidarigaaz had left the courtyard, taking wing with his mother. Together beyond the wall, they roared down from the skies, sending lines of fire and sulfur into the host there.

"There should be no more attacks from that quarter, unless they breach the wall again," Jhoira guessed. She strode toward the infirmary door. "The battle has moved inside. It'll be room to room now. Can you hold this one?"

"Yes," the man repeated.

"Good," Jhoira said and strode out into the hallway.

A great ruckus poured from the Hall of Artifact Creatures ahead. Sighing wearily, Jhoira ran toward the sound.

A room-to-room battle, with her friends in the rooms—Karn in the observatory, Teferi in the great hall, Diago in the master's study, Terd in the cellars, Barrin in the rectory, and Jhoira herself in the Hall of Artifact Creatures. A small smile played about her lips. What Phyrexian host could be a match for a group like that? She would have to remind Urza, as he constructed his flying warship, to make sure to man it with the best of crews.

Her face darkened. She would remind Urza if they both lived through the day.

* * * * *

Urza rose from the vile sludge at the base of the canyon. With an exertion of will, he sloughed the muck of dead fish and tenacious seaweed from his robes. The shallow lake churned with the flood that poured into the gorge behind him. Up in the Phyrexian city, though, all was still. Barrin had been right. K'rrik had thrown every able creature into the assault, wanting at long last to eradicate the school. The only Phyrexians who remained were ballistae crews, sentinels, and those incapable of passing the temporal barrier. Chief of those was, of course, K'rrik.

There would also be another crop of vat-grown monsters. Urza would not leave until they all were dead. From decades of observation, Urza knew where the mutagenic labs lay—deep within the basaltic extrusion on which the city was built. With a thought, he was in a dark, deep cavern.

An aisle of vats extended ahead of and behind him. Stonework stanchions stood between panels of smoky obsidian. Behind these panels were bays of glistening oil—Phyrexian blood and placental fluid. K'rrik had likely filled these cells by draining thousands of his citizens. The emptied husks would then have been diced and jerked to make food for the creatures developing in the tanks. Phyrexians had switched from natural to artificial means of reproduction when placentas began, in utero, to consume their mothers from the inside out.

The grotesque figures within these tanks seemed utterly capable of matricide. Though immature, most were the size of a full-grown human, with nictitating membranes over large and rheumy eyes, knobby shoulders, soft claws, oil-breathing lungs, and rows of legs, some thickening into actual limbs and others withering and dropping away, leaving only hip-nubs. In a number of the dark vats, vestigial leg bones hung from the half-formed teeth of the blind beasts, a snack between scheduled feedings.

Urza was sickened. He rose toward the cavern ceiling, out of the aisle of vats. It dropped away beneath him, revealing row upon row of vats beyond. One hundred, five hundred, twenty-five hundred . . . A network of bone catwalks ran above each row. Across the ivory causeway, machines scuttled, dipping probes into the glistening oil, dumping chips of dried meat onto the heads of hungry creatures, and skimming waste from the top. Urza recognized pieces from his falcon engines in the design of these nursemaid machines.

No wonder K'rrik has sent the whole city on this attack. In months of his own time, mere weeks outside, K'rrik would have a whole new city, a whole new army.

Not any longer—as Urza drifted up into the dark vault of the cavern, he lowered his hands, spread his fingers, and sent great blue flashes of lightning down into the vats. Where the bolts struck glistening oil, massive plumes of fire rose. The figures within the oil writhed. Blue-white sparks traced out their curved fangs and the venom sacks beneath their throats. Arcs leapt finger to finger, knee to toe. The creatures convulsed, churning the oil, feeding the fires. In moments, flames wreathed their exposed heads, and then mantled their shoulders, and then girded their hips. Thick skin burned and cracked and split and curled back, looking like bark. Muscle cooked. Bones burst. One by one, the waiting army of K'rrik stewed where they stood. At the last, as all the glistening oil flared into the air, the sudden intense heat change shattered the obsidian shells. Shards of glass and bits of burnt Phyrexian scattered down the aisles.

More lightning flared; more vats erupted. Half of them were gone. Urza panted, feeling the drain of power on him. He would recover quickly, of course, and needed only one spell to slay K'rrik. Until these all were destroyed, Tolaria would not be safe. Blue energy leapt from his fingers. Orange columns of fire blazed in the cavern night. Black clouds of soot and smoke belched up to roll at the height of the chamber. Dizzy with exertion, Urza blasted the last of the vats and watched as their inhabitants burned in putrid pyres.

This ought to flush out K'rrik.

Urza stopped breathing. The air in the space could be nothing but sheer poison. He lifted his eyes wearily toward the vault. There black smoke rolled in the deeper blackness of the cave. Something else moved there, too, something silvery and fleet and . . .

The shriek of the stooping falcon engine sliced through smoke and fire and oil. Urza raised his gaze just in time to see the creature's fierce eyes glinting above its knife-edged beak.

Impact.

Urza fell, struck from the sky like a sparrow. He crashed among oil-dripping glass shards. They were the least of his worries. His belly was filled with a mass of rending steel, macerated liver, and bone chips. The cometary creature had sliced into him and flung itself open. The whining whir of its shredding mechanism was unmistakable. The thing tore through muscle and viscera. It snapped ribs and rattled against backbone.

With a supreme effort of will, Urza stanched the flow of blood, reassembled tissues and organs, reconstructed himself out of the remembrance of being whole, but the machine was too quick. It destroyed any tissues that reformed.

Urza was being slain by his own invention, reprogrammed no longer to seek glistening oil but the smell of Urza's own blood.

It was his turn to writhe. He jittered across the shards of glass. Every moment, his mind threatened to blank out. There was not enough left of his physical form to sustain belief, to power the thought that would allow him to planeswalk and escape this horror. Perhaps if he had not spent such power on destroying the Phyrexian army, he could have mustered the strength. Now, though, he was pinned like a fly to a card. His gemstone eyes speckled with his own tossed blood. He struggled to reassemble himself, to draw each of those spots of blood back into the streams and vessels whence they came. The task was nearly impossible. He could not escape the machine, nor could he let himself merely die. He could only feel forever the ravening teeth of the device.

At least he had destroyed the army, if he hadn't destroyed K'rrik.

As though summoned by the thought, the man appeared. The term *man* could little apply to him now, though. K'rrik was little more than an animate skeleton. His time-vulnerable flesh had been mortified from his body over the centuries of his imprisonment. It had been replaced in patient succession by grafts of flesh from each new generation of negators. He had been slowly rebuilding himself, hoping some day to escape the gorge where he was imprisoned. His body now had a sinewy look to it, as though he were not a single man but a series of eels sewn together in the shape of a man. At the extremities of his figure—fingers, toes, knees, elbows, and brow—spikes had sprouted, most of them hollow-tipped and venom-dripping. Only the man's face remained roughly human in shape, and his eyes . . . they were bright and blue and human.

"After your last visit, Urza, I knew your weakness. Keep you near to death, and you cannot escape. Ballistae bolts and sword strokes are too clumsy, though. They leave moments of lucidity, and one moment is all it takes," K'rrik purred as he approached. His clawed and iron-heeled tread cracked chunks of glass as he walked. "This solution is much safer—and a nice piece of poetry. Thank you for the falcon engines. I have forty more, stationed around the gorge, should you succeed in planeswalking."

Urza, unable even to draw breath to respond, could only stare in stunned agony at his nemesis. As he focused his thoughts inward, on perpetual healing, one curl of his mind marveled that this monster spoke so well the tongues of men.

"That was your great mistake, Urza, coming here the first time. It taught us everything we needed to know. That has always been your great mistake, Urza, stumbling into our realm, letting us look you over, and then retreating while we prepared what we needed to kill you. You did it first in Koilos, and we followed you out. You did it again in Phyrexia, and we followed you out. You led us to Serra's Realm, you know. We attacked and invaded. They think they eventually defeated us, but we're still there. We've never left. We never leave a place, once you lead us to it. We've been engineering the transformation of Serra's Realm. The angels think they rule it still, but it is ours. It is one of our staging grounds for the full-scale invasion of your world.

"We've never left this place, either, and now, today, we have taken this island from you."

Urza wished his could spit his defiance. He wished he could remind K'rrik that his mutant army was dead, both inside the gorge and outside. He was left with only a handful of guards, and no matter how many modifications he underwent, K'rrik would never be able to squeeze his brain out of the time-cage where he was trapped. Urza wanted to say all this, but he could do nothing more than hold onto consciousness as he shivered across the rubble-strewn floor.

He didn't need to say any of it. K'rrik seemed to know. "By the way, you haven't destroyed all the vats. This is only the smallest chamber. I have three others. I have eight thousand warriors there. I have two thousand that are ready to emerge."

That was it then. K'rrik would taunt Urza awhile more, then draw his sword and lop off his head. Even if Urza could somehow muster the strength to planeswalk—which as that moment, he could not—he could not escape the time pit, could not even step beyond this death chamber. Three other falcons circled within the rolling black smoke overhead. That was it. Urza would die; K'rrik would live. Two thousand more Phyrexians would emerge to sweep away the final resistance. Six thousand more would emerge to make Tolaria a Phyrexian stronghold on Dominaria. The invasion Urza was only beginning to prepare for would be fully under way. That was it. All was lost.

"I see by the look in your . . . remarkable eyes that you have at last grasped your defeat, Urza Planeswalker. The seed of it was contained in those first moments at Koilos. From the beginning, you had lost everything." K'rrik advanced, drawing a scimitar with slow relish. "I had been hoping to watch your torment a bit longer, but it was only fun before you broke."

Urza shuddered with the unholy motion of the thing shredding his innards. He almost let go in that moment, if only to steal K'rrik's final victory, but an impulse arose in him to remain a moment more.

K'rrik towered over him now and lifted his scimitar high. "Good night, Planeswalker." The blade descended.

In the moment before it struck, a sudden surge of power filled Urza—strength from within him, but strength that was not his. Multani. It was strength enough for a single planeswalk. With the power came a whispered word, the one place to which Urza could planeswalk that would mask him from the falcons and give him the final victory.

K'rrik.

With a thought, Urza stepped out of space. He disappeared from the floor and the rattling creature. For a breath, he was in a nowhere place, but he did not linger there, lest the Phyrexian would understand. With a second thought, Urza stepped back into reality.

He emerged at the exact core of K'rrik's body. Urza's form of scintillating energy swelled into being from the spot, bursting the Phyrexian's flesh in a rain of meat and glistening oil. K'rrik exploded, and in his place stood an oil-drenched planeswalker. Bits of eel-skin spattered out across the ruined vats.

Urza held still, not daring to blink or breathe.

The falcon that had moments before been rending him rattled to a stop on the glass-strewn floor. It withdrew its gear-work wings and shredders, folded them against its sides, and turned its head quizzically. The machine seemed to sniff the air. It trotted forward a few paces and pecked experimentally at the glass shards. Then, in a rush of metal wings, the thing leapt into the air and climbed into the smoke clouds above, to join its counterparts.

Move quietly, came the voice of Multani within Urza. *We have three more chambers to cleanse.*

Urza complied. He rose quietly into the air, sought out a doorway leading from the cavern, and slid through the air toward it. As he drifted smoothly along, Urza sent a thought inward, toward the forest spirit that inhabited him. *Then we are allies?*

Multani's response came without pause. *You have known the agony of Argoth. We have known the agony of Phyrexia. If these are the creatures you fight, we are allies.*

A sigh escaped Urza. He watched nervously to see if any of the falcons would pick up the scent of his breath. When none did, Urza sent, *I am glad of it. I'll need your strength to finished cleansing the gorge.*

Multani replied, *When we are out of this pit, and back into the forested isle, I can conclude this battle for you.*

* * * * *

Jhoira had linked up with her old comrades as they purged the academy of Phyrexians. They had pursued the beasts out of every chamber and corridor in the place, at last cornering a knot of twelve monsters in the far courtyard. Here, though, the tide had turned.

The defenders of Tolaria found themselves fighting for their lives.

The situation was the same elsewhere. The Phyrexians had been forced from the battlefields by the drakes, runners, scorpions, and human fighters, but once in the woods, they held their ground, destroying whatever pumas dropped from the trees onto them. They would have slain thousands of Phyrexians, but whatever hundred survived would only return to the fast-time rent to rise again.

The defenders despaired.

The forests themselves rose. Tree branches swiped down to lash Phyrexian faces and tangle them in boughs and strangle them. Vines fastened around limbs and ripped them from their sockets. Mosquitoes and gnats and flies swarmed the monsters and flayed they alive. Leaves, hardened by some strange will, cut like daggers across fleeing legs.

Within the courtyard, the very grass beneath the feet of the twelve Phyrexians shot up in sudden life, piercing feet and slicing through legs and dragging the monsters down to their graves.

The shout that went up in that moment was weary and scattered, but it was the shout of victory.

Monologue

It is finished. The invasion of Tolaria is finished. I have never in my life felt so weary, incapable of even the simplest spell, incapable of even releasing this dagger I clutch so tightly.

But I did not save the island. Urza and his six-part alliance saved it, and if he can rally the folk of Dominaria like this, perhaps he can save the world after all.

—Barrin, Mage Master of Tolaria

Chapter 18

"They are in Serra's Realm, Barrin," Urza said nervously. Barrin was straightening the master's white and gold ceremonial robes, and all the fidgeting attention nettled Urza. "They've been engineering the whole decline of the plane, preparing it as a beachhead for their invasion of Dominaria. You aren't even listening."

Barrin released a long hot breath that only seemed to make the small pavilion tent more uncomfortable. "There will be time for war counsels later. Today is a day of alliances." He punctuated this speech with a snap of Urza's stole.

The master let out his own snort. Sweat seeped at his temples in the warm tent. He was so distracted with thoughts of devils among the Serra angels that he did not think to adjust his personal core temperature to be comfortable.

"They've followed me wherever I have gone. When Xantcha and I traveled the planes, wiping out Phyrexians, we were sewing them like seeds through the worlds. I tell you, the battle we have just fought is only the mildest prelude of the war to come."

"Yes," Barrin agreed placidly, dragging an errant strand of the man's hair back from his burnished brow, "and we just won the prelude. It is time to celebrate our victory with our allies." He backed up, looked the man over from head to foot, and nodded. "You look every inch the conquering hero."

"I feel defeated. There is no time to waste on ceremonies—"

Barrin grew suddenly stern. "To win the Battle of Tolaria, you had to enlist the aid of students and scholars, Viashino, goblins, fire drakes, and even the spirit of an ancient and distant forest. To win the Dominarian War, you'll have to enlist the aid of the whole world. The speech you give in the next few moments will cement the current alliance and lay the foundation stone for your planetary defenses. For once, Urza, don't run off to your clockwork contraptions. For once, Urza, be the statesman, speak to these delegates you have gathered. Reward them for the battle won and prepare them for the war ahead. Afterward, we can go sort things out in Serra's Realm."

The planeswalker's eyes flashed with something halfway between resentment and hurt. In that moment, Barrin remembered why it was that this great man, this near-god, so routinely retreated to his machines: among other humans, he was in fact a shy and fragile man.

"How do I look, Barrin?" Urza asked.

Barrin hitched his head. "You look ready."

Taking a deep and conscious breath, Urza clenched fists within his robe sleeves and strode toward the narrow, bright flap at the front of the pavilion tent. He emerged from the dark, stuffy enclosure onto a field awash in light and air.

The gathered delegates cheered.

Urza smiled. He could not help himself. There, arrayed before him in the bright glade, were the select representatives of his alliance: Jhoira, Teferi, and a contingent of Shivan students; Karn, Bey Fire Eye, Diago Derro, and the bey's personal bodyguard; Glosstongue Crackcrest, Machinist Terd, and the Destrou chieftain; Gherridarigaaz and Rhammidarigaaz; Multani and a contingent of Tolarian wood faeries; and of course Barrin with two other Tolarian scholars and a group of elite students. Sworn to secrecy about the location of this glade and what they would see here, the assemblage were nonetheless brought to witness for all their people the salvation Urza initiated for Dominaria. They represented the army of survivors. But they were more than survivors, they were victors.

Only a week ago, fires and Phyrexians, the dying and dead had filled the island. Tolaria's defenders had won the battle. They then had turned with equal vigor to scouring stones and rebuilding walls. The honored fallen of Tolaria now lay in decorous shrines about the old Teferi monument. The dead of Phyrexia had made a pyre that burned for three days, high and blue, beside the gorge whence they had come. Not even bones or carapace had survived that oil-fed flame. Thousands of spider artifacts, created by Urza and his associates in fast-time plateaus throughout the island, had been deployed to ensure that Phyrexians would never again plague the island, never again survive the rising of the Glimmer Moon. All that had remained of K'rrik and his negators was the vacant gorge and a reek that cleared away once the last ember of the funeral pyre was out.

There was no scent of death in this glade. Morning air shifted brightly. The forest was verdant, untouched by battle. Centennial trees hung green banners of leaf over the quiet space. Nature wore its finery.

The people did, too. Clothes of labor and mourning were gone, replaced by resplendent finery. The students' and scholars' robes of silk and linen shone in a panoply of ranks and colors. As they cheered, the fabrics flapped like flags in salute. The corps of Shivan humans were garbed in clean jumpsuits of red and wore expressions that were both grave and joyous. Bey Fire Eye's lizard warriors were clad in brightly dyed skins and carried the totems of their houses. Even Terd had submitted to a bath and a session with Tolarian tailors. At the back of the company, the fire drakes wore ornate red barding, surreal against the green jungle. Smoke drifted like dolorous incense up from their muzzles.

As the cheering died away, Urza found himself smiling again. He noticed the sweat was gone from his temples, and he took a deep breath.

"Children of Dominaria, welcome to this new dawn. We dwelt for a time in deep darkness, but now we have light. And I am thankful for the darkness if only in that it made us allies.

"I have hidden this island of mine from the world. I hide it still, that the forces of evil we have battled not find it again. But to you, my friends, it is open. The learning of this land—the clockwork and spell work—are open to you now, open to Viashino and Ghitu, to Grabbit and Destrou and Tristou, and to you, Gherridarigaaz and Rhammidarigaaz. The machines we have built will defend you as well as us. The knowledge we have gained will be shared among us all."

Applause answered this pronouncement, accompanied by eager hoots from Terd.

"By coming together—by ceasing our wars and burying our pasts—we arm ourselves for the future. Gherridarigaaz has regained her son not by slaying Viashino but by allying with them."

The ancient fire drake bowed her head in acknowledgment, and something akin to a grin spread across her toothy and fearsome face.

"The silver golem Karn—once owned by me and then by the lizard men—has won his freedom, proving himself in battle and service to us all."

Karn nodded his thanks to the Viashino bey stationed nearby.

Urza flung wide his hands in a grand gesture. "The Viashino, through our decade of alliance and with the guidance of Jhoira and Teferi, have produced this magnificent gift for the defense of our world."

He winked from existence for a moment. A murmur of uncertainty moved among the Viashino and goblins, but Teferi and Jhoira wore knowing smiles.

In the space of a long breath, Urza reappeared, hands still upraised. Before him, hanging in midair, was an ethereal ship. Glowing motes of blue magic outlined its long, sleek gunwales, its deep keel, its sideways-jutting masts and winglike spars and twining lines. Here and there, though, the ship was solid—metal pieces that gleamed like graphite but looked harder than steel. A sleek ram fronted the forecastle, trailing in its wake a series of floating portholes, joist plates, mast mountings, spar collars, cowlings, hinges, strike plates, doorknobs, and rivets. A large anchor and chain rested in the fore, just behind the ram. A pair of lateral sail mounts extended from the starboard and port walls. At the heart of the ship hovered a massive metal core that could only have been an engine.

There was no applause now, only sighs of wonder and open-mouthed stares.

"The workmanship of these fittings is superb. They will last an eternity. They will forever grow, drawn on by final causes from these fine beginnings into perfection. They will reshape themselves and become what is needed to save us all, to save our world.

"But this great ship, of course, is incomplete. It is not by artifice alone that our world will be saved. It is by life, too, by green mana. Our newest ally, Multani, spirit of the great and distant forest of Yavimaya, has brought with him a gift for Dominaria." Urza lifted a piece of wood, a large seed. "This is the Weatherseed, from the heart of the oldest magnigoth tree in Yavimaya, a tree that remembers the world before the Brothers' War, before the Phyrexians. It bears in it the essence of the ancient forest. It is the forest's heart."

A strange light had entered Karn's eyes. He stared at the Weatherseed as though it were his own affective cortex. In a way, the heart of Xantcha and the heart of Yavimaya were much the same. They would give life to Urza's machine.

The master held the Weatherseed high and strode to a clear oval of grass. "From this seed, through the aid of Multani, the ship's hull will grow."

So saying, Urza drove the wedge down into the soft earth. His arm disappeared to the elbow. When he drew forth his hand again, black soil clung, crumbling, all around it. He looked at the wound in the grass, seeing even then the forest spirit moving to weave the spot together. Urza stepped back as a bright cloud of shimmering creatures approached. Faeries. They strode from the woods, their very presence setting a hum in the air. They bore with them leaves folded into little cups. Gathered dewdrops glistened in each cup. As the faeries walked past the site, they poured the cool water onto the ground. The creatures bore their empty cups back into the woods as a continuing stream of their comrades followed with more water.

Once the line of cups ceased, other faeries marched out of the woods. Accoutered with slim battle blades and carapaced armor, they were stern-eyed and martial. They surrounded the spot where the Weatherseed had been planted, faced outward, and planted pikes.

Dumbfounded, Terd watched the fey creatures parade into position. The goblin wore a beatific grin on his face. His hoary claws twitched as though he wished to pluck at the faeries, but he resisted.

The Viashino, meanwhile, were watching the ground where the seed had disappeared. Already, silent and slender, a shaft had grown up from the mended hole. It spiraled up into the light, sending yellow leaves out to gather sunshine. In moments, the leaves deepened to green and proliferated. Twigs sprouted, swelling into branches. The small sapling shivered in a breeze that only it sensed and rose upward.

Urza made a gesture. With slow magnificence, the ethereal ship tilted, its prow rising into the air and its stern swinging down to hover over the growing tree. Soon, the great vessel stood on end. The questing boughs of the tree reached up to it, running along the metal plates and lines of force like rose branches up a trellis. They would spread out along the enchanted framework, taking inspiration from its design, melding without conforming.

All the while, quiet lingered in the glade. Urza's footsteps seemed loud as he retreated toward the tent. No one watched him, their eyes and minds and hearts captured by the spectacle of the ship taking form before them—the conjoining of mechanism and blossom, of artifice and nature, of history and destiny.

"Even now, the goblin tribes, once at war with Viashino and Ghitu and drake—"

"And each other!" shouted Terd. The group responded with laughter.

"And each other—these creatures are working on the matrix of a powerstone that will drive this great, saving machine."

Terd released a whooping cheer, which was taken up by Glosstongue and the Destrou chieftain, then spread to the rest of the crowd. There was accord in that sound. For a moment, they had ceased to be Viashino and goblin, human and machine. For a moment, they had become the voice of Dominaria. The cheer rolled out through the forests and startled birds from their placid perches.

The sound died away, and Urza spoke again. "To complete this great ship, I will need all of you, my allies, my friends. The Phyrexians are gone now from Tolaria and gone forever, but they are not gone from our world. Even now, they are taking over a world connected to ours, one step away from ours. I need your help to build this ship, but I also need your help to save another realm, for if it falls, so shall we."

Monologue

Well, I suppose I should have expected it. I'm the one who set this ball into motion. I am the one who insisted that Urza regain his past.

He began the road back to sanity when Xantcha provided him a facsimile for his brother—Ratepe. It was when this second Mishra died, again in an attempt to rid the world of Phyrexians, that Urza at last accepted the truth of his brother's death. He had begun to regain his sanity.

Then came the explosion of the time-travel machine. That blast did to Tolaria what the Brothers' War had done to Teresiare. In the dark hours after the blast, I had thought Urza was lost for good, but the death of Tolaria at his hands worked on him just as the death of Ratepe had. At last, in present-time microcosm, he had a facsimile of his past-time, macrocosmic mistake. With the destruction of the first academy on Tolaria, Urza began to understand the destruction of Argoth caused by the sylex and by the decades of war that made the sylex necessary. Urza returned to Tolaria to rebuild, to face the children of fury. He was nearer to sanity.

There was more penance to do. In its destruction and resurrection, Tolaria allowed Urza to make amends with the human world for the crimes against Argoth. He yet needed to be reconciled to the natural world.

Then came Yavimaya. Urza had gone there to seek the avatar of the forest, an entity that could grow the hull of his flying ship. What he got instead was a five-year penance for the agony of Argoth. Yavimaya remembered Argoth. Multani remembered Titania. He recognized Urza and made him pay for his past. In purging the guilt of Argoth, Multani returned Urza's sanity. And with his sanity, Urza could at last destroy the Phyrexian children of fury in his midst.

I've tried to tell him he is well, now. I've tried to tell him there is no more need to venture into the past, that now is the time to focus on the future. He only shakes his head and speaks of leading Phyrexians to Serra's Realm.

That will be Urza's next journey, perhaps his last. If K'rrik is to be believed, Phyrexians are there among the angels. I cannot imagine how Urza will survive, trapped between angels and devils.

—Barrin, Mage Master of Tolaria

PART IV

Between Angels and Devils

Chapter 19

Once again Urza descended. It was his preferred approach when arriving in unknown and hostile territory, and Serra's Realm, as it had devolved in the last few centuries, was indeed unknown and hostile.

It was still an empyrean skyscape, an arcing firmament stacked with rafts and mountains of cloud. Now, though, the once-blue sky was tinged in yellow and gray. A brimstone stink of Phyrexian glistening oil filled the air, and the realm's illusion of limitlessness had fallen away like a tattered robe. Heaven seemed cramped. The curve at the edge of it was just perceptible. The angel realm had once been a place of white cloud mesas, with large garden berms drifting placidly among them. Now the great berms had disintegrated into small clods, some only the size of shacks, and the sublime mountains had tumbled into pessimistic hills. Their color was muddied too, as though they were loosing their quintessence and transforming into dirt. All the lines had been blurred. Every constitution was diluted. Each ideal was debased.

Phyrexians were here. They excelled in such transformations.

Urza turned a slow spiral as he descended. Gemstone eyes marked out signs of habitation. At one time, the realm had needed no dwellings, for there was neither cold nor rain, night nor predators, and the very air nourished any who breathed it. Then, the only structures were built for sake of art or philosophical contemplation—pillared gardens, ivy-covered amphitheaters, high halls of state, groves of mana stones, galleries beneath the whirling heavens. Now many of those edifices clung in broken ruin to disintegrating clods of ground. Buildings not firmly rooted had fallen away in the tumbling chaos. Their foundations jutted like shattered teeth from rolling chunks of ground. Among these foundations new structures had been fashioned that seemed more the beige hives of mud-daubers than the homes of angels. They were hard-packed outside, and inside delved into spinning darkness—entrenchments against inclement weather and sudden night and marauding predators.

Phyrexians were here.

The smoke that rose from some of these deep hovels told of fires within to heat and dry the dark, cold spaces. The scent of flesh on that smoke told of creatures being hunted and slaughtered and eaten. No longer was breathing sufficient to sustain life. Now life had to be stolen from others who had it. Angels lived upon mortal flesh. The plane, once a living creature in its own right, had died. Every tissue and corpuscle of its being struggled to survive—preying on neighboring cells, drawing nourishment from the decaying body all around.

Phyrexians were here. They had killed the plane and taught the dying to eat the dead.

Only one fine structure remained, Serra's Palace. Urza glimpsed the palace, floating distant and dark within the gray sea of sky. It looked like an inverted question mark, a fact that had seemed fitting when Serra resided in the crystal aviary at its pinnacle. She had devoted herself and her realm to the constant debate of perfect society, perfect virtue, and perfect beauty. Questioning and discussion were an inescapable part of her realm. Now, though, the inverted question mark of the palace symbolized a place adrift, constant questioning become eternal doubt. It no longer meant debate, but confusion.

Toward that sign of confusion, Urza floated. As he neared the spot, he saw that it glinted more with rusted steel than silver. Its great banks of golden glass were shrouded in an orange grille, spiked and forbidding. Its ivory pilasters were chipped and yellow. The windows of its fanciful turrets had been knocked out to make space for batteries of ballistae and barracks of angel warriors.

These latter flooded out upon the acrid air, approaching the invader.

They were led by three archangels. Gigantic eagles' wings bore these creatures hurtling forward. In their hands glinted magna swords. Single-edged and curved at the tip, the blades were halfway between scimitars and axes. A carapace of massive silver plate armor covered each of them, and a skirt of metal mesh trailed behind. Silver masks hid their faces. In the wake of these three fierce defenders came a contingent of thirty-some warrior angels. Smaller and more lightly armored than the archangels, these creatures nevertheless bore wicked-tipped lances, round bracers, and expressions of fanatical loyalty.

Urza watched as they came. He readied the supernatural defenses of his planeswalking form. He would not fight these creatures, but they might fight him. Even if he could survive such a conflict, there would be more forces in the palace—archangels, angels, the Sisterhood of Serra, human warriors, and the citizens of the realm. He would have to win past them all and do it without fireballs and killing, to reach the embattled creature at the center of this collapsing plane. He had come not to conquer but to ally.

They swarmed up around him. Wings beat the yellow air. The three archangels formed a triangle that hemmed him in, and angel warriors orbited in a large sphere all around. Droning wings almost drowned out the stentorian command of the lead archangel.

"Approach no farther," the archangel said from behind the mask. Cold, ruthless, and almost metallic, the voice was neither male nor female. "You are uninvited."

"I am Urza Planeswalker," the man responded, his white robes of state stark against the brown clouds and fetid winds.

"We know," the archangel replied. "We remember the smell of you." The comment was spoken matter-of-factly, without humor or malice.

Urza's lips tightened. "Yes, but I do not recognize the smell of this place."

"Much has happened since you came. Much has happened because you came." With or without inflection, the implication of this statement was clear.

"That is why I have returned," Urza replied. "I have come to help restore the realm to its former splendor."

"It is not your concern, Planeswalker," the archangel said. "It is not your war."

"It is if I become your ally."

"Lady Radiant needs no allies."

"Radiant? Yes, I remember her. So, Radiant is in command now?"

"Yes."

"And she needs no allies?"

"Yes."

Urza cast an ironic glance around at the devolving realm. "It would seem to me she could use whatever help she could get."

"That is not for you to decide."

"Nor for you. Take me to her," Urza said in sudden command.

"You are uninvited."

"I could merely 'walk there." Urza lifted his hands threateningly to either side, and the sphere of angels widened just perceptibly. "I am Urza Planeswalker."

The angry buzz of wings deepened. Angels nervously fingered their lance hafts. The lead archangel drifted toward Urza. From behind its mask, air emerged, hot and steely.

"Come with us." The creature backed away from the planeswalker, its unseen eyes remaining ever on him.

Without further word, Urza followed through the droning air. All about him, angels hovered in static threat. Their shadows, pale and diffuse in the sickly glow of the sky, passed languidly over Urza as they went.

Ahead, the dark, overturned question mark grew. With each moment, its transformation was more apparent. Ogee arches above landing platforms bore boxy portcullises like iron false teeth. Fine traceries had been removed to make room for bulky grills. Crystal mana collectors had been replaced here and there by smoking chimneys. Lines of soot traced across buttresses, and blast points showed where the palace had sustained attack.

"Your palace has become a fortress," Urza noted, and he remembered a similar transformation of his academy.

"Only a temporary measure," the lead archangel said, maintaining his backward flight, "but, as you can see, the defenses are warranted."

Urza could see. He imagined Phyrexians swarming the palace, riding on their wicked skyships or flying on wings of steel. He could imagine salvos of bolts arcing from the engines and smashing against the floating city, could imagine angels much like these pouring from the shattered windows and staved walls. There was war in heaven, and he had brought it.

"Yes. Warranted. That's why I want to speak to Lady Radiant. Her foes are my foes. I know of the monsters lurking here, and I have armies of my own to help destroy them."

Behind its quicksilver mask, the archangel did not respond. It merely drifted backward, without apparent effort, toward a large landing platform at the base of the inverted question mark.

The platform jutted like an angry jaw from beneath a dark archway. Its edge was ringed with curved horns, the teeth of a great carnivore. A few flying machines hung in dock around it. Clusters of figures stood in their midst. Three were archangels and another handful angel warriors. Most of those on the air dock, though, were moiling crowds—angels and humans. They clustered together like fearful sheep. Guards strode around their group and jabbed with the butt of their spears. Some of the humans, packs on their backs, staggered up a wobbly gangplank and onto a waiting air boat. Meanwhile, in sad knots, angels broke from the rest, laboring out into empty air.

"Who are they?" asked Urza on the final approach to the landing.

The archangel before him sank lightly to stand on the crowded platform. Other angels around alighted as well. "Refugees, mostly, fleeing the rebels of the far reaches. They have come to the city for protection, but we have no room for them. Others are dissidents, heading for exile."

Urza nodded, setting feet to ground. The marble floor felt gritty, scored with stone chips broken off in some recent assault. "To what plane will they be exiled?"

"They will remain on this plane. No one leaves the realm, not even dissidents."

"And what of planeswalking visitors?" Urza prodded.

"Radiant awaits above," the archangel declared.

Walking backward in the midst of the landed flock, the angel guided Urza into the once-great city. The divine figure moved with a smooth ease, as though its feet still did not touch ground. It floated beneath yawning embouchment where refugees and dissidents huddled and brimstone breezes blew.

The spaces within were vast, dwarfing even the mob of angels around Urza. Tall, slender columns held aloft vaults of stone. When last Urza walked these halls, those vaults rang with lyric music and the sounds of lively debate. Now they roared with the shouts of sparring soldiers. Along the walls, rank upon rank of stone golems stood in mute insolence, ready to slay any army that might land upon the platform. The windows behind them were covered in black iron, giving the place a cave-gloom.

In the center of the main plaza, a great fountain stood, five stories high and ornately carved with angelic figures. If Urza remembered from his last visit, the statuary depicted the great virtues of Serra's Realm—Art, Discourse, Freedom, and Peace. No water flowed over that fountain anymore, though, and the figures representing these virtues stared out from beneath great rags of dust. At their feet, martial mounts—griffons and pegasi—drank from a half-full, stagnant pool.

Beyond the fountain, a great amphitheater sank into the floor. Urza remembered the glorious wall of golden glass that had stood beyond it. A rubble-and-mortar bulwark now sealed off the rear of the theater, protecting its users from aerial attack. A platoon of human holy warriors used the site. Before them paced an archangel, its sex-less voice instructing them in techniques for cleansing and sealing off Phyrexian catacomb complexes.

"—want to be certain none of them survive. Do not assume that any number of spell blasts will cleanse a warren. Enter, but do so with caution and in teams. Once within, there will be burned bodies. Make certain they are dead. Behead them. Do not let a single neck remain intact. Black mana spells can bring them back, even so. They heal with preternatural ease. Do not assume a warren is cleansed simply because all visible foes are dead and quiet. Search every space. They hide like rats. Look for secret chambers. Look especially for their offspring. These will be hidden best of all. Kill them. Behead them. Let not a single one remain, or it will become twenty and return to slay you. Use your soul torches to make certain the job is accomplished. . . ."

Urza reflected grimly on this advice, the same he would have given to anyone going with him into K'rrik's fast-time gorge—if anyone had been able to accompany him.

The archangel leading him glanced upward. The party had just reached a broad shaft that rankled upward past hundreds of floors and balconies and promenades. Even in its decayed state, the space was awe-inspiring, disappearing into blue distance a mile overhead.

"She awaits, above."

The angels, like a startled flock of doves, leaped suddenly into the air.

Urza accompanied them. As they rose, he saw the city in cross-section. The streets were deserted, the public squares taken over by encamped warriors, the windows darkened by plates or locked away in cages of steel. Hollow groans moved through the haunted struc-ture. Smoke seeped from forges. Boot steps echoed from armories. A jewel box no longer, Serra's Palace had become a weapon. It was a city under siege.

Urza thought of his distant Tolaria. It had once seemed as lost as this place. Now it was the nexus of a new alliance that spread across Dominaria. It had been a long battle to save the island. It would be a longer battle to save Serra's Realm, but it was a battle he would willingly fight.

They arrived. Urza drifted from the shaft into an enormous space, a circle of marble thousands of feet across. A vast hole in the center of the space opened onto a deep, verdant forest, a literal hanging garden, in which exotic birds flitted and sang. Above the marble circle rose mile-high windows of stained glass. All along the outer walls of the aviary tower, platforms and perches hung, where Lady Radiant's court conversed or planned or discussed. Banners of state, some with the sun-and-wing heraldry of Serra, and others with Radiant's own lantern-in-darkness design, floated on wires across the center of the tower.

Most impressive of all, the glistening-oil stink that tainted the air everywhere else was gone. Urza sensed the filtering work of great magic in the air.

He exhaled in awe. The aviary was the only pristine place in the realm—quite an exorbitance, given the aerial army it would take to protect the place. An angel nudged him with her staff and gestured toward the pinnacle of the aviary.

The archangel at the head of the party rose into the air. "Up."

As the contingent ascended up the tapered tower, the spaces around them closed in. Heat grew. In moments, palatial promenades gave way to large balconies. Golden windows narrowed. They changed too. As the party rose, simple triangles of glass gave way to powerful lenses. Light-bending enchantments lay thick on the panes. Some gave fragmentary views of other rooms in the palace. Others showed ruined gardens near the edge of the plane. Still more followed over the shoulder of one angel or another. Every floating continent, every tumbling clod, every shattered wall of the place had its own window. Figures—angelic and mortal—moved kaleidoscopically through the panes of glass.

All about Urza, angel warriors averted their eyes from the jarring mosaic of images. For them, the sight must have been dazzling and absurd. But Urza's multifaceted gaze could make sense of it. In this spot, he could see every corner of the realm. If he stayed here long enough, he could peer into every mind and heart in heaven. This all-seeing chamber had been the single most powerful tool at Serra's disposal. In it, she, or any other planeswalker, would be omniscient.

In the midst of the glaring windows hung her throne. The seat was grand, a pendulum dangling from the apex of the aviary. Its back was fashioned of pearl-inlaid gold. It was draped in red samite that curtained down into the hot space. It could pivot completely around and thus provide easy view of every pane of glass. The throne was politically well positioned too, requiring all supplicants to hover in air and crane their necks toward the one seated there.

The planeswalker Serra no longer occupied the throne. Now the seat held a mere angel—Radiant.

The woman sat the throne as though it were her eternal punishment. Myriad images shone from the windows and swam sickly over her. She endured their ceaseless caress, but her eyes showed no sign of deciphering the images. For her, the throne was no all-seeing seat but a torture chair dangling in the midst of an off-balance carousel. Her eyes were glassy from long exposure, and her hands clutched the throne like a pair of talons. She sat with the aspect of one terrified of heights and did not deign to look upon the company that hovered up beneath her. Golden hair and white wings draped in regal majesty about her, but her face showed nothing like royal grace—only desperate resolve. She had never been suited to rule the realm, not even at the height of her power. She had fallen far since then. The realm had decayed around her, and war had begun. She seemed grimly determined to see it through to the bitter end.

Though she did not look down, Lady Radiant recognized the prisoner. "Ah, Urza Planeswalker, returned at last to the scene of the crime?"

"Greetings, Lady Radiant," Urza said formally. He bowed in midair. "In a way, I have. I have returned for an alliance. I have returned to save you from your foes."

"Foes you brought to this place," Radiant pointed out. "Foes such as your consort, Xantcha."

"Xantcha was a friend, not a consort," Urza corrected placidly, "and she did not bring the Phyrexians here. I did. They followed me."

"They followed you and ruined us," Radiant said. "We drove them out once, but never has their taint left us."

Urza nodded in understanding. "Yes. The stench of Phyrexia is in the air. I sensed it the moment I arrived, faint but omnipresent. It is in the air, in the wind, off angel pinions, even in the lower palace. Only here, in this aviary, is the stench gone."

Lady Radiant's voice was strained. "It takes great feats of magic to make this air pure."

"But you cannot cleanse the whole realm. For that matter, you can never restore it to its old grandeur. With or without Phyrexians, all artificial planes collapse in time. This one is no exception. But I offer you salvation. I will bear you and all your people from this place and give you a new home on Dominaria. It will be as beautiful and grand as this place. And it will be yours. In return, you need only pledge your alliance to fight at my side against Phyrexia. Do not despair for this realm or for Serra's vision. Once the plane is empty, it can become part of our greatest weapon. It can charge the powerstone at the center of an airship that will defend our world."

"*Our* world," asked Radiant. Her eyes flashed with malice. "No. Dominaria is not *our* world. It is *your* world. *This* plane is our world. It is collapsing because of the fiends you brought here. I am fighting a war against those fiends. How dare you suggest we abandon our world? Would you abandon yours? Your old arrogance remains."

"Forgive me, Lady," Urza said, bowing. "Much of my old arrogance does remain. I did not realize how committed you were to this battle. I should have. I have just concluded my own private war against Phyrexia. They can hide in plain sight. They take human form, perhaps even the form of angels. There is no more insidious foe. In apology for my presumption, I would like to share with you the technologies I devised and the spells my mage master devised, to destroy them. If you will not ally with me on Dominaria, at least let me ally with you here. I offer myself, my machines, and my enchantments to aid in this private war of yours."

"It is exactly that," said a new voice, a man's voice, coming from a platform behind Urza. He pivoted in air to see a tall, thin man with a black goatee and eyes as slim and yellow as wedges of lemon. "It is a private war."

"Allow me to introduce my minister of war, Gorig," Radiant said regally.

The goateed man gave a shallow bow, though he never lowered his baleful eyes from the planeswalker. He gestured to his own features. "As you can see, I am a wielder of mana magic. I am also an able general. Our war is in hand, and it is private."

Urza demurred with a small smile. "I have learned no war is truly in hand."

Though she said nothing, Radiant suddenly drew all eyes to herself. Her face wore a strange, beaming intensity. "When first we knew you had returned, Urza, we expected you had come for war. You must excuse us for being so surprised by your offers of peace."

"It is a new man who stands—who floats before you," Urza explained.

"Yes," Radiant agreed, somewhat dismissive. "Before you commit yourself and your armies to this conflict, perhaps you would wish to accompany us on our next raid. We would like to view your combat strategies as well. Our next offensive will be launched in a few weeks. Stay with us and feast until then. Once we have battled shield to shield, as the saying goes, we will know if this alliance will benefit us both."

Urza nodded. "This counsel is well considered." He bowed low. "I gratefully accept your invitation."

At a motion from Radiant, the swarm of archangels and angels melted away beneath them, leaving only the planeswalker, the angel ruler of Serra's Realm, and the dark-bearded man, Gorig.

* * * * *

In one noisy wing of the Shivan mana rig, Jhoira and Karn peered through a glass port in the side of the crystal matrix chamber. Below the floor, magma engines channeled their searing heat into a concentrated beam of ruby light. It rose up a series of tubes, reflecting from panels of silvered glass positioned in exact alignment, and lanced into the matrix chamber. There the beam was split by a large lens, and split again, the four resulting bands of light rebounding through the space to sketch out in air the exact dimensions and cut lines of the airship's powerstone.

"An ethereal stone for an ethereal ship," Jhoira remarked acidly.

Karn glanced briefly toward her, wondering at her mood. "At the rate Multani is growing the hull, the ship is more than ether now. It's been over a month."

"I know," Jhoira snapped. She rose from the riveted superstructure, dusted off her hands, and whistled toward the scampering teams of goblins, signaling the magma pumps to accelerate. "Almost two. Urza is off on another of his endless journeys."

A quizzical gleam entered the silver man's eyes. "He has saved Tolaria. He has made alliances with Yavimaya. He has devised a great ship to save the world. Now he seeks to drive Phyrexians from another place. You can't fault him for that."

"I don't," Jhoira said impatiently. She stooped beside a pair of arguing goblins, entered the disagreement in their own dialect, pointed to a schema one of them held, delivered a pair of thumps to their heads, and sent them on their way. "It's just that Teferi is gone."

"He's what?" Karn asked.

"He'd said when we were leaving that he'd be heading for his homeland, Zhalfir. They were having a war of their own, and they could use a mage of his caliber. He wanted to say good-byes three weeks ago, but I put him off, said we'd have time when I'd returned from Shiv. I'd thought we would be here only two weeks."

"Perhaps he is still at Tolaria," Karn said. "Perhaps he is waiting for us to come back. What difference will a few weeks make?"

"Much difference, in time of war," Jhoira said. She angrily threw a great lever, sending lava into chutes around the matrix chamber. These channels of rock would solidify around the ionized center of the jewel matrix, providing a compression mold. "No, he's gone. He wouldn't wait for me. He couldn't wait for Urza. Last time Urza stepped out for a week, he was gone five years."

"He's changed, Jhoira," Karn replied. "Before that trip, he traded me away to the Viashino. Afterward, he negotiated to get me back."

Jhoira at last stopped working, letting labor slough from her shoulders. "This isn't about Urza; this is about Teferi."

Stomping up beside her, the silver man stood, awkward. He had long ago learned not to drape one of his massive arms over Jhoira in consolation, lest he crush her.

"We were best friends before Teferi. We can be best friends again."

She turned toward him, a trembling smile on her lips and tears welling in her eyes. "You're right, Karn. We've always been best friends. I was silly to think I needed more." A tremor of uncertainty underlay her words.

Hesitantly, Karn reached out to take her hand. "Urza has taken me back, and now you have as well."

"Yes," Jhoira said. She melted sadly against him.

Karn stood there, even more lonely than before. He was the only thinking, feeling machine among Urza's artifact creatures, and because of it, Urza had no idea what to do with him. Karn was not a colleague; nor was he a mere creation. He had been designed to journey through a time machine that no longer even existed. He was kept busy with a thousand duties, but he had no real purpose. Had he been any other artifact creature, Urza would already have junked him, melted down his parts, and made new machines.

Now, though Jhoira called him "best friend," her voice told of disappointment and resignation.

Standing there, Karn wondered if joining the junk pile would be a mercy.

Monologue

Teferi left just this morning. He took the refitted *New Tolaria*, and a small army of runners, pumas, and scorpions. I kept half the force—some five hundred units—but probably did not need to. The island has been cleansed of Phyrexians. Spider crystals fill the land. Zhalfir needs the machine warriors more than we do, but Teferi's ship would not hold more. As it was, I had to argue quite a while to get the proud young mage to accept the mechanical aid. I do not blame him. Though my association with Urza makes artifice a necessary study, I much prefer spell battles to mechanized ones. Of course, if one wants to win, one employs both.

I am seeing such necessary connections everywhere these days. The hull of the skyship is taking shape, day by day. Wood fuses with metal, and both grow together. I have spent many evenings with Multani. Weary in the suspiring night, he relates to me all he has learned from our fast- and slow-time forests. He speaks of young worlds and old, of the cycle of growth and decay. He tells how the blast that tore through Tolaria brought death in its first moments, and new and diverse life thereafter. He says that had it not been for the destruction of Argoth and the sinking of Teresiare, Yavimaya would never have risen. Life and death oppose each other, yes, but it is only in their opposition that either can exist at all. There is no death without life, and no life without death.

Magic and machine, metal and wood, life and death, Shivan fire drakes and Tolarian sea drakes, somehow, Urza has brought them all into alliance. Somehow, in the words of Multani himself, Urza has come to embody each of them. I have never had such hope for our world as I do now.

Urza has been gone too long in Serra's Realm. He seemed to think he would be able to quickly tell angels from devils. I have to wonder. If fire and water can become allies, perhaps good and evil can, too.

—Barrin, Mage Master of Tolaria

Chapter 20

Urza flew among echelons of Radiant's purification army. He wore a battle suit, much like the one he had devised for his assault on Phyrexia. The mechanized assault armor bore special protections against fire—he remembered well the conflagration of glistening oil in the gorge—and airborne poison. It was also proof against ballistae bolts. He bore a great black battle lance tipped with numerous blades, including a narrow axe and curved spearheads. From earlobes to toes, he was covered in black metal, scale mail, and power conduits. He realized with a certain irony that should he slay Phyrexian sleepers this day, he would seem more the monster and they more the humans.

Ahead of Urza to his left flew the commander of this echelon, an archangel as faceless and sexless as the others, its name unknown to Urza but its command unquestioned. It bore a magna sword that could cleave the head from a bull with one swipe. Behind the archangel, in a great cone, flew a contingent of fifty angel warriors, some armed with whips and nets, others with enchanted torches that flared blue-white and were said to turn the skin of Phyrexian newts yellow. The remainder carried swords for summary executions and head bags that would allow the dead to be counted and the skulls to be immolated, preventing grave magics from reviving them. At the rear of the party sailed an airship loaded gunwale to gunwale with white-suited holy warriors. These humans stood statue-still as the ship surged along. Their eyes stared golden and dead from their heads. Righteousness had been part of these warriors' demeanors when they first arrived in Serra's Realm, and ruthlessness had been learned along the way.

The flight of angels and avengers sighted their target ahead—a tumbled cluster of pulverized earth. What once had been an archipelago of aerial islands had been shattered into fragments of rock and grass. The remaining planetoids turned listlessly in midair. Some of them spewed uneven spirals of soot from the hovels dug in their sides.

"The Jumbles contain the single largest infestation of Phyrexians in the realm," Radiant had explained some days ago over a course of tea. The porcelain settings rattled with each stomp of boots drilling in the palace below. "They masquerade as angel folk and human outcasts—and to be sure, there are settlements of each among them—but there are wolves hiding among the dogs. You'll know them by their yellow-green cast in the light of the soul torches."

Urza lofted one such torch now. Others did the same. As yet, the light from the arcane brands was too distant and dim to pick out any creatures on the rolling boulders and hunks of ground. They would see soon enough. Angels swooped down with lightning speed.

The archangel commander made a series of crisp hand signals. The outer wings of the attack column broke away into sweeping lateral dives. Urza stayed with the leader, its core flight of twenty fighters, and the air barge. The other two units—fifteen angels each—soared outward to converge on their target like a pair of hammers. The main flight rose, following the archangel.

The field of rolling rubble dropped away beneath, revealing for the first time in its midst a series of larger aerial islands. The central force would land on the largest of these, purify it, and post a contingent there to secure it while proceeding to the second largest. Already refugee hives of mud and stick were visible below. The colony crouched in a hollow of stone beside a dead forest of gray stumps. The refugees must have been scavenging the ruined forest for firewood.

Another hand signal from the archangel indicated a flat rock bed just below the warren. They would land there. Like screaming falcon engines, the angels stooped from the sky. Their enchanted torches blazed all the brighter in the rushing air. The sight must have been horrifying from below—two-score sun-bright lights blazing down like comets, bringing with them a host of warrior angels and a boatload of angry humans. The sight must have seemed an apocalypse.

The angels came to ground at a run. They dashed up slope toward the gaping entry to the warrens.

Within, faces shone, yellow-green and wide-eyed. They flashed away into shadow.

The angel warriors homed in on those fleeting faces. Their strides lengthened. Their blades rose. There came no shout of fury or terror, as comes from mortal armies on the charge. Only the sizzling torches and the relentless boots announced their coming. Blue-white light bleached the gently rolling landscape. Glaring circles spilled into the shabby warren entrance.

As the charge closed, a mighty crunch and thud sounded behind. The ground leapt. The barge of holy warriors had beached itself. A clank and boom announced the fall of the troop door. Then came the human roar of fury and fear.

Meanwhile, Urza and his archangel commander had reached the warren's entrance. They charged within and rounded a corner. A pair of desperate blades swung weakly out toward them. The first caught on the archangel's massive shoulder plate. The second scraped dully against Urza's armored flank before clattering loose to the floor. The wielders—two young human-looking males—staggered back from the assault and flung up hands to ward off the archangel's torch-cudgel. In the blue-white glare of the torch, the young men glowed a ghastly shade of green.

A spell arced from the angel's gloved hand, pinioning the limbs of both men on spits of lightning. They paused only a moment before bursting outward in a rain of charred flesh. White flashes of life-force flared from the falling bodies and were drawn violently into the torches. Without pause, the archangel strode over the smoldering forms and into the narrow passage beyond. It was a spiraling descent that led into the heart of the aerial island. Urza followed.

Behind them, the main body of angel and human warriors entered. Two warriors took post at the cave mouth.

"They live in cold, squalid darkness down there, afraid of the light, of the truth," Radiant had said as she nibbled on a corner of toast. She had followed the comment with a wistful sigh. "It is as though the air that had once nourished all of us is poison to them."

The archangel led Urza and the rest of the cleansing contingent down the spiraling passage. It let out into a large central chamber. It was deserted. Five small fires leaked smoke into holes in the ceiling. A few middens of bone and trash lay near disheveled sleeping mats. From this central chamber, many dark side passages opened.

The archangel drifted regally into the middle of the cavern. He signaled the troops after him to scour the passageways. Two by two, the warriors pressed into the darkness. Torches flared. Voices cried out in terror. Lightnings crackled. Teams emerged.

Efficient, rapid, and ruthless.

Except that something was very wrong. As they had descended into the cavern, the Phyrexian stench of the air lessened until it was gone.

Urza swept quickly ahead of the brute squads, into a dark passage. His gemstone eyes dismantled the darkness, and he saw:

A very human family huddled in that tiny alcove—mother and father and child. Phyrexians did not make sleepers to resemble children. These folk clung to each other, cowering against unyielding stone. They stared through the blackness at the hulking figure of Urza. They muttered prayers to their angels.

Then the killers arrived. They swept past Urza. Their torches sent mirror-shards of blue and white scattering across the wall. Urza saw his own shadow cast, huge and malevolent, over the family.

Then torchlight broke out over them, and their skin glared yellow-green.

An axe rent the father's head, and a spear impaled mother and child both. Red blood came from them all in the moment before the incinerating blast. White fire gave way to black smoke and red welts in the eyes. In the midst of it, spinning ghosts poured from the cloven forms and were sucked away into the beaming torches.

An angel cast another sorcery. Glowing motes of sand followed the inner contours of the wall, seeking secret doors. When none were found, the killing team gave the all-clear whistle, shouldered their weapons, and marched out past the holy warrior posted at the entrance.

Urza followed them out. He soared to the archangel who hovered in the cavern midst. Arriving beside the commander, Urza spoke rapidly.

"Those torches don't work. They show human skin to be yellow-green also."

The archangel's response was unimpassioned. "We have no better way to proceed."

"You are killing your own folk. You are killing humans and angels, not Phyrexians!" Urza insisted.

"This is a private war," the archangel replied flatly.

"I can smell their blood."

"We cannot send you like a scent hound into every burrow—"

"You cannot keep killing innocent people—"

"You have done so—"

"I have done so to battle Phyrexia!"

"Phyrexia is here. You said it yourself!"

"The reek isn't here. It is in the palace—"

And then he knew he had said too much.

Even as the lightning bolt jagged out from the archangel's fingers, Urza stepped into the space between worlds and walked the halls of chaos.

* * * * *

Urza emerged in the height of the aviary. He was alone, for the moment. Radiant's throne stood empty. The nearest angels or guards lingered on platforms hundreds of feet below. He was alone, save for hundreds of spell triggers, silently tripping, one after another. He felt their sorcerous hooks drawing over him and retracting into the walls. He waited—for Radiant, for her personal guard, for whomever would answer the alarms. In the all-seeing panes of glass around, Urza glimpsed images of slaughter and death. The cleansing squads had not ceased their labors.

A globe of light leapt into being around him. Its surface roiled with fire. A score of angels rose in a fierce circle from the floor and, in moments, hemmed him in with spears.

She arrived. Whatever other enchantments lay upon the space, Radiant apparently maintained a summoning alarm. She appeared, seated in her punitive throne, wings and hair drooping over her sides. As her robes of state spread across the high throne, a darker being took form just behind Urza. Minister of War Gorig drew his tall, lean figure together from empty air and strode to the edge of the platform. His lemon-wedge eyes glared balefully at the planeswalker.

"To what do we owe this intrusion?" Lady Radiant asked from her lofted throne.

"Forgive my effrontery," Urza said, sketching an elaborate bow, "but the situation is urgent."

"You were to accompany our cleansing army at the Jumbles," she said. "You were fully provisioned and briefed. That battle is even now in progress. Why are you here?"

"Your cleansing army is killing humans and angels as well as Phyrexians," Urza said urgently. He flung a hand toward the images in the windows. "Look! See for yourself!"

Radiant involuntarily peered toward the scenes, and then reeled, her eyes swimming with violent images.

Gorig blinked in irritation. "There will always be civilian casualties in such operations. There are weeds among the grain. To root out the weeds, a few heads of grain will be lost. But to leave the weeds, they will all be lost."

"I sensed no Phyrexians in the main cavern we entered, and yet every living creature within was being slaughtered. They were humans. They were angels. They were not Phyrexians, and yet they died all the same."

Gorig's response sounded like a growl in his throat. "They were dissidents. They were traitors to the state. They were in league with Phyrexia, were in all respects but physiology Phyrexian. You do not know their crimes against the state and so cannot judge their fates. This war is a private matter."

"If you wish to be rid of these refugees—"

"These dissidents," corrected Radiant serenely.

"—these dissidents, I will prepare a place for them on Dominaria."

Radiant's fair features were tainted with distaste. "You would bear them to your world, even knowing Phyrexian sleepers hid among them?"

"Yes," Urza said without pause. The response seemed to surprise even him. "I would do my best to root out whatever Phyrexians lurked in their midst, but better the multitude of mortals survive to shield a handful of monsters than that they die to eliminate them."

Radiant glanced a question at her war minister.

Anger jagged across Gorig's features. "How can you possibly make this offer? If even one of the beasts survives, your whole world could be destroyed."

"I know that very well," Urza replied sternly, "and yet I make the offer. Lady Radiant, do you give me leave to rid you of your refugee problem?"

The woman's face had regained its placid composure. "I suppose it would save us casualties and weaponry merely to ship out the dissenters—"

"No," interrupted Gorig. "No one leaves. The doors of the realm are closed and will stay closed. No one leaves."

A protest formed itself on Urza's lips but never emerged. In a sudden flash, Urza understood. "No one leaves except me."

Even as he stepped across the dimensional threshold into that shifting space between worlds, the roar of Gorig followed him out, "Return and you will be slain. You are an enemy of the state, Planeswalker. You are Phyrexian!"

* * * * *

"Phyrexian sleepers are indeed in Serra's Realm," Urza said as he paced in his private study, "and they are transforming it, using it to prepare their invasion of Dominaria, but not as we had thought."

Mage Master Barrin sat grimly at the black-wood table. The shadows of the high study gathered about his shoulders. Beyond the window, in a distant glade, the nearly completed hull of the airship creaked in its slow, final expansions.

"The sleepers have fomented rebellion in the realm. They have sparked a civil war. They've done it not by stirring up dissidents among the citizens but by filling the palace with fear. Their leader is War Minister Gorig, who has shut down the discourse and debate that once filled the terraces and gardens of the realm and replaced them with tribunal and terror. Every day he declares more citizens traitors to the state and evicts them from the palace. They cannot leave the realm, though, and flee to refugee camps on broken islands at the edge of the plane. There they are hunted down as though for sport. All the while, the realm shrinks."

Barrin was nettled. He ran a hand through his ragged hair. "How does any of this advance the Phyrexian invasion?"

"White mana," Urza said. "Phyrexia has discovered a way to decant it, draw it off, and convert it into black mana. By slaying the refugees, they are harvesting white mana, drawing it into sorcerous torches that store the power until it can be taken to Phyrexia. Between raids Gorig must empty the torches into a soul battery. All the while, Serra's Realm is shrinking, and Phyrexia's reach is growing. Gorig will allow no one to leave because he is harvesting their souls."

A specter crossed Barrin's eyes. "Harvesting them . . ." He shook his head, dumbfounded. "How much has the realm shrunk?"

Urza rubbed his jaw in consideration. "It has already fallen below its critical mass. Its collapse is inevitable."

"If all of that white mana is harvested by Gorig and reaches Phyrexia—"

"We are doomed," Urza finished.

Barrin could sit no longer. He bolted to his feet, chair toppling behind him. He paced feverishly.

"If we could find Gorig's stores of white mana and divert them into the powerstone for your flying ship . . ."

An astonished look crossed Urza's face. "I can't believe what you are suggesting. It is Argoth all over—using the souls of others to power my own private war."

"No," said Barrin. "No, this is different. This is no longer a private war, Urza. And you would not be harvesting souls. You would be resurrecting them. They are gone already. You would be bringing them back, saving them from Phyrexia, and giving them new life in the heart of your ship. You would be giving them a chance to avenge their own deaths."

"Perhaps," Urza allowed. His eyes glowed with remembered atrocities. "Perhaps."

"This is not Argoth at all, Urza," Barrin assured. "We're too late to save Serra's Realm. The Phyrexians have already destroyed it, but you can still save her people."

Urza's voice was fervid as he picked up the thought. "I'll find where Gorig is storing the souls—they must be in Serra's Realm, perhaps in the palace. But he'll know I've come back. He'll know what I'm looking for. He'll tighten his defenses. I'll have only a few chances. Perhaps I can bring back some refugees each time. I could take a hundred at once if they would gather together—but there are thousands." He looked up. His eyes sparkled intensely. "We need the ship, Barrin. Once I find the battery of souls, we'll need the ship to go get the rest of them. How soon can it be ready?"

"The hull is almost complete. The engine and metal pieces are already in place. The sail crews finished months ago. By now Jhoira and Karn will have completed the powerstone core. We've got to train a crew, of course. Find the soul battery, and I'd say we could fly in a month. Three weeks, if we work day and night."

"I'll find the battery . . . and save those I can . . . and muster the rest."

Barrin smiled broadly, rubbing his hands together in astonishment. "I had thought our victory over the monsters in the gorge had been your crowning moment, my friend. But you have made wars before, and it takes no great man to kill. It takes a great man to save, Urza. It takes a great man."

* * * * *

The cranes were in place around the upended airship, block and tackle threaded through great straddling braces of metal. Terd kicked the base of one of the stanchions, scratched his head in vexation, and shouted instructions to his gray-skinned comrades. They scurried up about him and stared in puzzlement at the bottom of the metal beam. It sat almost but not quite atop the stone it was supposed to rest on. As his workers looked downward at the spot, Terd took the occasion to fling his arm out, winging them all in the back of the head. More shouts followed, and the workers turned to a set of ropes stabilizing the great piece of machinery.

Meanwhile, Diago Deerv and Barrin consulted diagrams spread across the field table. They discussed torque and stress loads. Diago assured the master mage that the metal cross members could support two flying ships. If any aspect of the arrangement were insufficient, he insisted, it was the network of ropes. With a quirked lip, Barrin likewise assured the Viashino engineer that Tolarian hemp was extraordinarily strong in all of its applications.

Nearby stood another table. It was stout and stone. Four runners surrounded it, a watchful scorpion was stationed beneath it, and falcons circled high above it. Atop the table lay a black cloth, beneath which huddled a mass the general size and shape of a man. To one side of the table stood Karn. Though he was utterly still, the focus of his eyes shifted nervously across the crowd of students, lizard men, and goblins clustered beyond the ropes.

Jhoira sensed the tension in her friend. "Relax, Karn. There are no Phyrexians among us today."

"The stone is priceless," Karn said. "It wouldn't take a Phyrexian to try to steal it."

"It would take a mammoth," Jhoira pointed out.

"I'll just feel better when the stone is in the engine," he said.

Jhoira shook her head wonderingly and teased, "You're constantly complaining about having a purpose in the grand scheme of things, and once you have a purpose, all you can do is worry."

"Perhaps my affective matrix is flawed," Karn said in impressive deadpan.

A shout came down the line of goblin laborers. Ropes that had been slack went suddenly taut. The great hull of the ship creaked as lines tugged it in cross-directions. Long and slender, the ship quivered within its drydock framework. Its bowsprit wavered, three hundred feet up in the blue sky, and with a tremendous groan the prow tilted down toward the horizon. More shouts came from the goblins, and lines shuddered with the strain. The curved metal stanchions overhead bowed just slightly beneath the tipping burden.

Mage Master Barrin sent streamers of blue magic out to wrap themselves around points of stress. Scintillating power sank into metal or hemp, adding magical strength.

The tapered stern of the airship, once lying against the ground, tilted upward, showing a row of windows and an insignia shaped like a giant seed.

"The Weatherseed," Jhoira said, pointing to the spot.

"Yes," Karn agreed.

"Multani says the ship is complete but unfinished," Jhoira said. "It's still alive, still growing. It is as much a creature as it is a machine."

Karn was silent.

Jhoira pressed. "You are no longer alone, Karn. Urza has designed and built his second living machine."

"No, Jhoira, you are wrong," Karn said. "I'm a thinking, feeling machine, but I am not alive. This ship is Urza's only living machine. It is always growing, integrating new parts into its structure. I am not growing. I am disintegrating."

Jhoira sighed heavily. "Disintegrating—aren't we all."

Masts and spars that had for long months jutted sideways from the upended ship stepped into the sky. With a final shudder and thud, the vessel settled atop the landing spines. Ropes that had eased it downward grew slack. The teams hauling on those lines leaned forward and let them drop to the ground. There was a sigh from workers and artificers and even the ship herself. Upright for the first time, the sleek-raked craft looked large and muscular against the whispering forests of Tolaria. Crews reverently approached it, staring in awe at its glimmering portholes and its elegant webwork of lines.

Then the commands started again. Workers set ladders to the side of the vessel and climbed aboard. Ramps were hauled into position to ease loading. Weapon crews swarmed the various beam weapons embedded in the prow and along the length of the gunwales. Master Mage Barrin levitated himself into the air and floated along the curving rail of the craft, surveying it on all levels.

"Well, Karn, let's get this stone inside," Jhoira said.

She pulled back the black cloth, revealing a massive and beautifully shaped stone, configured in a long lozenge like the Weatherseed itself. It caught the sunlight, amplified it, and sent it stabbing outward in a blinding corona. Karn leaned down, gathered the heavy gem against his gleaming chest plates, and hoisted it into the air. The combination of silver and crystal was dazzling. Karn was transfigured, a man made of lightning. He walked reverently toward the ramp that led into the ship, and a cadre of four runners surrounded him.

Jhoira fell back, astonished by the bright spectacle. It suddenly occurred to her that Karn and the airship were of a piece. They were not two different generations of invention but one continuum. Perhaps Karn didn't realize it—perhaps Urza did not even realize it—but the silver man and the skyship would go down together through time, parts of a single legacy.

Urza crouched in a dark chamber in Serra's Palace. Gorig's forces had located him and were closing in. Their boot steps rang in the hallway. He still had not found the soul battery. He had not even discovered where Gorig kept charged soul torches. Time grew short.

With sudden violence, soldiers' boots pounded against the barred door.

Urza stepped away. He crossed the echoing crawlspace between worlds and emerged in the empyrean reaches of Serra's Realm. Here the palace was only a distant black speck drifting on the horizon. Ahead of him, the Jumbles formed a chaotic sea of tumbling stones.

A golden regatta of troop landers and angel wings glinted above one of the larger masses. They descended toward a refugee hive. Their white-blue soul torches trailed smoky crazings in the air. There, just beneath a green ridge where grasses clung to a ruined temple, was the entrance.

With a mere thought, Urza disappeared from the spot where he hovered. He stepped in a flashing moment into the mouth of the hive.

A handful of young guards started at his appearance and pivoted to hurl their crude spears. One man fell in a tangle of grimy clothes. Four others managed to send their spears Urza's way.

The planeswalker swept his hand in an arc before him, and the spears cracked from a sudden, invisible barrier. They rattled to the cave floor.

"Save them for the cleansing army," Urza advised. "Like it or not, I am your ally against them. I am going within to take with me any who wish to escape to a new place." He retreated quickly down the passage while the sentinels stared, stunned, after him.

One of them, a young angel warrior, rose on her wings and followed. Urza sped away from her. She shouted in his wake.

"Who are you?"

"I am Urza, the planeswalker." The broadening cave walls picked up the announcement, bearing it inward to the people clustered about fires there. Without pause, Urza continued his oration, "The armies of Radiant are coming. They will kill anyone they can find in this place. Any who wish to escape, gather here beside me."

His summons was met with only dull stares.

"There is no time. If you would live, gather here."

Though most of the folk beside the fires—grimy men and women and dispirited angels—stayed where they were, a few young folk rose tentatively and made their way toward Urza. Behind him, several metallic thuds sounded, and then came the distant roar of warriors charging. More of the cavern's inhabitants gathered to the stranger's side, a group of nearly twenty. Flashes and shrieks sounded from the mouth of the cave. Now no one remained by the fires, either fleeing to Urza or fleeing away to the dens carved into the rock off the main hall.

"Those who will not come," Urza shouted out as he focused his mind on the coming planeswalk, "if you survive, get yourself to the colony farthest from the palace—the Arizon colony on the aerial island called Jobboc. I will return there in two weeks' time to save you and anyone else you can bring with you."

Gesturing the fearful, starving mob into a tight cluster, Urza extended his consciousness to surround them. Just as the air began to flare and spark with lightning, Urza folded them into two dimensions and 'walked with them from the world.

* * * * *

Radiant sat on her throne at the height of the aviary. In the last few weeks, it had become a much more soothing place.

When Urza had joined the rebel cause, Gorig at last convinced Radiant to fortify the aviary. She let him surround the glass tower in a web of steel grills. That measure did not satisfy Gorig though. He pointed out that any flying creature with a crossbow could slay her on her throne by sending a bolt through the glass. Radiant relented. She allowed Gorig to fasten thick plates of steel atop the grillwork. Of course the aviary grew dark. The plants died. The birds fell into an unnatural slumber from which they never awakened. The place became cold and dank, but at least it was safe—except for those cursed windows and their violent images. Last of all, Gorig had convinced Radiant to let him dispel the far-seeing enchantments and convert all the panes in the aviary into mirrors.

Now Radiant sat in a dark and safe aviary. The only light came from her glowing presence. The mirrors all around her shimmered with her image. For the first time in centuries, she felt at home on the throne of Serra. Here she sat, searching the eyes of a multitude, the eyes of Radiant.

"Lady Radiant," came a voice from below. It was Gorig. He had emerged on his audience platform. The whine of servos told that he yet wore his battle armor. There was another sound, too, the untidy whisper of a large and heavy bag being drawn along marble. "I have something to show you. Something that will please you very much."

"Not now, Gorig," the angel said distractedly. "I am seeing the future. I am gazing into my own eyes."

His voice was impatient but as sly as a serpent. "Look down for a moment and you will see the future."

"No. The future is here. It is in my eyes. That's where Urza Planeswalker will find his fate. He will look into my eyes. This war will come down to us. I will fight him myself. He will look into my eyes and see the beauty there and remember what this place was when Serra sat this throne, what this place was before he brought death here—"

"We had a successful harvest today—"

"I will look into his eyes and understand at last what madness makes a man bring devils to heaven and then return to aid them."

Gorig's voice was suddenly hesitant. "I would advise you not to look directly into the eyes of Urza Planeswalker, my lady. They are unnatural things—like the eyes of a bug. They will only hypnotize you."

"No, Gorig," Radiant said with a bitter smile. "I will look into his eyes, and he into mine, and we'll know which of us is right and which of us is mad."

"Please, dear lady," begged Gorig, "forget about Urza for a moment. Look down and see what I have brought you." His entreaty was followed by a clattering sound, as though the bag he dragged disgorged hundreds of large wooden balls.

Her curiosity piqued, Radiant at last glanced down. Her eyes lit with delight. "Oh, heads! There must be two hundred heads! Oh, how beautiful, Gorig. How beautiful!"

Monologue

In the last three weeks, Urza has gotten four hundred and twenty-three refugees out of Serra's Realm. He estimates that at least that number has been slaughtered by Radiant's cleansing army. He also believes each of his intrusions into the embattled plane only accelerates Radiant's genocidal war. All of the large concentrations of refugees have been harvested—aside from the Arizon colony on Jabboc. It holds thousands.

For them, there is only one hope—the airship. Once it is fully operational, it should be able to hold most of the remaining Serran "rebels." The trouble is, the vessel will be fully operational only when we find the soul battery.

Urza still hasn't located it. He has searched Gorig's private chambers. He has penetrated the deepest vaults in the palace. He has fought his way into and out of the best-defended sections of the realm. Still, nothing.

On one of his journeys, Urza was forced into a showdown with an angel contingent. After the smoke had cleared and the bodies had fallen to dust, he recovered twelve mana-charged soul torches. A week's study, night and day, revealed the trick of them. They held enough white mana to provisionally charge the ship's powerstone. We estimate the vessel will be able to fly, planeshift once, fire a few bolts from the deck-mounted energy ports, and maneuver to the refugee encampment.

The twelve emptied torches are now mounted along the lines of the hull, power conduits running from them to the core of the ship.

Urza hopes they will draw enough white mana from the air of Serra's Realm to recharge the stone for another planeshift—with the refugees aboard. The power will not last, of course. We need the soul battery to permanently charge the stone. But Urza is less concerned about completing his airship than he is about rescuing refugees.

He acts as though these folk are modern-day ambassadors representing the bygone thousands killed in his wars. Perhaps they are. Perhaps in saving them, he is saving himself.

—**Mage Master Barrin of Tolaria**

Chapter 21

The day of launch had arrived. A great crowd filled the Tolarian glade—student and scholar, elf and artifact engine, Viashino and goblin, angel and human. Half of them were refugees from Serra's Realm. They pinned all their hopes on the rescue force at the center of the glade. The other half of the crowd had worked for years to assemble that force. Now the work was done. All that remained was to wait and watch. The crowd pressed inward, just out of reach of the war-barded drakes but as close as they could get to the great sky-ship.

Aboard the vessel, Master of Engines Karn made his rounds in preparation for launch. He peered down into the open hatch.

Artifact creatures clustered in the hold, shoulder to shoulder—two hundred runners, twelve pumas, two hundred scorpions, and a hundred modified Yotian warriors. These creatures formed the planetary defenses meant to guard the refugees as they boarded the ship. The mechanical men shifted in the close quarters, some of them packed so tightly they could not stand. There would be no room for them on the return trip, Karn knew. They would be left behind to be blasted into nothing, or captured and dissected and melted down. Barrin seemed impressed by Urza's willingness to sacrifice the artifact creatures, speaking of Urza's newfound humanity. Karn felt only saddened by it.

Disintegration.

He drew the hatch closed over the main hold and turned away, striding across the narrow deck to the roosts where three hundred falcon engines awaited release. They would perform a new task, providing aerial cover for the fleeing refugees. In addition to this function, they would home in on Phyrexian blood, impaling themselves in any target, and shredding the creature from the inside out. They would also fight any foes that threatened the refugees. Just in case the falcons did not purge the plane, Urza had filled bombards with modified spider capsules, which would resonate in the presence of strong white-mana sources.

He spoke of saving the refugees and cleansing the plane.

Of course, Karn thought darkly, neither the falcons nor the spiders would be returning either.

He moved along the gunwale toward the first bank of fog-cutting lanterns along the bow. They were fitted with focusing lenses and parabolas that rendered their light into powerful beams. In tests, these ray weapons could ignite clothing from two thousand feet away, could make deadfalls burst into flame, and could etch stone. The lantern crews were goblins, selected due to their familiarity with the Thran ray technology used in the crystal forge. Terd and a pair of gray, stumpy Grabbits manned the lantern Karn checked over.

"Everything in order here, Master," Terd declared with a salute snapped so rapidly that his fingertips left welts on his forehead.

Karn only nodded, continuing his inspection of the device. "The sighting mechanism is dirty."

Eyes widened into saucers on Terd's face. In a gibbering tongue, he upbraided his companions. He stomped on one's foot and twisted the other's ear before returning his attention to Karn. A toothy grin crossed his lips.

"It so clean, you see your face in it—" the thought shimmering in his eyes grew a bit cloudy. He blinked uncomfortably "—or not. We not shine ray at your face. You shiny enough, it bounce off anyway! 'Course, it then kill everybody else. We not shine at your face. Malzra say angels got shiny faces, too. We shoot for whites of eyes. Wait, we not see whites of eyes—"

Karn left the creature in midsentence, following the rail to the glasspitter—an invention of Jhoira's. She had been inspired one day by the deadly sprays of molten metal that occurred when water dropped into a blast furnace. The bombards hurled spheres of glass-covered energy among enemies. Where the balls burst, melted shrapnel was flung outward. Her design was finished and presented to Urza before she had fully thought through the lethal consequences. Before she would allow the devices to be built, she made Urza promise they would be used only against dire and deserving foes. She got her wish—and command of the flying ship.

Even now, Jhoira crouched in the prow beside the ship's final ranged weapon—an acid atomizer. The device used an unstable energy field to dispersed a caustic spray among foes. Karn approached her.

"Is the atomizer in working order, Captain?" Karn asked.

Jhoira startled. She stared at Karn, blinking stupidly for a moment before shaking the visions from her eyes. "Sorry, I was just mentally preparing for the coming battle. What were you saying?"

"The acid atomizer, Captain," Karn repeated, "is it ready?"

Jhoira nodded, crossing arms over her chest. "Yeah, but don't call me captain. Call me Jhoira. Just because I've been given command of this vessel and crew doesn't make me a captain. As for the atomizer—the fog from this thing will be as destructive as a blast of the fire drakes' breath."

They both reflexively cast glances toward Gherridarigaaz and Rhammidarigaaz, positioned on either side of the long, sleek ship. The fire drakes would provide an aerial defense of the ship and the refugees. The beasts would be planeswalked into Serra's Realm by Urza himself.

Just now, Urza was to starboard tightening saddle straps on the ancient drake dam. To port, Barrin packed wands and tomes into the saddle bags of the young dragon. Though Jhoira was in charge of the ship, Urza and Barrin would direct the entire operation, employing an arsenal of white-mana spells from the backs of the fire drakes.

Urza even then stood in the drake saddle and made a gesture to silence the buzzing crowds. "They will call us invaders," Urza said, his voice amplified by a quick spell from the mage master. "They will call us invaders, just as they have called their own citizens traitors. They have even called us Phyrexians, so powerful is the web of delusion that traps them. We will not listen to what they call us. We will listen to what history calls us. We will save them despite themselves."

A mild ovation answered these words.

"We are not invaders. We are defenders. We are the alliance of Dominaria. We are human and divine, Viashino and goblin. We are builders and enchanters. We are the power of the forest and of the sea, of the mountains and of life itself. We have cleansed our own island of Phyrexian hordes, and we will cleanse Serra's Realm as well. But, most of all, we will return, and bring with us the rest of her refugees, a new army of allies."

A roar of joy began among the humans and angels gathered there. It swept through the ranks of lizard men and goblins, elves and artifact creatures, students and scholars, until the very forests and oceans echoed the shout.

As the sound mounted up, Jhoira nodded to Karn. "Initiate the startup sequence, Master of Engines."

"Aye, Captain," Karn replied.

He crossed the narrow deck to reach the bulkhead where stairs descended into the hull of the ship. In moments, he had reached the engine room. Diago Deerv and three other red-scaled Viashino came to awkward attention as Karn entered.

"Initiate startup sequence," the silver man ordered.

The Viashino snapped salutes and scrambled to their posts. Switches were flipped, levers adjusted, and gyros set into motion. Groans came from the massive engine. A chatter of commands and verifications arose among the lizard men.

Karn meanwhile moved to the center of the curved console

bank, beneath an ornate speaking tube that led directly to the bridge. Before him, a pair of deep ports delved into the inner reaches of the engine. Karn inserted his hands into the holes, feeling for the twin bars at their bases. He found them and clasped his hands. When turned, the rods would trigger the engine's start up.

"Open the superfluid manifold," Karn ordered.

He pivoted both handles inward, and felt the mechanisms engage and lock. A great warmth was abruptly born within the engine. In moments, it had drowned out the ovation outside.

Before Karn could withdraw his arms, bracers emerged from deep within the machine and fastened over his wrists. Small wire probes slid smoothly into the joints in his knuckles. Magnificent surges of energy prickled along his hands. Jolts moved up arm and shoulder conduits, converged in the silver man's chest, and fountained into the powerstone at the center of his head.

Suddenly Karn could sense the green superfluids coursing through the great engine block before him. He could feel the warm bath sluice around the glimmering powerstone at the heart of the machine. He could see out the fog-lanterns of the ship, fore and aft, starboard and port. He could kinesthetically sense the weight and alignment of the ship's hull, its sails, its lines, even its young, strong captain as she stood at the ship's wheel. The airship had become a second body for him. Its engines and controls and defenses were suddenly his own.

Integration.

To welling cheers, Karn lifted the great skyship into the air. It rose amid the red-flapping wings of the fire drakes. It ascended into the bright skies over Tolaria, the bright skies of Dominaria.

* * * * *

Jhoira felt small and overawed as she stood on the bridge of the airship. As yet, there was no need to steer. The vessel was merely rising into the blue Tolarian sky. Not until it made headway would the warping of sails and the bending of airfoils make any difference at all to the craft's movement. But clutching the wheel now made a definite difference to Jhoira's position: it allowed her to stay standing.

Beneath her feet, enormous, hot engines labored. They dragged into clear air a payload of five hundred war engines and a crew of thirty. She tried to forget that the fully loaded ship weighed four thousand tons. She tried to forget that this was the vessel's first time aloft—its shakedown cruise. She tried to forget that she would be sailing this vessel into a war with angels.

Something huge and red arced with sudden violence above the ship's rail and then disappeared again. It returned, a leathery mountain, translucent—the bones of a great drake visible through it. The wing dipped a second time. When it reappeared, it brought the red-mantled head of Gherridarigaaz above the rail. A gray snort escaped one craggy nostril as the she-drake pulled herself higher into the sky. Urza, standing in his saddle, lurched into view. He held something in his hand, something that looked like a club but sparkled like a wand. His face was clenched with effort, and he drove the drake toward the prow of the ship.

Something is wrong, Jhoira thought, clinging to the wheel. Something has come loose—or something that was supposed to come loose hasn't.

Gherridarigaaz surged toward the bow of the ship. Urza leaned so far in the saddle he appeared in danger of falling. He swung the shimmering club at something clinging to the prow. A dull thud sounded, and then a wet shattering sound.

"I name thee, *Weatherlight*," Urza declared, holding aloft the fragmented neck of the bottle. His mount soared away over windswept treetops.

Jhoira laughed. There was no monster, nothing amiss. The planeswalker was merely blessing and naming the boat on its maiden voyage. Jhoira felt the weight of dread and impossible futures sag away from her and drop among the rattling leaves below. She laughed.

"Full ahead! Follow that drake," the first captain of *Weatherlight* commanded.

Gherridarigaaz darted out over the forests of Tolaria. Rhammidarigaaz slid into her wake. *Weatherlight* followed them both. Wind coursed over the prow and back to reach Jhoira. She drew the fresh air into her lungs and remembered another place she used to stand—at the edge of her world. She remembered an earlier time, when young courage filled her heart and she dreamed of a soul mate. The man had never arrived, but she had lived a full life without him, and now, young courage poured again into her heart.

Gherridarigaaz was merely a crimson jag on the horizon. Rhammidarigaaz was just behind her. *Weatherlight* gained on them both. The helm had grown active in Jhoira's grip, tugging at her the way an eager horse pulls at the rein. She returned its forceful play, holding the ship against cross winds.

"Trim the sails," Jhoira commanded the human crew. They scampered to cleats and drew on lines. "Reconfigure the port and starboard fans into airfoils." More workers clambered onto the lateral rigs to rework the canvas.

With each tug on slack lines and each shift of sail, the ship gained speed. It coursed above the green sea of trees with greater velocity than any water-bound craft. A turgid wake of tossing treetops spread out aft. The wind washing over the deck threatened to blow the lighter crew members overboard. Terd and his diminutive comrades hunkered down beside the rail. Lines throughout the rig hummed in the bluster. The ship's hull creaked as it eased itself into the stresses of its new orientation.

Jhoira smiled. She had almost caught up to Urza and Barrin. At the shoreline of Tolaria, the drake riders nudged their steeds to match the ship's speed. Gherridarigaaz and Rhammidarigaaz flew wing and wing. Churning storms of air spread in twin cones behind them. Jhoira steered the ship past the shore and into the twin gales. Wind lashed brutally across the deck.

"Hang on!" Jhoira shouted to her crew. "We will slow once we enter Serra's Realm."

Until that time, they had to fly in close formation. Urza's planeshift would barely encompass both drakes, and it could be tracked by *Weatherlight's* apparatus only if the field effects over-lapped. Whitecaps thundered below, and gray cumulous clouds thundered above. The very air seemed to turn solid, tearing at sail-cloth and hemp, wooden hull and metal fittings. It clawed also at the captain at her wheel, but now she felt only exhilaration.

A bubble of magical might swelled out from Urza. In a heartbeat, it stretched to encompass both drakes. Already they shimmered, punching into the portal.

"Planeshift!" shouted Jhoira.

Another bubble welled up from the heart of the ship itself. The curtain of magic cracked out, whiplike, and dimmed sea and sky. Blue Dominaria glimmered for one tiny moment more, and then it was gone. The roar went with it. Black chaos swept in to displace all. Beyond the ship's rails lay only a churning world of emptiness, and the laboring wings of two great drakes.

And then blue and black both were gone. In their place came a vast skyscape of tinged light, sulfuric cloud, and troubled, tumbled chunks of land.

"Serra's Realm," Jhoira said into the sudden roar of wind, the edge of Serra's Realm. She reached down to a slot in the deck and drew forth a glass-encased map of the Jumbles. The cartography was unmistakably Urza's—detailed, turbulent, overworked. It showed three landmark isles. One was pear-shaped, and it tumbled in rapid succession. Another was long and flat like a great stone knife. The third, lying just beneath the descending brow of sky at the utter edge of Serra's Realm, was the rock called Jobboc.

There, on that distant and broken world, in a colony called Arizon, waited a thousand souls.

"Start a rapid swing round to starboard on heading ninety-five, three twenty-eight, eight. We're heading for Jobboc." Steersmen trimmed in the airfoils and Karn, below, channeled what remained of the ship's power into the banking descent. "Release spider bombards from alternate sides every thirty seconds begin-ning on my mark." The bombard crews scrambled to load their first salvos.

Meanwhile, Terd clambered up the ladder to the main deck and grabbed at Jhoira's sleeve. "They are here already, Lady. Lightning bugs!"

Jhoira peered out along the line of the goblin's gnarled finger. To port, she glimpsed a beautiful and terrible sight. Glimmering in air like gold dust, were the cleansing armies of Radiant.

"Mark!"

* * * * *

"They've released the first spider bombard," shouted Barrin. He brought Rhammidarigaaz through a sweeping turn to the flank of Urza.

"Good," Urza called back from atop Gherridarigaaz. "We'll know who we're fighting." He looked to his left, where the cleansing army of Radiant swarmed. Their wings making a distant drone in the air.

"How many do you think there are?"

"Hundreds," Urza called back, "perhaps thousands. We will need every advantage."

Urza flung out his hands, drawing to himself the white mana of the many places he had traveled in the realm. He fueled a pair of powerful spells. White lightning crackled out from his fingers and spread across the two drakes, feathering around them in a thousand leaping lines. Power surged through them. The enchantment made scales seem gossamer feathers, made red mantles seem rainbowed coronas. There was a sudden glorious aspect laid on the beasts. They were transformed into divine figures, terrifying in their beauty and power. With another gathering of white-mana magic, Urza cast a scintillating aura around each rider, a whirling circle of what appeared to be snow.

"That will protect us from white-mana spells or creatures," Urza explained.

Barrin, unfamiliar with the realm, drew on blue magic instead of white. He summoned a pair of Tolarian drakes. Giant kin of fire drakes, these two dragons had skin as smooth and translucent as reef water. Their wings flashed blue against the yellowing clouds. Their spiky manes, as barbed as tridents, oscillated in the roaring wind. Barrin reached into the core of his memory, tapping memories of the forests of Tolaria. He thought of Jhoira's Angelwood and the Western Reaches and the many fast-time subarctic scrub forests, and cast an enchantment on the two creatures. Green scales sprouted across the backs and bellies of the summoned drakes, providing them additional protection against attacks, magical or mundane.

"Impressive," shouted Urza over the growing buzz of angel wings approaching.

"I have a leviathan up my sleeve, if things get really desperate, though summoning it would tax my every reserve."

There was no time for more discussion. The approaching army's drone had become a roar. They grew from golden motes into arrows of flame.

The angel army of Radiant arrived.

They soared in with the speed of falcons. Two score archangels led the vanguard, each bearing a magna sword, broad as an axe but long as a lance. The archangels came in a vertical circle and held their blades inward like a ring of fangs. Behind them, forming a lethal gullet, were hundreds of angel warriors bearing lances. A great leviathan in its own right, the cleansing army of Radiant opened its toothy maw to swallow the drakes and their riders.

"I'll meet you on the other side!" Urza yelled as he plunged into the hailstorm of white fangs and silver masks and flashing steel.

The other side of what? Barrin wondered.

The angel thicket closed around him.

Magna swords struck the tip of the fire drake's pale muzzle and sparked along its scaly neck. The enchantments held, repelling steel. Even so, the blades converged, tracing their way toward the rider.

Barrin yanked hard on the drake's rein. Rhammidarigaaz curved broadside to the speeding angels. His leeward flank arched away from attack, and his windward flank became an impenetrable wall against which archangels and angels smashed in bloody wreck.

Barrin urged Rhammidarigaaz back into his charge. The beast surged his wings, flinging loose a pair of angels who had swarmed up behind him, and vaulted deeper into the throat of the attack. He breathed a great gout of fiery breath into the onslaught, and angels fell from the sky like burning pigeons. Rhammidarigaaz plowed into the vacated space.

The dragon's side was dotted with blood, most of it angelic, though there were a few long wounds where swords had broken through the enchantments. Instantly, Barrin cast a healing spell on the drake, and the gory gashes along his sides knitted together with threads of white energy.

Another blast of fire emerged from the beast. More angels tumbled in black smoke and melted quill. Silver masks cleaved to screaming faces. Magna swords fused with skeletons.

Distant in the fight, the flames of Gherridarigaaz carved an equally hellish swath through the swarm of angels.

The blue drakes fared less well. Their steam breath killed many, but the press of bodies and the hack of swords ripped the creatures to rags. A bolt of healing radiance leapt from Urza toward the beleaguered Tolarian drakes, but another sorcery, cast by an archangel warrior, deflected the spell en route.

Barrin was beginning his own healing enchantment when an angel choir shrieked down upon him and laid to with swords. A familiar sorcery leapt from his fingertips. The kindled fire arced across the pitching air into the face of an angel warrior, waking flames in her mouth and eyes. He unleashed a second spell of the same kind, drawing additional power from the first. A third conflagration blazed out to strike an archangel, blasting a hole through its armor and out the other side. Three bodies tumbled away, but twenty more clung to the drake's back and attacked with swords and barbed whips.

Massive blades descended. They struck Barrin in head, neck, belly, and back. Magna swords rebounded from his enchanted flesh as though they had struck stone.

Barrin sent Rhammidarigaaz into a sudden dive, flinging free the attackers and bringing the beast's fire breath against new clouds of the foe. Exhilaration moved through the Mage Master of Tolaria—until he saw the bleeding hulks of the Tolarian drakes.

They were below and behind, their carapace enchantments dispelled, and their blue hides marked with gashes as numerous and ominous as hieroglyphics. The killer angels still clung to the beasts, maggots on dead corpses, until their wings at last gave out. In quick succession, the summoned beasts dropped from the sky. Angels peeled themselves from the falling forms.

Chastened, Barrin brought Rhammidarigaaz soaring back into the fray, fiery breath and steel-hard wings slaying angels in their hundreds. The master mage cast sorceries, death blossoming all around him. He would kill as many as he could as quickly as he could, hoping to keep them from the refugees.

Suddenly, black and grotesque in the midst of that angel throng, there came a beast that could win right past Barrin's white mana protections. Bewinged, befanged, and Phyrexian, the monster dropped like night from the sky onto Rhammidarigaaz's neck. It reared up, and Barrin recognized the lemon-wedge eyes Urza had described.

The man otherwise was utterly transformed—his figure hulking and muscular, fitted with countless implants and weapons—halberd arms and dagger-tipped feet and scythes at the elbows. The greatest weapon of all, though, was built right into the beast's torso—a black manifold that blazed in twelve places with the white-blue fires of soul-stealers. He drew white mana into his very being, storing it, harnessing part of it to transform himself. He grew more powerful with every creature he killed.

Gorig *was* the mana battery.

Barrin had time to see no more. Gorig lunged atop him.

* * * * *

Karn felt *Weatherlight*'s fading power as a torpor in his own frame. The soul torches weren't gathering enough white mana from the surrounding air to recharge the stone. It only glimmered weakly within its superfluid bath. The ship had enough energy to fly, perhaps enough for a few brief bursts from its ray weapons, but the vessel would not planeshift again.

"We'll need more torches, Jhoira," he called into the speaking tube over his head. The sound of his voice was empty and weary, made doubly so by the metal pipe work. "Just to carry the refugees away, we'll need power from more torches."

"Aye," came the clipped reply from above. "Prepare for landing."

Below the ship—Karn still saw all the world through the ray weapons at bow and stern—the aerial island called Jabboc floated black and forbidding against the descending dome of Serra's Realm. It was a dark place. The eternal light of Serra was failing in these reaches. The life-giving air was thin and tainted. The very edge of the plane hovered only a scant mile beyond the black rock. In ever-changing array, its frayed fabric showed the gray chaos that lay between worlds.

"Reduce speed," Jhoira's order came.

Gratefully, Karn scaled back the power flow from the tepid crystal.

"Decrease altitude."

Sails shifted, the prow rose just slightly, and the ship's keel eased downward. The massive aerial island swelled to fill Karn's field of vision. He saw there a twilight roil of hills and rocks. Dead fields lay gray within the perpetual murk. Tangled trees stood in dead woods across the isle. It seemed Hades or Sheol, a place of shadows, sunless land of the dead.

"Lanterns ahoy! Bring the ship to ground beside those lights."

Through the eyes of the ship, Karn saw the flickering glow of lanterns, oil and wick pushing back the darkness. The tepid light traced out arches against the dark—the entry to the Arizon colony. Light reflected in tiny gleams from something clustered within. They seemed almost wasp eggs, piled inside the mud-daubers' nest, but with a certain wonder and dread, Karn realized what they were—

Faces, thousands of faces—waiting and hoping for salvation.

Karn drew upon the strength of his own power matrix to bear the ship across the cold reaches before the cave. A black vale below led past a field of rubble and a forest deadfall. The *Weatherlight* nosed through the tangle of trees and to the flat plain, just below the cave. Landing spines emerged from the lower sweep of the hull. Easing the ship slowly down, Karn felt in his own being the vast shudder of the hull settling.

"Open hatches! Release falcons! Deploy runners and pumas and scorpions! Ready cargo holds! Ready ray weapons!" There was a new urgency in Jhoira's voice.

When Karn peered through the stern lanterns, he saw why.

Angel armies descended on them in a golden cyclone.

* * * * *

Urza stood in Gherridarigaaz's saddle. The Tolarian drakes had plunged out of the battle there, where the swarm was thinnest. They had tumbled away into the gray-blue depths and, some mile below, flashed out of existence entirely.

Only a mile below . . .

The plane had shrunk considerably before their arrival, but it was dissipating even more quickly now. Urza drew hard on the reins, sending Gherridarigaaz into a blistering attack. Angels tumbled from the dragon's blazing onslaught, white and inconsequential like popped maize from a steaming kettle. They, too, dropped away and disappeared in the ever-nearer edge of the world.

With every angel death, the plane was collapsing. The more fiercely the drakes battled the main army, the less time any of them had. Soon the mana depletion would reach a critical threshold, and then the collapse would take only moments. Any living thing left in the plane would be destroyed.

"Hold fire!" Urza commanded the drake. He reined her in a huge circle. "To Rhammidarigaaz, to Barrin!"

The dragon entered a shallow dive that would speed her toward her son and his rider. Angels flung themselves in dense clouds about her, but she held back her killing breath. Magna swords shrieked across her armored hide. Some bit through the enchantments and sliced open long rents. Urza's magic healed them even as they formed, letting not a whisper of air spill from the drake's wings.

Even so, agony won through. Gherridarigaaz roared, smoke trailing from her jowls. She barely contained the fires that ached to spew forth. She focused her fury instead on the battle ahead and on Rhammidarigaaz caught in it. Another three surges of wing brought her to soar just beneath him.

Urza shouted toward Barrin, saddled above, "Break off! To the *Weatherlight*."

In a flash, they were past. The drake sliced through air and angel both as they made their way along. Air made small booms at the trailing edge of the drake's wings. The thickest swarm of warriors fell away. Gherridarigaaz punched through the final wall of them and shot into the gray spaces beyond. Ahead lay the Jumbles. At its distant end hung a large floating isle, and on it glinted the lights of *Weatherlight*. Those lights were dim beneath the gold and white shimmer of angel warriors and soul torches.

Another army.

Urza urged his mount to greater speed. Even as they closed on Jabboc Isle, he could see the advancing curtain of chaos at the edge of the plane.

There was less time than he had thought.

* * * * *

Jhoira helped a staggering old man into the hold of *Weatherlight*. He was garbed in tatters, his face drawn into a scowl of concentration, his eyes turned down from the loud battle that raged only a thousand yards aft. How anyone survived in the Jumbles was a mystery to Jhoira, let alone how an old, infirm man had. How old had he been when he was cast into that world of flotsam? Perhaps he had lived in the isles for years, perhaps all his life.

"Quickly, please, Grandfather," she urged gently, "and move as far aft as possible."

"Is there sunlight where we are going?" the man asked, tottering a moment on the steps.

"Yes, sunlight, water, forests—everything," Jhoira assured as the man moved forward. She stared across the bow at the snaking column of refugees.

There were too many of them. They were too slow, too weak. Beyond their desperate cave-colony, the crackling wall of chaos verged nearer and nearer. Soon it would not matter that there were too many of them. Soon the edge of the plane would begin its disintegrating march across the isle.

Matters aft were just as grim. The falcon engines fought fiercely, dropping angels from air atop the front line of ground combat. The ranks of runners thinned, their crossbow quarrels already spent, their scythe blades snapping out to trap their foes. Orange explosions crackled out along the line. Clutched together, angels and machines both blazed into nothing.

Soul torches fell to ground at the front and crackled and spat, absorbing the hundreds of souls that perished there. The infernal devices blazed, white hot.

The mathematics were against Jhoira. Even if each machine destroyed one warrior with its blast, Radiant could overrun them with hundreds more.

"Karn, can you muster enough power to use the ray weapons?" Jhoira called.

The answer sounded dower and hollow. "I have barely enough power to lift off."

Jhoira stared at the infernal line of battle and considered. She had been told, as commander of the ship, she was not to leave it, but if she didn't, there might well not be a ship to leave. They needed to charge the stone, and only a thousand feet away, power lay sparking and crackling.

"I'm going to get some torches," Jhoira told Karn, her voice hushed. "I'll bring back as many as I can carry."

Karn's response was slow—too slow—but Jhoira did not need to hear it to know what it was. He as much as forbade his captain.

It is mutiny, pure and simple, thought Jhoira ironically as she dropped amid the lines of scorpion engines, marching into oblivion.

A scraggly figure leapt from the rail to land at her side. "You need fighters, I think," Terd said, matching her stride for stride.

"You're right," said Jhoira kindly.

"The more torches, the better," added another familiar voice. Diago Deerv blinked placidly at their looks of surprise. "After all, my folk built half this ship."

Side by side, the woman, the goblin, and the lizard man waded forward through the press of metal, heading toward the burning front.

* * * * *

The Phyrexian smashed atop Barrin, breaking ribs and flinging the man from his drake saddle. The Mage Master of Tolaria tumbled across the dragon's spread wings and fetched up, broken, in the crook of one reptilian elbow. His mind whirled, unable to fasten on anything. Wind roared over him. He clung to the drake's wing, shaking his head to clear it.

Gorig crouched on the saddle, jowls drawn back in a dagger-toothed leer. Long, barbed legs drew up beneath the insectoid creature. The twelve soul-stealing ports along its manifold torso flared in hungry anticipation. Its wings spread outward, and again it lunged.

The first blast of air over Barrin brought with it thought of a spell. He summoned his memories of distant Tolaria and hurled before him a wall of air. The creature smashed heavily against the sudden gale. Gorig roared. It tumbled helplessly backward, away from the mage master and his mount.

Rhammidarigaaz rolled beneath the turbulent barrier. Barrin could only cling raggedly to the drake's wing. Rhammidarigaaz pivoted and soared out from the angel swarm. His fiery breath carved an avenue of soot and burning flesh before them. Barrin could not care. He could only hold on, inching slowly back toward the saddle.

"Urza ordered the retreat," Rhammidarigaaz gasped out between breaths. "*Weatherlight* is under attack."

Barrin nodded dizzily. He clawed his way back to the saddle and clung, gulping ragged breaths.

A ferocious roar came behind them. The bright blaze of the wall of air shattered. Out of the heart of that conflagration came the shrieking Phyrexian. Gorig soared, faster than even the archangels who followed in a shrieking cone behind. Devil and angels alike, every last staff and wing and magna sword was intent on destroying Barrin, Mage Master of Tolaria.

He could not care. He could only hold on and stare at the battle that raged around *Weatherlight*. If he reached Urza, the ship might be saved.

Monologue

Death is not so horrible a thing when one is broken and clinging to the burning back of a fire drake and plunging through a heaven that seems in all ways hell. Death is not so horrible at all.

—**Mage Master Barrin of Tolaria**

Chapter 22

The front lines were thick with angels and scorpions engines, so thick that Jhoira had to battle her own forces to reach it. From behind she grabbed a scorpion's stinger and let the darting tail fling her up onto its back of metal carapace. She caught a foothold and sent her sword swinging into the epaulet of the angel warrior before it.

The creature was fast. His soul torch clattered up and hurled her blade to one side. He followed the stroke with a dagger slash. Jhoira reared back from the strike. She kicked the creature's dagger hand, spinning him to one side, and stabbed with her sword. The angel grasped his side and whirled. The soul torch swung in a blaze toward Jhoira's face. She staggered, trying to bring her sword to bear, but she was too slow. With a white-blue sizzle, the torch impacted. Jhoira instinctively crumpled atop the scorpion's back and cradled her face, expecting to find only charred tatters of flesh. Her skin was whole and healthy.

The torch had impacted the scorpion's intervening stinger. The metal tail thrust back the magic brand. It slid from the angel's grasp and toppled. The sizzling tip of it fell against the wound in the angel's side. In a white-blue flash, the creature's soul was sucked away. Lifeless, the angel collapsed. The torch flared.

Jhoira scrabbled across the scorpion's back and snatched up the torch. She lifted it, just in time. The brand blocked a descending magna sword. The broad blade clattered aside and sliced deep into the scorpion's back plate. Jhoira rose. An archangel towered over her, struggling to wrench its magna sword from the collapsing scorpion. She rammed the white-hot tip of the torch up beneath the archangel's silver mask, catching it in the fold between throat and jaw.

The archangel shuddered, caught between a snagged blade and an incandescent death. Then, in a terrific clamor of wings and armor, the creature convulsed its life away. The torch shuddered and trembled as it drew in the powerful being's life-force. Jhoira gritted her teeth in determination to hold on to the too-hot handle. A roar erupted, fury and agony embodied, and death clutched the archangel. Its own soul torch dropped, and Jhoira let go of her dagger to catch it. Meanwhile the angel toppled back, a great tree falling in a forest. Its wings cleared a broad path beneath it.

As Jhoira caught her breath, she saw Terd scurry out upon that fallen giant and snatch up three more torches lying among the angel dead. They were overflowing with power, having drawn into themselves the souls of hundreds of warriors. Terd used the ragged end of his tunic as a hot pad to grab the torches. He scuttled back just as another angel descended to strike him down. One wave of the three sputtering brands pushed the creature back among its cohorts.

Jhoira grabbed Terd's collar and hauled him away from the front.

In his turn, Diago caught Jhoira's collar and hauled her back. Moments later, a fireball struck the spot where she and Terd had been, driving the destroyed scorpion into a blackened crater.

"I have two torches," Diago gasped out as he drew back his comrades in retreat. The lizard-man's scales stood on end in the heat of battle. "You have two torches, and the goblin has three. That should be enough. We have to get back to the ship."

"Yes," Jhoira agreed, breathless from fighting and from holding onto the cometary torches. "Back to the ship. . . . This will be enough to get us flying . . . shoot some deadly shots. . . . Maybe even to planeshift."

Jhoira looked toward the ship. It was a carnival-lit hulk on the hillside, beside the glowering caverns of Arizon and the black masses of refugees, crowding into the ship. Behind that tableaux, the curtain of chaos gnawed at the edge of Jabboc isle.

"Maybe even to planeshift. . . ."

* * * * *

"Cease this battle!" Urza cried imperiously. His figure blazed with light aback Gherridarigaaz. Dragon and rider descended in a column of mana energy before the storm of angels and falcons. "Cease this battle or be destroyed! I am Urza Planeswalker!"

"Tremble before him!" came a voice in mocking answer from among the angel horde.

Radiant emerged. Her figure was lit with an incandescent heat equal to Urza's. A group of archangels accompanied her, four before, four behind, and four more around the ruler of the realm. Her appearance brought a sudden hush to the battle lines. She was strange-eyed, beautiful, and terrifying.

"Tremble before this petulant god-child, this despoiler of worlds, destroyer of planes. Urza has come, my children, and when Urza comes, death always follows."

"I have come to take you out of death. I have come only to carry away those I call refugees, those you call refuse," Urza shouted from the hovering drake. "Let us leave in peace, and we shall kill no more."

"It is too late for bargains. Your war is collapsing our plane around us." She gestured with her war staff toward the advancing curtain of chaos. "You come first bringing Phyrexia, and you come last bringing destruction."

Urza lifted his own battle staff. "Forgive, fair lady. I brought Phyrexia here, true, but you have given it a home in your war minister, Gorig, and throughout your court. The very spells you created to drive the stink of Phyrexia from your palace are the spells that allowed Phyrexia to dwell there and surround you and turn you against your own people. Your plane shrinks not because of me, but because of these soul torches of yours, harvesting the life of your people, your plane, for Phyrexia. That is why chaos threatens. That is why your plane is dying."

In the echoing stillness of the battle, whining servos and pulsing wing beats gave the air a dead drone. Beyond that sound hovered the approaching rumble of matter giving itself over to chaos.

"Come with us, all of you. Come with us to another world. Come where all who are good can live and where Phyrexians, beneath the Glimmer Moon, will die. Come with us, Radiant. Cease this senseless war, and come with us."

She seemed to consider, her face for a moment lovely amid swirling hair and wings of light. Then she spoke, and death followed her words. "Kill them all. To a man, kill every one!"

Radiant herself made good the command. She hurled a wall of force from outstretched fingers. The vast wave of energy ate the very air. It arced toward Urza, too fast to stop, too huge to escape. It would not kill him, but it would stun him long enough that angelic death could fall on him from the sky.

Gherridarigaaz rose. The ancient fire drake spread her wings in a giant shield before Urza. He had to cling to her back not to be thrown from the vertical saddle.

The blast struck Gherridarigaaz full in the belly and chest. Scale and skin and muscle disintegrated. She dissolved away as though in acid. Ribs hung for a moment, vacant of flesh, and then dripped into white smears. Gherridarigaaz released one last, long wail before lungs and throat and head all were gone. Wings, too, vanished. By the time the wave spent itself, all that remained was spine and shoulder blades and half a pelvis.

She had sacrificed herself. It was the highest honor among lizard folk.

Urza escaped the tangled traces of the saddle just before Gherridarigaaz's remains plunged away. He roared too. He roared as though she were his own mother.

The time of negotiation was done.

The time of moderation and sanity was finished.

The time of killing had come.

Gathering magical might, he hurled himself at the tyrant of heaven.

Radiant was ready. She hung in the skies, savoring this moment. Her eyes gleamed madly in the fray. Lithe hands swept out to her sides and forward, as though in a curtsey. Her fingertips trailed long lines of archangels in their wake. They converged on Urza.

Heedless, he shot toward her. With a thought, his flesh turned adamantine. Magna swords fell in a flurry upon him. Their broad blades rang and clattered. His head smashed them back like a soaring cannonball. What archangels managed to hold onto their blades shuddered in nerveless jangle. Others lost their swords. A few even lost their arms. Urza blasted past them all and ran headlong into Radiant.

A lesser being would have been torn in half by the attack, but Radiant had been waiting for this moment. She dodged back in the instant of impact, grabbed hold of the rocketing planeswalker, and with a surge of her wings, hurled herself along with him. She clawed at his face, seeming surprised at its impenetrable warding. Then, hands soft as silk clutched his sides, and lightning arced from her fingertips. It traced out nerve and muscle and bone, a storm within the planeswalker.

He trembled, enervated. Electricity possessed his every tissue. Aside from spasms, he could not move.

Smiling bitterly, Radiant carried him above the boiling cloud of angels and falcons and into the wheeling heights. "You are not welcome here, Urza, not now not ever."

Those soft hands turned iron hard. She flung the paralyzed man upward, into the descending ceiling of chaos above the realm. As he went, the last jags of lightning danced across his frame. A white tempest cycloned from her upraised hands. The storm bore him fistlike into the shredding curtain. Urza smashed into the verge. He dissolved away. Chaos grated muscle from bone. He was gone as quickly as Gherridarigaaz had been. The wind dissipated, and Urza

Planeswalker was not even a stain on the dark chaos.

Radiant shook her head and brushed her hands off.

Something suddenly was between those hands. Urza took form against her. One hand caught her beneath the jaw. The other arm wrapped her waist. No longer adamantine, those limbs were still implacable, inescapable. He flipped her over and dragged her back down into the roaring battle, down toward the struggling refugees and the battle-torn ship. He forced her to gaze at the sight.

"Look, Radiant. Look who you are killing. Look what you've become."

"I know what I am," she gasped out. "I know what you are too."

She cast a quick series of spells, prepared and laid aside for this very moment. All defenses were stripped from Urza's head. Her fingers grew as long and sharp and curved as daggers. She drove them into his skull. They punched through bone and into his frontal lobe.

Urza roared, reconstituting shattered bone and ruptured brain.

She was not done, though. Her fingers curled into claws. She raked through gray matter and shattered sinuses and optic cavities. She scooped up the gemstones that were his eyes. With a brutal yank, she hauled them forth.

Blind and gaping, his head staved, Urza struggled against tumbling walls of pain.

He clutched to her. She was all that kept him aloft.

He had to heal.

He had to rebuild his being.

He could not. Part of that being—the only part that was not a mere projection of his mind—had been ripped away. Those gems defined him. They were at the heart of the Brothers' War: Mightstone and Weakstone. They had been his eyes since the blast at Argoth. They had been his eyes since he had become a planeswalker. They were at the heart of his madness, his power.

Even in his dying agony—for, yes, he was dying: his power was also his weakness—Urza realized how like Karn he was. They were both defined by stones set in their heads. Both lived with them and died without them. Mightstone and Weakstone—they were Urza's affective and cognitive cortex. Without them, he was destroyed.

Radiant knew it. With relish, she hoisted the gory things overhead, beyond Urza's feeble reach, and she actually laughed. "Gorig had told me about these. He had told me you were like Xantcha. She had had a Phyrexian heart, and you have Phyrexian eyes. I told Gorig I needed only look into these eyes to know that you were mad, that I was right. Yes. This is my moment of triumph. I've found the Phyrexian in my realm, Urza. I've found the Phyrexian, and it is you."

She smiled, a faint and wicked thing that Urza could no longer see.

"I've won, madman," Radiant said, staring into the glimmering crystals. In their bloody facets, the battle below played itself out. "My work is done. Gorig will finish off your forces and our rebels. He will cleanse the realm. That is his job. He will even capture your ship—what a curiosity! And with these powerstones—the Eyes of Urza—I will restore my heaven." A thought occurred to her. "Funny that you tried to destroy my world to charge a powerstone, but in the end it is your powerstone that will save it." She glanced down at the convulsing body of Urza, clinging to her in its death throes. "I rather like whispering these things into your dying ears. Perhaps I will take you with me. Yes, no better way to assure you are dead."

So saying, she cast a final spell and disappeared from the decaying heights of her plane. She took with her the Mightstone and Weakstone and the dying body of the planeswalker.

* * * * *

Before *Weatherlight's* bow roared a wall of absolute destruction. Entropy ground rock and grass and tree to nothing, nothing at all. Behind the ship's stern roared another wall—angels turned demonic, rending the machines thrown hopelessly against them. Both walls advanced, closing in on the ship and her overflowing hold.

"There's no more room!" shouted Terd from the hatch. His webbed foot stomped on the shoulder of one refugee as if he could pack them more tightly.

"Then let them stand on deck," Jhoira replied testily.

She lifted the third soul torch over the exposed conduit. They'd had to tear up planks beside the wheel to find where the lines of power descended to the crystal. The ship had shuddered with each stripped board, as though it felt the wound in its very being. Beneath the planking ran a channel of metal sinews, like an exposed nerve bundle. It led down to the powerstone in the core of the engine. Taking a deep breath, Jhoira lowered the sizzling torch so that its butt contacted the conduit. With a lightning jolt, the torch emptied its charge, and the tip of it went black.

"How's that?" Jhoira called down the speaking tube to Karn.

"Better," came the metallic reply. "Almost enough to lift off. We'll be top heavy. We'll need more power to keep the ship upright. How many more?"

"Two more torches," Jhoira said, casting the emptied one aside and lifting another.

"No, how many more refugees?"

As energy surged into the conduit, Jhoira looked at the almost-full deck and the crowd struggling to reach the ship. "Too many. Too many."

"They've broken through!" shouted Terd. He clung to the rails of the ship and pointed at the sky. Angels flooded down in a great storm. "Permission to fire? Permission to fire!"

Jhoira fitted the last torch into the slot. "Fire! Fire!"

Between goblin fingers, fog-lanterns rattled violently. Their parabolic plates slid into position. Twin red beams stabbed out from them and tore into the cascade of angels. Fire erupted among them. The down-rushing wave faltered a moment. Roars of rage turned to howls of despair.

Jhoira glanced over her shoulder. The final hundred passengers were rushing up the gangplank and packing themselves in on deck. In moments, the ship was fully loaded. "Castoff the gangplank.

J. Robert King

Castoff the grapples. Draw the anchor. Prepare for liftoff!"

Power surged blue-white through the exposed conduits. Jhoira backed away. She caught hold of the ship's wheel and shouted, "Take us up, Karn! Bring us around in a quick turn to port, heading one sixty-five, thirty-one, sixteen. Lantern-rays, clear us a path through the battle. Hold on!"

A tremor of anticipation moved through the crowd and through the great hull itself. The tremor turned into a rumbling groan. The engines below decks growled to life. A grinding noise rose between landing spines and ground. Knees buckled under the first jolting advance of the vessel. Ponderous and clumsy, *Weatherlight* nosed up and away from the rocky niche where it had sat. Energy coursed in dazzling rivulets along the exposed conduits. The prow curved dangerously near the advancing curtain of chaos.

"Hard to port!" Jhoira shouted.

The ship listed away from ravening oblivion. The refugees crouched on the deck clung tightly to the rails and each other. With a magnificent roar, the ship nosed up and away from the planar envelop. A ragged cheer moved wavelike across the deck until the new danger came to the fore. Flights of angels and archangels converged on them, magna swords swung toward the refugees like scythes to heads of wheat.

"Down, everyone!" Jhoira ordered, her voice raw. "Fire at will."

Beams of killing light erupted from shuddering lanterns and cut jagged lines across the vanguard. The acid atomizer dissolved away any creatures that lingered. Angels tumbled from the skies, their spirits whirling ghostlike from their riven forms and into the soul torches along the ship's hull. With each new life, *Weatherlight* gained speed.

Still, the beams did not catch them all, and angels poured over the rails. Refugees shrieked. Magna swords sliced into them. Red fountains erupted.

"Glasspitters fire! Beams fire! Fight, all of you! Fight!"

Swords and belaying pins and chains—the crew led the charge. Viashino and goblin and human, they fought. Great blasts of

332

molten glass belched out from the bombards, catching and slaying angels in their hundreds. Rays of crimson light burned through feather to muscle to bone. Still they came. Out of the throat of heaven came the killer angels. Spirit after spirit poured from sundered bodies into the torches, into *Weatherlight*'s powerstone. Out of it flowed red beams that slew all the more. Every death fed the killing machine.

"Faster, Karn!" Jhoira shouted. "Punch through them. Planeshift speed!"

There came no answer from the speaking tube, only the roar of engines and the hot smell of heat-stressed metal.

* * * * *

Radiant reappeared in her throne room, her sanctuary. Ever since Gorig had cast mirror spells on the windows, this room had become her refuge. Now into her refuge, she had brought the dying form of her foe and the gems that were his life.

It was a simple enough thing to decide what to do with Urza. She stripped him from her waist and tossed his crumpled figure to a nearby platform. She wasn't much interested in Urza anymore. He had been merely the package that had carried these stones. Now, broken open, he lay discarded on the floor.

These stones, though . . . Radiant lifted them in a gory hand. She had not spent the energy it would take to transform her fingers from the dagger-claws they had become. She rather enjoyed them in their fierce aspect. They looked so powerful like this—reflecting the gentle glow of the stones and mantled in the planeswalker's blood.

Radiant glanced up. The mirrors were full of her glimmering victory. From every angle, the darkness gave back fragmentary visions of her beauty. A forest of eyes gazed at her—no longer merely her eyes, but the Eyes of Urza too.

"You were like Serra, weren't you?" Radiant said. Her quiet voice echoed ceaselessly off the dark mirrors. "You could see in this room—even when the windows were lenses. You could make sense of the visions of this throne. Of course you could. Your eyes had a facet for every window, and now your eyes are mine."

Urza did not move. His sundered head leaked blood and brain onto the floor.

"Gorig will be sad he was not here to collect your soul," Radiant said wistfully. "Ah, but I have your eyes. Such beautiful eyes."

The crystals rolled languidly apart on her hand. She saw only then the ragged point of fracture between the two stones. She had known the Mightstone and Weakstone were halves of a whole, but seeing how they might be joined intrigued her. Taking one crystal in each hand, she studied them.

"It looks as though they fit together just like—this—"

* * * * *

Breath failing, strength failing, Barrin had crawled to the saddle of Rhammidarigaaz and strapped himself in. The young fire drake struggled toward one army of angels and away from another. Before him, a refugee ship fought through the battle, mantled in spectral lights. Behind him a furious demon labored at the head of a hellish legion.

It was a unique vantage there, suspended in the relative calm between two deaths, between pain and despair. Barrin knew he was done for. He could not fight. He could not escape, but he did have one final spell and the power to bring it into being. The question remaining was one of timing and focus. What would be the best use of the spell? Perhaps he could compel Radiant to kill Gorig, or Gorig to kill Radiant, or an archangel to make a suicide stand to cover the ship's retreat.

Gorig was more than a Phyrexian monster. He was the soul battery.

Suddenly Barrin knew what he would do. He rolled onto his back. Gorig labored down toward him out of the darkening heavens. The beast's torso blazed blue-white in anticipation. There was a simple ratio—something about the velocity of A minus the velocity of B divided by the distance between them over against the velocity of B plus the velocity of C divided by the distance between them—something Urza could have calculated with a mere thought. Barrin was more mage than mathematician, and he had trouble breathing, let alone calculating. Instead, he simply waited until the demon—eyes ablaze and dagger-teeth drooling over the mage master's legs—hovered just out of reach. Summoning the last bit of his strength, Barrin cast a ray of command.

The fury in the beast's eyes shifted from Barrin down to the approaching *Weatherlight*, down to the main deck, where the captain stood. With new, ardent speed, the Phyrexian monster dropped into a dive and screamed his way toward the beleaguered ship.

* * * * *

Mightstone in her right hand and Weakstone in her left, Radiant slowly brought the two together. As the rough facets of the split edges approached each other, the light in the crystals redoubled. They suddenly glowed brightly in her hands. They cast her shadow, giant and menacing, through the aviary. In a million mirrors, Radiant glimpsed herself transfigured by the light.

A glinting smile crossed her teeth. "Such power. Such power."

She brought the stones closer together. Light flared brighter still and brought with it heat. Intense beams leapt out of each facet of the stones. They struck silvered glass and ricocheted through the aviary. The vast structure seemed the interior of a giant gemstone, glimmering brilliantly around Radiant. Light bathed every dark corner. It shone across the ruined gardens below. It danced on bodies of dead birds. It gilded the still form of Urza Planeswalker. Refulgent, nimbic, luciferous, radiant light.

"If they were lenses instead of mirrors," Radiant mused idly, "all this light would spill outward and be lost. But, clever me, it remains here. It is mine."

She turned the Weakstone slowly, matching its fracture marks exactly with that of its brother. With a final slow ecstasy, she eased them together. . . .

The stones never touched. Lightning awoke between them. The glare was blinding. The heat was incinerating. The crystals, glimmering faintly when apart, were holocaustal together. Their effulgence filled every mirror. The light had nowhere to go. Each moment grew exponentially brighter. Each instant grew exponentially hotter.

Radiant tried to pull her hands apart, but the stones called to each other. They burned out her eyes.

"I'm the mad one!" she gasped.

Next moment, it did not matter. Angel flesh seared away. Angel bone exploded. Blood flash boiled. Innards puffed into black smoke that itself was bleached white and then dispersed altogether.

Radiant was gone. The lantern in darkness had burned herself out from within.

Someone else was there in her place. Someone hovered there, the embodiment of the stones, the creature created and sustained by them. It was the conflict between those stones—the world-shattering conflict of irreconcilable opposites that were even so halves of a whole—that granted Urza life. It immolated his old flesh, and in the same flash, fitted him with a new body, a glorified body. It formed around the locus of his being. It formed around the stones that were his eyes.

And next moment, the core of heat and light could no longer be contained. Every mirror in the mile-high atrium shattered. Hunks of silvered glass flung outward and crashed into the grids and plates Gorig had said would save Radiant. They buckled out and flew away, insubstantial as paper. The blaze followed them. It arced through air. It filled the yellow and shrinking skies.

Urza gazed out through the blinding brilliance. He saw the explosion peel back the skin of Serra's Palace. He saw it pulverize walls within. He watched as blast lines punched holes deep into the floating citadel. Shattered and crushed, the palace listed slowly. Streamers of force tore through its web of levitation spells. The place released an horrific moan and rolled over. The massive hand of gravity tightened its fingers around the thing and dragged it downward. It receded. A coiling sea of smoke trailed behind it. The broken hull soon seemed only the falling, spinning seed of a maple tree.

Then it struck the rising floor of the plane. Chaos swallowed it whole.

All around Urza, the edges of the blast were disappearing against the closing. Before the tide of destruction could sweep him under, Urza stepped from the dying realm.

* * * * *

Only moments after the deafening explosion that destroyed the palace, Jhoira heard an even more ominous sound. Through the groan of overheated engines and the shriek of dying refugees and the howls of rabid angels, she heard a high, keening wail. Something was falling out of the sky, too fast to avoid. She looked up. The meteor hurtled through the angel throng, ripping wings from bodies and rending anything it stuck. It grew larger, its maniac teeth glinting in the moment that it hung above deck. Its eyes were yellow as lemon wedges.

With a sudden, horrific boom, the demon creature struck the white-hot powerstone conduits. Its head was pulverized by the impact. Its wings peeled away, but the thing's massive metal torso remained. The soul-portals on either side of it flared, emptying their charges into the engines.

Weatherlight lunged forward. The beam weapons stabbed out with twice their previous intensity. Whole flights of angels disintegrated. Souls *en masse* flooded into the flashing torso. The ship gained speed. Angels flung themselves away from the juggernaut and hovered in stunned terror in space for a moment before realizing the curtain of chaos had closed on them.

The plane was disintegrating. The point of critical collapse had been reached. Nothing would stop it now.

The white mana that rained from the folding skies poured into the powerstone of *Weatherlight*. Every creature caught by the advancing curtain turned into a spiral of life-force, which was drawn into the sparking torso of the beast, into the engine.

Jhoira could do nothing but stand and stare in grotesque fascination and awe.

The angel armies fell back as the refugee craft sped into the clear space beyond.

To starboard appeared Rhammidarigaaz, with Barrin lashed to him. There was no sign of Urza. Unless the dragon flew just above the ship at the moment of planeshift, it and Barrin would be left behind.

"Planeshift before final collapse!" Barrin shouted. "Any mortal left in the plane will die!"

"I know! I know!" Jhoira returned. "You hear that, Karn! We need full speed! We need it now."

"Too many passengers," Karn roared from below. His voice was strained, as though he propelled the ship by main strength. "Too much weight!"

Before the bow, another army of angels hung. They were disintegrating before another collapsing edge of the plane. And suddenly they were gone.

Only the *Weatherlight* and Rhammidarigaaz remained in the collapsing plane. Curtains of chaos closed ahead and behind them.

"Now or never, Karn!" Jhoira shouted.

They reached the wall. The prow of the ship sank into chaos and dissolved. In the breath afterward, the ship and all those aboard were gone.

* * * * *

The invasion force had been gone eight hours, and the sun had at last quit the skies over Tolaria. The crowd that had had gathered for *Weatherlight*'s launch had remained, but their high spirits had dissolved. The festive morning had given way to a speculative noon, which in turn surrendered to a fearful and prayerful evening. Night now lay full and cold over the academy walls. Someone had fetched candles from the great hall, but a mocking wind put out the hopeful little lights moments after they were coaxed to life. A few lanterns had replaced them, glaring baldly across the mulling multitudes. The quiet prayers were becoming whispers of doubt.

A restless breeze moved among the trees. The crowd turned its attention to the distant deeps of the sky. Something moved there among the lazy clouds of night. Something large. The shape grew rapidly and silently on the wind.

The crowd that had lingered throughout the long, hot day began to draw back in dread. Those lurking in doorways withdrew inside, and those out in the open pressed back toward doorways. A reddish streamer of flame outlined devilish jowls and a great, rapacious eye.

"It's a demon!"

"Yes, but one of ours."

The dragon's figure was clear now, above the treetops. In moments it soared over the walls and flapped ferociously above the courtyard. Rhammidarigaaz! In his wake, black against the blue-black of night, there came a giant hull. From its sides jutted smiling faces and waving hands.

The *Weatherlight*.

* * * * *

It was some months later when Jhoira stood again at the prow of the ship, feeling the sea winds in her hair. She breathed deeply and remembered a time long ago when she stood in her secret spot, on the prow of Tolaria, and dreamed of far-off places and soul mates. Her girlhood dreams had not come to pass and had in fact brought her much pain over the years. Life had been good nonetheless. She was among the greatest artificers in the world, a trusted companion of Urza Planeswalker and, for the time being, the ad hoc captain of the grand ship *Weatherlight*. She had explored earthly paradises, had run forges in hell, had fought wars in heaven, and had traveled the planes with a silver man and a skyship.

"How are things looking down there, Karn?" she asked through the speaking tube that emerged at the prow.

"The crystal's supply of energy is limitless," Karn replied.

His energy had also increased of late. The orphaned child of Urza had at last found his home, at the heart of the ship he feared would be the end of him. The planeswalker had returned from Serra's Realm chastened by his victory. Unexplainably to anyone, he had begun to show a fatherly affection toward Karn, saying the silver man was formed in his own image. Whether by plan or happenstance, Urza's first thinking, feeling artifact creature had become the heart of his Legacy for the world.

Karn had even learned a little bit about humor. "Is there anything you'd like me to shoot?"

"No, thanks, Karn," Jhoira said. "Steady as she goes."

"Aye, aye."

Yes, it had been quite a life so far. No soul mates, but quite a life—or were there soul mates?

The tip of Zhalfir jutted just ahead, a rocky prominence behind which stretched a broad and bountiful land. The civil wars were concluded, thanks to the wisdom and power of a certain Tolarian wizard, and the country had pledged a tract of land for human refugees from Serra's Realm. That was the purpose of this trip. Jhoira, Karn, and the crew of *Weatherlight* were conducting three hundred and sixty-three human refugees to their new home in Zhalfir. Jhoira's mind, just now, was not on any of those three hundred and sixty-three, but rather on the figure that stood, red-swathed and magnificent on that prominence of stone.

Heart catching in her throat, Jhoira shouted the order that would bring the ship slowly up to hover just above the prominence. Smiling broadly despite herself, Jhoira called out to the man standing there. "Teferi! Excuse me, Lord Mage Teferi of Zhalfir! Good to see you again."

"And you!" came the genuine reply. With a simple flip of his arm, the man levitated up to the ship board. He spread his cloak in wide majesty as unseen arms of magic lowered him to stand before Jhoira. He bowed low, returned her smile, and set hands on his hips. "I hear you have some new citizens for my nation."

"Yes," Jhoira said. "Three hundred and sixty-three."

"Fine. Fine. I do hope you are planning to help them settle in."

Jhoira tipped her head regretfully. "I can stay the day. Urza wants his ship back for other . . . errands."

Teferi nodded, his eyes darkening in disappointment. "Some other time then, perhaps."

"Why don't you come back with me to Tolaria?" she suggested. "You have lots of friends there. Arty Shovelhead is aboard. He would be happy to see you."

"I'm lucky to be alive, after all I did to him." Teferi wore a chagrined smile. "It's hard to believe a hundred-pound kid would pick on a twelve-hundred pound golem. Still, I'll have to see him again later. Anyone can fight a war. It's maintaining peace that takes all the real work." He looked her up and down. "Well, Jhoira of the Ghitu, let's take these people to their new home."

"Yes, my friend," she replied. "Yes."

Monologue

I'd really hoped Jhoira and Teferi would get together. After all, a master artificer and a master mage would make natural partners. Oh, well, perhaps it will come in time. And on Tolaria, time is one thing we will never run out of.

—**Barrin, Mage Master of Tolaria**

Epilogue

At last, Urza is sane.

He remembers battling his brother Mishra, three thousand years ago, and regrets the destruction they caused. He remembers the death of his surrogate brother, Ratepe, and his best friend Xantcha, and is grateful for their lives together. He is capable at last of true regret and gratitude, and that goes a long way. He is at last capable of having true friends.

Urza not only remembers his past, he has taken responsibility for it. He resurrected time-ravaged Tolaria, did penance for Argoth, destroyed a small corner of Phyrexia, and even saved the refugees of Serra's Realm.

As I write this, I sit with Urza in his high study. The evening winds of Tolaria are hot and pregnant with life. The sound of night-birds has begun, haunting and beautiful. The Phyrexian gorge lies quiet, empty now for nearly a decade. The only other sound comes from the great hall. There is a dance tonight, and a whole new generation of Tolarian students are having fun. I tap my foot absently to the distant sound of rebecs and drums.

The master raises his face from the book he is reading. It is his wife's account of the Brothers' War. He has been reading it very gravely during the last month, his thoughtful expression broken at moments into wistful remembrance. The smile that appears on his face now is something different, though.

"How late does the dance run tonight?"

I shrug. "I said they could dance till the Glimmer Moon went down—well after midnight. If the sound is bothering you—"

"No," Urza says with an off-putting hand. "It's just that I've been rereading this wedding sequence. I remember the dances from that day, long ago. I don't imagine modern music would quite accommodate the same steps. . . ."

I rise. "Oh, if not, we can teach the players a few of the old tunes."

Yes, Urza is sane. Now, I suppose I'll see if he can dance.

—**Barrin, Mage Master of Tolaria**

Get the story behind the world's best-selling game.

The Brothers' War
Artifacts Cycle Book I
Jeff Grubb

It is a time of conflict. Titanic dragon engines scar and twist the very landscape of the planet. The final battle will sink continents and shake the skies, as two brothers struggle for supremacy on the continent of Terisiare. And one alone survives.

Planeswalker
Artifacts Cycle Book II
Lynn Abbey

Urza, survivor of the Brothers' War, feels the spark of a planeswalker ignite within him. But as he strides across the planes of Dominia™, a loyal companion seeks to free him from an obsession that threatens to turn to madness. Only she can rescue him from despair and guilt. Only she can help him fulfill his destiny.

Time Streams
Artifacts Cycle Book III
J. Robert King

From a remote island in Dominaria thousands of years after the Brothers' War, Urza tries to right the wrongs he and his brother perpetrated against their homeland. His task is immense, and his enemies are strong. Only a mighty weapon can turn the balance of history.

Bloodlines
Artifacts Cycle Book IV
Loren L. Coleman

Urza's weapon lacks but one component: a human hand to guide it. As the centuries slowly pass, he patiently perfects his plans, waiting for the right moment—and the right heir. The heir to his legacy.

www.wizards.com

The Official
URZA'S LEGACY™ Game Guide

Full-color reprints of all the *Urza's Legacy* cards.

Direct from Wizards of the Coast®, *The Official Urza's Legacy Game Guide* contains everything players need to know about the newest expansion for **Magic: The Gathering,** the world's most popular trading card game. From a strategy guide to a card reference, this book has it all.

- Written by Will McDermott, editor of *The Duelist*® magazine.
- Includes a foreword from a lead developer of the card set.
- New strategies from the designers of the **Magic: The Gathering** trading card game.

www.wizards.com/Magic

Questions? Call 1-800-324-6496

For a store near you check out:

<http://locator.wizards.com>

Release: April 1999   Price: $9.99 U.S.   Product#: TSR 21353   ISBN: 0-7869-1353-3